Though I Stumble

A Promises of God Novel

Kim Cash Tate

Cover Design: Jenny Zemanek at Seedlings Design Studio

Scripture quotations are taken from the NEW AMERICAN STANDARD BIBLE ®, Copyright © 1960, 1962, 1963, 1968, 1971, 1972, 1973, 1975, 1977, 1995 by The Lockman Foundation. Used by permission.

Scripture quotations marked (NIV) are taken from the Holy Bible, New International Version®, NIV®. Copyright © 1973, 1978, 1984, 2011 by Biblica, Inc.™ Used by permission of Zondervan. All rights reserved worldwide. www.zondervan.com The "NIV" and "New International Version" are trademarks registered in the United States Patent and Trademark Office by Biblica, Inc.™

Tate, Kimberly Cash.
Though I Stumble / Kim Cash Tate.
ISBN 978-1-946336-00-2
1. African American women—Fiction. 2. Christian fiction.

ALSO BY KIM CASH TATE

Heavenly Places
Faithful
Cherished
Hope Springs
The Color of Hope
Hidden Blessings

DOWNLOAD:

"IN HOT PURSUIT: A Mini-Devotional Study For
The Journey"

at

kimcashtate.com/inhotpursuit

The LORD makes firm the steps
of the one who delights in him;
though he may stumble, he will not fall,
for the LORD upholds him with his hand.

PSALM 37:23-24 (NIV)

CHAPTER ONE

Saturday, May 7

The closer it got to five o'clock, the more Stephanie London's insides skittered with anticipation. Her husband's return shouldn't be an event, but that's what it had become. She'd counted the days, deep-cleaned the house, asked off from the Main Street Diner, and this morning got her hair done, all while telling herself things were going to be better now. At least, once they'd addressed a few things. But none of that today. Today, if she could keep a right attitude, she would simply celebrate that Lindell was home.

She turned toward the diner, her last stop, and a good thing since a gaggle of balloons obstructed her rearview. She'd gotten them on impulse, seeing the party store near the hair salon, and carefully crammed two dozen into her Camry. Not that balloons were her thing. But she needed a carefree, fun vibe. If it took props to get her there, so be it.

She parked and strolled toward the entrance under a bright blue sky. On days like this, Stephanie felt good about Hope Springs, North Carolina. Perfect mix of gentle breeze and warm sun. Family and family friends eager to gather—they'd be over later. Even this diner. At her lowest point it had given her a place to work and stay sane. But after almost three years in Hope Springs, this town was more heartache than good. She needed Lindell to see—it was time to get out of here.

The bell clanged in the doorway, causing Sara Ann to look over from the table she was serving. Patty, the hostess, waved from a distance.

"Ooh, look at you." Sara Ann topped off the water glasses at her table then walked her water pitcher to the counter with Stephanie. "Love your hair like this." She tousled it a little. "Full and curly. Why don't you wear it like that more often?"

"Girl, two hours under the dryer? Ain't nobody got time for that every week. Lindell better appreciate it." Stephanie laughed, glancing around. The diner was near full, mostly Saturday regulars.

"Hey, Mel!" Sara Ann rose on her tiptoes, calling across the counter. "Table seven wanted a fruit cup instead of fries." She turned back to Stephanie. "You're not supposed to be here. But I know, we're hard to resist."

"I just need to learn how to make Mel's meatloaf as good as Mel."

"Ah, Lindell's favorite." Sara Ann had worked at the diner for years and knew just about everyone's favorite dish. "With mashed potatoes, light gravy, and sweet corn."

"And bread pudding." They said it in unison.

"I know he's looking forward to home," Sara Ann said. "I

love his heart for medical missions, but it can't be easy. The people of Haiti stay in my prayers . . . one devastation after another."

"It's heartbreaking," Stephanie said, thankful for Sara Ann's comment. This was what she needed—to focus on the good that Lindell was doing. Haitians truly did experience crisis after crisis. And Lindell's training as a doctor provided an immense benefit. If only her marriage weren't suffering in the process.

"Here you go, Steph." Patty brought her a handled bag, the aroma escaping through piping hot containers. "Mel said I must've heard wrong. He put biscuits in there anyway."

"See why I can't get away from these hips?" She looked at Mel, who gave a wink. "You're not right, Mel. You know I can't say no to those doggone biscuits."

Mel placed an entree in the service window. "Only looking out for my buddy Lindell."

"Whatever." Stephanie chuckled. "All right, hate to leave y'all with this late lunch crowd." She headed for the door.

"I'm so sure." Sara Ann moved toward a table that had just been seated. "See you later tonight."

Stephanie headed home, less than a five-minute drive; as she neared the end of their country road her phone rang. Probably Lindell on his layover in Miami. She parked in her usual spot, on the gravel to the side of the house.

Lifting the phone from her bag, she glanced at the name and winced. It was her sister.

"Um, what had happened was—" Stephanie chuckled.

"You know you're wrong," Cyd said. "You were supposed to get back to me a week ago."

"Not *wrong* wrong." Stephanie got out of the car, grabbing the carryout. "I wasn't blowing you off. I just can't make up my mind." She headed inside.

"It wouldn't be a problem if the hotel wasn't booked. But last-minute registrations are rolling in, and we're trying to make room for people. Momma said she'd give up her room and stay with me, if you're not coming."

"Oh, you called to tell me you're booting me out." Stephanie put the food on the kitchen counter and went back out. "No big deal. Just the first ever women's conference for my home church, which my sister happens to be hosting. And a chance to see family I haven't seen in, how long?"

"Okay, awesome, you're coming then?"

"Well. No." Stephanie laughed a little as she opened the back door to her car. "I really want to. But Lindell gets back today, and he's been gone so much lately . . . I'd rather not have one of us leaving town again in two weeks."

"Is everything okay? You sound a little funny."

"Things are good," Stephanie said. With thirteen years between them, Cyd was more like a second mom than a sister, her radar always in tune. But even if Stephanie had wanted to talk about what was happening, she wouldn't know where to start. "Listen, I need to finish getting ready before I pick up Lindell from the airport." She gathered the balloon strings.

"I'm sad you won't be here but I understand," Cyd said. "And you're right, it's been way too long. Either we need to get down there, or you and Lindell need a trip home to St. Louis."

"Right? It's ridiculous. I'm calling you as soon as the conference is over so we can make a plan."

"Which means I'll be calling you," Cyd said.

"Whatever." Stephanie smiled as she clicked off and put the phone in her back pocket.

She eased the balloons from the car and made her way to the house as a light gust of wind kicked in, sending them flying and knocking about. As she was wrangling them through the doorway, her phone rang again. When she had the gang safely inside, she grasped the strings in one hand and checked her phone. Her pulse quickened a little.

"Hey, you're in Miami?"

"Not exactly," Lindell said.

"Your flight got delayed?" She set the balloons, anchored to three weights, on the dining table and picked up scissors to trim the lengths of string.

"No, it's not that." Lindell hesitated. "Something came up. I'm still in Haiti."

Stephanie felt her hand trembling a little and lowered the scissors. "What happened?"

"A couple of emergency cases came in last night," Lindell said, "and they're still touch and go. I couldn't leave."

Stephanie lowered herself into a chair. "But . . . aren't there emergency cases coming in all the time? I'm trying to be understanding, Lindell, but you've been gone for a month and a half on what was supposed to be a two-week trip."

"I know. I'm sorry, Steph. I can't control the circumstances. I just know they need me."

His words tugged at emotions she'd been trying to stuff. "What about the fact that *I* need you?"

"Here we go." Lindell sighed. "Steph, do you understand the situation down here? Do you know what these people have to go through to get medical care and how few doctors are available? We're talking life and death. That's a real need. Yet you always want to whine about your own perceived needs."

Silent tears fell. He was right. Her needs didn't compare, and she felt guilty for voicing them. But why did it feel like he didn't care at all?

"I was just . . . looking forward to seeing you." She paused. "So when will you leave now, in a day or two maybe?"

"It's doubtful. I want to make sure these patients are stabilized, and one already needs another surgery." Lindell moved away from the phone as he spoke with someone else. "Hey, I need to run. I'll let you know when I'll be home, as soon as I know."

And he was gone.

Stephanie held her phone, the quiet suddenly engulfing her. The house was never quiet on Saturdays. She and Lindell lived there with her cousin Janelle, Janelle's husband, and their two kids, an arrangement that came about after their grandmother died. Stephanie and Janelle had cared for her while she was ill, and then decided to move into the house where their own parents had grown up. With Janelle's kids and the neighborhood kids running in and out, there was never a dull moment. But today they'd gone on an extended day trip so Stephanie and Lindell could have time to themselves. They'd be back later tonight . . . for the celebration.

Stephanie's eyes fell on the *Welcome Home* balloons that dominated the bouquet. She stood and poked each one with her scissors, watching the life drain from them. Next up, the *You're Amazing* ones. What possessed her to include those anyway? And the festive gang of neon lime, ruby red, and sunburst yellow. *Pop. Pop. Pop.*

She walked to the kitchen, picked up the Main Street Diner bag by the handles, and dropped it into the trash. Then she went to the bedroom, to their one closet, and pushed aside the shoe boxes on her side of the top shelf. She stared at it, the last of the wine she'd bought the last time Lindell was coming home—and didn't.

Stephanie grabbed the bottle by the neck and went to find the corkscrew.

CHAPTER TWO

Saturday, May 14

Treva Langston should have known better than to take the main entrance onto the University of Maryland's campus. She'd gotten caught up in the frenzy of getting Hope across town to a tween spa day, in bumper-to-bumper traffic, moving her youngest daughter to tears because she was sure she'd miss the facials. Her middle daughter, Joy, had to be dropped off next, at an eighth-grade graduation party, after which Treva waded through more DC area traffic to get to College Park, where her oldest needed to be moved out of the dorm by evening.

Taking the main entrance helped avoid congestion at the rear, near Faith's dorm. But once Treva made the turn, she had an entirely different problem—a slew of emotional triggers.

She drove around the manicured M, every landmark a reminder. This was where she'd met her husband. Where she and Hez had fallen in love. Where she'd learned to open up and trust. They'd walked miles on this campus, along this very route, past the library, Student Union, and Cole Field House, where he first held her hand. Her heart traveled back, remembering everything about that moment. The Terps scoring on Duke, students going wild, Hezekiah's hand slipping into hers, as if she wouldn't notice. That one touch took her breath away, though she would have never admitted it at the time.

Treva rounded a bend and her insides clenched. The education building, where Hezekiah had returned to work as a professor.

Her car slowed as that day from two years ago replayed in her mind. He'd called before he left the building. Said he would meet her at Faith's high school senior banquet. Treva could hear the excitement in his voice. Every milestone related to his girls excited Hezekiah, but this was a dream come true—his daughter about to attend school at his alma mater, which was now his place of employment as well. He'd teased Faith about how much he'd get on her nerves, showing up at the dorm when least expected, asking her professors how she was doing. Faith balked even as she welcomed it. It was a big reason why she'd chosen Maryland, because her dad was there.

Treva navigated traffic near the dorm, grief loading from different places of the heart. It hurt more than her own memories of Hezekiah on campus—the fact that Faith wasn't able to create her own. Hez's life ended that night, in a car accident.

She spotted a car pulling from a spot and waited, her finger stemming the onset of tears. She couldn't do this right now. She needed to be upbeat for Faith. How on earth did her daughter deal with it, being up here every day? Treva prayed for her regularly, tried to talk to her about it, but Faith had kept her grief mostly to herself. Still, she'd done well. Treva wanted to focus on celebrating a successful sophomore year.

Crates, refrigerators, and luggage moved past her as Treva made her way to the dorm with two empty suitcases of her own. The secured doors had been propped open, so she moved through them and up to the fourth floor. She walked into the room, a single, and found Faith pulling the bedding from her mattress.

"There she is." Treva set down the empty luggage and hugged her daughter. "Finished her last final, now officially a junior. I'm so proud of you."

"Not official yet." Faith hugged her back. "I'm waiting to hear how I did on my Renaissance Lit final. It was way harder than I expected."

"You say that every semester and wind up on the dean's list— I'll take care of the bed, sweetie." Treva took a sheet and started folding. "We'll walk on the wild side and celebrate tonight anyway, at Del Frisco's. I made reservations for two."

"Really?" Faith stuffed clothes from the drawer into a suitcase, her natural hair in a cute Afro puff atop her head. "Just the two of us?"

"Your sisters have sleepovers tonight, so I get you to myself." Treva folded the plain yellow comforter and stacked it with the sheets. "Seems like we haven't spent time together in the longest.

You were coming home all the time freshman year, but you must have found your groove this year. That's a good thing."

Faith worked on the next drawer. "Yeah, I guess."

Treva watched her daughter with a slight smile. She loved that Faith was her own person. Baggy sweat pants. Random *Star Wars* tee. She'd never cared an iota about style or fashion, a marked departure from her mom. But her features—especially her chocolate complexion and five-eight height—were all Treva.

"Oh, guess who I talked to yesterday?" Treva moved to the closet. "Cyd London."

"You talked to Cyd London?" Faith said. "She called you?"

"Well, she left a message, and I had to call her back."

"That's so weird, that you actually have her phone number."

Treva chuckled as she removed a couple of jackets from hangers and put them in the second piece of luggage. "Why are you acting like that woman is a rock star or something?"

Faith was quiet a moment. "I remember the Bible study of hers I did last year, the one on being steadfast. I wasn't sure how a whole study could be done from that one word, but it was impactful. She's amazing to me."

"And you're amazing to me." Treva grabbed Faith's robe from a hook. "When I think about where you are compared to where I was in college . . . believe me, I wasn't thinking about the Bible." She looked at her daughter. "I feel like God has such special plans for you."

Faith looked at her mom, then looked away, moving to collect flip-flops and tennis shoes from under the bed. "So what did Cyd London say?"

"Oh, she said the conference team is providing transportation for speakers, and though I'm not exactly a *speaker*, she'll be picking us up from the airport next Thursday. Pretty cool, huh?"

The resident assistant popped her head into the doorway. "Hey, Faith, don't forget to stop by before you leave. I need to get your key and go over a checklist." She moved on to the next room.

Treva glanced around, noting that the work was almost done. "I should start loading up," she said.

She piled the bedding atop a crate of books and carried them to the car. She hadn't taken time to appreciate it before, but the spring weather was gorgeous. With Faith back home, Treva would have her outdoor walking buddy once again. So many little things she'd missed.

She headed back to the room and was surprised to find the door closed. Opening it, she saw Faith on the floor beside her bare mattress, curled in a ball, in tears.

"Sweetheart, what happened?" Treva closed the door and went to her. "What's wrong?"

Faith kept her head buried. "It all hit me at once . . . the conference, that Bible study I did—you saying I'm *amazing*." She swiped tears with the back of her hand. "I'm nowhere near amazing. And whatever awesome plan God had for me, I've messed it up." She lifted her head a little, staring into the distance. "I don't know what to do. I feel like I'm drowning."

Treva lowered herself to the floor and put an arm around her. "Tell me what's wrong, sweetie, we'll work it out. It can't be as bad as—"

"I'm *pregnant*."

Treva was struck silent as the words sank in.

Faith turned toward her. "See, it *is* that bad. Your face says it all."

"I'm just . . . shocked, sweetie. I didn't know you were even dating anyone. So I admit I'm a little . . . thrown. Are you sure? How long have you known?"

"A week."

"Wow . . ." Treva hugged her tighter as a hundred thoughts and questions swirled in her mind. *Lord, help me not to say the wrong thing.* "Oh, sweetheart, I know it feels like you're drowning—I can't even imagine all that you must be feeling—but I promise, we'll get through this. I'll be with you every step of the way."

Faith looked up at her. "I thought you'd be upset."

"Well, I'm not *not* upset, Faith, but my main concern right now is you and making sure you're okay."

Faith stared downward, tears streaming still.

"Sweetheart, tell me about the guy. I know you started going to a campus Bible study last semester. Did you meet there?"

Seconds lapsed before Faith replied. "No. It's Jesse." She exhaled. "Jesse Edmonds."

Treva sat up a little, looking at her. "Carolyn's son? How do you even know him?"

"He goes here, Mom." Faith wiped her nose. "Well, just graduated. And he was at our house for the Christmas potluck."

"That's right. I forgot he was there." Carolyn had recently joined the Bible study at Treva's home and had brought her son to their annual gathering. Treva knew all she needed to know about Jesse from a prayer request his mom had shared. "You two started seeing each other after that, and you never mentioned it?"

Faith stared downward as conversations rolled in Treva's mind. So many, between Hezekiah and Faith especially, about the kind of guy Faith would choose one day. It had always impressed Treva that Faith was often the one to bring it up. *Well, Daddy, what if* this? *And what if* that? At one point she had resolved that she didn't want to date anyone seriously unless her parents—her dad especially—thought he was good for her. And she had always been adamant about saving sex for marriage.

"Does Jesse know?" Treva said. "What's he saying?"

"He was shocked, like I was," Faith said. "We found out in the middle of finals, graduation . . ."

"Wait," Treva said, looking at her. "So he wasn't using protection?"

"It just *happened*, Mom, and it was only two times and—"

"Lord, have mercy . . ." Treva's head fell in her hand. "And he's shocked you're pregnant? I'll be shocked if you're not dealing with more than that."

"What is that supposed to mean?"

"Faith, how well do you know Jesse? He's really not the sort of guy—"

"Mom, just stop. How well do *I* know him? You don't know him at all." Faith moved to her feet. "And just so you know, I'm in love with Jesse."

"In love?" Treva stood as well. "No, I don't know Jesse personally, but trust me, I know enough. I'm just saying, Faith . . . All the times you've talked about the kind of guy you want in your life—you know Jesse Edmonds isn't it."

Faith walked past Treva to the closet. "This isn't even up for discussion. Jesse and I are together. And we're having a baby. We'll figure out the rest as we go." She pulled shirts from hangers and tossed them into a suitcase.

Treva sighed at how quickly things had turned. Seeing that the second suitcase was full, she zipped it and carried it off as her heart found a million reasons to break. How would her daughter be able to bear an unexpected pregnancy? Having lost her father, Faith had already been on a tough road. Now Jesse Edmonds was along for the ride?

She stepped onto the elevator, pondering that last bit. Faith and Jesse? How would *that* play out? Treva could only imagine more heartbreak.

She walked to the car and put the suitcase in the trunk, then lingered, taking in the sights and sounds of the campus around her. Thinking for the thousandth time, *If only Hezekiah were here.* He'd know what to say and do. Her heart reached for him always, in little things and big. As much as she knew God was there, she longed for what she'd had for more than two decades . . . the love and care her husband so consistently gave.

Maybe it wasn't so much that her heart was breaking—but whether it would ever be given the chance to heal.

CHAPTER THREE

Tuesday, May 17

Jillian Mason divided six pounds of chicken breast pieces into three groups and seasoned each with the mixes she'd prepared—sriracha, barbecue, and spicy mustard. She began adding them to a lined baking pan, separated by aluminum foil "sticks."

She paused and lifted the iPod from her apron pocket, needing to hear that last bit again. She had Cyd London in her ear, teaching the weekly lesson her Bible study group would watch later that morning. Jillian liked to order the audio in addition to the DVD, so she could listen in advance while she cooked and did other chores. Something always struck her that she could use to ignite discussion among the women.

She rewound thirty seconds and listened again as she resumed adding chicken to the pan.

"We have to stay there for a minute, don't we?" Cyd said. "I was fine when God was passing judgment on the Babylonians, talking about all the stuff they'd done. But why did He have to tell Habakkuk, 'But they will be held guilty, they whose strength is their god.' That got personal, didn't it? Do you take pride in your own strength? In your ability to handle—"

"Hey, babe," a voice said, and Jillian turned to see her husband heading for the coffeepot.

She paused the audio again and took out her earbuds. "Morning, babe. I brewed the light roast this morning. You were talking about how bitter the other one was tasting."

"Oh, thanks." Cecil eyed the baking pan. "What do you have going there?"

"Meal prep, since I'll be gone Thursday through Sunday. I did sriracha, mostly for you." She pointed. "Honey mustard for Trevor and Courtenay, barbecue for Sophia and David. You can put it over pasta, rice, spaghetti squash, whatever you like. I'll also make some—"

"Mom, David hid my math book, and he thinks it's funny." Trevor, her youngest at ten years old, yelled from downstairs.

"He *lost* his math book," David countered, "and yeah, it's funny, because he never remembers where anything is."

Jillian walked to the top of the stairs. "Trevor, you had it at the dentist's office yesterday. You didn't leave it there, did you?"

"Oh, it's in the car!" Trevor came bounding up and headed for the door that led to the garage.

"And you know what?" Jillian called after him. "You wouldn't have had to take it to the dentist's office if you weren't wasting so much time earlier in the day. When I get back from Aunt Treva's, I'll be checking to see how much you've gotten done."

Cecil poured coffee into a mug. "Are you looking forward to

your girls' getaway this weekend?"

"Well, I was, but now Faith says she's not going." Jillian added the rest of the chicken to the pan. "And Treva's hinting that she might not go either."

"But you'd go anyway, by yourself?"

"I don't *want* to go by myself," Jillian said, "but we've paid for it. And you know we've been doing Living Word Bible studies for years. I'm excited they're finally doing a conference. This trip means a lot to me."

Cecil held his mug, looking at her. "This trip means a lot to you."

Jillian frowned slightly. "Why'd you say it like that?"

"Nothing, Jill." He grabbed a banana from the fruit basket.

"Mom," her oldest, Courtenay, called from upstairs. "Did you get the stuff I need for my chemistry experiment? I texted it to you."

"I'll have to stop by the store on the way home from Bible study." Jillian saw her husband leaving. "Cecil, seriously, why do you sound funny? Are you upset because I said I might have lunch with Tommy?"

"Why would I be upset about that?" Cecil said. "You haven't seen him since college, and he was like a brother to you. I get that."

"Then what is it?"

"Mom, my math book's not in the car," Trevor said, back from the garage. "Maybe I did leave it at the dentist's office."

"I need to finish getting ready for work," Cecil said, moving toward the stairs.

"Mom, you have to call and see if they have it."

Jillian sighed. Cecil's words kept playing in her head. So calm and unaffected. But somehow they bit.

⁓ ❀ ⁓

"So you've decided? You're not going?" Jillian popped the disc for the lesson into Treva's DVD player in the family room. "Did something else happen?"

"We had a blowup late last night." Treva looked at her sister from the kitchen as she measured out coffee. "Faith walked in at three in the morning, and I asked if she'd been with Jesse. She said she was almost twenty and too old to be questioned."

"Faith said that?" Jillian came closer. "That doesn't sound like her."

"*Then* she said Jesse used to spend the night in her dorm, so if she stayed out all night, it wouldn't be a big deal." Treva blank-stared her sister. "Has she lost her mind? I said, 'Uh, no, ma'am, not while you're living in this house.'" She pushed the button to start brewing. "I'm trying my best to be supportive, Jillian. But somehow all of the focus is on Jesse now, and I'm the bad guy for having an issue with him. Honestly, I'm not sure what to say to Carolyn when she gets here. And it's awkward because there are only the three of us today."

"I thought about that on the way over," Jillian said. The other two women had called over the weekend to say they couldn't make it. "I'm sure Carolyn was as shocked as you were by all this."

"I want to know more about what she alluded to last fall." Treva took bottles of water from the fridge. "Jillian, she asked us to pray because his girlfriend had had an abortion."

"I know." Jillian's voice was almost a whisper. "Did you tell Faith that?"

"I couldn't," Treva said, "since whatever's said during Bible study is held in confidence. But maybe she already knows." She looked at her sister, worry etched in her face. "I'm wondering, is this other girl still in the picture? Is Jesse serious about Faith? What's the deal?"

"I doubt Carolyn knows the answers," Jillian said. "And anyway, you can't go quizzing her about her son."

"So we're just supposed to pretend this isn't happening?"

"It's complicated, that's for sure. But I don't understand why it means you can't go to the conference."

"I feel so bad, because we were all looking forward to it. But I feel like I need to be here for Faith. As much as she wants to act like she's grown, I saw how she broke down in her dorm room. She's overwhelmed." Treva pulled coffee mugs from the cupboard and set them on the counter. "The whole thing makes me sad, because Faith is the one who found out about the conference and suggested we go. I think she backed out because she's

21

feeling ashamed, but I bet the conference is the very thing she needs."

"It makes me sad too," Jillian said. "I know what Faith is going through. I remember it vividly."

"I was surprised you shared that with her yesterday. And *she* was clearly surprised to hear your story."

"I had to tell her," Jillian said. "She's committed to having this baby, and I wanted her to know how much I admired that since . . . I didn't make that choice." Her mind flashed back to that time, but it was too painful to stay there. "And I agree. The conference is exactly what she needs—you too. Besides, how *can* you back out, since you're on the program?"

"I'm only sharing for a few minutes about my life," Treva said. "Wouldn't be hard for someone to take my place."

"But your story is unique," Jillian said. "That's why they picked you."

"Well. Can't argue with that. Not too many people grow up with a mother who can't stand them because of the color of their skin."

Jillian nodded a little. It hurt still to think about it, but that was their reality. Jillian, with her fair skin and features, had been the favored one. Treva, older by two years, had been treated with disdain. Still, the two of them had always been close.

"It's pretty exciting that you'll be able to share what God did," Jillian said. She heard her phone and went to check the message. "I guess you're not the only one feeling awkward. Carolyn says she can't make it today."

"I'll call her later," Treva said. "This can't be easy for her eith—"

"Mom, Grandma Darlene said you're not going to the conference now?"

Jillian and Treva turned to see Faith standing near the entrance to the kitchen, looking as though she'd just rolled out of bed.

"I let her know this morning," Treva said, "so she could make other plans for the weekend instead of staying here. She texted you?"

"She said she was surprised to hear I wasn't going," Faith said. "Mom, are you staying home because of me?"

"Of course," Treva said. "With everything going on, it doesn't seem right to leave."

"Nothing will happen over the course of one weekend," Faith said. "You were doing these studies way back when I was in middle school. You said yourself you feel like you know Cyd London and Pastor Lyles from the DVDs. It doesn't make any sense for you not to go."

Treva eyed her. "You're not trying to get rid of me, are you?"

"Oh, stop," Jillian said, smiling. "You're right, Faith. And I wish you would reconsider going yourself. It's probably true that nothing will happen over the course of one weekend—here at home. But we've been praying about the conference. I'm believing God can do a lot in one weekend there."

Faith's hand went to her stomach. "I'm actually feeling a little nauseous," she said. "I'm going to lie back down."

"Do you want some crackers?" Treva said. "Let me get you some water."

"Maybe later." Faith started down the hallway toward the stairs.

Treva looked at Jillian. "I guess the girls' getaway is back on, for the two of us anyway."

"Don't sound so excited."

"I wish I could be excited. I doubt I'll be able to focus on anything when we're there."

"I'll keep praying," Jillian said. "I really do believe God will be moving in awesome ways this weekend. The timing is no coincidence."

"You sound like Darlene," Treva said. "You know how she is. When I told her I wasn't going she said, 'God is in no way surprised by any of this. Carry on with the original plan and watch Him bless it.'"

Jillian smiled. Treva's mother-in-law was like a mother to both of them. She always spoke straight. "That's Darlene. And she's right. I can't wait to get there."

Cecil's words floated through her mind—*This trip means a lot to you.* What *was* that about? Did he have a problem with her going? It couldn't be the kids. Even when the four of them were small, he'd never seemed overwhelmed caring for them. Said it wasn't Tommy. So why would he have an issue?

CHAPTER FOUR

Tuesday, May 17

Faith made her way up the walkway Tuesday afternoon, wondering why she felt so nervous. This was Jesse, the guy she'd spent countless days with over the course of the semester. They'd gotten to know one another, not only in a physical sense, but in a friendship sense. That was how it had started—just talking, talking about everything.

But it seemed the clock struck midnight at the close of the semester. Everything had changed. Jesse graduated. Faith moved back home. And aside from a few brief text messages, they hadn't connected. That would've been hard regardless, but now that she was pregnant, it was crushing.

She rang the doorbell, which set off immediate barking inside. *Jesse has a dog?* She waited, glancing over at his car. She'd taken a chance coming, not knowing if he'd be home. He hadn't been last night. On a whim, she'd driven by on her way to a gathering at a high school friend's. When her mom asked if she'd been with Jesse, all she could think was how much she wished she had.

Footsteps approached and seconds later the door opened, but only partway.

Jesse looked out, wearing athletic shorts and a frat shirt. "Faith, hey. You scared of dogs? It's a big one, but he's friendly."

Faith caught sight of the dog trying to get to her, barking still. "A big one? Uh, yeah, that's a Doberman."

"He's lovable, though." Jesse winked. "Like me."

"Whatever." Faith felt her arms trembling slightly and held herself to calm them. "And no, I'm not afraid of friendly, lovable dogs, as long as it's true."

Jesse opened the door wider, and Faith walked in.

"Hey," he said, hugging her.

She lingered a moment, looking into his eyes. Medium height and build, he was only slightly taller than she. He leaned in, his almond brown cheek touching hers, and kissed her lightly. She looked down, realizing the dog had stopped barking and was sniffing her jeans.

"What's his name?" Faith backed up a little, keeping her eyes on the dog, just in case.

"Lancelot."

"Okay, really?" She raised her gaze to Jesse. "Did you name him?"

"Of course I did. What?"

"As if you know anything about the character?"

"Oh. Nice." Jesse couldn't contain his smile. "More English major snobbery. Nobody else could possibly be familiar with classic works."

"Oh, like when I couldn't possibly be familiar with the fundamental theorem of Calculus? Math major snobbery." Faith ran her hand across the dog's back, warming to him. "Tell me, then. Who was Lancelot?"

"*Sir* Lancelot," Jesse said. "Fiercest knight of King Arthur's Round Table. Mad skilled with the sword. Irresistible to the queen."

"Sounds like you admire that part."

Jesse shrugged. "Just stating facts. Also known for being strong, kind, and loyal—at least, until the thing with the queen—which is why the name got passed on to this guy."

"I'm impressed." Faith crouched down, rubbing Lancelot behind the ears. The dog moved to a sitting position, eating it up. "Aww, sweet boy, you're definitely lovable."

Jesse looked at her. "I've missed you. You're the only one who brings out this side of me."

Faith looked up at him. "What side is that?"

"I don't even know how to describe it." He shrugged. "But I wish you had texted first so I could have saved you a trip. I'm actually on my way out."

Faith stood. "I took a chance because it's been hard for us to connect. And we haven't really talked since, you know, the news."

"I know." Jesse ran his hands down his face with a heavy sigh. "Have to say, I'm still processing. There was so much going on, with graduation and family in town all last week." He nodded vaguely. "But we do need time to talk."

"How about this weekend?" They could drive somewhere,

maybe Annapolis, and spend the day. "I was supposed to be in St. Louis, but I decided to stay home."

"You were going to St. Louis?" Jesse said. "My buddy Aaron has been trying to get me to visit. That could've been timely."

"You're thinking we could have made the trip together?"

"Yeah, I could've helped with the driving, and we could've carved out time together."

"I was flying actually." Her mind switched gears. Out-of-town together sounded much nicer than Annapolis. They could tour the city, take a ride up the Arch . . . "We could check to see if there are any seats still available. We'd be leaving in two days, though, on Thursday, staying till Sunday."

"That's no problem," Jesse said. "But I can't afford a last-minute ticket."

"It can't be that much," Faith said. "I can take care of it." Perks of the college fund her dad had set up for her.

"What's in St. Louis for you, family or something?"

"It's a women's ministry conference thing." Faith wasn't sure that she'd attend, but that was another matter. "I registered last fall with my mom and Aunt Jillian."

"Have you told your mom about . . . everything?"

Faith nodded.

"And you'd show up with me? How do you think that would go over?"

"I can't worry about that. It's a chance for us to spend some time." Faith hesitated. "I've . . . missed you too."

"You miss me, huh?" Jesse eyed her. "Help me figure something out. How do you show up over here in regular ol' jeans—not even fitted—regular ol' T-shirt, no makeup, not your best hair day, just keeping it real, yet still *fine*." He took her hand and brought her closer. "That's my problem with you. You drive me crazy."

The thickness of his voice sent chills through her. "Why is that a problem?"

Jesse stared into her eyes, traced her brow. "I don't even want to think about that right now." He put his arms around her and touched his lips to hers.

Faith pulled back a little. "I thought you were on your way out." Part of her had been comforted by that.

"I was," Jesse said, kissing her again. "You throw my whole world into chaos."

His arms tightened around her waist, and Faith told herself this was as far as it would go. She couldn't keep to a path she knew was wrong.

But being around him was intoxicating.

Jesse kissed her neck, ran a finger up the bare skin of her back. "You want to go upstairs?" The whisper caressed her ear.

His voice, his scent, his touch . . . every aspect of him diluted her resolve.

She gave the slightest nod and allowed him to lead her by hand.

CHAPTER FIVE

Wednesday, May 18

Stephanie dialed her sister as she waited for her takeout order, hoping to leave a message. She wasn't in the mood for conversation. Or questions. But she needed to let her know.

"Steph, I'm in a meeting about the conference, can I call you back?" Cyd said.

Stephanie moved aside as someone else came to place an order. "You could've let it go to voice mail, you know."

"You don't usually call in the morning," Cyd said, "so I figured it might be important. Is it? Or can I call you back?"

"It's not *important*. Just wanted you to know I'm on my way."

"On your way where?"

"To St. Louis, for the conference." Stephanie waited a few seconds. "Hello?"

"Sorry," Cyd said, "I had to step out of the meeting to make sure I heard you right. You're on your way here? What happened to change your mind?"

Stephanie picked up her order, sighing inside. One of the

questions she didn't want to answer. "Long story, but Lindell wasn't able to make it home as expected." She stopped at a counter for condiments, tasting a fry to make sure it was hot. "It hit me last night that it wasn't too late to come, so . . . Here I am, at a rest stop on the Kentucky border."

"Wow," Cyd said. "Talk about impromptu. But how is Lindell? Is he okay? That was a week and a half ago he was supposed to be home. When's he coming now?"

Stephanie headed to her car, trying to slide a straw into her milkshake with one hand. More questions. And she didn't have an answer to a single one of them. "We'll see. He's got a lot to tend to down there."

"Okay," Cyd said, in that tone that said she could ask more but would leave it. "Well, I get to see you, so I'm excited. And your nephew will be super excited. Chase loves his Auntie Stephie. Okay, gotta go. Drive safely, and I'll see you soon."

Stephanie settled herself in the car, putting the burger and fries on a napkin in her lap so she could drive and eat. She didn't want to waste any time. The closer she got to St. Louis, the farther she was from Hope Springs.

And with every passing mile, she was more sure of her decision.

CHAPTER SIX

Thursday, May 19

Treva boarded the plane from Baltimore-Washington International to St. Louis with a heavy heart. Less than a week ago she'd been looking forward to Faith coming home for the summer. Her hang-out buddy. The daughter who loved chick flicks and legal thrillers, raw cashews and kale smoothies, and reading everything from poetry to slave narratives—all just like her mom. She'd even talked about going to law school, as Treva had.

But Faith had influenced her mother as well. Faith loved the Lord from an early age—thanks to her dad and Grandma Darlene—and possessed an unshakable faith. She knew who she was and didn't care to please anyone but God. Her dedication inspired Treva . . . which was why this whole thing was so surreal, and so painful. Tuesday evening especially—when Carolyn called to say she'd walked in on Faith and Jesse in his room. Faith wouldn't talk about it, and last night she'd said she was staying with a friend. Treva hurt for her—as a mother, of course, but just as much as a sister in Christ.

"Treva?"

She looked. Jillian had stopped a couple feet in front of her.

"I said, how's this row?"

Treva nodded. "Fine."

Jillian scooted in, taking the window seat. "I know you like the aisle. If it's not a full flight, maybe we can keep the extra room in the middle." She put her tote bag under the seat in front of her and settled in.

Treva stashed her carry-on overhead and moved into the aisle seat. She checked her text messages.

"Anything?" Jillian asked.

"Nothing." Treva checked e-mail too, though she knew it was the last method of communication her daughter would use. "I just want to know that Faith's okay before I leave town. I don't understand why she's not responding."

Jillian looked at her. "Lots of reasons. She's upset that you have a problem with her seeing Jesse. She's embarrassed about what happened with Carolyn—"

Treva held up a hand. "If we never mention that again, I'll be just fine." She looked at her sister, dumbfounded. "I'm still just . . . Is that not the *last* thing you'd ever expect . . ." She shook her head. "I just can't."

"I keep imagining myself in Carolyn's position. She pops her head into her son's room to ask why he's home instead of picking up his little brother like he was supposed to, and—boom." Jillian shook her head. "I don't know what I would've done. To

Carolyn's credit, she handled it well."

"I don't know what I would've done either," Treva said. "But I would've had a *real* hard time simply apologizing and closing the door."

"It worked well, though," Jillian said. "Faith was out of there in five minutes flat, without having to be any more embarrassed than necessary. And Carolyn gave you a heads-up so you could be there for Faith."

"Oh, I agree it was the best way to handle it. Still. You know me. No telling what my reaction would've been in the moment." Treva gave her sister a look. "Girl, I might've forgotten I was saved."

"The best thing you can do for Faith now is pray and trust God. He's well able to take care of her."

Treva was quiet a moment. "That's what Hezekiah would have said. But then, if Hezekiah were still here, she wouldn't have fallen for someone like Jesse."

"Oh, Treva, you can't go there," Jillian said. "First of all, you don't know that for sure. Faith's learning what it means to have freedom and responsibility. She could have made the same choices."

Treva shook her head. "I just can't see it. You know how close they were." She lowered her armrest and put an elbow on it. "I don't think I'll ever understand why God took Hez. Everything just feels so . . . wrong. Honestly, sharing my story at the conference feels wrong. It's basically a sham."

"What? Why would you say that?"

"I'm telling these women about the pain I suffered growing up and how God did a miracle, bringing forgiveness and healing in our family. Yet here I am struggling *right now* and wondering where God is. I don't want the women who hear me to think everything has a happy ending, because it doesn't. My oldest daughter is becoming a stranger, and the only man I've ever loved is gone."

"No way am I letting you believe that lie. It would be a *sham* to testify about what God did? Did He do it, or didn't He?" She looked at her sister. "He did a miracle in Momma's heart—and yours and mine too. He did way beyond what we could ask or think. Just like I'm believing He'll do this weekend. Those women will be blessed by what you share."

"Ladies and gentleman," a flight attendant announced, "we need everyone to find a seat and stow your bags so we can push back from the gate on time."

Treva leaned her head back and closed her eyes. Jillian could believe in conference miracles all she wanted. That's who she was, ever the optimist. All Treva hoped was that she could get through the weekend without worrying herself half to—

"Oh my goodness, is that Faith?"

"What?" Treva sat up and looked, leaning one way, then another to see past people in the aisle. "I don't see—wait, I *do* see her." She looked at Jillian. "Can you believe it? She came after all."

"I told you," Jillian said. "Beyond what we ask or think."

Treva watched her daughter make her way toward them. The line was backed up, moving slowly as people took vacant middles and searched for space overhead for their bags. Faith finally came near and Treva rose from her seat. "Sweetheart, I'm so glad you decided to come." She gestured to their row. "We've got an empty seat right here."

"Mom, thanks, but . . ." Faith gestured over her shoulder—and there was Jesse, a couple of people behind her.

"We decided to come together. He has a friend in town and—"

"Ma'am." The flight attendant tapped Treva's arm. "I need you to take your seat so people can move through the aisle."

"Sorry." Treva moved into the row, head spinning. "Faith, honey, the plane is crowded and you need to sit somewhere. You can still sit here with us, can't you?"

Faith looked to the flight attendant. "Are there two seats together anywhere?"

"Very last row," she said, pointing backward, "if you don't mind being by the bathroom."

Faith pushed forward, and Treva sat back down, stunned. She looked at Jillian. "I don't even know what to say."

"Hey, good to see you, Mrs. Langston."

Treva looked up at him, the boyfriend who'd been hidden, the father of her future grandchild. Looking cute, preppy, and harmless. "Good morning, Jesse," she said.

The person behind him, one of the last to board, indicated he wanted their middle seat.

Treva moved into it herself and allowed him the aisle. She buckled her belt and turned to Jillian. "Did that just happen? Is she planning to go to the conference? And is she staying with us?"

"You don't have to figure everything out two miles down the road. This is huge, Treva. Faith is on the plane. She'll be in St. Louis."

"Yeah." Treva let her eyes fold to a close. "With Jesse."

<hr />

The moment the wheels hit the runway in St. Louis, Treva powered up her phone and speed-dialed her mother-in-law. "Ma, you won't believe this."

"I know," Darlene said. "I'm still waiting to hear from Faith myself, but—"

"No," Treva said, her voice a whisper. "She showed up. With Jesse."

"Showed up where? At the airport?"

"*Boarded the plane.* They're here, in St. Louis."

"What in the world?" Darlene said. "Where are they planning to stay?"

"You know she didn't tell me her plans. If she's going to the conference, I feel like she's got to stay with us at the hotel."

"And how would you accomplish that exactly?" Darlene said. "Gunpoint?"

Treva moved into the aisle and pulled down her carry-on. "So all we can do is stand back and watch her make bad decision after bad decision? She doesn't even know this guy, not really. But she acts like it's Faith and Jesse against the world."

"Chile, that's not all we can do," Darlene said. "We are *praying*. And you better believe God is up to something. How do you think she got on that plane?"

"But she's with Jesse."

"And she's in St. Louis. I'll be praying she gets to the conference."

"Why do you and Jillian always say the same things?" Treva looked back at her sister as they made their way up the aisle.

"Treva, listen." Darlene had her fighter voice. "Don't be shaken by what you *see*. It won't be pretty. No telling what Faith might say or do this weekend. But you have to keep the faith."

The well of emotion rose. "I'm trying, but you have no idea how hard this is without Hezekiah. I didn't think it was possible, but I miss him now more than ever."

It took a moment for Darlene to respond. "I know." Her voice was thick. "Treva, you know how much I loved Hezekiah, and I loved the way he loved you. But sweetheart, Hezekiah was never your strength. God is your strength, and He's still with you."

Treva sighed. "My head knows it. I just wish my heart could

feel it." She made her way up the Jetway. "I'll call later when the girls are out of school."

"I'm hoping you'll be having too much fun to call. We'll be fine. I'm cooking up all their favorites as we speak."

"Spoiling them is what you're doing."

"That's my right."

"Love you, Ma."

"Love you too, baby. Praying hard."

Treva hung up and turned to Jillian, who was on her phone, then cast an eye beyond her for Faith. She didn't want to miss her, in case they bypassed baggage claim. She wanted to hear their plans.

"Oh, really?" Jillian was saying. "Yep, just landed. Okay, sounds good." She hung up. "Hey, Treva, that was—" Her eyes lifted along with Treva's as Faith and Jesse came out of the Jetway.

"Jesse," she said, reaching out. "We met briefly at the Christmas party. I'm Faith's aunt, Jillian Mason." She shook his hand. "How are you?"

"Real good, Mrs. Mason, thanks."

Treva cleared her throat. "So Faith, are you coming with us, and Jesse's going with his friend?"

Faith sighed. "No, Mom, that's not the plan. We booked a room at the conference hotel."

"Booked a room . . . for the two of you?"

"Yes," Faith said. "They had a couple cancellations."

"Excuse us, Jesse," Treva said, then looked at her daughter. "Let me talk to you a minute."

Faith hesitated before following Treva a few feet away.

"I don't understand anything that's going on right now," Treva said. "You're registered for a Christian women's conference and staying at the conference hotel with a man who's not your husband, like"—she threw her hands up—"no big deal? I feel like my daughter's been invaded by an alien."

"Mom, how is it a big deal? Jesse and I are having a baby. Obviously this won't be our first night together."

Treva stared at her daughter. "Where is God in all this? Do you even care about Him anymore?"

Faith made a face, as if incredulous. "Of course I care about God, Mom. Everything is not as big a deal as you make it."

Darlene's words flashed in Treva's mind—*Don't be shaken by what you see*. Treva wouldn't win this, and she'd only do damage trying. "You know what? You'll be twenty this year, and I have to let you make your own decisions. I'm glad you're here." She wanted to ask whether Faith was going to attend the conference, but she bit back her question.

Faith glanced at a notification on her phone. "We've got to go," she said. "Jesse's friend is waiting for us." She rejoined Jesse, who'd been talking to Jillian, and together they walked toward one of the exits.

"What were you two talking about?" Treva headed toward baggage claim with her sister.

"He's actually kind of funny," Jillian said. "They had a chatty Uber driver on the way to the airport. They told him they were going to St. Louis, but the driver kept saying St. Croix. Then he referred to Faith as Jesse's wife." She veered to the right, following the baggage claim arrow. "So Jesse said, 'On the off chance that dude was a prophet, I'm thinking I should note the date somewhere, in case Faith and I get married and honeymoon in St. Croix.'"

Treva looked at her. "How is that funny?"

"O-kay," Jillian said. "Moving on . . ."

"Treva?"

A woman waved at them, approaching baggage claim from a different direction.

Treva smiled. "Cyd?"

She'd only seen Cyd London in a picture on the conference website, but this had to be her. With all the Faith and Jesse drama, she'd forgotten how much she'd been looking forward to meeting her.

Cyd came toward them, beaming, and they embraced like old friends.

"You look just like your picture," Cyd said, "except taller than I expected."

"And you're taller than I am," Treva said. "What, five nine? And you cut a few inches of your hair too. Looks cute."

"Exactly right on both counts," Cyd said. "And you must be Jillian." She hugged her too. "I feel like I know you two after

41

reading Treva's story."

"Isn't it amazing?" Jillian elbowed Treva. "I had to hound her to get her to submit it."

"You're kidding," Cyd said.

Treva looked sheepish. "It's true."

The conference website had asked attendees to share stories of how God had used a Living Word Bible study in their lives. Sharing personal stuff had never been easy for Treva, but it wasn't purely Jillian's hounding that moved her. It had been a chance to express gratitude to the ministry that had made a huge impact on her life. She was floored when Cyd had called to ask Treva to tell her testimony at the conference.

"I hope this doesn't sound weird," Cyd said, "but the story really comes alive seeing you two side by side."

Treva nodded. "Jillian needs to stand next to me while I tell it, as a visual aid."

"I'll be whatever you want me to be," Jillian said. "I'm just excited you're doing it." She looked at Cyd. "And I have to say, I am such a fan. The last two Living Word studies our group has done are the ones you wrote, and we love them."

"That means a lot," Cyd said. "Pastor Lyles asked me a few years ago to write some, but then I got married and had a baby." She gave them a look. "*In my forties.* For a while I was too tired to write my name. And that little boy's still got me hopping. Tell me things calm down in a year or two."

This time it was Treva giving Cyd the look. "Girl. My nineteen-year-old daughter is driving me crazy. So umm . . . no."

"Gee, thanks."

The three women laughed, and it felt good. The past week had held little humor.

"Luggage from flight 2952 from Baltimore-Washington International now being delivered to carousel two."

As the women moved to the carousel, Cyd said, "If you two aren't doing anything this evening, we're having an impromptu cookout at my house. My sister's in town, and we're having a few friends over. I could come get you from the hotel around six." She paused. "But if you have plans, I understand."

"I'd love that," Jillian said.

"You have no idea," Treva said. "That would be the perfect carefree thing right now. But honestly, you've done so much, just picking us up from the airport. And you've got the conference starting in the morning. We can easily grab something near the hotel."

"No trouble at all," Cyd said. "But speaking of your daughter, wasn't she supposed to be with—"

"Jilli-Jill!"

All three of them turned to see a guy walking toward them with a wide smile.

"Is that Tommy Porter?" Treva cocked her head. "Talk about a blast from the past."

"Tommy-Tom!" Jillian met him halfway. "So good to see you!"

Treva watched as he enfolded her sister in his slightly husky frame.

"Okay, small world," Cyd said. "You all know each other?"

"Tommy was like a brother to me when we were in college," Jillian said. "How do you know each other?"

"We attend the same church," Tommy said.

"This is crazy," Jillian said. "And Tommy, you remember Treva, right?"

"Definitely," Tommy said, hugging her. "And I remember two things—you were about the best dressed woman on campus, and I had the distinct impression that you didn't like me."

Treva's eyes widened. "Why would you say that?"

"Oh, maybe because when all of us would hang out, you never really . . ." Tommy shrugged in a funny way. "Spoke."

"Oh my," Treva said. "I feel bad. It wasn't personal. I had a lot of . . . issues." She couldn't help but chuckle.

"Oh! I see our bags." Jillian grabbed hers from the conveyor belt and Treva's right after.

Tommy looked at Jillian. "So, you ready?"

Treva eyed her sister. "You've got plans?"

"We just made them when Tommy called, after the plane landed. I was about to tell you, but Faith and Jesse— Anyway, we're just grabbing lunch. I'll meet you back at the hotel in a few."

Cyd checked her watch. "Then, Treva, we should get going

so I can get you checked in and take care of a few things before this evening."

"Absolutely." Treva looked at Jillian. "Guess I'll see you . . . in a few, then."

CHAPTER SEVEN

Jillian followed Tommy outside and into the parking garage, feeling the warmth of the St. Louis weather. "Why do you look exactly the same?"

Tommy grinned over his shoulder. "You don't have to sound so disgusted."

Jillian laughed. "It's not fair, having the same build you had in college. But I see you trying to hide the gray by shaving your head."

"Oh, it can't be because it's cool or suave—I have to be hiding something." He turned, eyeing her. "Meanwhile, you're working that Clairol honey auburn."

"You are so wrong."

Tommy stopped at a beige Lexus and popped the trunk. He put Jillian's bags inside and led her to the passenger side. "Let me officially welcome you to The Lou," he said. "I can't believe you've never been here."

"I've never been a lot of places." Jillian sank into the beige leather seat. "I'm one of those boring people who likes sticking close to home."

"That's cool, though," Tommy said. "Proverbs 31 in full effect."

"I didn't say all that now."

Tommy got in on the other side and started the car. "Seriously, I love it. You said you've been married, what, nineteen years?"

Jillian nodded. They'd had a long catch-up conversation a week ago, their first in two decades.

"Four kids," Tommy continued. "You stay at home *and* homeschool. Girl, what else you got to do to be P31 certified?"

"I'm thinking a couple of handmaidens would help. Maybe learn how to sew."

"Well, shoot, might as well grow a vineyard too."

Jillian chuckled. "It's funny how we get right back in the flow."

"Yeah," Tommy said, "but you were kind of guarded at first when I called."

"I think it just felt weird," Jillian said. "It's been a long time. But hey, you sounded a little guarded yourself."

"All I knew was my sister called, all excited, saying she saw you at this church she visited." Tommy changed lanes. "Then she says you're coming to St. Louis, and I need to be a good host and show you around the city." He glanced at her. "I didn't know if it was her idea or yours. And if it was yours, I felt bad because I was about to shoot it down."

"I had no idea she was going to call you," Jillian said. "She mentioned you lived in St. Louis. I mentioned I was heading there in a couple weeks. But honestly I wasn't thinking of getting together."

"Yeah, my first thought," Tommy said, "was that you're my girl, but hanging out with a married woman on an out-of-town trip? I have this neon sign in my mind, 'Be careful how you walk.'"

Jillian waved a finger at him. "That's what it was. I was trying to remember what you said. I was like, wow."

"Which is when you asked if I'm a Christian now, then started quizzing me to see if it was legit."

"I did not quiz you."

"Please. You were like, 'Share your testimony in one hundred words or less, and I'll be listening for the key words: *Jesus. Repentance. Changed.*'"

Jillian cracked up. "I seriously can't stand you. All I said was, what's your testimony?"

"What you wanted to know was whether I'm the same guy I was in college."

"Nope," Jillian said. "I would hope you're not the same guy. We're twenty years older. But there's a difference between being changed by maturity and being changed by the Spirit."

Tommy glanced at her, nodding. "When you asked about my testimony, that told me how serious *you* are about the Lord." He gave her a look. "Because don't act like you weren't a trip in college."

Jillian shook her head at the memory. "When I think back to that time . . . You know better than anybody, all the stuff I shared with you."

"So after all that, here you are in my car." Tommy laughed.

"How did that happen?"

"It seemed crazy *not* to get together after all the reminiscing and testifying. You're the one guy who's been a brother to me, and now you're my brother in Christ." Jillian paused, thinking about the blessing in that. "I'm glad we got together. I feel like I needed this. And I'm not even sure why."

<hr>

"I had no business eating that peach cobbler after fried chicken, mac-n-cheese, and collard greens," Jillian said. "I'll have to work out tonight, tomorrow morning, and whenever I get a break in the conference."

"I can't eat like this regularly." Tommy leaned back, tossed his napkin on the table. "I only do Sweetie Pie's when people come to town. I get more requests to come here than the Arch."

Jillian had never seen the reality show that had made the soul food restaurant popular, but one of the women in their Bible study had said to check it out.

"In your case," Tommy continued, "I thought of it more as a mission trip."

"A mission trip?"

"For the deprived child who grew up without soul food."

Jillian laughed. "I can't believe you remember that."

"Who could forget?" Tommy said. "I was shocked."

"You wouldn't have been so shocked if you had ever met

my mother," Jillian said. "She turns her nose up at anything she deems 'common.' As kids we had to act a certain way, dress a certain way, eat a certain way . . ." She sipped some sweet tea. "But you can rest easy. After college, Treva's mother-in-law became my mentor, and she specializes in soul food. Made up for everything I missed."

"Oh, yeah, she's the one that led you to the Lord, right?"

"Yep. Darlene Langston. That woman changed my life. Kind of like your story, with what's his name?"

"My pastor, Lance. Lance Alexander. Definitely changed my life." He grew reflective. "I wish things had changed a little sooner, though, before I wrecked my marriage."

Jillian knew he'd married and divorced in his twenties, but didn't know the details. She looked at him. "Sounds like it was pretty bad."

"I was caught up with work, trying to make it as an entertainment reporter. A lot of late nights, a lot of travel." He paused. "I found out my wife was having an affair."

"I thought you said *you* wrecked your marriage."

"Of course I didn't see it that way at first," Tommy said. "I put all the blame on her for a long time. But God showed me my marriage wasn't the priority it should have been. I wasn't there for her."

"Did you ever think about going back? Trying to work things out?"

"Couldn't. She married the guy the minute it was legal to do so." Tommy drank some lemonade. "I did call her, though, several years later, and apologized for my part." He played with his straw. "Felt like I had to."

"You think you'll marry again?" Jillian asked.

"I don't know." A slight twinkle entered his eye. "I'm seeing someone though."

"For real?" Jillian leaned in. "I know you're not trying to be coy about it. Details, details."

"Well. I've been taking it slow. We were just friends for a long time, but in the last few months . . ." He shrugged. "Might be getting serious."

"She's here in St. Louis?"

"She is," Tommy said. "I wish you could meet— Heyy, we're going to an old-school concert tonight. One of the perks of having an entertainment column—free tickets to everything. I've got four to this one. You and Treva should join us. And you can meet Allison."

Jillian shook her head. "I'd love to meet her, but Cyd invited us to her home for a cookout this evening. Who's headlining, though?"

Tommy paused. "New Edition."

"No way."

He pointed at her. "Don't even go there. That was the most embarrassing moment of my life."

Jillian tried to stifle a laugh. "I just never understood why you agreed to be in the talent show. I mean, you *knew* you couldn't sing."

"I said I'd do it because my boys needed a fifth guy, and you have to admit I could do the dance moves. We *told* the sound guy to keep my mic off."

"But why did you started singing lead?"

He leaned in. "Because I thought my mic was off!"

Jillian was outright laughing now. "The way you got into those dance moves, though, all loud and off-key."

"You know what, you can walk back to your hotel." Tommy laughed with her. "I told Allison, and she thought I was exaggerating."

"Oh, I would love to confirm that it's true." She thought a moment. "I actually think it would be fun to go. Cyd said it was informal, no big deal if we couldn't make it. I'm sure she'd understand." She paused again. "But Treva probably still wants to go, and I'd hate to be a third wheel on your date with Allison."

"She's really easygoing and she loves people," Tommy said. "I know she'd want to meet you." He pulled out his phone. "I'll call her right now."

"Well, don't ask her while I'm sitting here. That's so—"

The phone was already ringing.

"Hey, how was lunch with your college friend?" Allison asked.

"It's good, we're still here actually. I've got you on speaker."

"Okay, what's up?"

"New Edition concert tonight," Tommy said. "I didn't think you'd mind if I invited Jillian and her sister. But her sister has other plans, and Jillian doesn't want to be a third wheel—"

"Oh, not at all," Allison said. "We go to concerts all the time. Hey, Jillian! I'd love for you to come so I can meet you."

Jillian smiled. "I appreciate that, Allison. I'd love to meet you too. And I can't remember the last time I went to a concert."

"It's a must then."

Tommy pushed a button and took her off speaker. "Thanks, Al," he said, his voice softer. "I'll call you back in a little bit . . . Love you too."

Jillian gave him the eye when he hung up. "*Might* be getting serious?"

"Just a little."

"Look at you blushing."

"A black man can't blush." Tommy put down a tip and rose from his seat. "And I told you, I'm taking it slow."

"Uh, huh." Jillian got up, grabbing her purse. "Just don't leave Cecil and me off the guest list."

Tommy paused. "This is actually really cool."

"What is?"

"Being back in touch. God is full of surprises."

"I know," Jillian said. "I'm glad to have my brother back."

CHAPTER EIGHT

Faith stood at the picture window in the hotel room, staring at the view from the fifteenth floor. "Can you believe
how nice this is?" She glanced at Jesse, who was sprawled
across the king-sized bed doing something on his phone.

"I didn't know we'd be right downtown." He looked up, his
eyes sweeping the room. "This has to be expensive, Faith. I told
you I could've stayed with Aaron, while you stay with your mom
and Aunt Jillian like you planned."

"And I told you," Faith said, "it's no problem." She was well
under budget for the semester, and besides, this was what she'd
wanted, the two of them together. "So what should we do? The
Arch? We're within walking distance. Or we could walk by the
river. Or get something to eat." She plopped on the bed. "What
do you think?"

Jesse seemed to ponder it. "What do I think?" He sat up
and put his phone on the nightstand. "I think we've got some
elephants in the room that need to be dealt with. We said we
needed to talk, right?"

Faith's heart pounded slightly. "You sound so serious."

"It is serious, Faith. You're pregnant."

She looked down. "I know."

"And we never talked about what happened Tuesday with my mom."

Faith groaned. "I don't ever want to talk about that. What she must think of me . . ."

"She's got a lot of respect for you."

Faith tossed her eyes. "Right."

"I'm the one she had an issue with." Jesse glanced down. "She said . . . well, she said a lot of things . . . but one was that I needed to be honest with you."

Faith stared at him, listening.

"To be honest, this pregnancy couldn't have come at a worse time. You have to be thinking the same thing."

"Well, it's not optimal, that's for sure."

"So the question is, what do we do? We need to look at our options."

Faith's brow lifted. "What options?"

"You're only about four weeks along," Jesse said. "Nothing's even formed yet. We could put this behind us and move on—"

"Are you talking about an abortion?" Faith said. "That's nowhere on my radar."

"Well, neither was sex. I'm just saying. Sometimes one unexpected choice leads to another."

"There's no way I'm having an abortion, Jesse." Faith got up and paced a little.

He was quiet a moment. "Then adoption needs to be the

next option."

"Really?" Faith turned to him. "It might be *your* next option, but it's not mine."

Jesse's expression turned grave. "Are you saying you want to keep this baby? You're ready to be a parent?"

"Of course I'm not ready," Faith said. "This wasn't planned. But there's a life growing inside of me, and it's *part* of me—and part of you. I can't wrap my mind around giving the baby away."

"Do you even understand how selfish you're being?"

"How am I being selfish?"

"What *you* want is all that matters," Jesse said. "You don't care about a single thing I'm saying." He took a deep breath. "I'm not ready to be a parent, Faith."

"Did you think about that when we were having sex?"

He got up and walked to the window, staring out at the city.

Tears welled in Faith's eyes. "I'm just trying to handle this the best way I know how."

Jesse turned suddenly. He grabbed his phone from the night-stand and headed for the door. "I need some time to think."

"You're leaving?" Faith followed him. "Where are you going?"

"I'll have Aaron come get me."

"But—"

The door closed behind him, and Faith stopped just in front of it as the tears fell. All she could think was how much she wanted her dad.

CHAPTER NINE

Stephanie was sure her head would explode. She'd thought St. Louis would be an improvement. This was home. And being around Cyd had always been good for her, even when she was too rebellious to realize it. But not this time. All the conference frenzy was making things worse.

"What do you mean, you're not going?" Cyd stood by the kitchen counter, chopping carrots and broccoli for a veggie tray. "I thought that's why you came this weekend."

"Because when the conference team was here a little while ago, I got a taste of what it'll be like." Stephanie sat at the kitchen table, her fingertips pressed to her throbbing temples. "Endless questions about whether I'll ever be able to move on with my life."

"Oh, Steph, nobody asked any such thing."

"That's what all the questions were really about."

"They genuinely want to know how you're doing, that's all. Some of these women have known and loved you since you were a little girl." Cyd looked over at her. "Anybody who went through what you went through . . . It's a lot to move past."

That's what it was. When they saw her, people here were

reliving the Hope Springs Tragedy, as news outlets had dubbed it. Which made those events from almost three years ago fresh again. On top of her current sucky life.

"And ooh," Stephanie said, "did you hear Miss Shirley's little comment? 'Be careful about making food your comfort'—like I don't know I've gained weight." She stewed over it anew. "Folk get on my last nerve."

"I'm with you on that," Cyd said. "I guess she meant well, but it wasn't necessary."

The doorbell rang, and the screen door opened and clanged shut. "Hello," a voice rang out.

"Hey, Lance, we're in here," Cyd called.

"Wait till you see how the shirts—Steph, hey!" Lance rounded the bend with a big box. "I didn't know you were in town."

"It was kind of a last-minute decision." *A dumb one, apparently.* She got up to hug him. "It's good to see you, Lance. Or should I say 'Pastor Alexander.'"

Lance set the box down, looking every bit the same in faded jeans and a graphic tee. They were both in their thirties, and Stephanie had known him since he first came to Living Word over a decade ago. Now he was pastor of a Living Word church plant—Living Hope.

"Don't even try to get formal on me." He gave her a big hug. "I'm still Lance."

Stephanie's heart went out to him. "I don't even know what to say." She held his gaze a moment. "I was really happy when I heard about the church plant—I mean, who didn't know you'd be a pastor one day? But knowing what you've been through, losing your wife. I can't imagine . . ."

"Thanks, Steph," Lance said. "It's been a roller coaster for sure. But I remember thinking the same about you, that I couldn't imagine what you were going through down there in Hope Springs." He shook his head. "So sad what happened to that sweet girl. What was her name? I followed the story on CNN."

"Her name was Sam." Stephanie's heart reacted whenever she spoke her name, as the headline rolled in her mind: *Teen commits suicide after date rape video goes viral.* "And she really was a sweet girl. I only knew her for a few months, but we had gotten close."

"Lance," Cyd said, "I was actually thinking about the fact that you and Steph have both experienced loss recently. I was wondering if you could, you know, maybe talk to her or recommend a good—"

"What Cyd means is she thinks I've never quite rebounded."

"Steph," Cyd said, "I just don't think the counselor you had down there was a good fit. And as I've been saying, there's nothing wrong with needing ongoing help after a life crisis."

Lance was nodding. "What you experienced was traumatic, Steph. Weren't you the one who helped Sam the night of the rape?"

"And she was there the next day when they found Sam had taken her own life."

Lance looked at Stephanie. "It goes without saying. I'm here if you ever want to talk. I can also put you in touch with a friend who's an excellent grief counselor."

Stephanie nodded, then moved to the cabinet to look for headache medicine. Cyd meant well, but she had no idea. Her issues went way beyond the tragedy.

"Did Lindell come with you?" Lance asked.

How timely. "No." Stephanie poured a glass of water. Maybe if her own husband had been there for her after what happened with Sam, she would've rebounded a lot sooner. "He's in Haiti."

"Still doing medical missions, huh?" Lance sounded impressed. "That's awesome."

Stephanie threw a pill to the back of her throat and downed some water.

"So, the shirts," Cyd said, moving toward the box. "I'm so excited to see how they turned out."

"Thanks again for using the guy I recommended," Lance said. "I remember what it was like trying to find work when I got out of prison. An order like this means a lot, and he does great work." He pulled a shirt from the box and held it up.

Cyd gasped. "Oh, I love it. Steph, look." Cyd took the shirt from him and held it out. On the front the words *In Hot Pursuit* were emblazoned with an artsy font and logo, and on the back *Living Word Women's Conference.*

"Your friend did amazing work," Stephanie said. "That fuchsia and brown combo sets it off."

"What size do you want?" Cyd reached into the box. "You

can have yours now."

"Um, that's okay."

Cyd gave her a glance, then turned back to Lance. "I can't believe it's all come together. It was just a seed of a thought for so many years, then it formed more and more in my mind, but it seemed it would never happen." She held up the shirt again. "But tomorrow morning it actually kicks off—the first ever Living Word Women's Conference!"

"The Living Hope women can't stop talking about it," Lance said. "They feel like it's their baby too."

"It *is*," Cyd said. "It's been amazing having women from both churches get behind this."

"Why wouldn't they, Cyd?" Lance said. "You're a natural leader."

The back door opened, and a burst of energy entered the kitchen—Cyd's husband, Cedric; their four-year-old son, Chase; and their dog, Reese.

"Hey, man," Cedric said, slapping hands with Lance, "you ready to work? I'm getting the grill ready."

"How is it every time you have a cookout, I get put to work?"

"Consider it a compliment of your growing skill level," Cedric said.

"Oh, *growing* skill level. Okay." Lance looked at Cyd. "He refuses to admit I'm the one who taught him everything he knows about grilling, but it's cool."

"All I know," Cyd said, "is when the two of you get busy out there, the food is delicious. So indulge him, Lance, so we can eat well." She winked at her husband. "I've got to pick up one more person from the airport. Be back shortly."

Chase tugged at her shirt. "I wanna go with you, Mommy. Can I go?"

Cyd bent down and hugged him, kissing his forehead. "Not this time, little man. I thought you were helping Dad."

"Exactly." Cedric spread his arms like he was hurt. "You were ready to leave me like that, Chase?"

"It's hot outside, Daddy."

Cedric laughed. "Boy, if you think eighty-five is hot, wait till next month. Come on, let's find the water guns so I can soak you."

"Yayyy!" Chase raced off to find them, Reese on his heels.

Stephanie watched her nephew and felt herself growing sadder. As much as she adored him, it was hard to engage the way she normally would.

"You want to ride along, Steph?" Cyd said. "I'm picking up one of the worship team members."

Stephanie rose from the table. "I think I'm going to take a nap."

"Sounds good. I hope you'll feel better."

Stephanie could feel Cyd's eyes on her as she took to the stairs. Worrying about her little sister, as usual. She was happy for Cyd. She'd been quietly mentoring women, and by example, Stephanie, for as far back as she could remember. It was no surprise that she was now writing Bible studies and leading a conference.

But by contrast her own life looked bleaker than ever. No purpose. No passion. No plan. Not that she'd ever had a clear vision for her life. That's why she'd moved to Hope Springs, to start fresh, to *get* a vision. And she thought she had. Working as a substitute teacher at Hope Springs High had filled her with purpose in a way she'd never known.

And it drained like a sieve within months.

Stephanie closed the blinds in the guest room and lit two fragrant candles she'd found earlier in the kitchen, placing them on the nightstand. It wasn't just Cyd on her mind, but Lance as well. In the midst of his own tragedy, he'd found purpose. He was thriving. And Lindell. As much as his time in Haiti had gone way beyond what was reasonable, it sprang from passion.

Stephanie got her phone, scrolled to a light jazz playlist, and inserted her earbuds. Then she sifted through a large piece of luggage, between a pile of shirts, where she'd placed a bottle inside a carrying case.

Reclining on the bed, candlelight flickering, smooth saxophone playing, she tipped the mini-bottle of white wine to her lips and savored the liquid as it went down. She'd be fine like this all weekend. This was how she found a modicum of peace.

CHAPTER TEN

Treva couldn't believe what she was hearing. "I thought this was supposed to be sister time. But you're ditching me *again?*"

"I'm not ditching you." Jillian lifted her shirt over her head and changed into another. "I asked you to come too."

Treva gave her a look. "Are we not here for the women's conference? Did we not talk about how cool it would be to meet the woman who wrote the Bible studies we've been doing?" Her gaze followed Jillian as she got ready. "Now this same woman is inviting us to her home, which you were excited about. And suddenly you'd rather be at a concert?"

"You had to be there," Jillian said. "We were reminiscing, and he mentioned New Edition and that he had four tickets . . . I never do things on the fly like this. It sounded like fun." She paused. "But now I feel bad. I know we've made a big deal for months about having a girls' getaway."

"Now you're making me feel bad for making you feel bad." Treva chuckled. "Fine. Go. You're right, you never go anywhere."

"Hey, thanks."

"So, about you and Tommy . . ." Treva slipped on an indigo

maxi dress. "Was there ever anything between you two?"

"Me and Tommy?" Jillian threw her a surprised look. "No. You would have known."

"Well, I didn't know you got pregnant until a few years back."

"I tried to tell you at the time."

Treva sighed. She was in law school then, always grinding, too busy to return her own sister's calls. "I know. But that's my point. I might've missed the news that you and Tommy had a thing."

"Not at all. Brother status only."

"You tell Cecil you're going?"

"Yes, Mother. Cecil knows I'm going to a concert with Tommy *and his girlfriend.*" Jillian moved to the mirror, ran her fingers through her hair, a blunt cut that hit below the ear. "What's with the third degree?"

"I don't know, it's just weird, you going out with another guy."

"*And his girlfriend.*"

Treva put on her sandals. "Don't mind me. I'm always thinking of questions I should have been asking Faith. I guess I'm trying to make up for it through you."

"Have you talked to her since the airport?"

"No," Treva said, joining her at the mirror. "I keep telling myself to give her space, not to call. I am wondering what room they're in, though."

Jillian got a text and checked her phone. "Tommy and Allison just pulled up." She grabbed her purse. "Please give Cyd my apologies. I want to hear all about it."

"Have fun, girl."

Treva's phone dinged with a text as Jillian went out the door, and Cyd London's name lit the screen.

Hi Treva, be there in ten. Meet you in front.

Treva finished freshening her makeup and hair and went downstairs. The lobby was full, people going to dinner, milling about, grabbing Starbucks. And mostly women, groups of them, wearing conference badges and chattering with excitement.

Treva moved toward the door so she could watch for Cyd's car—and spotted Faith sitting a little ways away. She sat in a grouping of chairs looking out a big picture window that faced the hotel's circular drive. Treva watched for a moment, moved by this glimpse of her daughter. She was beautiful, her hair in a pretty puff, her face natural and flawless.

Treva walked over. "Sweetheart, hi." She stood over her, feeling strangely without words.

Faith looked up. "Oh, hey." Her eyes fell again.

Treva wanted to ask what was wrong, but she knew the answer she'd get—*nothing*. "What are you up to?"

"Waiting for Jesse to get back so we can get something to eat."

"Okay."

Faith looked at a notification on her phone. "Great. He was supposed to be here an hour ago, now he's saying at least another hour before his friend can drive him back downtown.

I'm starving."

"Why don't you go with me to Cyd's? I'm sure she wouldn't mind. They're having a cookout tonight."

"Cyd London? You're going to her *house*?" At Treva's nod, Faith stared outside again. "I don't think so. I can wait."

"Okay."

Treva's tongue was growing thick. So much she wanted to say, like *Why are you building your existence around Jesse?* And *If you're starving, you have a baby to consider.*

Faith looked up again. "How long do you think you'll be there?"

Treva hid her surprise with a shrug. "The conference starts at nine in the morning, so I doubt it'll be late."

Cyd's car approached in the semicircular drive. "That's her," Treva said, looking at Faith. "You think maybe?"

"Yeah, I guess."

They walked out together, and Treva opened the front passenger door. "Hi, Cyd, Jillian sends her apologies. She wasn't able to come. But I hope it's okay to bring my daughter."

Cyd smiled. "Of course."

Faith got in the back, and Cyd turned. "So good to meet you. I'm Cyd London."

"Very nice to meet you, ma'am." Faith extended her hand. "I'm Faith Langston."

Cyd navigated her way through the semicircle to the main road. At a red light she glanced back. "I think your mom said you're nineteen?"

"Yes, ma'am."

"Wow, you're one of the youngest attendees," Cyd said. "I'm so excited you're here. Have you done Living Word Bible studies yourself?"

"Yes, I got a group together in my dorm last year," Faith said. "We did the one on the faithfulness of God. I did the 'steadfast' one too."

Cyd beamed. "You go, girl. We prayed specifically for younger women who were fired up for the Lord to come, get even more fired up, then go home and impact the people around them. I love that you're letting God use you."

Faith didn't reply. And Treva stared out the windshield, wondering what God might be up to.

"So, wait, how old were you when you got pregnant?" Treva leaned in, deep in conversation with two other women at Cyd's kitchen table.

One of the women, Kelli, sat across from her. "Eighteen," she said. "Senior in high school. My boyfriend and I got carried away in the moment. Then I got scared and had an abortion because he left me."

Dana, the other woman, pointed. "That's him, headed out back."

Treva followed her finger, eyes wide.

"Yeah." Kelli smiled. "Brian and I are married now."

"That's beautiful," Treva said.

"It was a long road, though," Kelli said. "I loved the Lord in high school and wanted to stay celibate. When that happened, I couldn't forgive myself."

Treva took a quick glance around, wishing Faith were hearing this. Last time she saw her, her daughter was outside with Cyd's son and dog. She'd even eaten with Chase in his wooden fort. He'd found a playmate, and Faith had found an escape from questioning adults.

"Well, why in the world am I giving my testimony?" Treva said. "You should be giving yours. It's incredible."

"Oh," Kelli said, "actually, my husband and I travel and tell our story all the time. And I'll be doing a breakout session at the conference on forgiving yourself."

"And besides, Treva, you *have* to give your testimony," Dana said. "When you tell it, it's like"—her jaw dropped—"wow. And this is funny. When you walked in, I whispered to Kelli that you were gorgeous—then you tell us how your mom called you ugly because of your dark skin. Crazy."

Kelli nodded. "Both you and your daughter are striking. It's hard to believe your mom felt that way. Thank God that's all changed."

"By the way," Treva said, "how do you two know Cyd?"

"She's my sister-in-law," Kelli said. "Cedric's my brother."

"And Cyd and I have been best friends since we were young," Dana said. "She talked me into doing a session on forgiving others." She gave Treva a look. "Don't even ask. We don't have time." She chuckled.

"*Mom.*" Faith came through the back door, breathless. "Can you believe I just met Alien? He's actually here."

"You met an alien?" Treva said.

"No, I met *Alien*, the Christian rapper. I have every one of his albums. I can't believe he's here."

Kelli was smiling broadly. "That's my Brian. Alien is his artist name." She got up and hugged Faith. "I'm Kelli. It's so good to meet you. Let's stay in touch, and next time we're in the DC area, you'll have to come to a show and hang out with us backstage."

Faith's eyes lit up. "Oh, wow, I would love that."

Treva's heart lifted. Staying in touch with Kelli would be great for Faith. She looked at her daughter. "If you're a fan you've heard their story, right? About Kelli getting pregnant in high school?"

Faith hesitated. "I think I do remember hearing it," she said.

Treva watched the wall slide back up, as if Faith thought the world was plotting against her. Her phone vibrated with a call, and she stepped back outside to answer it.

"Hey, hey! Who's ready for more barbecued chicken?"

Treva looked as one of the guys came in from the grill.

"I've been waiting," Kelli said. "Nobody grills chicken like you do." She looked at Treva. "You've met Lance, right? Pastor at Living Hope?"

"I only saw him in passing," Treva said, "and didn't know he was a pastor."

"Well, come on then, Kelli, and get it piping hot." He set the pan down and walked over. "Lance Alexander," he said, extending a hand toward Treva.

"Treva Langston," she said. "Nice to meet you."

"You as well," Lance said, backing up. "Don't mean to be rude." He aimed a thumb outdoors. "I've got burgers coming off too."

"Now that's what I'm waiting for," Dana said. She grinned at Kelli. "Did you see that young woman slide out the door after Lance? I'm not even sure who she's here with, but she's had her eye on him all night."

Kelli looked amused. "St. Louis's most eligible bachelor. If I hear one more—"

"All day I've been talking about how well things have gone." Cyd walked in, looking harried, phone in hand. "Just found out some sad news. One of our breakout leaders had a death in the family. She can't come."

"Which one was she leading?" Kelli asked.

"Interestingly, the one on recovering from loss. Her husband died six years ago." She pondered a moment. "Not sure what I'll do. She was a great fit for that one. She's even started a grief ministry."

"I think Treva would be a great fit also," Kelli said.

"What?" Treva looked at Kelli. "What makes you say that?"

"Well," Kelli said, "you just shared how God helped you heal from everything you went through with your mother. Now you've lost your husband, which was astounding to hear. I see so much grace on you as you recover from that too. I could see you leading that breakout session."

"Um, sorry," Treva said, "but there's no way, not that Cyd would have agreed anyway. I can share about my mother and my upbringing, but it's too soon to talk about losing my husband."

"Actually," Cyd said, "you wouldn't have to talk about it, not like you're doing with telling your story. You'd be facilitating a breakout session—"

"Oh, goodness." Treva shook her head. "I could never prepare for that. Too short notice."

"Just so you know," Cyd said, "all the session leaders have a packet of materials already prepared. We'll be leading the ladies through a new study, focusing on different aspects of it, like forgiveness, which Kelli is doing. All you have to do is look over the materials and share a little of your story at the beginning. Doesn't have to be in depth. And then there's the discussion part."

"I'm really not the right person for this," Treva said. "I don't facilitate our Bible study sessions back home. Leading discussions, all that . . . that's my sister's thing . . . gift . . . you know what I mean? But mostly," she went on, "it's the subject matter. I'm just not ready to deal with it."

She almost added that she'd seen the breakout session listed as an option on the website and decided she wasn't even ready for it as an attendee.

Cyd nodded slowly. "I'm hearing you," she said, "but I have a question. Are you willing to pray about it overnight? The more we talk about it, the more I just feel this might be a God thing." She raised her hands. "But I could be completely wrong. If you say no tomorrow morning, no problem."

Treva could feel anxiety rising at the thought of it. She knew what her answer would be, but how could she not agree to pray?

"Deal," she said. "I'll pray. And I'll be searching you out first thing in the morning."

CHAPTER ELEVEN

Jillian was sure she wouldn't be able to hear for days, and her feet, aching in the heels she wished she hadn't worn, screamed for relief. But right now, none of it mattered. New Edition was belting "Can You Stand the Rain?", the song she'd been waiting for all night, and she—and the rest of the concert hall—were on their feet, swaying to the beat.

From her spot in the third row she could see clearly that the members of the group had aged, but she couldn't tell from their moves. They were the same smooth guys she used to watch thirty years ago in the videos.

She looked to her right, where Tommy and Allison were in the aisle doing a two-step. He still had the moves too, and Allison looked good with him. He pulled her closer, and they swayed to the beat. Then Allison stepped back, grabbed his hands, and sashayed back to him.

"I see you, Allison!" Jillian called over the music.

She laughed. "Girl, I gotta work to keep up with this guy."

Tommy held her. "Trust and believe . . . not even possible!"

The two women shook their heads at him.

Jillian wished Cecil were here. He'd loved New Edition back

in the day too, and at one point had said they should look to see if they were coming to DC. But she doubted they'd actually go.

"Good night, y'all! We love you!" the lead called out as the song was winding down.

Nobody was fooled. They hadn't sung their main hit yet. Voices from the audience started calling out "If It Isn't Love"!

Tommy and Allison were back by their seats, and Allison turned to her. "So this is the infamous song, right?"

"One and the same." Jillian looked over at Tommy, on Allison's other side. "The one he'll never live down."

"If we get married," Allison said, "I'll walk down the aisle to it."

Tommy almost choked with laughter. "Don't think I won't propose just to see it."

The crowd roared as the band struck the familiar tune. New Edition moved immediately in synch with the same signature moves they'd done on the video so many years before.

Tommy was hamming it up, doing the moves with them, the ones he'd learned for the talent show. Jillian laughed, mimicking him.

"You know the moves too?" Allison said.

"I dated a guy who was in their 'New Edition' group," Jillian said. "I saw these moves a million times."

"Y'all need to go on out there," Allison said, pulling Jillian toward the aisle where others had gathered.

"Noooo." Jillian pulled back. "I'm not a big dancer. I'm just being silly."

Tommy looked. "Jill's trying to be shy?" He reached for her. "Come on, girl."

Allison whooped as Jillian followed him. They claimed a spot in the aisle, where the crowd looked like an extension of the stage, everyone moving and singing along with an infectious energy.

"Hey, here comes your part," Jillian said. "Ready to hit that falsetto?"

"Should I go grab the mic?" Tommy said.

He lip-synched it, pretending his voice was going up high. Jillian wondered if the lead in New Edition might be lip-synching himself. Probably not easy to hit those notes live, especially after all these years.

The band broke down a new beat, and the guys in the group came forward on the stage, rocking to the beat.

"Let me see you throw your hands in the air," one of them said, "and wave 'em like you just don't care."

The crowd went wild again, recognizing the familiar call. Tommy grabbed Jillian's arm and raised it high, and Jillian moved over so she could grab Allison's.

". . . somebody say 'Oh, yeah!'"

"Oh, yeah!"

"Thanks, y'all, for coming tonight!"

The crowd knew it was for real this time. Cameras flashed and arms waved as people yelled appreciation. New Edition did some final choreographed moves, including a bow, and left the stage as the band continued playing.

Tommy looked at Allison and Jillian. "I've got all-access passes if you two want to meet them and take pictures or something."

The women both looked intrigued.

"But it takes a while before they get to the meet-and-greet room," Tommy said, "and you can count on a line."

"If we could get a picture right now and leave, that would be cool," Jillian said. "But I'm just realizing how hungry I am. I haven't eaten since Sweetie Pie's."

"You know, me either," Tommy said. "Let's get something to eat instead." He took Allison's hand and led her up the aisle, with Jillian right behind.

"I'd love to," Allison said, "but I ate before you picked me up, and I've got a flight in the morning." She looked at Jillian. "That's why I can't be at the conference. I'm headed out of town."

"I can grab something around the hotel," Jillian said.

Allison checked her watch. "It's ten thirty. I'm not sure what'll be open down there." She looked at Tommy. "What about Hazel's? They're quick, food's good. And it's near me, so you can just drop me off beforehand."

Tommy pouted. "You're just gonna bail on us like that?"

"I know, that's bad." Allison pouted too, and their puckered lips touched. She turned to Jillian. "But this was fun, wasn't it?"

"Definitely," Jillian said. "So glad I came."

Allison smiled at her. "I'm glad you came too."

Tommy guided Allison through the lobby crowd and out the door, his arm around her.

And Jillian found herself eyeing them, surprised by what was rising up inside her . . . a hint of sadness.

***

"So how's Cecil doing with the kids?" Tommy asked. "Everything okay?"

Jillian sat opposite him in the booth. "We've got three teenagers now, so other than coordinating crazy schedules, he should be able to handle it."

"So let me ask you," Tommy said, "what would you say is key to the longevity of a marriage? I've been trying to get wisdom from people whose marriages have lasted long."

Jillian gave a wry smile. "Yeah, I didn't miss Allison's reference to walking down the aisle."

"I was waiting for you to mention it."

She thought about his question. "Only one thing?"

"As many as you think are key."

"Okay," she said. "For sure, Jesus."

"Be specific."

"Knowing Jesus," Jillian said. "Growing in Him. Looking to Him."

Tommy nodded. "That's good." He waited.

"And communication."

"Be specific."

Jillian narrowed her eyes at him.

"Hey," Tommy said. "I'm learning everyone doesn't mean the same thing when they use these words."

"True," Jillian said. "I mean being able to share your heart with each other—"

"See, 'share your heart' is not how guys describe communication." He chuckled. "But this is good. That's why I'm after a female perspective too."

Jillian continued. "Being able to talk about anything, and being able to do so in love, whether you're happy, sad, mad—because those times will come."

Tommy nodded.

"Let's see, what else . . ." She took a sip of ice water. "Continue dating." She added quickly, "I know, be specific."

"Definitely want specifics on that one," Tommy said. "I like that. How do you and Cecil do that?"

They looked up as their server arrived with their omelets. Jillian considered her answer as their plates were set before them. She only knew Tommy had prayed for the food by his "Amen."

He dug in immediately, forking up some of his mushroom omelet, and looked at her, waiting.

Jillian moved the side of potatoes around with her fork. "On the dating thing, to be honest, we could actually . . . do better with that."

"Don't you think most people feel that way? That they could

be doing better?"

"I don't know. I guess." Jillian tasted a tomato from her omelet, her thoughts overtaking her appetite.

Tommy looked at her. "You okay?"

She gave a quick nod. "Why do you ask?"

"Oh, I don't know," Tommy said, "maybe because I know you. It may have been a couple of decades, but some things never change."

"Such as . . ."

"You're never quiet, at least around me. You've always got some comeback, some question, usually a nosy one, always counseling and encouraging. But when you *do* get quiet? Something's wrong."

"I don't think that's true. I'm not *always* running my mouth." She cut her eyes at him playfully.

"Sophomore year I knew something was wrong, remember?" Tommy leaned forward. "You'd been quiet for two days, and I kept bugging you till you finally opened up."

The memory was sobering. Jillian had just found out she was pregnant. Tommy knew before the guy she'd been dating. "I was afraid to tell anybody," she said. "You gave me courage to deal with it."

"That's how we rolled," Tommy said. "Brother and sister." He looked at her. "I'm not asking for details, Jill. I know things aren't the way they used to be, and they don't need to be. I just want to know if you're okay."

Jillian stared at her omelet, trying to make sense of the feelings that were swirling as she thought about Cecil and her marriage. She looked up finally and said, "I'm not sure."

CHAPTER TWELVE

S tephanie spooned a good heaping of baked beans onto her plate, alongside the barbecued chicken, ribs, macaroni and cheese, and green beans, daring anyone to comment on how much she was eating. She'd make food her comfort to her heart's content. She put it in the microwave as her mom walked into the kitchen.

"Hey, Sweet Pea," Claudia said. "We were wondering if you were okay. You slept through the cookout held in your honor."

Stephanie opened the microwave, savoring the mouth-watering aroma. She'd vaguely remembered Cyd twice trying to rouse her, but the headache and the wine had helped her hold fast to sleep, which wasn't a bad thing. If Cyd had asked, she would've said she preferred to be alone this evening.

"I'm a little better now," she said. She joined the others at the table and dug in.

"So is everyone driving straight from here to the hotel?" Kelli asked.

"I'm not staying at the hotel," Claudia said. "I told Stephanie yesterday she could have my spot in Cyd's room. I sleep better in my own bed anyway."

"Momma Claudia, you might regret it, though," Dana said. "It's nice to have somewhere to go during breaks, maybe even take a power nap."

"Well, thanks for the tip," Claudia said. "I'll come to your room."

Dana smiled. "I'll get you a passkey."

Cyd checked her watch. "Wow, it's after ten already. Steph, after you eat, we need to get Treva and Faith back to the hotel and check in ourselves. Are your things ready to go?"

Stephanie gave her a look, one that said they'd already had this discussion. "I'm not going to the conference. Remember?"

Heads turned Stephanie's way.

"Since when?" her mom asked.

"Since today," Stephanie said. "I'm not up to it. People have too many questions."

"I thought you'd still share a room with me," Cyd said, "even if you're not going to the sessions."

"And as soon as I'm in the hotel, you'll say 'You might as well come down to the conference since you're here.'" Stephanie picked up a rib. "I'm good. I'll babysit Chase and Reese."

Claudia looked concerned. "I think you should go, Steph. It might be just what you need."

"That's what I told her," Cyd said. She turned to Stephanie. "I know you didn't leave Hope Springs and drive thirteen hours only to be holed up in my house."

Stephanie glanced at her briefly, agreeing in principle. There was much more to her leaving than that.

"Hope Springs." Treva eyed Stephanie. "I kept wondering why you looked familiar. We were riveted to the story of that young girl who committed suicide."

"Ohh . . ." Faith let the word hang as it registered. "I thought you looked familiar too. I was about Sam's age when it happened. I still remember her name. That really shook me."

Stephanie focused on Faith for the first time. Till now, the girl had been mostly on her phone, texting or something. "So you're about nineteen?" Stephanie asked.

"Yes," Faith said. "I still think about Sam sometimes—" She looked at her phone and jumped up. "Oh, Jesse's here. I have to go."

Treva looked at her. "Jesse's *here?*"

"We were texting, and Miss Cyd gave me the address so he could come get me."

"Well, why would he need to come get you?" Treva said.

The doorbell rang, and Reese's barking took over as the dog bounded toward the door.

"I got it," Cedric called, moving from the family room where he and a handful of guys had retired to watch an NBA playoff game.

Stephanie watched as Treva eyed Faith, and Faith looked away.

Moments later, footsteps approached the kitchen.

"Faith," Cedric said, "a guy named Jesse's here to pick you

up."

Jesse walked into the kitchen behind Cedric. Young, handsome guy. Neatly dressed in a short-sleeve collared shirt and jeans.

Faith went to him. "Um, everyone, this is my friend Jesse."

Jesse acknowledged the room. "Nice to meet you all."

Cyd walked over. "I'm Cyd London. Nice to meet you." She shook his hand. "I don't know if you've eaten, but please, we've got lots of food." She gestured toward the counter. "Take a plate to go if you want."

"That would be awesome," Jesse said. "It looks delicious."

"I can get it," Faith said, grabbing a plate.

"So, Jesse, you live here in St. Louis?" Cedric said.

"No, I live in Maryland," Jesse said. "I flew here today with Faith."

"I'm so glad we got to spend time with her," Cyd said. "She's amazing. I'm a college professor, and I don't meet many young women as grounded as Faith and hungry for the Lord." She smiled. "But I know you already know how special she is."

"I do." Jesse looked over at her. "I was just telling her this afternoon."

Faith glanced at him, pausing for a second by the macaroni and cheese.

"When she makes up her mind about something," Jesse said, "she's unshakeable, ready to run with it." He looked at Faith. "I'm sure you told them, right?

Faith grabbed the aluminum foil and pulled out enough to

cover his plate. "I'm not . . . sure what you mean."

"About the baby," Jesse said.

"*Jesse.*" Treva's voice was a whisper.

Stephanie watched Jesse and Faith, studying them.

A car horn sounded outside.

"We'd better go," Jesse said.

Plate wrapped, Faith moved toward the door, saying a quick thank-you to Cyd on the way.

Cedric walked them out, and silence hung over the kitchen momentarily. Stephanie watched as Treva let her head fall into her hands, and then, a brief moment later, popped out of her seat.

"I'm sorry, Cyd," Treva said. "Do you mind if we get ready to go?"

"Absolutely," Cyd said. "But Faith's okay, right? You know where she's staying?"

"At the conference hotel."

"Okay, good." Cedric's packed up the car for me already, but let me get one more bag from upstairs and we'll get moving."

Cyd was halfway up the steps when Stephanie rose and called after her.

"Cyd?"

"Yes?"

"I'm coming too."

CHAPTER THIRTEEN

Friday, May 20

Ten minutes before she needed to be downstairs, Treva was changing for the third time. Stepping into a pair of black slacks, she listened as Faith's phone rang through the speaker.

"This is Faith, sorry you missed me. Leave a message."

Treva grabbed her cell from the bed and clicked off. "The phone is ringing," she said, trying different shoes, "which means it's on, she sees who it is, and she's ignoring me. I've been calling since last night."

"I'm sure she's okay," Jillian said, pulling on a pair of jeans.

"I don't know. You should have seen her face. It wasn't just embarrassment—she was hurt." Treva eyed the new combo in the full-length mirror. Nothing seemed right, but it was better than the dress.

"Oh, no," she said. "I've been so focused on Faith, I forgot to call Cyd to tell her I'm not doing the breakout session. I'll let her know downstairs." She looked at Jillian. "I told you about that, right?"

Jillian nodded. "You told me last night."

Treva paused. "Are you okay?"

Jillian frowned a little. "Why?"

"Normally, you would've been hounding me about it, making sure I said yes. And you'd be chatting nonstop about the conference. Last night I thought you were just tired. What's going on?"

Jillian shrugged lightly, powdering her face. "It's nothing. You've got enough on your mind."

"No, I want to know," Treva said. "Wait, did something happen with Tommy last night?"

"It's got nothing to do with Tommy," Jillian said. "Not really. It's just—"

"Oh, I hope that's Faith." Treva's phone was blaring, and she looked about, trying to remember where she'd put it. Finding it in her purse, she looked and breathed a sigh of relief. "Sweetheart, I've been trying to reach you."

"Mom, I know." Faith sounded tired. "Please stop calling every ten minutes. It's ridiculous."

Treva felt the stab. "I was worried," she said. "I could tell you were upset. Why did Jesse—"

"It's fine, Mom. I'm fine."

Treva waited a beat, wishing she could penetrate the wall. She wanted to hear Faith's heart. "So, I'm headed down to the conference. What's your room number? It's a little early, but I can stop by and pick you up, and—"

"I'm not going to the conference."

"But last night you said you were," Treva said. "You were even asking about breakout sessions."

"I think it was just, being at Miss Cyd's house . . . I changed my mind."

"But . . . remember I'm giving my testimony this morning?"

Faith sighed. "Mom, I know your testimony. I lived through much of your testimony. I don't have to attend the conference for that."

Tears stung Treva's eyes.

"I have to go," Faith said.

The phone went dead.

Treva got her purse and tote bag and snatched a couple of tissues from the bathroom.

Jillian hugged her. "I'm almost ready. I'll be down in a few minutes."

Treva nodded into her shoulder. "Okay." She hastened to the elevator, emotions pulsing.

Lord, I was trying to be encouraged that Faith is here, just the bare fact that she's here. I was trying to look past the person she's here with, the situation they're in, the fact that they're staying together, because I was praying she'd go to the conference and get something out of it.

The elevator opened, and Treva squeezed in with a bunch of women wearing conference shirts. She nodded a smile as they chatted about who would save seats and who would get Starbucks. The way things should have been, Treva, Jillian, and Faith riding down, having light conversation, eager for the day to begin.

Lord, this is just hard. On top of everything else, Faith is so distant. Help me break through to her. I don't know what to do.

The doors opened and Treva proceeded to the escalator, which would take her to the conference area. On the way up, she could see a huge banner—*Welcome to the Living Word Women's Conference*—and scores of women entering the main ballroom. Amid all the turmoil she felt inside over Faith, a flutter rose. She'd be standing before these women within the hour.

She shook the nervousness from her hands. It was silly. She had experience with public speaking. As an attorney, she'd argued before judges and juries for years. But that was another world entirely, one in which she'd had training and skill, even a measure of confidence. Her spiritual life was different. She'd been surrounded by spiritual giants—her sister, her husband, her mother-in-law. Treva never felt she measured up.

She stepped off the escalator and paused, trying to remember where the e-mail had said to go. She walked past the ballroom and made a left, then down to almost the end of the wide hallway, where she heard voices. She pushed open a door that was slightly ajar and entered the "green room," as they were calling it, a place for conference participants and workers to gather, get last-minute instructions, and replenish with food and beverages.

Cyd waved from the other side of the room where she was huddled with two women with clipboards, and motioned for Treva to join them. Unassuming in dark slacks and a pretty white poet blouse, her hair bouncy with loose curls, she exuded an indescribable mix of warmth and power.

"Hey, good morning," Cyd said, hugging her. "Did you eat yet?"

"I haven't," Treva said. "I'm not real hungry, though." Maybe if her stomach wasn't so jumpy.

"We've got bagels, pastries, fruit. Help yourself," Cyd said. "In a little bit, Tammy here is going to get you mic'd up. We'll have praise and worship, I'll say a few words as an intro, and we're going right to your testimony."

Treva took a breath. "Okay."

"Also, I made sure we reserved a couple of seats up front for Jillian and Faith." She paused. "How's Faith this morning? I've been praying."

"I guess she's okay," Treva said, "but she's not coming to the conference now."

"Oh, Treva, no." Cyd pulled her aside. "I hope she doesn't feel she shouldn't come because of what her boyfriend shared. If you want me to talk to her, I will."

"I appreciate that, Cyd. Honestly, I don't know if it would help or not."

A guy in a black shirt and black denim approached, beckoning Cyd. "We need you to check something backstage ASAP."

Cyd turned to Treva. "I'll be right back. We still need to talk about the breakout session."

Treva nodded. She felt bad saying no, but she had prayed about it. And her overriding feeling was that she didn't know enough to be natural with the materials, to answer questions, to feel like she was doing the women a service. She needed to get it over with and tell Cyd so she could find someone else.

Treva sent a quick text to Jillian, telling her she had a seat up front, and to Faith as well, hoping. She poured a cup of coffee, glad to soon get the testimony part over with so she could enjoy the rest of the conference, anxiety-free.

"Hey, Treva!"

Treva turned and saw Kelli waving her over.

"Hey, what are you doing here?" Treva set her coffee down and took an open chair beside her.

"Oh, I thought I told you," Kelli said, smiling, "I'm on the worship team." She nudged her. "You ready?"

"No." Treva laughed a little at her fast answer. "Do you ever get nervous before you sing?"

"All the time," Kelli said.

"Really?" Treva drank some of her coffee. "That surprises me."

"When I feel like I *know* I've got this down," Kelli said, "it doesn't go as well. But when I'm a little anxious, it prompts me to pray and trust God."

"That's good," Treva said. "I needed to hear that."

"Hey, how's your daughter?" Kelli's eyes were warm. "She was on my heart last night, after her boyfriend made that announcement."

"I wish I could tell you," Treva said. "I'm trying not to worry—and worrying at the same time."

"It brought back so many memories," Kelli said. "I can imagine what she's feeling. And what you must be feeling." Her eyes were sympathetic. "I just wanted you to know I'm praying."

"Conference kickoff in twenty!" the guy in black called out.

"Which means the praise and worship team needs to leave in five," Kelli said. "I'd better run to the restroom. I'll see you a little later."

Treva sipped her coffee, wondering herself what Faith was feeling, and what she'd do today, since she wouldn't be at the conference.

"Treva Langston? Good morning."

She turned. "Oh, yes, we met briefly last night." She shook the hand he extended. "Pastor Lance, right?"

He smiled a little. "'Lance' is good." He moved Kelli's chair out and sat, casual in faded denim and a button-down shirt. "I just ran into Cyd, and she wanted me to share an idea for the breakout session, the one on recovering from loss."

Treva hesitated. "Okay."

"I know we're short on time, and we can talk more on the next break, but—"

"Actually," Treva said, "you should know I'm going to tell Cyd that I can't do it."

"Oh," Lance said. "Okay, then."

"But I'm curious," Treva said. "What was the idea?"

His eyes grew thoughtful as he leaned in a little. "Well, I lost my wife to cancer almost two years ago."

"I didn't know," Treva said. "I'm so sorry."

"I appreciate that," Lance said. "Cyd told me you lost your husband, and I was sorry to hear that as well."

Treva nodded, wishing she hadn't asked about the idea. Now wasn't the time to dwell on this.

"Cyd asked if I'd be willing to lead the session if you weren't able to. And I said, 'What if we do it together?'"

"Together?"

"Well, she mentioned it's a difficult subject for you right now, understandably. It's hard for me too."

"Really?" Treva said. "I wouldn't have thought that. You seem so . . . together."

"Right," Lance said. "So do you. I mean, look at you. If I knew nothing about your life, I'd think everything was cool. But some days you're dying inside. Some days *I'm* dying inside. And nobody knows."

His words landed unexpectedly. "That's true," Treva said.

"And if it's true for us, it's true for others who are here this weekend," Lance said. "To be honest, when Cyd asked, my first thought was that I didn't want to do it either."

Treva listened, waited.

"I get in front of people every week and talk, but I never talk about the loss of my wife. I just don't. It's too painful."

Treva nodded. She knew exactly what he meant.

"But I don't know," Lance said, "maybe it's not about us having enough of the grief behind us in order to lead the session. Maybe we need the session ourselves. And in the process, God can use us to help others get back in the race. Which is what this conference is about."

Treva could only nod, the weight of the moment descending. She wasn't ready to deal with her grief openly, but it wasn't about her. *Pray and trust*, Kelli had said. And everything Lance had said seemed targeted just for her.

"I guess this is the answer to my prayer," she said, "even if it's not the one I wanted. It won't be easy. I'm feeling all the emotions already."

"And I'm supposed to take you backstage now to get mic'd up," Lance said. "My timing wasn't cool at all."

"No." Treva pulled a tissue from her bag. "Actually, I think it was perfect."

CHAPTER FOURTEEN

S tephanie walked through the hotel lobby toward the restaurant hoping breakfast was still being served. French
toast would be awesome, with thick-sliced bacon. Or maybe they had an omelet station, in which case—

Three women came toward her, chatty, *In Hot Pursuit* blazing
on their chests. From the first time she'd seen those words, they'd
been kicking at her, accusing her. She wasn't in pursuit of much
of anything, let alone in "hot" pursuit. She turned slightly, watching them, drawn to the purpose in their steps . . . remembering
the purpose she'd felt when she first moved to Hope Springs. It'd
been a bold act, but she and Lindell had heard God's call, or so
she thought. And that sense of purpose seemed clearer as she'd
walked the halls of Hope Springs High. She would make a difference in the lives of those young people.

Right.

Stephanie's gaze cut away as the women disappeared up the
escalator. She continued on to the restaurant. What a joke, thinking she could hear from God, that she could make a difference.
Her days were empty. Her marriage was empty.

Might as well eat a good breakfast.

"Hi, table for one, please." Stephanie looked past the host at the fairly light crowd.

The woman grabbed a menu. "This way, please."

She didn't go far, leading Stephanie to a two-top near the entrance. Stephanie checked the menu and smiled—*Breakfast served till 10:30 am*. It was ten after.

"Good morning, my name is Kelsey and I'll be your server," a young woman said. "Can I get you some coffee, water?"

"I'll take a glass of ice water." Stephanie hesitated. "And a glass of white wine."

It was the woman's turn to hesitate. "Um, sure . . . would you like to see our wine menu?"

"No need," Stephanie said. She'd checked from the room. After telling her what she wanted, she added, "You might as well bring the bottle."

"O-kay." Kelsey jotted something down. "I'll be back shortly for your order."

Stephanie perused the menu and settled on her order, then stared out into the lobby. Seconds later, she sat up straighter. Faith had just come down to the lobby. She found a chair and perched on the edge, her phone to her ear, making agitated motions with her other hand.

What in the world?

"Ma'am, are you ready with your order?"

"Oh." Stephanie turned and saw that her server had brought the water and wine. As Kelsey poured, Stephanie ordered her

French toast and bacon then brought the wine glass to her lips to taste. "Perfect," she said.

The server walked away, and Stephanie's eyes darted back to Faith—except Faith wasn't in the chair. Stephanie scanned the lobby and spotted her standing, arms folded, staring out the hotel window. On impulse, Stephanie left her table and the restaurant itself, and went to her.

"Excuse me. Faith?" Stephanie touched her shoulder to get her attention. "I'm Stephanie London. We met last night at my sister's."

Faith turned around. "Oh, yes, hi."

"I happened to see you out here." Stephanie pointed toward the restaurant. "I'm about to eat breakfast. You want to join me?"

Faith glanced outside and back to Stephanie. "I was waiting for Jesse. He said he'd be here in a few minutes."

"Have you eaten?"

Faith shook her head. "Not yet."

"Well, either way, you have to sit," Stephanie said. "So you might as well sit and eat some breakfast. From where we're sitting, you'll be able to see when he comes in."

Stephanie led her to the restaurant, asked for a menu, and they situated themselves at the table.

The bottle of wine seemed larger. Stephanie wondered how it looked, but sipped anyway when the server came to take Faith's order.

When she looked up she caught Faith's eyes on her. "What?"

Stephanie said, setting the glass down.

"Nothing."

"You're surprised I'm having wine with breakfast?"

"Well, I've never seen it. But if that's your thing . . ." Faith shrugged.

"I wouldn't say it's my *thing* . . ."

Faith glanced at the bottle, then moved her gaze to the lobby entrance.

Stephanie took another sip. "So, wait, you're not at the conference."

Faith shook her head.

"Because your boyfriend announced that you're pregnant?"

Faith looked down at her water.

"Congratulations, by the way."

Surprised eyes met Stephanie's. "You're the first person who's said that."

Stephanie shrugged. "May not be ideal circumstances, but there's a little life growing inside of you. Life is a miracle, you know?"

Faith seemed to ponder that.

"But hey, I get it," Stephanie said. "You thought you'd be dealing with looks and comments. That's why I'm not there."

Faith looked puzzled. "Why would you be dealing with looks and comments?"

"For me this isn't just a conference," Stephanie said. "It's home. I've known a lot of these women my entire life. And they're kind of whispering and wondering when I'll get my life back."

She took a long sip, still ticked that one had had the nerve to ask how long she'd be working at the Hope Springs diner, as if something was wrong with that. She didn't tell her she'd quit the day before, since then she would've had to explain it to Cyd.

Faith seemed unsure how to respond. "Because of what happened with Sam?"

Stephanie nodded into her glass. "But your situation? You're not even showing, and only a handful of people know. And I can vouch for those people. If anything, they're praying for you. So don't let that stop you, if you want to go."

Faith's gaze wandered back to the lobby as the server brought their food. She set Stephanie's entree before her, and buttermilk pancakes, turkey sausage, and orange juice for Faith. From habit Stephanie bowed her head and prayed for her food, and glimpsed Faith doing the same.

Faith poured syrup on her pancakes. "Can I ask you a question?"

"Shoot." Stephanie cut into her French toast.

"You seem a little different from your sister."

"Are you asking or telling?" She gave a slight chuckle. "Very different. Thirteen years apart, so she's more like a mom. And she's always been God's girl, while I played the rebel." She lifted her glass as Exhibit A and took a sip.

"But I saw you on CNN. You were the one who took Sam

to Bible study and led her to the Lord. That doesn't sound like a rebel to me."

"Well." Stephanie swirled her French toast in syrup. "For a minute there, I really felt like God was moving, but . . . Okay, can we get to your actual question?"

Faith swallowed a bite of pancake. "So, I was always 'God's girl' too, and now I feel more like the rebel. And it's not like I'm *trying* to be, but things are so confused. I can't make sense of anything, even within." Her eyes, full and pretty, grew earnest. "For some reason I feel like it would help to talk to you, so I just wondered . . . and this is only because of something I saw in one of your news interviews, but I know it's kind of strange . . ."

"Faith, spit it out."

"I remember Sam didn't have any friends and, as unlikely as it seemed, since you'd just met and you were a lot older, you offered to be her friend. I wondered . . ."

Stephanie felt her stomach dip. "If we could be friends?"

Faith nodded, glancing down.

"I . . ." Stephanie knew she needed the right words. "Actually, Faith—"

"I know. I'm sorry." Faith forked up more pancake. "It was a dumb question. I can't believe I even—"

"Faith, no. Not dumb at all." Stephanie leaned in. "It's me. I don't think I can be a friend right now. I've *lost* friends because of where I am. At first it was dealing with the tragedy with Sam, then it got compounded with so much other stuff." She sighed.

"I would hate to bring anyone into this mess that's my life."

"I understand." Faith focused on her food, followed it with juice.

Stephanie's heart caved. "I'm not saying we can't—"

"Seriously, no worries," Faith said. "I'm good."

They ate in silence a few moments, and Faith's gaze turned toward the lobby. "There goes Jesse," she said, jumping up. "I need to talk to him."

"Don't you want to finish eating?"

Faith glanced at her plate. "I ate a good amount," she said. "I'm feeling a little queasy anyway." She took a final sip of her juice. "Thank you for breakfast. I really appreciate it."

"You're welcome," Stephanie said, though Faith was already out of hearing range.

Stephanie blew out a breath, staring after her as she moved in the direction of the elevators. She'd wanted to tell her yes. She was drawn to Faith, inexplicably so. Watching her last night was what compelled her to come. She felt for the girl, her baby, their situation. But she couldn't open herself up to a friendship. She had nothing to give.

Faith had no idea . . . Stephanie couldn't make sense of anything either.

She tipped the bottle and watched more wine pour into her glass.

CHAPTER FIFTEEN

Faith walked into the hotel room as Jesse looked through his luggage and pulled out his toiletry bag.

He looked over at her. "I thought you'd be at the conference."

"I didn't feel like going." Faith watched him head into the bathroom. "Where are you going now?"

"Aaron's picking me up in about an hour, after he runs some errands," Jesse said. "I'm about to shower and get ready."

"But you just spent the night at Aaron's." Faith had wanted Jesse to pick her up at Cyd's, to be sure they met back up. But as upset as she was about what happened there, she was more upset that Jesse had decided to stay with Aaron, and they simply dropped her off. "I thought we were going to spend time together. And not just time where you're calling me selfish and making me look bad in front of people I admire."

Jesse walked back out. "About that . . ." He sat down on the bed, and moments passed before he spoke. "All I could think as I listened to you yesterday was that every one of my plans was in jeopardy. Like my entire life was being squeezed." He hesitated again then took a deep breath. "I'm the one who's selfish. That was another thing my mom said to me the other night: 'All you think about is yourself. One day . . .'"

Faith moved closer. "One day what?"

"She said, 'One day God'll bring you to the end of yourself, and you'll find out how real He is.'" He shrugged. "So, yeah, it's me, not you. I apologize. I've never felt this much stress. I have a lot to sort out."

"Um, I'm the one who's carrying this baby. I have a few things to sort out myself."

"I know. And clearly you're better at it than I am." Jesse looked up at her. "Any normal person would've come in here and cussed me out for the way I acted yesterday. You still want to spend time together. What's up with that?"

"I guess I'm just 'quirky,' as you always say."

Jesse smiled a little. "That's fair."

"We had never argued before. I don't like holding onto things like that." She sat next to him on the bed. "Plus, I had a different vision for this trip." Her heart beat wildly as she leaned in and kissed him.

Jesse leaned back a little, eyeing her. "You've never done that."

"What?"

"Kissed me like that, on your own."

"Okay. So?"

Jesse stared downward a moment, then looked at her again. "If I ask you a question, will you answer it honestly?"

"Of course."

"No follow-up questions, no hemming and hawing, you'll just answer?"

"Yes."

"How do you feel about me?"

"You mean before yesterday?"

Jesse smirked a little.

"That's not a fair question," Faith said. "It's too complex, and you don't just *ask* people how they feel. That's the kind of thing that unfolds over time and gets spoken in the right moment."

"Wow." Jesse focused on her. "I guess they don't teach English majors how to follow rules. So, what? If it's multiple choice, you turn the exam over and write an essay?"

"I just don't see why you're asking," Faith said. "Why do you want to know?"

Jesse gave her a confused look. "Excuse me, did we not just—?" His mouth made a sound, like a tape rewinding. "If I ask you a question, will you answer? Of course. No follow-ups, no hemming and hawing—*yes*." His eyes rested on her.

"Okay." Faith sighed, returning his gaze, her heart beating a mile a minute. She'd said it to herself dozens of times, to her mom, even her Aunt Jillian. Why not tell the man himself? "How do I feel about you? I'm in love with you."

Jesse stared off into the distance.

"Why? Why did you ask?"

"I can't explain it. I guess I wanted to know if . . . if this was as new and different and . . . deep as it seemed." He focused on nothing in particular for a moment. "I meant it when I said you throw my world into chaos, and it's not just the pregnancy. You stir things in me that I don't even understand." He looked at her. "No matter what happens, Faith, I just want you to know . . . I love you too."

Faith kissed him again, and this time Jesse returned it, taking it deeper. His phone sounded, and he looked at it, then typed something quick. "Aaron can wait," he said, pushing the phone aside.

He lay back on the bed, bringing Faith closer, and she was sure she'd never forget this moment. He *said* it. The man she loved—loved her.

CHAPTER SIXTEEN

“ ‘‘I can’t believe I almost canceled.”

Treva rode with Jillian down the escalator to grab a sandwich, with women in conference tees all around, as far as she could see.

“What was that?” Jillian cupped her ear. “You’re seeing you were meant to be here?” She beamed. “I know I was there for much of those stories you told, but I didn’t know how you would tell them.” She looked at her sister. “Phenomenal. See how many women came up to you at the break? You struck a chord.”

“All I can say is God took over, because I didn’t plan to tell it all that way,” Treva said. “But I’m not even talking about that part. The praise and worship, the way Cyd broke down what the conference and this study are about. I didn’t realize how much I needed—*oh*.” She stepped off the escalator and continued walking beside Jillian. “I didn’t tell you I’m doing the breakout session now.”

Jillian stopped in her tracks. “The one about recovering from loss? Are you serious?” Someone bumped into her from behind. “Sorry,” she muttered, continuing on. “You were so sure you weren’t doing it.”

"I know, but there's this pastor, Lance Alexander. He was at Cyd's last night. Anyway, he told me he lost his wife to cancer and—"

"Oh, wow," Jillian said. "Tommy mentioned him yesterday, and it didn't click. You remember the story about him and his wife, don't you? Their wedding was all over the news."

"It was?"

"Girl, google it. It was beautiful. I think her name was Kathy, Kendall, something like that. Anyway, her fiancé dumped her a month before the wedding because she was diagnosed with Stage IV cancer. A few months later, she and Lance fell in love."

They rounded a corner and gaped at the line that snaked outside the hotel sandwich shop, and took their spot at the end.

Treva spoke in a softer tone. "So he married her knowing she might not have long to live?"

"Yes, girl. And if I recall, she only lived about a year. But what does this have to do with the breakout session?"

"Cyd asked him in case I said no, which I was about to do. Then he suggested we do it together, and I was still about to say no—"

"Excuse me," a voice behind her said. "Treva?"

She turned. Two women had taken the spot behind them.

"Yes?"

"I just had to tell you how moved I was by your story. You have no idea." The woman, who appeared older than Treva, looked to her friend, who nodded confirmation. "My issues with my mother were different, but same effect. She made me feel like I was nothing, and you helped me see that I hadn't yet forgiven her. Thank you."

"Thank you for sharing that," Treva said. "I can tell you first-hand that God is able to transform that situation. I never imagined having the kind of relationship my mother and I have now."

Jillian nodded as she dug out the conference notepad from her bag. "What's your name and your mom's name? I'll put you on my prayer list."

"Oh, bless you."

They inched up in line as Jillian got the information. That was her sister. She didn't just talk about praying. She prayed.

"Wait till Momma hears about all this," Jillian said. "You know she wants you to call her as soon as you're able."

"I wish she could've been here," Treva said. "I'm sure she's enjoying herself in Palm Springs with her friends. But okay, enough about all that. What was going on with you this morning in the room? And then I saw you slip into the ballroom late, just as I was starting to share."

Jillian waited, let them move up a little more. "I broke down in the room after you left," she said finally. "Couldn't stop crying. I lost track of time."

Treva lowered her voice. "I knew something was wrong. What's going on?"

"It's hard to explain." Jillian stared ahead.

"That sounds like something I would say," Treva said. "Just

go step by step, from the beginning. We've got time."

Jillian took a deep breath. "So, last night I was with Tommy and Allison."

"Right."

"And you know how it is when you're newly in love. Lots of hand-holding, hugs, stolen kisses. And by the end of the night, I felt myself getting sad and couldn't understand why."

Treva kept her eyes on her sister as they moved into the sandwich shop.

"This morning," Jillian continued, "I realized it was because Cecil and I don't have that."

"But you said it yourself," Treva said. "They're newly in love. You've been married nineteen years. It's not going to look like that."

"Not exactly like that, but it should look like *something*."

"So what are you saying?" Treva felt a hand to her shoulder and turned.

"I'm sorry to interrupt," the young woman said, "but I spotted you and had to come in."

"No need to apologize," Treva said. The woman reminded her of Faith—young, beautiful dark brown skin. "What's your name?"

"Erin. And I'm trying not to cry again . . ." She sighed. "My mom always loved on me and told me I was beautiful, but it was the world that told me differently. The way I was treated at school, names I was called. I always wondered why God would make me this color. As if He'd cheated me." Erin was wiping tears now, and Treva put an arm around her as they moved closer to the counter. "I felt like this morning was just for me."

Treva hugged her, understanding the weight of her words.

"Next in line," the woman behind the counter said.

Jillian stepped forward and started placing her order.

"Can I get a quick picture?" Erin said, holding up her phone.

"Here, I'll take that," a woman behind them said.

She snapped it, and Erin said, "Thanks again," as she left.

Orders in hand moments later, Treva and Jillian searched for some place in the lobby to sit.

"Hey," Treva said, "let's go up to our room. We can relax a little before the conference starts back up, with no interruptions. I want you to finish what you were telling me."

"There's not a lot more to tell," Jillian said. "I'm still processing."

"Then we'll process together."

Back in their room, Treva kicked off her shoes, perched herself on the bed, and opened her turkey club sandwich. "I remember exactly where we were," she said. "Tommy and his girlfriend looking madly in love, me saying you can't expect a long-term marriage to look like that—"

"Except, as I think about it now," Jillian said, turning in the swivel chair to face her, "you and Hezekiah had that. That's one of the things I always admired about you two."

Treva's mind called up those moments, the way Hez would

slip an arm around her waist, take her hand. "So you don't feel there's enough affection between you and Cecil?" She gripped her sandwich with both hands and took a bite.

"Any," Jillian said. "I'm saying there's not *any*." She seemed to be coming to grips with it even now.

"That's not true. Just last month at Trevor's piano recital, you two were hosting dinner together, taking pictures, looking cuddly like you always do."

"That's what we do well," Jillian said. "We cook together, host dinner parties, take great pictures. None of that is affection." She set her sandwich down. "I had to think back today, because I wasn't sure. It's been at least three months since we've made love."

Treva's eyes showed her surprise.

"Exactly. I'm like, what is wrong with us?"

"Jill, it's the busyness of life. You have four kids, two of them in high school, and you homeschool. You're not superwoman. Sometimes things slide, and then you realize it and work to get it back to where it needs to be."

Jillian wiped her mouth. "When you say it like that, it doesn't sound so bad. I was distraught this morning, feeling like my marriage was falling apart and somehow I'd missed it."

"You and Cecil, falling apart? Not hardly. You just need to hit that refresh button." Treva popped a chip into her mouth and let it crunch. "When we get back, bring the kids over for the night—better yet, for the weekend—so you two can have some special time together."

"I can't remember the last time we did something like that."

"And we'll go shopping so you can blow his mind with some new lingerie."

"Definitely can't remember the last time I did that."

"Girl, you've got perks that Allison and Tommy don't have. You just need to dust them off and use them." Treva's phone rang then, and she hopped up to get it. "Maybe it's Faith." She'd tried not to linger on her disappointment from this morning. It had been hard staring out at that empty reserved seat.

An unidentified number was flashing on her screen.

"This is Treva," she said.

"Treva, hi, this is Vicki with the social media team." Her words had a fast clip to them. "I know this is short notice, but we're filming promo spots for the breakout sessions and realized we hadn't scheduled yours. We'd like to do a short promo with you and Pastor Lance for your session tomorrow afternoon. Can you come down to the green room right now?"

Treva hustled to the green room, knowing time was short before the conference started again. Vicki was waiting when she walked in, typing on her phone.

"Treva, hey there," she said, looking up. She walked toward her. "We're actually heading to another room down the hall."

Vicki led the way, still engrossed in her phone. She looked back at Treva. "Hey, are you on Twitter? The women have been tweeting like crazy about your testimony, and many are asking what your Twitter handle is."

Vicki paused, showing Treva her phone. She saw comments with her name and the word *powerful* in them.

"I had no idea," Treva said. "No, I'm not on social media. I've never been real . . . social."

Vicki laughed. "That's refreshing, actually."

She led Treva to an area where studio lights and chairs had been set up, behind them a backdrop with the conference logo. Cyd wasn't there, but Treva recognized others from the conference team.

"Howdy," Lance said, walking in just behind.

"Oh, good," Vicki said, "I didn't know if you got my message or whether you'd already left." She focused on the two of them. "So we're trying to make these promo shots as painless as possible. It'll be short, no more than two or three minutes. You'll introduce yourselves, tell the women briefly about your workshop on grief and what you hope they'll take away."

Treva's eyes widened. "Vicki, I've hardly had time to skim through the material. I have no idea what to say."

"Ah, true. Everyone else has had weeks to prepare." She chewed her lip, thinking. "Let me talk to my crew. One second."

"I can't believe I agreed to this." Treva stared in Vicki's direction, mumbling to herself. "The testimony was stressful enough.

Now this."

"That testimony, though . . ."

Treva looked at Lance. "You heard it? I thought you had a meeting."

"I did," Lance said. "Got held up talking to someone backstage and was finally on my way out when you started. I couldn't leave."

Treva frowned slightly. "Why?"

"I'd never heard anything like your story," Lance said, "and your upbringing was way different from mine. But so much was familiar."

Treva gave him a look, but he was already nodding.

"I know, I need to explain," he said. "My background is really—"

"Okay, here's the deal." Vicki was marching back toward them. "Since your session is tomorrow afternoon, we can film it before the morning session if you want. You'll be going over the materials this evening anyway to prepare. This way, you can also be planning what you want to say for the promo."

"Okay," Treva said. "That sounds good."

"Does that work for you, Lance?" Vicki said.

He nodded. "That works."

Vicki hurried off to her next task, and Lance turned back to Treva.

"I was thinking," he said. "It makes sense to prepare for the session together, the promo too. But the only time we re-

ally have is this evening." He held up his hands. "You've probably got something scheduled, and I'm not trying to 'spend the
evening' with you—" He grimaced. "That sounded dumb. You
know what, forget it. It'll come together somehow."

"No, no, don't be silly," Treva said. "It's a joint workshop. It
would be crazy not to plan it out, and even talk about how much
of our personal grief we should share." She gave him a look.
"Plus, you can finish telling me about your way different, familiar
background."

"So we're hitting my grief and my past in one evening? On
second thought . . ." He stuffed his hands in his pockets, chuckling a little.

"Exactly," Treva agreed. "The two things I least like to talk
about, I'm talking about this weekend—in front of a crowd of
strangers. I think it's safe to say God is up to something."

"And I hate to tell you, the weekend is just getting started."

CHAPTER SEVENTEEN

Stephanie closed her eyes to transport herself from her current scene—knees to a dirty floor, slumped over a nasty toilet, swallowing every other second to keep down whatever remained in her stomach. Thankfully this thing had an automatic flush, and nosy Miss Gertrude seemed to have left. If she had to hear one more time, "Stephanie, is that you in there? Are you all right?"

Did it sound like she was all right?

Stephanie hadn't answered, because she couldn't and the couple of moments she could've, she didn't want to. Maybe Miss Gertrude really wasn't sure who it was in here. Stephanie just wanted to keep it together long enough to get up and get out of there without notice.

The outer bathroom door swung open just as she started to heave again.

"Steph, are you in there?"

Her eyes shot open, along with her mouth, as more contents spilled out. Her hair dangled over the bowl, and she swiped it aside just in time.

The clicking of heels moved closer. "Steph, is that you? Are you okay?"

Unbelievable. Stephanie grabbed some tissue and wiped her mouth as the toilet dutifully flushed. "What are you doing in here, Cyd?" Her own voice surprised her. Sounded like a croak.

"Miss Gertrude came and got me. Said she was pretty sure she saw you rush in and start vomiting in the toilet."

"So she hunts down my sister and reports me like I'm five?"

"It wasn't a report. She was worried. And why are you being defensive?"

"I'm not." Stephanie moved to her feet, but the lightheadedness made her wobbly. She leaned against the stall wall. "And I'm good. You don't have to wait."

"Steph, open the door."

Stephanie steadied herself. Nothing else was coming up. Her hand jiggled the lock and the door tipped open.

Cyd opened it further. "Did you get food poison or—*oh, my goodness.*" She batted the air. "What is that smell?"

"It's called vomit."

Cyd took Stephanie's hand and led her out, sniffing in the process. "Have you been drinking? You vomited because you were *drunk?*"

Stephanie washed her hands and splashed her face with water. "Between you and Miss Gertrude, who needs the FBI?" She dried her face.

"When did you start drinking again?"

"Nice. Go back a decade and throw it in my face."

"I'm not throwing anything in your face, Steph. I'm asking a question."

"And to your point," Stephanie said, "I do think something was wrong with the food, because I wasn't drunk."

"What were you drinking?"

"Just white wine."

"How much?"

Cyd stared at her, until she felt like she was five.

Stephanie felt tears gathering. "I just don't understand why God doesn't like me. I make a mistake, I get busted, every time."

"Are you serious right now?" Cyd said. "The conference is starting back up in twenty minutes, I'm giving a message I've been preparing for months, and you're having a pity party about getting busted because you decided to drink the day away?" She pulled her phone from her pocket. "I'm calling Mom to come get you."

"Oh, come on. She's the last person to call. I'd never hear the end of it." Stephanie held her arm. "I'm fine. I'm heading up to the room."

Cyd paused, staring again. "I kept asking you to talk to me. I knew you were going through a lot." Her voice broke, and she embraced her sister. "We'll get through this. I promise we'll get through this."

Stephanie's tears flowed now. "I'm serious, Cyd, God doesn't like me. Even when things turned around and I was trying to serve Him—you *know* I changed—it ended up a nightmare."

Cyd rubbed her back. "Listen, I can see there's so much more going on than I knew. But one thing I do know is that you don't need to be in a hotel room right now. You need to be at the conference. In fact, this message might be just for you."

Stephanie sighed. "I am *not* going to the conference. And anyway, if you smelled alcohol on me, so will everyone else."

"Go upstairs, change, and freshen up, including a long gargle with mouthwash. There'll be a seat waiting for you on the front row."

"And if I don't come back down?"

"Mom'll be at the door, with my passkey."

~ ❧❦❧ ~

Stephanie took her time getting to the ballroom. After a long, hot shower, she dressed then stopped at Starbucks for coffee and a bagel. She was sure she'd missed at least half of Cyd's message, until she glanced at the conference booklet. Praise and worship had opened up the afternoon session.

Stephanie opened the ballroom doors and slipped in, flashing her badge to the attendant. The lights were dimmed, and Cyd was on the platform, her voice booming. For a moment Stephanie was riveted. She'd never seen her sister like that, speaking before hundreds of women.

"And I remember when I hit a low," Cyd was saying. "I was turning forty, and I had been praying for *years* for a husband.

Some of you know how it is when you've been through *every* season as a single. The season where you thought you found the one, and in hindsight, you must have been out of your mind . . ."

"Girl, preach!" rang out near Stephanie, along with other shouts and nods of agreement.

Stephanie continued to the far right side of the ballroom and headed up the aisle toward the front.

"And the super-spiritual season. 'Lord, I don't need anyone but You. If I'm called to singleness, just let me be about the work of the Kingdom.'" Cyd paused. "And that season lasts about a minute, right?"

Laughter rang out.

Stephanie looked down the front row and saw a couple of empty seats. She headed for the one next to her mother.

Claudia leaned over and whispered, "I'm so glad you decided to come."

"But the main season, at least for me, was a season of waiting," Cyd said. "Some days easier than others. But I'd never been as low as when I turned forty. And here's why." She paused. "I was turning forty." She laughed a little with the women and continued. "Seriously, it felt like life had passed me by. *Plus*, my much younger sister was getting married. On my birthday. And I was her maid of honor."

Stephanie heard the sympathetic groans, but only vaguely. She was trying to figure out how she'd missed all this. As far as she remembered, Cyd had been happy that day. But that would have been like Cyd to suppress her own feelings for her sister's sake.

Cyd walked to the other side of the platform. "I hit an emotional wall that weekend. I didn't understand why God would do this to me. He could have easily sent me a husband in my twenties . . . in my thirties . . . Instead, I spent decades alone while everyone else got married and had kids. I was upset with God, in tears, crying out *Why?*"

In tears? Stephanie tried to picture it. Had she ever seen Cyd in tears? She was always so strong.

"Why am I sharing all of this?" Cyd said. "Because we all hit a wall at some point—of disappointment, grief, heartache, failure . . . And let me tell you, when you're upset with God or mad at God, it's hard to stay in hot pursuit. The only thing you might pursue at that point is a pity party."

"Ha," a woman near them said. "I'm real good at that kind of pursuit."

Cyd looked out at them. "This morning I talked about the theme of this conference, all about running the Christian race. We looked at several verses and broke down what it means to *run* and *press* and *pursue*. As challenging as those words are, that's what the Lord expects of us. Now I want you to think about your answers to a few questions." Cyd paused. "Here's the first one: Do you even want to run?"

Stephanie grunted within. No need to think about it. *No.*

"Maybe you're fine with a stroll. With chilling in the stands.

Ask yourself—Am I truly willing to die to self?" She let the question settle. "Am I willing to accept the Lord's will, no matter what?"

Women were rising to their feet in agreement. Easy to agree in theory, Stephanie thought. She wondered if they'd ever been through anything.

"See, we have to know where our hearts are because this is a *race*. Many of you know I'm a Classics professor, and I teach Greek. So beware, because dissecting words gives me life." She smiled. "But seriously, this word *race* is amazing. It's *agon*, from which we get the word *agony*. When the Bible says we're running a race, the mere choice of that word is the Holy Spirit saying to you, listen, this is going to be hard. This Christian life is a struggle. When you hit a wall, you better be determined to get around it and keep moving. You better be like David and say, 'by my God I can leap *over* a wall.'"

"Yes!" rang out across the ballroom, and more women were on their feet.

Stephanie stared vaguely ahead, Cyd's words swirling. She knew all about hitting a wall. She was still staring at the wall. With the faint taste of alcohol on her breath.

CHAPTER EIGHTEEN

J illian had no doubt that these messages were for her. She'd barely made it to the opening session because of the pain of realizing her marriage wasn't where it should be. That quickly she'd gotten stuck. If it weren't for needing to be there for Treva's talk, she would have missed it altogether. But this word from Cyd had her so pumped she could do a few laps right now around this ballroom.

"The scripture says 'run with endurance the race that is set before us.'" Cyd was standing almost directly in front of them. "You have your own unique race set before you, and it's planned out by a sovereign God—every mountain, valley, swamp, and patch of quicksand. I didn't like mine in that season, but that's what God gave me. I had to run it." Cyd paused. "What are you dealing with?"

Treva leaned over and whispered to Jillian, "This is so good. I can't believe Faith is missing all this."

"You'll have to get her the audio."

"Good idea, assuming she'd listen."

Cyd was wrapping up. "We all have different issues related to the course set before us. We're praying there's a breakout session that speaks to where you are, and will motivate you to *run*. Even if you've been stalled out . . ."

Jillian's phone lit up and she looked at it then sighed. Facebook friend request. Not Cecil. She was excited about Treva's idea to drop off the kids so they could spend special time, and she'd thought to take it a step further. Plan a getaway weekend, maybe several days. It didn't have to be someplace exotic; they couldn't afford that anyway. And the timing was good, given that Cecil was a teacher. Though he worked over the summer, his schedule would be more flexible. She'd texted him the idea and couldn't wait to get the ball rolling.

"This is what I really want us to get." Cyd looked out over the ballroom. "The Bible says nothing about a perfect race, a pretty race, a speedy race, or even a—"

Cecil's name flashed on her phone, snagging Jillian's attention. Smiling, she brought her phone closer.

His text was one line: **Where is this coming from?**

Jillian blinked. *What kind of response is that?* She unlocked her phone and thumb-typed, **What do u mean? Thought it'd be good for us.**

She waited, her heart beating confusion, Cyd's voice fading to white noise. Several minutes seemed to pass.

Then: **So did I . . . over a year ago. And again a couple months ago.**

Jillian stared, dumbfounded. She whispered to Treva, "I have to call Cecil," and scurried out. She speed-dialed his number before she cleared the ballroom doors.

He answered on the first ring. "Jill, I can't right now. I have a meeting in fifteen—"

"Are you talking about the conference you wanted me to go to in March?" Jillian strode across the lobby outside the ballroom to a quiet corner. "When there was a conflict because the kids had practices, games, recitals . . . ?"

"Jill, we have four kids involved in endless activities. There's always a potential conflict." Cecil spoke calmly, always his way. "Your mom or Treva could've stepped in and helped, but you didn't want to ask."

"You said it yourself. We have four kids with endless activities. It's hard to ask for help when it requires so much."

"But now you're saying Treva offered to take the kids for the weekend."

"Yes. She *offered*. That's the difference. She's got three kids herself, and things are hard now that she's alone."

"But why did it come up *now*?"

Jillian hesitated. "I guess, at the concert, seeing Tommy and his girlfriend, kind of made me think about . . ." She searched for words.

"The way things used to be."

Something in his tone. And it wasn't a question.

"That's what I was trying to get back to," Cecil said. "Last year it was spring break. I said we should go somewhere, just the two of us."

"But the timing was bad then too, remember? Momma had her trip to Greece, and there's no way I would have asked Treva at that point. She was a wreck, understandably."

"I offered to ask Darlene myself," Cecil said.

"You did," Jillian said, "but she was helping out so much with Treva's kids."

"It's always something that interferes," Cecil said. "When was the last time we had a date night?"

"Why are you throwing this at me like it's my fault?"

"No, Jillian. I just want you to see what's been happening. I know I'm to blame as well. Honestly, I fell back and stopped trying to plan date nights because there was always a conflict. Since you manage the kids' calendars, I figured I'd leave the planning to you."

"I can't argue. I didn't make it a priority. I see it now." A lightbulb came on. "Is that why you made that comment, when I said this weekend meant a lot to me?"

"You know I'm glad for you to attend the conference," Cecil said. "But I just . . . wished the trips with me had meant that much."

Jillian blew out a sigh. "I'm sorry, Cecil. But now I'm even more excited to plan this weekend for the two of us. Be thinking about where we should go."

Seconds ticked by.

"I can't right now," Cecil said.

"I don't mean right this minute. I'm just saying think about it.

An island would be really nice, but it doesn't have to be that. We can spend time somewhere close even."

"Jillian, I'm saying I just don't know."

"About the trip?"

"I don't know about *us*."

Jillian's heart constricted. She felt her legs giving out beneath her and moved them, robot-like, toward an empty grouping of chairs. "So we miss some date nights, don't go on a couple trips, and now you don't know about us?"

"Really, Jill? Is that all it is? How about, there's no intimacy between us. How about, we don't talk about anything other than the kids and schedules. Anything but us." He sighed. "I didn't want to get into this right now. I really have to go."

"You tell me our marriage is in trouble, and then you just hang up?" Hunched in a cushioned chair, she kept her voice low, tears welling, mind racing. "Cecil, is there someone else?"

The silence moved her tears to a stream.

"Jill, we need to have this conversation, but obviously not now. I'll call you this evening."

The phone went dead, and Jillian trembled in the chair. He could've said no, there's no one. Why didn't he just say, "No"?

She replayed the conversation, then past conversations. She could hear Cecil asking her to go to his conference. *Let's find a way to make it work,* he'd said. *I really want you to come.* Tender, almost pleading. That was less than three months ago. What had happened since—

The ballroom doors swung open, the noise level ratcheting upward as women began pouring out.

Jillian looked up. She'd left her things on her front-row seat, but she couldn't deal with the crowd right now, or even Treva.

Three women came near, conference brochures open, chatting about which breakout session they'd attend. They were gone as quickly as they'd come, and two others took their place.

Jillian felt her phone vibrate and looked down at it. "I know," she said, answering. "I left my things in there."

"Where are you?" Treva said.

"Right outside the ballroom."

"I'm still in here, talking to Stephanie."

"Who's Stephanie?"

"Oh, I forgot you didn't meet her. Cyd's sister. And check this out—she asked how I'd feel about her reaching out to Faith, building a friendship. She said Faith *asked* if they could be friends."

"That's awesome, Treva."

"Is everything okay at home? Why'd you have to rush out— oh, Stephanie, wait."

Jillian stood. "Treva, I need you to grab my Bible and tote bag, and I'll get them later."

"The breakout session starts in thirty minutes. Aren't we headed there together?"

"I can't right now."

"What? Jillian, what's going on? Just come in here where we were sitting so I can find you."

"I'll call you after the breakout."

"Jill, wait—"

Jillian hung up and headed up the escalator toward their room, too aware that her feet had hit quicksand. And she was going down . . .

CHAPTER NINETEEN

Something inside of Faith stirred when the server set her Dreamboat Float in front of her on the outdoor patio table. Fitz's was known for its root beer made on site, but it was this that caught her eye—orange soda with vanilla ice cream. The treat her dad used to whip up to celebrate one of his made-up occasions.

Because you persevered after that disappointing chemistry test.

Because I saw how you helped your little sisters clean their rooms.

Or the one Faith would never forget—*Because you'll always be my baby girl.*

He'd grab the stash of Sunkist—soda was otherwise banned—and the Blue Bell vanilla and do what he did best . . . make her feel special.

"How do you like it?" Stephanie asked.

Faith tasted, savoring the flavor. "It's really good." She looked across the table. "How did you know about the floats? My mom told you?"

Stephanie's brow bunched. "Your mom didn't say anything about floats. What's the deal?"

Faith stirred lightly with her spoon. "It was a special thing with my dad."

Stephanie sat back. "No way." Her gaze fell on the passersby for a moment then she looked at Faith. "I haven't been in a good place with God for a long time. But after I threw up in the hotel lobby bathroom and Cyd made me go to the afternoon session—"

"What?"

"Girl, I wasn't kidding when I said my life was a mess." Stephanie sipped her green tea then continued with a sigh. "At the end of the session, I felt like I needed to get in touch with you, which was odd—because even back when I *was* hearing from God, or at least thought I was, I wasn't the type to reach out and make friends."

"Except with Sam."

"Except with Sam." Stephanie echoed it lightly. "So I asked your mom for your number and prayed, even though I wouldn't really call it *prayer*. More like, 'Okay, God, I guess I'm calling Faith, and I don't know what she'll say or whether she'll talk to me. But if she does agree to talk, I'd rather go someplace away from the conference, maybe show her a slice of St. Louis.'"

Faith waited for her to finish.

"Next thing I knew the Loop came to mind." Stephanie gestured around her. "That's what we call this area. And Fitz's is a favorite spot because I love root beer. Then we got here, and you said root beer wasn't your thing, so I felt bad for choosing all wrong."

Faith shook her head. "It couldn't be more perfect. I haven't had one of these since . . . Well, since before my dad died."

"Tell me about your dad."

Faith took her time, spooning up soda and a bit of melted ice cream, savoring it as it went down. "He was everything to me," she said. "I'm the oldest, and I was the only child for about five years, so he and I did everything together. Even after my sisters were born, Dad and I were tight. He just had a way of spending special time with each of us."

"Were you tight with your mom too?"

"Not until the last few years," Faith said. "She was never home. She worked late nights and weekends. It's part of her story, how she tried to prove herself through her career because of all she went through with her mom."

"Wow," Stephanie said. "I wish I'd heard it this morning."

"My dad made everything fun. Even when he cooked, he made it fun, playing word games, doing silly dances." She smiled. "And he was patient. Like, unbelievably patient. When I was little and I did something I shouldn't have, he'd sit me down and ask what I thought about it. Then he'd get the Bible and say, 'I wonder if God has any thoughts on this.' He was super calm, but it was excruciating because you're like, 'Am I getting a punishment or not?'"

Stephanie was smiling too then sobered a little. "Faith, what happened to him?"

"A car ran a red light and slammed into his car on the driver's side." Faith took a breath. "He was on his way to my school for the senior awards banquet."

"Oh, Faith . . ."

"It was two years ago last month," Faith said. "I started college at Maryland that fall, where he'd been a professor. And it was hard. The whole year was hard."

Stephanie shook her head. "I can't imagine losing my dad. I'm so sorry, Faith. I see why you said you couldn't make sense of anything."

"Well. Obviously things are even more complicated now. Jesse, the baby . . ." Her hand grazed her tummy.

"So how did you and Jesse meet?"

"My mom and Aunt Jillian have been part of a Bible study for years," Faith said, "and Jesse's mom joined last fall. She brought him to the Christmas party at our house." She thought back. Only a few months ago, but it seemed like ages. "We found out we were both at Maryland."

"You'd never seen him around campus?"

Faith shook her head. "Maryland is big, and I'm not the type to hang out." She scooped more creaminess and swallowed it. "At the end of the night he took out his phone so we could connect on social media, but I've never been into all that. So we exchanged numbers. I was surprised when he actually texted me once we got back from break."

"Why surprised?"

Faith shrugged a little. "He was older, a senior. He's super cute. And he asked if I wanted to go out, which was kind of new."

"You're not saying you'd never been on a date."

"Mainly group outings," Faith said. "I was a late bloomer, not really into guys."

"Okay," Stephanie said, nodding. "So he's your first in a lot of ways."

Faith nodded. "Then two weeks ago I find out I'm pregnant."

"Oh wow. I didn't realize it was so recent."

"That's why I'm confused about pretty much everything."

Stephanie leaned in. "What's the biggest thing?"

"The mixed signals I get from Jesse. Sometimes days go by and I don't hear from him. Or that thing he pulled last night, telling everyone I'm pregnant—it was sort of 'revenge' because I'd told him I wouldn't consider giving the baby up for adoption." Faith felt tears rising and wiped her eyes. "One minute I'm thinking he doesn't care. Then he'll say or do something that blows me away. Like today, after breakfast."

"What happened?"

"He asked how I felt about him . . . and I admitted that I love him."

"That's pretty deep," Stephanie said. "What did he say?"

"He told me he loved me too."

"Okay, wow, it just got really deep." Stephanie leaned in. "So you love Jesse, and he loves you. You're having his baby. Tell me about him—is he everything you've dreamed, the answer to your prayers—what?"

Faith sat back with a sigh. "My mom says no."

"What do you say?"

Faith played with the spoon in her drink. "I'd have to say . . . not exactly?"

"Hmm. What does that mean?"

"I used to pray for a guy who loves the Lord," Faith said. "Not just on Sunday, going to church and all that. But every day, living for Him. You know?"

"Okay," Stephanie said, waiting.

"Jesse grew up in church, but he questions some things. He says his church had too many rules, so he stopped going. And he feels like my parents were too rigid with me, didn't give me room to flex and grow and learn who I am."

"Do you agree?"

Faith shrugged. "Not really. A lot of what he saw in me in the beginning wasn't because of my parents. It was because of my relationship with God."

Stephanie looked at her. "In the beginning. Did that change?"

Faith hesitated. "If I'm honest, it's nowhere near the same. I'm not sure I can ever get back to what I used to have with God." She looked at Stephanie. "And you thought your life was a mess."

"Hey, I've got you beat today at least. I didn't hear you mention camping out on a nasty floor, spilling your guts in a porcelain bowl."

Faith gave her a wry look. "If nothing else comes of this weekend, the two of us should at least win some kind of award. Instead of 'In Hot Pursuit,' we're 'Most Likely to Bring up the Rear'."

Stephanie laughed. "Right. And I'm so out of shape I'd claim the very back of the rear." She took a sip of tea, staring out at the passersby. Several seconds passed before she turned to Faith again. "So, this is your first full day in St. Louis, and I'm sure it's not what you envisioned. No conference. No quality time with Jesse. But you've still got tonight, all day tomorrow, and part of Sunday. What now?"

"What now . . ." Faith echoed the words with a sigh. "I have no idea."

"I can't believe I'm saying this, but we could go to the conference together."

"You're going to the rest of it?"

"Well. I went to the one session to get Cyd off my back," Stephanie said. "But I have to admit it roped me in a little. And Lance is speaking in the main session tomorrow morning, so I kind of want to hear where he takes it." She drained the last of her tea. "We could sit way back in the rear, where we belong."

Faith heard herself chuckle. "I see why Sam loved you. You really are one of a kind."

"I wish it had made a difference in the end though."

"I thought it made every difference," Faith said. "Didn't her diary say she gave her life to Jesus because of the time she spent with you?"

Stephanie gave a slight nod, her eyes closed.

"She doesn't have an end because of you," Faith said. "She stepped from this world into Jesus' arms."

"I just keep thinking about what I could've done differently," Stephanie said. "So she could still be on this side, in college like you, living her life." She waved it away. "I can't go there right now. And anyway, you're supposed to be saying, 'Yes, Stephanie, it's you and me at the conference tomorrow.'"

Faith exhaled long. "I guess."

"What was that?" Stephanie leaned in. "I couldn't hear you."

"Fine," Faith said, her voice up an octave. "I'm nervous about what to expect, but I'll go."

"Oh, trust me," Stephanie said, "this is scary for me too. This morning I was sure of two things: I wasn't going to the conference, and I wanted a drink. Now it feels like I'm inching back into space I can't control."

"Except," Faith said, "you weren't in control in that bathroom, were you?"

Stephanie put a hand to her hip. "How is it you're confused about your own life, but you're clear all day about mine?" She looked long at Faith. "I might need your friendship more than you need mine."

CHAPTER TWENTY

"Okay, tell me again why this is all the rage." Treva stared at the square slice in her hand, poised to be a good sport and take another bite.

Lance gave a deep chuckle. "You didn't hear me say it was all the rage. But when you described the St. Louis-style pizza you wanted to try, I knew you were talking about Imo's."

Treva let the sausage and mushrooms in that second bite go down. "When we lived in Chicago, I had a coworker who was always battling with the natives about pizza, raving that St. Louis thin crust beat Chicago deep dish hands down." She examined it. "I don't even know if you can call this a crust. It's more like a cracker."

"You sound like Kendra," Lance said, on his second slice. "She used to say Imo's pizza was more like nachos because it didn't have a real crust."

Treva looked across the booth. "Was this a favorite spot for you two?"

"No, we never went to Imo's." Lance's gaze was on the pizza between them. "Actually, we never went to any pizza place. She couldn't eat it." He looked up, mustering something of a smile.

"I'm sorry, Lance, I wasn't thinking."

"It's a natural question. We just never experienced a lot of the everyday things couples experience."

"My sister told me your wedding was big news, because you married Kendra knowing she might not have long to live." Treva paused. "How did that happen, if you don't mind my asking?"

"I don't mind at all," Lance said. "That's why we're here." He took a slow sip of lemonade. "I needed a place to stay, and Kendra's dad needed someone to look after his home—and keep an eye on Kendra's brother—while he was overseas. I was Trey's youth pastor, and I knew Kendra from high school." He paused. "I should say I knew *of* her. I wasn't in her circle. Anyway, she was living in DC, but soon after I moved in she showed up, and I found out she'd been diagnosed with Stage IV cancer."

Treva stared, eyes wide. "I don't know which question to ask first. What do you mean, she showed up?"

"She got the diagnosis, her fiancé left her a month before their wedding, and she had nowhere to turn. Coming back home was a last resort."

"So the two of you were thrown together in the same house."

"Exactly. She was scared about the diagnosis and all that it meant, getting intense chemo but too stubborn to ask for help, dealing with the hurt from her fiancé's rejection. I wanted to help however I could, but it was rough going for a while." He lapsed into memory. "I fell in love with her without trying."

Treva picked up another slice of pizza. "What did you mean,

you weren't in her circle?"

"Ah, that background I mentioned." Lance reached for a napkin and wiped his hands. "Kendra and I were from different sides of the track. She grew up with every advantage, went on to become a lawyer. I grew up with a drug-addicted mother, dropped out of high school, and ended up in prison."

Treva ran it all back in her mind. "I don't think I've ever been left speechless this many times in a single conversation. But wait, what was it about my story that sounded familiar to you?"

"That feeling of isolation growing up. Nobody understands. All the insecurities." Lance looked at Treva. "I looked and acted tough, but it was hard to admit even to myself how insecure I was." He folded his napkin absentmindedly. "Kendra used to check me all the time about that. To be honest, I still grapple with it."

"How so?" Treva caught herself. "Scratch that, it's too personal. And I should know better, as private as I am."

"Normally I wouldn't be talking about any of this," Lance said. "Maybe it's a shared grief thing . . . grief from death, grief from the past. Or maybe it's that I won't see you after this weekend and won't have to be embarrassed." He gave a wry smile. "For whatever reason, it's not hard to talk to you."

"I get it," Treva said. "That 'only this weekend' thing is huge."

Lance took another drink of lemonade. "So, my insecurities . . . I'll always be a high school dropout. Will always be an ex-con. I pastor people way smarter than I am, even the college students, and I wonder how I could possibly help them. If you want to know the truth, after hearing your testimony and all you've accomplished, helping you with the breakout session sounded like a joke." He spread his hands. "There you have it. The thoughts that go through my head."

"You're not alone," Treva said. "I'm realizing this weekend that I'm still battling insecurities from things my mother said growing up. I was never good enough. Could never measure up to my sister. And Jillian became a believer before I did; she knew the Bible backwards and forwards before I'd ever opened one. And she's always been the Christian standard for me. Honestly?" She took a breath.

"Take your time."

"I didn't want to do this breakout session because I didn't want to relive the grief. But I would've hesitated no matter the topic. This is *Jillian's* territory, sharing about the Bible, helping others spiritually. And then . . ." She gave a sheepish look. "Okay, confession. I listened to one of your sermons online before you picked me up. And yes, helping me with the breakout session *did* seem like a joke. I was ready to tell you to do it all by yourself."

Lance looked surprised. "You listened to one of my sermons? Why?"

"Talk about embarrassing." Treva sighed. "A couple things you said earlier stayed with me, and I was intrigued as to what your preaching was like. And since this is already awkward, I might as well say you need to get over that education insecurity thing. You are *gifted*." She nodded slowly. "I'm glad Kendra used to check you on that."

"I appreciate that," Lance said. "If it weren't for her, I doubt I would've planted a church. She kept encouraging me to do it, before she passed." Twice he looked up, about to say more, but didn't. Then finally, in almost a whisper, he said, "Sometimes I just really miss her."

Treva saw a tear fall and grabbed hold of one of his hands, surprised by her own gesture. But she knew the pain of those simple words. Knew the depths from which they sprang, endless days and nights wrapped around the unbearable reality of loss.

Lance swiped his face. "I can't believe I broke like that. It hit me out of nowhere."

"Out of nowhere?" Treva pulled her hand back. "This was what we feared, right? Talking about it. The stuff we *never* talk about. The soul dredging." She looked at him. "Lance, it's okay to break down. It has to be."

"Did I just say this wasn't hard?" He looked up at her briefly, eyes clouded. "You talked about your husband in the session this morning, how God used him in your life. I could tell he was an amazing man."

Treva nodded. "He's the only man I've ever loved. And he loved me with everything in him. I know he did, even when I was selfish and didn't deserve it. I found out how strongly God loves me, because of Hezekiah."

"How long were you married?"

"Twenty-two years," Treva said. "He died two years ago in a car accident."

Their server appeared, topping off their water glasses.

"Twenty-two years," Lance repeated. "I had less than two with Kendra, and the grief was heavy. I can't imagine what you went through."

Treva blew out a silent breath. She knew they'd get to this, knew she'd have to say things she'd never said out loud. Her heart was hemorrhaging already.

"I felt like a little girl again. Alone. Afraid. And I went through a crisis of faith because I was supposed to be leaning on God. I was supposed to *know* I wasn't alone. I was supposed to be strong for my three girls, telling them God is with us and He cares and He'll see us through, and I *couldn't*, not when I was wondering, *does* He really care?"

She paused, but Lance waited for her to continue.

"I felt we had an unspoken promise, that Hezekiah was my special gift and I'd be able to treasure that gift for as long as I lived. I had already been through a lifetime of pain, and now God allowed the worst pain of all." Treva took a breath, head bowed, as she waited for the emotion to pass. "Sorry," she said.

"Treva," Lance said, "it's okay to break down. It has to be."

She narrowed her eyes at him. "That only works when you're not the one breaking down. Or the one wearing mascara."

"I could protest that, but I'm sure I'd lose."

Treva smiled a little. "As hard as it's been, and as much as I've questioned God, I have to say He's been good. I thought I'd have to go back to work, but the girls had grown accustomed to my being home. And we'd grown close. I'd been sad thinking they'd lost their dad and would also lose our time together. But Hezekiah had insurance policies I didn't know about. He'd provided for us." She paused. "*God* had provided for us. That's what's kept me going, seeing God's faithfulness. I write it down in a journal."

"I love that. Grief had knocked you out, but Treva, you got back up. You got back in the race. You did what this conference is about."

"Yeah, but . . . nowhere near 'in hot pursuit.' I *might* be at a slow crawl."

Lance grabbed his notebook from the materials on the table. "That's exactly the point we need to make. Sometimes the pursuit *is* a slow crawl. And it's a good thing. Forward progress is a win." He scribbled some notes.

"What about you, Lance?" Treva said. "For me, it absolutely felt like grief had knocked me out, and I always felt a big part was because it was unexpected, a tragedy that upended our lives." She spoke carefully. "What was it like for you, given that you had this diagnosis and had been walking through this painful illness with Kendra? Would you describe it as feeling knocked out? And how did you get back in the race, even starting a church plant?" She added quickly, "Sorry. That's a lot."

Lance took a moment to respond. "They said it was terminal, but I was believing for a miracle. I felt God *wanted* me to believe she'd be healed, and there was a brief period after chemo when she was cancer-free. But even when it came back . . ." He tapped his pen on the page, as if it would help stifle the emotion. "I was still believing. I knew God could . . . I knew He was able." He looked at Treva. "It knocked me out."

Tears welled in Treva's eyes. "Did you talk to anyone? Besides God, of course."

Lance shook his head. "It wasn't the same even talking to God. I couldn't get back to what we had. Didn't know what to pray for or hope for anymore. And everyone's looking at me like I'm this strong man of God. I wanted to scream, 'Are you all crazy? You have no idea what I'm going through right this second.'"

"You loved her deeply."

"I always will."

Treva knew the comfort in those words. She felt the same about Hezekiah. "How much time passed before you planted the church?"

"Kendra died in October, and our first service was in May. We already had a team, a small group that had been meeting at the house for Bible study. We had the support of Living Word, where I'd been youth pastor. That was huge. And a church even gave us their building. Everything fell into place."

He focused on her. "You asked how I got back in the race. Treva, I was on autopilot. I was doing what I always did. I still had teens showing up every week, texting me, telling me their issues. I couldn't say, 'I can't help you, I'm grieving.' I had to be there for them." He sighed. "As I talk about it now, I think some parts of me stalled out. I can't even tell you what that means. It's just now hitting me."

Treva tried to sort through the jumble of thoughts that were rising up in her mind. "I keep thinking I'm overstepping," she said. "We're practically strangers, sharing deep things we haven't even shared with people close to us. But I'm wondering . . . can we pray? You said maybe we need this session ourselves. I think that couldn't be more true." She searched for words. "I've never really prayed with someone about my grief, and I don't want to be presumptuous, but if you could use that too . . ."

Lance extended his hands across the table, took hold of Treva's, and bowed his head, ignoring the tears that fell. "You start," he said.

CHAPTER TWENTY-ONE

J illian watched as people all around her in the church stood, hands raised in worship. Three gospel artists were performing tonight, and the enormous sanctuary was packed with people who'd come to praise. For Tommy it was work, though he too was on his feet. It was also part rescue mission after she called him, having driven herself half crazy in the hotel room. She must've sounded desperate, because it didn't take him long to announce that he was on his way. In the car he told her about the concert, said it'd be good for her. And it was. But her focus was her phone, again. Cecil should have called by now, and she had a lot she wanted to say.

She peeked up at Tommy and turned her phone sideways. He'd told her to stay off Facebook, but she couldn't help it. Cecil was seldom on Facebook, and when he was, he rarely posted. But in the hotel room Jillian had looked at his timeline from March, when he'd gone to the education conference. Someone had tagged him in a group picture, about seven of them at dinner, and a woman sat next to him. Jillian didn't think much of it until the next picture, captioned *Between sessions—enjoying the River Walk in San Antonio.* A small group was seen from behind, walking, and again Cecil was near the same woman, Regina Miller.

Jillian had clicked to the woman's profile page, hoping to find more conference pictures. Scrolling through, she saw yet another with Cecil and Regina, along with others, at the River Walk. She'd looked to see where Regina lived and whether she was married. And it was about the time she'd ventured over to Instagram and Pinterest to look her up that she knew she was losing it, and called Tommy.

But it just occurred to her that if something *was* going on, it might've started at last year's educators' conference. She needed to check Regina's Facebook timeline again, to see if she'd gone too, and posted pictures. With another quick glance at Tommy, she began scrolling down Regina's page, past happy poses with her own husband, which Jillian was glad to see. She was also glad Regina lived in Cincinnati, but what difference did any of it make if conferences were her and Cecil's rendezvous—

Tommy swiped Jillian's phone from her hand, and she looked up, realizing it was intermission.

He turned her phone toward her, a picture of Regina smiling at her. "Really, Jillian?"

Jillian took it back, closed the app. "You wouldn't understand."

"My wife cheated on me," Tommy said. "I understand. I also understand that this'll drive you mad with speculation because you don't actually know anything yet. I was hoping the concert would take you to a different place."

"What if Cecil is talking to her right now, trying to get his story straight?" Jillian said. "What else could he be doing? His work day ended hours ago."

Tommy looked at her. "What else could he be doing? With four kids? How much idle time do you have when you're home?"

"But given the way the conversation ended," Jillian said, "he should've been calling me first thing."

"You know what I think?" Tommy sat down. "I think you should go home. Maybe see if you can change your ticket and head back in the morning so you and Cecil can talk face-to-face."

Jillian bit her lip, thinking. "I hadn't considered that. That might be exactly what I need to do." Her phone vibrated and Cecil's name flashed on the screen, stirring an unusual mix of relief and dread.

Tommy handed her his keys. "Use my car for privacy."

Jillian headed quickly up the aisle, answering once she got to the lobby area.

"It took this long to call me back?" She regretted her tone, but he had to know how much she needed to talk.

"I know, I'm sorry," Cecil said. "You know how Fridays are around here. I was trying to wait until everyone was where they needed to be, so I could talk without interruption."

Jillian's insides settled a little. "I understand," she said, making her way across the parking lot.

"What's happening at the conference? Are you and Treva at dinner?"

"Treva had to prepare for her session tomorrow," Jillian said, "so I'm at a gospel concert with Tommy." She unlocked the door and hopped into the passenger seat, wincing at the way that sounded.

"You're with Tommy? Two nights in a row?"

"Last night I was with Tommy and his girlfriend. Tonight he picked me up because I was in the hotel distressed over our conversation. He was trying to help."

"Okay, so if I'm understanding correctly," Cecil said, "Tommy is now your confidant and counselor with respect to issues in our marriage."

Jillian looked at the phone in disbelief. "How did this become about Tommy and me?"

"Maybe because Tommy is spending more personal time with you than I have in months."

"Tommy has never been anything more than a brother to me," Jillian said. "You know that. And we wouldn't be here tonight if you hadn't left my question dangling in the wind . . . which drove me just a little crazy." She took a breath. "I asked you if there was someone else."

Her heart beat louder with every silent second that passed.

"I'm not having an affair, if that's what you're asking."

"What does *that* mean?"

"I don't know what you want me to say, Jill." Cecil's voice rose an octave, out of his norm.

Jillian steadied herself. "What's her name?"

Two seconds. Four. "She's just a friend. Regina."

Right. The woman with the happily married pics.

"We met at a conference last year," Cecil continued, "and I saw her again this year. This time we sort of stayed in touch. As friends."

"Meanwhile, you don't know about *us*, because you've been growing close to *her.*"

"It's not like that," Cecil said. "You and I have our own issues, and they've been building for quite a while."

"Have you kissed her?"

"What?" Another octave.

"At the conference, or wherever else you might've met up . . . Have you kissed her?"

"We haven't met up anywhere, Jill. I've only seen her at the conference."

"Have you kissed her?"

Long seconds passed. "Only once. It just . . . happened."

Jillian's eyes folded to a close. Her mind filled with images of Regina, arms around her husband, her lips against his. "I'm coming home in the morning."

"You don't have to cut your trip short," Cecil said.

"Really? Because I feel I *need* to, if I care anything about my marriage. We need time together, Cecil."

Cecil was quiet a moment. "I could use this time alone," he said, "to think deeply about things, to pray."

"Wow." Emotion clogged her throat. "You're telling me not

to come home?"

"I'm simply saying let's keep the current plan."

A couple walked toward the church building. Jillian's gaze blurred as she watched them. "You talked to her today, didn't you?"

"Jillian, don't do this," Cecil said. "It's not productive—"

"Did you or didn't you?"

"Okay, yes. We talked today."

The couple reached the front door and went inside. Jillian still stared . . .

Then she hung up the phone.

⁂

"I still can't believe he told me not to come home." Jillian lay in her hotel room bed, staring at the ceiling, her emotions roiling.

In the bed across from her, Treva rolled over. "To be fair, Jill, he said he wanted time to think and to pray. That's not a bad thing."

"Think and pray. Right. In between chats with Regina." Jillian rolled her eyes in the darkness. "And he had the nerve to question me about Tommy?"

"I think staying for the rest of the conference will be good for you anyway," Treva said. "These messages are right on time for helping you fight the spiritual battle at home."

Jillian closed her eyes again as Cecil's words replayed in her head. And more than his words, his tone. The way he so calmly seemed to be moving on. "If I'm the only one fighting, what's the point?"

"What's the point?" Treva propped herself up on an elbow. "That doesn't even sound like you."

"This morning I was distraught when I realized my marriage wasn't where it should be." Jillian sat up. "I told Cecil we should go on a trip. He shot me down. I was ready to fly home early. He shot me down. Waited hours for him to call. He's talking to *her*. And in the middle of it all I find out my husband was *kissing* another woman." She plopped back down. "I'm not distraught anymore. I'm mad. And I'm not fighting anything if he's just going to blow me off."

"So the marriage would end, just like that?" Treva said. "Easy win for the enemy."

"And easy for you to say. Hezekiah was never anything less than super devoted to you. You never heard him sound as if your marriage meant next to nothing to him. You have no idea how that feels."

"True. But I know what the flip side looks like. I was the one who acted as if the marriage meant nothing. And if it hadn't been for Hezekiah *fighting*, we would have divorced years before." Treva swung her legs over the side of the bed and looked at her. "Jillian, I'd be mad too, you *know* I would. And you would be the one working my nerves, telling me to pray and to get in the Word."

Treva reached for her arm and held it out. "You must have *Our struggle is not against flesh and blood* tattooed on here somewhere, as often as you've reminded me of it over the years. Girl, Cecil is in a battle. *You're* in a battle. Soldier up and *fight*."

Jillian turned over and stared at the wall. Cecil's words were resounding louder than Treva's. He was right. Their issues had been building for some time. Lack of intimacy and lack of real conversation were the norm, grooves worn into the rhythm of their lives. They were parents, household managers, social partners. But when was the last time she'd shared anything with him from the soul? When was the last time she'd longed to be with him, for even a simple evening stroll?

Her weekend getaway idea had come from the realization that something was wrong, from a need to problem-solve. It hadn't sprung from a desire to rekindle the fire.

It was hard to fight for a dying ember.

She didn't even know if she wanted to.

CHAPTER TWENTY-TWO

Treva lay back down, praying for her sister. She'd never seen Jillian like this, but then, Jillian had never seen a trial such as this. Why was God taking them through one hard thing after another, things that came out of left field and knocked them for a loop?

She thought about Faith and the long, hard months ahead. What would happen with college? With Jesse? How would they raise this baby? And would they get married?

I know, Lord, I can't help it. Seemed the main thing the Lord spoke to her heart these days was, "Be anxious for nothing." But who could do *that* when the "somethings" were so huge?

She heard the soft sound of a text notification. She'd turned the volume down but not completely off, since she'd hate to miss a call from Faith. She hadn't heard yet whether she and Stephanie had gotten together. And as much as she'd wanted to hear a report, she'd told herself to try a hands-off approach. At least for a minute.

She looked at the text and rubbed her eyes to read the name again. Lance?

Up praying and was moved to take care of something. Texting so u can hold me accountable. Tell u more in the am.

Treva set her phone back down and stared into the darkness, wondering what the "something" was. Had to be big for him to text, and at one in the morning. But then, they'd only left the restaurant at about eleven forty-five, as it was preparing to close.

She'd never had an evening like that, where hours held the depth of months, and words tumbled without fear. In the moment it seemed right. Unavoidable even. But the aftermath of feeling exposed, with a man she'd only met yesterday . . .

Treva's mind whirled, recalling thoughts exchanged, feelings shared, reminding herself that it was all for the sake of ministry. And truly, they'd gotten a lot done, digging into the materials after a time of prayer. But even after they'd declared themselves finished, they'd lingered. Talked. Shared more about their lives. On the way back, with the motor running in front of the hotel, one exchange led to another, to another.

Even now she was telling herself not to reply to his text. He was up, burdened about something, probably something they'd touched on. And he assumed she'd be asleep. She could find out right now what was going on. But somehow she knew—if she responded they could easily fire off a string of text messages.

And that would be an entirely different matter, texting Lance Alexander in the middle of the night.

With the slightest heart flutter, she forced her eyes closed and turned toward sleep.

CHAPTER TWENTY-THREE

Saturday, May 21

The sound of voices stirred Stephanie awake. She opened her eyes, got her bearings, and realized it was only Cyd talking on the phone. She looked at the clock—7:15—and turned over. Another forty-five minutes of sleep would be perfect. Then she'd get ready to meet Faith for a quick breakfast before the first session.

"Are you serious?" Cyd was saying. "No, I had no idea. I knew she was going through some things, but . . ."

Stephanie's eyes popped back open.

"No, she's definitely here," Cyd said. "Okay. I will. Thanks."

One, two—

"Steph?" Cyd came next to her bed.

Stephanie thought about feigning sleep, but she knew her sister. Cyd wouldn't give up until she got an answer. Stephanie turned over. "Yeah?"

"What's going on? Are you leaving Hope Springs?"

"Well, sort of." Stephanie's voice sounded half awake. "Why, who did you talk to?"

"Cousin Janelle just called," Cyd said. "They were looking for something and happened to check your room. She said they were shocked that most of your things were gone."

Add one more to the FBI roster.

"When she couldn't reach you this morning, she called me to make sure you were okay." Cyd paused. "And what does 'sort of' mean?"

"It just, all happened quickly, and I wasn't ready for any big announcement."

"And you quit your job too?"

Stephanie groaned. "You can't do anything in a small town without the world knowing. It's ridiculous."

"How have you been here since Wednesday night and not said a word about any of this?" Cyd said. "And where are you moving to?"

"Here," Stephanie said. "Back home."

"Really?" Cyd perked up. "So Lindell's already got a new position? Wait till I tell Cedric his brother's coming back."

"*I'm* coming home."

It took a moment to register. "Steph . . . Are you leaving Lindell?"

Stephanie gave her a blank stare.

"Oh, Steph." Cyd sat beside her. "What happened?"

Stephanie sighed. "No single big thing. Just a bunch of little things ever since, you know, what happened with Sam."

"I know it's been hard for you down there," Cyd said, "but I didn't know it was affecting

your marriage."

"I would get sad and depressed, and Lindell acted like I needed to just get past it. Move on. I think he didn't know how to handle everything I was going through, so he started pulling away. And we'd argue, about everything." Stephanie shifted to sit up. "Then I noticed his trips to Haiti were lasting longer, and becoming more frequent. Like he was trying to get away from me." She looked at her sister. "Do you know how much that hurt, Cyd? At a time when I needed him most, he basically abandoned me."

Cyd's face was filled with sadness and concern.

"I told him we should move back to St. Louis if he was going to spend so much time away. I thought it would help to put space between me and Hope Springs. To be around you and Momma and Daddy."

"What did he say?"

"He said he couldn't live life according to my whims. That we left St. Louis for Hope Springs to be near my family down there, and we weren't going to uproot again and go back."

Cyd was quiet a moment. "And what did he say when you told him you were leaving?"

Stephanie looked away. "He doesn't know."

"He doesn't know you're here?"

"He was supposed to let me know when he'd be home," Stephanie said. "Whenever he finds time to call, I'll tell him."

Cyd stood and paced a little. "This is heartbreaking. I hate that things have been so rough for you. You don't know how many prayers I've prayed—and I've actually prayed that you would return to St. Louis." She looked at Stephanie. "But not like this, not without Lindell. I'm speechless."

"Not for long, I'm sure," Stephanie said. "I already knew you'd be telling me this wasn't the way to handle things."

Cyd gave her a look. "That goes without saying." She came closer. "When did you start drinking again?"

"A few months ago. Christmas Day."

"Christmas?"

"I thought Lindell and I were spending Christmas together in Hope Springs. I'd been looking forward to it. Lots of family coming to town, plus those who live in the area."

"I remember," Cyd said. "Cedric and I thought about going down ourselves."

"He was in Haiti and was supposed to be back Christmas Eve. Then he sends"—she paused as emotion sneaked up on her—"he sends an *e-mail* saying he'll be delayed till the day after Christmas." Her voice rose, the incredulity flooring her still. "House full of people, and I'd never felt more alone. I drove to the convenience store, got a bottle of wine, and drank it late that night in my room."

Cyd sat next to her again and hugged her long. Her tears, trailing Stephanie's neck, caused Stephanie's to fall.

"I'm glad you're here with me right now," Cyd said. "I love you. I just wish I knew how to help you."

Stephanie pulled back a little. "You're already helping me. I hate to admit it, but you were right. I needed this weekend. Both of your messages yesterday . . ." She looked at her, eyes brimming. "They were for me."

"But you were only at the afternoon session."

"Yeah, well, I got the audio from both, and Faith and I listened last night."

Cyd stared at her.

Stephanie smirked a little. "Just when you thought I was completely hopeless."

"No, ma'am," Cyd said, shaking her head. "Why would I think such a thing? I *know* the hope that you have. I've been praying for *you* to know." She eyed Stephanie. "I know God has a plan for you, that He's going to work this extended trial for good in your life, that His love for you is deeper and wider than you can imagine, *and* that He's using you even in the midst of it all."

"Using me?"

"Treva was so disappointed that Faith missed the conference yesterday, and you got her there, by audio."

"I'm afraid to have another young person get close to me, though," Stephanie said, "especially now, when my life is in shambles." She felt the pang of remorse. "Do you know I was drinking an entire bottle of wine in front of Faith yesterday? I'm actually a bad influence."

"If there's one thing I'm fully persuaded about," Cyd said, "it's that God knows how to use us, warts and all. If your life looked perfect, Faith would have steered clear of you. But she's drawn to you, Steph. That's God."

"Can you just pray I don't do anything to ruin her life?"

⁂

"Hey, how're you feeling this morning?" Stephanie side-hugged Faith in the Starbuck's line.

"Good," Faith said, smiling. She looked cute in jeans and a long-sleeved red Maryland Terrapins shirt. "Sorry I'm late."

"You see you didn't miss anything," Stephanie said. "I've been slowly inching forward. These women don't play when it comes to getting their coffee in the morning."

Faith took a glance around. "It's weird," she said. "Day Two of the conference, but for me it feels like Day One. I was surprised to wake up feeling a little excited."

"I'm not surprised at all," Stephanie said. "You told me you were the one who suggested coming. You've been doing the studies. This is *you*."

"Well," Faith said, "the me I used to be."

Stephanie waved her comment away. "It's you at the core. That girl is still in there, ready to let loose." She nodded at the conference tote on Faith's shoulder. "Where'd you get that? I haven't seen those."

Faith leaned in. "I think they only had a limited number. Miss Cyd gave it to me at her house."

"Humph. She didn't give me one."

Faith smiled. "Didn't you tell her you weren't going?"

"And I was adamant about it." Stephanie chuckled. "So Jesse's already gone for the day?"

"He didn't come back to the room last night," Faith said, "because he stayed with his friend again." She smiled. "But we're going to dinner tonight, so I'm excited about that."

They moved forward and placed their orders, then nabbed the seats of two women who were leaving.

Faith pinched off a piece of bagel and popped it into her mouth, looking at the conference schedule. "So what breakout sessions are you going to?"

"Let's see," Stephanie said, turning the program partway. "Kelli's doing one on forgiving yourself later this morning. That's gonna be good."

"That's Alien's wife, right?" Faith said, adding quickly, "I mean, Brian's."

"Yep," Stephanie said. "And my sister-in-law."

"So, wait," Faith said, "your husband and Miss Cyd's husband are brothers? And Kelli is their sister?"

"Right." Stephanie sipped her vanilla latte. "Cyd was the maid of honor at our wedding, and Cedric was the best man. That's how they met."

Faith blew steam from her decaffeinated tea. "I love that."

Stephanie sighed inside. Her wedding seemed like yesterday, and now the marriage was ending.

Faith looked at the schedule. "I wasn't ready to hear what Kelli was saying the other night. Not sure I'm ready today. But it might be what I need."

"Good thing the breakout sessions are being recorded too, because I might need to hear all of them." Stephanie kept skimming then pointed at the paper. "This one on grief with your mom and Lance . . ." She took a breath. "I don't know. I would lose it in there. That might be one to listen to in a room alone with a box of tissues. A year from now maybe. If then." She looked at Faith. "Are you going to that one?"

"I don't know. My mom might get all weird if I show up. And there's this other one at the same time, on killing sin."

"Okay, for real, where's the light and fluffy session?"

"Funny," Faith said, "that's what excited me when I first read about this conference—the fact that it was meaty and I would grow. Now it's scaring me."

"Yeah, I'm starting to think we're *being* pursued, whether we're ready or not."

CHAPTER TWENTY-FOUR

The promo shoot for the breakout session was done, and Treva stood waiting for Lance, who was chatting with the camera guy. Lance had arrived with little time to spare, so they hadn't yet had a moment to talk about his wee-hour text.

From a distance her eyes fell on him and his easy demeanor. He'd shown up in denim again, and a light plaid button-down shirt, an interesting video contrast to Treva's beige linen skirt and embroidered white top. His smile was easy too. Accessible. She hadn't seen him in a conversation yet where he hadn't worn it. It was hard to believe he was once hard and closed.

He glanced over at her and held up a finger, letting her know he wouldn't be long, a two-second gesture that highlighted another thing—his deep brown eyes. Set against a warm, honey colored complexion. Enhanced by an athletic physique. She hadn't sought to draw a conclusion but it was inescapable—he was quite handsome. Not that it mattered. Her chest suddenly beating, she looked away.

What is wrong with me?

Lance finished his conversation and came over. "Sorry, hopefully you've still got a minute?"

They moved into the hall area, which was largely vacant. Praise and worship was about to start.

"More minutes than you," Treva said, "since you'll be speaking in a few."

He checked his watch. "Oh, man." He pulled her to the side. "Okay, here's the deal. You had us pray last night about our grief, where we are, where we need to be . . ." His eyes were animated. "And as soon as I got home, I was burdened with something I need to do."

Treva waited.

"I haven't packed up Kendra's things," he said. "Her dad and brother have already taken the things that are meaningful to them. But I haven't done anything myself, and I felt so clearly that it was time. I sent you the text because I knew I'd wake up with a ton of reasons why I couldn't do it today."

"You're doing it *today*?"

"I want to do it this evening," Lance said, "after our session. I'll already be on a wave of emotion, so might as well keep riding. It'll be hard, but it'll feel good to have it behind me." He looked at her. "Have you taken this step yet?"

"I have," Treva said. "About four months ago. The girls and I went through everything, along with Hezekiah's parents. I needed that team effort."

"That's what I figured," Lance said. He paused. "So I was hoping you'd help me."

Treva's insides reacted. "Me? Why?"

"You're the only one I can talk to about it, definitely the only one I can break down in front of." His expression was part sheepish. "Which is another reason I wanted to do it tonight—you're leaving tomorrow."

Something about that struck Treva. So much was happening in one weekend, and tomorrow it would all end.

"Did you have something planned for tonight, though?" he asked.

"Nothing concrete," Treva said, "but my sister's going through a hard time. I'd hate to leave her."

"Oh, absolutely." Lance shook his head. "I understand totally. Forget everything I said."

"I feel bad though."

"Don't. I've waited this long. Another time will come."

"How about this?" Treva said. "I should know more by our afternoon session. Can I let you know for sure then?"

"That'll work."

They started walking together.

"I just realized," Lance said, "this is the second night I'm basically proposing we spend the evening together, this time *at my house*." He laughed a little. "I promise. No hidden agenda. And just so you know, my brother-in-law is in town and will have a slew of friends over, so"—he smiled at her—"you're safe."

"Pastor Lance," Treva said, "that's about the last thing I'd be worried about, that you had some hidden agenda."

Lance moved toward the back entrance to the platform as Treva started toward the ballroom's main entrance, exhaling hard. No, she wasn't worried about anything out of control happening with Lance. The fact that she felt so safe with him—that's what gave her pause.

CHAPTER TWENTY-FIVE

"**S**o this is the infamous Lance Alexander." Jillian watched as he took the platform after Cyd's introduction.

Treva looked at her. "Infamous? Because of the news story about his wedding?"

"No," Jillian said. "Because he's the first man I've ever known my sister to spend time with other than Hezekiah Langston."

"To prepare for a conference session."

"Till midnight."

"Whatever."

"I know you," Jillian said. "If you were 'just' prepping for a conference session, you would've found a way to end that thing by nine." She eyed her sister. "I might've been upset last night, but don't think I didn't notice."

Treva stared ahead. "I thought you were still upset."

"Not such that I can't comment."

"How's everybody this morning?" Lance stood on the platform, looking out at the faces. "Okay, right off the bat, by a show of hands," he said, "how many of you thought this was a slumber party and stayed up half the night gabbing with your girlfriends, drank a gallon of coffee before the session, and are still wondering if you can stay awake?"

Laughter rose along with a good smattering of hands.

"All of you with your hands up," Lance said, "come closer to the front so I can keep an eye on you and throw stuff to wake you up, if need be."

Jillian leaned over. "How interesting. He happens to be engaging and good-looking as well."

"If you don't be quiet . . ."

A handful of women actually moved up closer to the front, as Lance had suggested. Jillian chuckled. She'd thought about staying in her room, but Treva had been right—she would have only moped the day away. And the thought of moping while Cecil and Regina chatted—as she was certain they would—made her even madder.

"This conference is all about being 'in hot pursuit,'" Lance was saying. "And I have to tell you, I remember vividly what it was like when the police were in hot pursuit . . . *of me*." He paused as some of the women seemed to sit up and take notice. "I know, Cyd gave the nice 'pastor of a church plant' intro, but I'm a man who's been rescued from some stuff. Can we be real this morning? Who else in here has been rescued from some stuff?"

Hands went up all around the room, including Treva's.

"Amen to that," she said.

"I was nineteen," Lance said. "I had gotten into some trouble, and I was in a car chase where the police were literally pursuing me. So I know a little about what 'hot pursuit' looks like. It's close—they were following right behind. It's continuous—trust me, they didn't take a doughnut break. And it's intense—all of their focus was trained on *me*." He added, "And by the way, they caught me. I did time, and prison was where I gave my life to Jesus."

Applause rang out, which seemed to surprise Lance. He pointed upward. "Amen. Give Him glory!"

Jillian looked at Treva. "Did you know he spent time in prison?"

Treva nodded, her eyes on the platform. "He's had an amazing journey."

"So I'm locked up," Lance said, "and I'm going to this weekly Bible study, getting fired up about what I'm learning, and then I get depressed. And I'm depressed because I can't do the things I want to do for God. I can't be used the way I want to be used, because I'm confined to a small, dark, nasty cell. And it's because of my own failures." He took his time, walking and talking. "So I started looking to the future. When I get out, I'll be able to run. When my circumstances change, I can get in the game. When this season has passed, *then* God can use me. Anybody else been there?"

Lance looked out among the faces of the women, who were giving their undivided attention. "Not in a prison cell," he said, "but because of your circumstances? Because of the season you're in? Maybe because of your own failures?"

Heads nodded soberly throughout the room.

"I think for many of us, it's a perpetual state," Lance said. "I mean, we can probably think of a time or two when we were running hot. Going after the things of God." He paused. "But how long does *that* last? There's always *something* to disable us. Disappointment. Fear. Doubt. Heartbreak. Betrayal. Failure. *Boom.* You're on the sidelines."

Lance moved to the other side of the platform, animated. "Let's be real, the sidelines become the norm. We hear, 'in hot pursuit' and it's like, what? It sounds unrealistic. Who *does* that? Yeah, we can do a few sprints and spurts, but mostly, we're doubled over, cramped up, nursing a pulled hamstring . . ."

"Or a sprained ankle!" a woman called out, smiling as she lifted up her bandaged ankle from the front row.

Lance laughed. "Or a sprained ankle. Yes, ma'am." He looked out. "Hey, I bet we've got a lot of sprained ankles in here, women nursing some sort of injury in the spirit. Can anybody testify to that?"

The words resonated with Jillian. She hadn't thought of it that way, but the imagery was apt.

"But here's the thing," Lance said. "We won't hesitate to use the injury as an excuse for why we can't run. Will get *mad* if somebody expects us to run because, '*You don't know what I'm going through.*'" He stuck out his leg. "'*You don't know how much this hurts!*'"

Lance came front and center, to the edge of the platform and looked out at the women. "We're basically saying, 'Let me live a substandard Christian existence instead of the supernatural one Jesus died to give me." He paused, taking his time. "I'd rather stay disabled with my pulled hamstring—my broken heart, my difficult trial, my failure—than look to God who's my enabler. I'll ride the bench this season rather than run.

"You know what God spoke to my heart in that prison cell? One sentence, from First Corinthians 9:24: 'Run in such a way that you may win.' He said, 'Lance, run! Right where you are!' The race wasn't suspended because I was behind bars. God's always working, everywhere!"

Lance walked the platform. "Your race isn't suspended because the storm blew in. God knew the storm was coming. He knew your heart was about to break, your health was about to be challenged, your child was about to become a prodigal, your job status was about to change. He knew! And He says, 'Run! Right where you are!' He's given you grace to run *despite* your circumstances. He's got work for you to do *in the midst of* your circumstances."

Women were standing all over the ballroom, some with tissues to their faces.

"The good news is we don't run in our own strength. We're running by the power of God. Our job is to believe and by faith keep moving. It's about endurance."

Lance took a drink of water from a bottle on the podium and wiped his face with a towel. "So, that was my intro." He smiled. "Seriously, I just want to break this down a little so you can leave here with tangible ways to run so you can win. Amen?"

"Amen!" sounded all around.

And Jillian knew. With a message like this, she'd normally be moved to stand and say amen. She'd be taking notes and her mind would be filling with ways to apply what she was hearing. But right now, she didn't even have her Bible open.

She was numb.

CHAPTER TWENTY-SIX

Faith couldn't stop weeping. Head bowed to her lap, she was shaken by an onslaught of emotion rushing so quickly she could hardly decipher it. It had started with silent tears near the middle of Lance's message, and now, as he ended, her body was wracked with sobs.

Stephanie had an arm around her. "It's okay, Faith. Let it out."

Faith cringed, knowing she must be drawing stares. She wasn't one to cry, certainly not like this.

A woman passed tissues into her hand, and Faith glanced up and smiled as best she could. Maybe she should go out, but that might draw more attention, at least until she could get herself under control.

"Faith?"

Mom. Faith buried her head further. She couldn't deal with questions, especially when she had no answers.

"Oh, Faith." Treva slid into the seat on her other side, empty now that people were moving to the breakout session. "I didn't even know you were here." She draped an arm over her, crossing with Stephanie's.

"It was a powerful message." Stephanie spoke above her.

"It really was," Treva said. "Touched a lot of people."

Faith felt another hand rubbing her back. She took a quick look. Aunt Jillian.

She swiped her face with a tissue, blew her nose, and buried her face again, feeling the weight of the last few months. Choices she'd made. Paths she'd taken. All of it coming together at once, crushing her.

"Hey, what's going on? Is she okay?"

"Lance, hey," Stephanie said. "This is all your fault. In a good way."

"You met my daughter the other night, didn't you?" Treva said.

"Oh, this is your daughter?" Lance took a chair and turned it around to sit in front of her. "Faith, right?"

Faith nodded from under her arms, tears flowing still.

"Not trying to intrude," Lance said, "but if it was something in the message, and you think it would help to talk it out, that's what we pastors love to do."

Faith sniffed. She wasn't ready to talk to her mom or Aunt Jillian. And though she could talk to Stephanie, there was something about talking to Lance that resonated. Maybe because it was his message that sparked this.

"Just let me know," Lance said, getting up, "I should be—"

"Maybe," Faith said, looking up. "If you have a minute?" She glanced around, surprised to see that the ballroom was practically empty.

"I sure do," he said, taking the seat again.

"We're going to head to the breakout session," Treva said. She hugged Faith. "I love you, sweetheart. I hope we can talk later."

Faith nodded. "Thanks, Mom."

Stephanie leaned in. "Should I meet you at Kelli's session?"

"Actually," Faith said, "do you mind staying?"

"Whatever you want me to do."

Faith blew her nose again and two-fisted the stream of tears. "Sorry," she said, looking at Lance.

"Don't worry about that at all." Lance leaned in, elbows on his thighs. "Tell me what's on your mind."

"I don't know if you heard my boyfriend's announcement at Miss Cyd's house," Faith said, "but just to put it out there, I'm pregnant."

"No, I didn't hear him announce it," Lance said. "Okay."

"And . . ." Faith felt more tears coming and fought to hold them in. "You talked about being real, so I hope this doesn't cross the line . . ."

Stephanie squeezed her hand. "You can talk straight with Lance. He was a youth pastor for years. He's heard it all."

Faith exhaled. "Up till a couple months ago, I was a virgin. You could probably say I was 'running to win,' bringing people together in my dorm for Bible studies, praying with them, sharing the Gospel. I just really . . . I loved the Lord. And then . . ."

Faith waited for a wave of emotion to pass. How had she

gotten to this place? How had she moved so far?

"You met a guy." Lance's voice was calm.

Faith nodded. "And I love him, but . . ." She searched for the words. "It's messed up my relationship with God. And the thing is, at the beginning at least, I knew I couldn't have both."

"What do you mean?"

"I knew I couldn't be intimate with God *and* be intimate with a man, outside of marriage anyway. I *knew* that. And the boundaries kept getting moved, and moved. And I started telling myself it was okay to go *this* far and maybe just *once*. Even yesterday right here at the conference . . ." A fresh wave of tears fell. "And now . . ."

Lance looked at her. "What's the now?"

"Now I'm so far from God that I don't recognize myself. My mother said it, and I got mad at her, but it's true." She looked at Lance. "You said 'run to win.' I don't know what it looks like to run *period* anymore."

Lance took a moment to respond. "You said you *loved* the Lord, past tense. You still do, don't you?"

Faith looked at him with tentative eyes. "Clearly not like I should."

"Have you ever loved God 'like you should'?" Lance tilted his face a little, showing a slight smile. "I know I haven't, not with *all* my heart, mind, soul, and strength." He sat back, crossed a leg over the other. "Tell me about God's love for you."

"What do you mean?"

"Sounds like you've studied your Bible. What does it say?"

"Unconditional. Nothing can separate me from it."

"Do you believe that?"

Faith stared down and exhaled, then looked at him and nodded.

"Okay," Lance said, "and when did God first love you?"

Faith hesitated. "Always?"

"Did He love you because you were running to win?"

"No." Faith's brow furrowed. "What are you trying to say?"

"God loved you before you knew Him or loved Him. He saved you, and by His Spirit, taught you how to run." Lance looked at her. "Do you think He can't teach you how to run now, in *this* season? You might not recognize yourself, but in God's eyes you're that same girl He's been loving on since time began."

Faith let his words soak in, remembering times her father would reassure her of God's love.

"Sin threw you off course, Faith, but you're still in this thing." He leaned in. "It's absolutely possible for you to run and even run to win. The question is, do you want to?"

Faith felt her insides bubbling, as if her answer was crucial. "I do," she said.

CHAPTER TWENTY-SEVEN

"I guess this was our breakout session," Stephanie said as she and Faith left the ballroom.

"I'm sorry," Faith said, "I should have told you to go ahead."

"No," Stephanie said, "I was serious. So much of what he said was for me, too." She looked at her watch. "There might be time to catch the last bit of Kelli's session, though."

"At this point, I'd rather listen to the audio from the beginning," Faith said. "I need to call Jesse."

"Wow, right now?"

"We've got to make some changes," Faith said, "or at least I do. And I want to talk about it while I'm feeling strong enough to say it." She looked at Stephanie. "But can you stay here with me? I'm not *that* strong."

"Let's go over here," Stephanie said, leading the way to an empty grouping of chairs.

Stephanie sat as Faith walked a little ways, phone to her ear. Seconds later, she was back.

"His phone didn't ring," Faith said. "Went right to voice mail." She stared off for a moment. "I'm calling his friend Aaron.

He called me Thursday when he couldn't get Jesse, so I have his number. I'm feeling an urgency, like I need to get this done." She paused. "I haven't felt this in a long while, that feeling like God is moving you. It feels good."

Stephanie checked her own phone, saw a couple of social media notifications and another text from Janelle. Nothing from Lindell. She wasn't sure what she'd say at this point if he did reach out.

Faith walked back with a weird look. "Aaron said he hasn't seen Jesse since yesterday morning, when he dropped him at the hotel."

Stephanie sat up. "What? You sure that's who Jesse said he was with today?"

"And yesterday afternoon," Faith said. "And last night."

"Did he mention knowing anyone else in St. Louis?"

"No one."

Stephanie thought for a moment. "You said you're not into the social media scene—but do you know what he's on?"

"A bunch of things," Faith said. "Facebook, Twitter, Instagram. Snapchat too."

"I'm not on Snapchat," Stephanie said, "but I've got the others."

She got his last name and searched Facebook first. His profile page was public, and she saw lots of graduation photos, mostly where others had tagged him. But nothing from this weekend. She checked his Twitter account next, which had nothing for the past month.

"Looks like he's not very active."

She tried Instagram next and found his page. "Huh."

"What?" Faith said, bending to look at Stephanie's phone. "Oh, he posted a picture of him and Aaron on Thursday."

Stephanie scrolled down. "You two don't take many pictures, I see."

"Yes, we do." Faith showed Stephanie photos of the two of them on her phone.

Stephanie kept her next thought to herself. The more accurate statement was that Jesse didn't *post* pictures of the two of them.

She went back to the one from Thursday, captioned *Landed in the Lou*. Aaron was tagged, so she checked his pictures but saw nothing of interest. She went back and checked the comments on the Thursday photo. One from BrandyB said simply *Yay*. With a click, Stephanie was on Miss BrandyB's page—and her breath caught.

She looked first at a single picture of Jesse, posted Thursday. The caption—*Tomorrow. Can't wait.* Yesterday she'd posted a goofy picture of the two of them at the Arch. And—Stephanie checked the time of the post—less than an hour ago—the caption—*With my sweetie at Sweetie Pie's*, with a picture of the restaurant.

"What is it?" Faith said, noticing her reaction. She bent down again to look, then took Stephanie's phone. "That's where he is right now? With her? Who *is* this?" Faith kept scrolling. "Looks like she's a law student . . . And she went to Maryland—she's got a sweat shirt on in this one . . . And she's got pictures of her and Jesse at Jesse's graduation."

Faith handed back the phone and stared into the distance.

Stephanie stood. "Faith, you've got a couple of options right now, and I'll tell you the option I'd choose, even though it's not your style."

"What's that?"

"I'd be hightailing it over to Sweetie Pie's to catch his behind eating fried chicken with BrandyB."

"What's the other option?" Faith said.

"Stay here, cry over a boxed chicken salad sandwich for lunch, and wait for Jesse to *maybe* show up for the dinner the two of you are supposed to have."

Faith's eyes bore the surprising look of steel. "How far is Sweetie Pie's?"

If it were possible, Stephanie was more upset than Faith. Faith had just spent the morning coming to terms with how much she had compromised her relationship with God for Jesse—a relationship that itself was apparently a sham. Stephanie sped out of the parking garage, thankful she'd driven her own car to the conference. At the time, she'd wanted the freedom to escape, if need be. She couldn't have guessed she'd be crashing Jesse's lunch date.

Come on. She'd hardly gone anywhere, with traffic bottle-necked near the hotel. She wanted to make it to Sweetie Pie's before they left. She wanted Jesse to have to face the lies he'd told. The heart he'd broken. The only problem was, Stephanie wondered if he'd even care.

She glanced at Faith, who'd mostly been stoic. "Faith, I keep thinking about what you told Lance, that the boundaries kept getting moved. What did that look like?"

"Well, the first time we went out I met him for lunch in the Student Union." Faith stared out of the window. "That was a boundary I had. I didn't want any guys coming to my room. Then one evening he dropped by my dorm. He said he was thinking about me and wanted to see how I was doing." She looked at Stephanie. "It meant something, you know? Knowing I was on his mind. And I felt silly saying *No, I can't see you.* So we hung out in my room and had really good conversation."

Stephanie nodded slightly. She could already see the trajectory.

"So he started dropping by from time to time," Faith said, "and one evening he asked if he could stay because he had an early class, and it was easier, instead of driving home."

Stephanie swerved around a car and into a different lane to beat the red light. "What did you tell him?"

"I was really surprised. I told him it wasn't a good idea." Faith grew quiet a moment. "I should have flat out said no, but to be honest, I was conflicted. I was feeling things I'd never felt. I could tell I was falling for him, even though I was trying not to. And he was a real gentleman, because at that point he'd been there a few times and hadn't even tried to kiss me."

Mm-hm. "What did he say when you said it wasn't a good idea?"

"He said he cared about me and enjoyed spending time with me. Then he hugged me, and that's when . . . That's when he kissed me."

"So he ended up staying."

"Another boundary gone," Faith said. "But nothing happened that night. By the third time he stayed, things had been going farther than I wanted. And I told him that." Faith looked at her. "I told him I wanted to stay a virgin, but at the same time I was so drawn to him. I was praying for God to give me strength, but . . ." She looked out the passenger window. "I couldn't stop crying afterward."

Stephanie glanced at her. "I know this is hard."

"I just wish he hadn't said he loved me. I guess everything's been a game to him."

They drove the rest of the way in silence. Stephanie found herself praying for Faith. This wasn't a matter of a simple breakup. With a baby involved, there was a complicated road ahead.

As they approached the restaurant they could see a line snaking out the door and around the corner. She found a parking spot a block away. Turning off the motor, she looked at Faith. "We don't have to go in," she said. "It might hurt too—"

"No, I want to," Faith said. "I still think it was God that led me to call Jesse, so I could find all this out. I need to see it through."

They walked past the people in line, up to the hostess stand.

Stephanie smiled at the young woman. "Hi," she said, half scanning the dining room, "we need to get a message to a friend who's here. Can we look for him real quick?"

The woman shrugged. "Sure, no problem."

They divided up, Faith looking to the right in the restaurant and Stephanie moving left. At a table for two on the far left, Stephanie saw them. She signaled to Faith, and they started in that direction.

Jesse jumped up the second they came near. "Faith, what are you doing here?"

"I was about to ask you the same question," Faith said.

Bewilderment shone in his eyes. "How did you know where I was?"

Stephanie moved closer to the table. "Let's not make a scene. Jesse, have a seat. By the way, my name is Stephanie."

Jesse sat down amid stares, and Faith moved in closer.

"What is going on here?" Brandy looked irritated, her green eyes flashing. "Jesse, who are these people?"

Faith stood beside him. "I'm wondering the same, Jesse. Who is she?"

"I can tell you who I am," Brandy said. "I'm his girlfriend, of three years. And you?"

Faith's hand went to her stomach. "I'm the mother of his baby."

Brandy's jaw dropped, and she stared at Jesse. His gaze fell to the remains on his plate.

"I asked if you had a girlfriend, and you told me no," Faith said. "I would've never gotten involved with you had I known. But I'll own my part, because I shouldn't have gotten involved with you anyway. I've asked God to forgive me, and I pray you do the same. I just hate that for the sake of this baby, I'll still have to deal with you." She started to leave, then turned back. "And no need to come up to the hotel room. Your things will be waiting for you at the front desk. I need your passkey."

Stephanie's eyes widened a little. *Whoa.*

Jesse handed it over, and Stephanie followed Faith out, putting an arm around her as they walked. Stephanie noticed she was trembling.

"That was hard," Stephanie said, "but you handled it ten times better than I would've. I'm proud of you."

"I was so naive. And stupid."

"You were refreshingly inexperienced, and he took advantage."

Faith stared at the sidewalk. "I don't know what I'm going to do. I never thought I'd be pregnant by a man who's with another woman." She looked at Stephanie. "I'm trying to hang on to the things Lance said this morning, but I'm losing my grip already."

CHAPTER TWENTY-EIGHT

Jillian spotted Tommy in the crowded hotel lobby and waved her hand. She moved toward him, hugging him when they came near.

"Thanks for bringing that," she said, taking from him the jacket she'd left in his car last night.

"No problem." Tommy's eyes rested just beneath the rim of his ball cap. "Glad I could catch you between sessions. How are you today?"

Jillian's eyes fell on the people coming and going. "I don't know."

He cocked his head slightly. "You don't know? Drill that down a little."

She looked at him. "I'm good, but it's probably not a *good* good. I'm not feeling anything right now."

"Are you praying?"

Jillian looked away again.

"But it helps, being at the conference, right? I heard Lance's message this morning was fire."

"I loved his message," Jillian said, "but . . . nothing is really penetrating. People were raving about the breakout session we went to this morning too, but I was kind of just . . . there." She shrugged. "That's why I wasn't in a rush to get to the main session after lunch."

"It's going on right now?" Tommy said. "Jill, you should be there. That might be the very one you need."

"I'll get the audio," Jillian said. "Do you have a few? We should get some coffee."

They walked to the Starbucks in the hotel, which was nearly empty. After getting their drinks, they settled at a table by the window.

"One thing I can say," Jillian said, holding her mocha latte, "is this has been one needed highlight of the weekend—the two of us reconnecting."

Tommy nodded, sipping freshly brewed coffee. "It's still hard to believe we went so long without any contact."

"Let's not ever do that again." Jillian tasted her latte. "By the way, I didn't tell you what Cecil said last night."

"What was that?"

"He got an attitude about us spending time together—*the nerve*—and made a snide remark about you being my confidant and counselor." She took another sip. "But you know what? I'm grateful for that. You're the one person besides my sister who truly gets me."

"Jill," Tommy said, "you and I didn't talk for a couple decades. I know you're upset with him right now, but your husband is your main confidant and counselor."

"Being my husband doesn't make him that automatically," Jillian said. "I've never been able to talk to Cecil the way I talk to you. This weekend reminded me of that."

Tommy stared into his coffee cup a moment, then brought his eyes to Jillian's. "You know I care for you and want the best for you. Right?"

"Always."

"And I have absolutely loved being able to spend time with you this weekend." Tommy smiled. "You will always be my Jilli-Jill."

Jillian felt a wad of emotion gathering in her chest.

"But after today, after this right here—we have to cut it off."

"What? Why?"

"Hearing what you just said. I don't want to come between you and Cecil."

"How does this even make sense?" Jillian said. "You don't want to come between me and Cecil, but he's already got Regina between us. And contrary to what *they've* got going, you and I are friends, brother and sister. What could be wrong with that?"

"I can't be the one you turn to, Jill. You haven't even been praying." His hands rested on his cup. "If Cecil isn't your main confidant, then Jesus needs to be."

"I don't see why it has to be so extreme." She looked at him, eyes brimming. "Cut it off? Like, never talk again? Our friendship is one of the few things giving me life right now. Why are you being so cold?"

"You know what, Jill, that neon sign is going off in my mind right now—*Be careful how you walk.*" Tommy leaned in. "You're my friend, my sister, my *girl.* You think I don't feel the same about being able to talk to you? We vibe when *nothing's* being said." He stared into her eyes. "But can *you* guarantee it would never lead to more? An emotional affair, at the least? Because I can't. I know how sneaky temptation can be."

Jillian couldn't hold his gaze. She turned, staring into the distance.

"But even if it never became more . . ." Tommy's voice was soft. "Even at this level, it's a lot, Jill. I could feel it this weekend. I would be there for you in a heartbeat, and that's not my place." He let silence engulf them for a few seconds. "I need to respect your marriage. I need to fade."

Tommy put his hand atop hers and squeezed it as he rose from his seat.

And he was gone.

Jillian could feel her face contorting as she gulped back a wave of tears. She wished she and Tommy had never reconnected. Now she knew they still had that something special—which could never be. How was it possible that she missed him already? And what did she have to look forward to? Tomorrow. Heading home. She looked forward to seeing the kids, but she couldn't say the same about Cecil. Her mindset had devolved to his—she didn't know about the marriage.

Her phone dinged, and Jillian read a text from Treva.

Where are u? We're outside the ballroom. Faith & Jesse broke up. Crazy story.

Jillian moved immediately, tossing the bulk of her latte, wiping water from her lids. The area outside the ballroom was crowded as women spilled out of the main session. Jillian threaded her way through, spying Treva first then Faith.

"My sweet niece," Jillian said, hugging her long. "This has been quite a day for you."

"He had a girlfriend the whole time." Treva had an I-told-you-so look. "Spending time with her right here in St. Louis. Faith saw them at Sweetie Pie's."

"What? Oh, Faith." Jillian hugged her again. "I know that hurts. How are you holding up?"

Faith gave a single shrug. "Okay. I was glad Stephanie was with me." She looked to the woman on her other side. "Have you two met?"

"It's good to meet you finally," Jillian said.

"Likewise," Stephanie said. "It's only been a couple of days, but it feels like I've known Faith and Treva forever. Where've you been hiding?"

"Ha," Jillian said. "You don't even want to know. It's been a rough two days."

"Oh, trust me," Stephanie said. "I feel you." She shook her head. "What is the *deal?* I thought women's conferences were supposed to put you on a spiritual mountaintop. Sounds like all three of us are going through. We need to ask for our money back."

"Right," Jillian said. "Or at least get a little label on our badge so we can spot everybody else who's going through, and stay away from the mountaintop people."

Stephanie chuckled. "'Cause you *know* misery loves company." She got a look in her eye. "But you know, that's a good idea."

"The label?"

"No, the company . . . misery lovers . . ." Stephanie grinned. "That didn't come out right, but you know what I mean. One second." She took out her phone and dialed someone.

Jillian glanced at Treva and Faith, glad to see them talking.

"Hey, are you still in the ballroom?" Stephanie spoke into her phone. "Okay, that girls' hangout tonight? We need to add Treva and Jillian. Okay, cool." She dropped her phone into her bag.

Stephanie looked at them. "So, Cyd invited a couple of people up to our suite this evening to hang out, mainly for my benefit, kind of a pick-me-up. I told her we needed to add Faith." She put an arm around her. "You two need to come too. It'll be a full-fledged crazy, silly, eat-too-much-pizza, girls' kind of night."

Faith was smiling. "I can't wait. I need crazy and silly right now."

"I'm loving this plan," Jillian said. "I missed the gathering Thursday night, but this one is right on time." She looked at her sister. "Treva?"

"I love it too," Treva said. "Definitely timely. But I'll have to bow out myself." She checked her watch. "Ooh, I've got to run to set up for the session. I'll see you guys later." She dashed off.

"Well, I'm excited you two can make it," Stephanie said.

"Me too," Jillian said vaguely, her gaze following Treva. What did she have going on tonight?

CHAPTER TWENTY-NINE

Treva felt a tinge of relief that the breakout session was coming to a close. The room was full and the discussion had been lively. But that was why she had one eye on the clock. Everyone's situation was so deeply personal that it was difficult to give answers she felt were satisfactory. She and Lance had prayed about it beforehand, and she'd been shooting up silent prayers throughout. Now she'd simply be relieved when it was over.

She stood to one side as Lance fielded a question. For the question and answer portion, they'd been alternating, an idea Treva had opposed. She wanted Lance to take all the thorny questions. Actually, *all* the questions. If there was any mercy, he'd craft a long, drawn-out response that closed the hour.

For the hundredth time, her gaze drifted to her daughter. It meant so much that she'd come, not for Treva's sake, but because Faith seemed to have turned a corner. Now, if she could only keep moving. Jesse's presence was such a wild card.

Lance clapped his hands one time. "Okay, I think we've got time for one more question."

Treva's stomach dropped and she exhaled softly, looking out

at the faces, each second gnawing at her. Jillian was out there too, which was a comfort. Maybe she would shoot a softball question her way.

A hand went up. Stephanie?

Treva walked down the aisle a little. "Stephanie, what's your question?"

"Okay, so I knew this would be a hard session for me. In my grief over a young friend's suicide, the question I keep coming back to is why would God allow this? Why would He let a young girl take her life? I just can't get past that."

As others in the room nodded, Treva looked back at Lance for a lifeline. He gave her a go-ahead nod instead, indicating that she could handle it, which was absurd. If there were a question she feared most, this was it.

Treva sent up a prayer as she cleared her throat. "Well, first," she began, "I don't have the answers. None of us does. I think when it comes to grief especially, we have to grow very comfortable with *not* knowing the answers." She sighed, feeling the weight of it. "I asked the same question about my husband. *Why would you take him, Lord?* He was raising three daughters, and raising them *well*. Serving in the Kingdom. It still makes no sense to me."

Treva's eyes caught the clock. Time was up, but no one was moving.

"One thing God keeps speaking to my heart is that we can never understand all that He understands. There's a verse in Romans that I've memorized because it brings me peace. Romans 11:33—'Oh, the depth of the riches both of the wisdom and knowledge of God! How unsearchable are His judgments and unfathomable His ways!'" Treva glanced upward. "His ways are higher. I think that should be a comfort to us."

Lord, please help me. Treva's heart was beating out of her chest. Were her words coming together right?

She let her eyes pass around the room then looked at Stephanie again. "Even though we don't have all the answers, there are some things we know for sure. We know God wants to be glorified. We know He wants people to be saved. So look what happened with Sam."

Treva addressed the whole group, though she moved closer to Stephanie's row. "I know a little about this story, and Stephanie's young friend taking her own life wasn't the whole story. It wasn't even half the story. The *story* was that she received *eternal life* the night before, because Stephanie led her to the Lord. See, in our minds, death is the worst thing that can happen. But Sam left this earth and stepped into Jesus' arms."

Stephanie had tears in her eyes, nodding. Faith held her hand.

"The *story,*" Treva said, looking at Stephanie, "was that you got to be on CNN telling everyone *her* story, impacting even more people. So God was glorified. Sam was saved, and through Sam, probably many others. And that's only the tiny, tiny bit that we know." Treva exhaled. "I hope something in there made sense."

"It did," Stephanie said. "Something clicked for me as you

spoke. I just need it to stick. Thank you."

Lance dismissed everyone after a quick prayer, though hardly anyone left. Given the stories people had shared, everyone seemed to want to mingle and comfort one another.

Jillian came up to Treva. "Awesomely beautiful," she said, hugging her.

"That might be a little over the top," Treva said. "But thanks for coming. I appreciate the moral support."

"Sorry, but I wasn't here for moral support. You and Lance talked about how grief is loss, and not just from death. I'm dealing with loss in my marriage, and today, the loss of a friendship. I needed this."

"Loss of what friendship?"

"We'll talk," Jillian said. She inched closer. "And by the way, what plans do you have tonight?"

Treva gave her a look. "We'll talk."

Stephanie came up then and hugged her. "Seriously, Treva, I don't know where y'all came from, but you and your daughter dropped into my world at the right time."

"No, you dropped into my daughter's world at the right time," Treva said. "And by the way—Faith is one of those people impacted by your telling Sam's story."

When the last of the people had left, Treva gathered her papers back into her bag.

Lance came into her peripheral vision, arms folded. "'I can't handle the thorny questions,' she said."

Treva gave him the eye. "I couldn't believe you didn't rescue me."

"You didn't need rescuing."

"I was scared out of my mind."

"It was beautiful."

Treva looked down at her papers. "I'm just glad it's over."

Lance went to gather his things as well. "So what are you and your sister doing this evening?"

"Oh." Treva turned to him. "I didn't have a moment to tell you. She's spending the evening with Cyd, Stephanie, and some others. I told them I couldn't make it." She paused. "That is, if you still want to move forward with your plan."

"Weren't you supposed to be holding me accountable if I didn't?"

"Then, yes." Treva ignored a flutter. "Tonight it is."

~ ❊ ~

The soft evening breeze tickled the back of Treva's neck as she sat on the outdoor patio. She'd changed following the session, donning jeans and pony-tailing her hair, and was glad to have some time to soak up a beautiful St. Louis evening.

"I didn't know you were doing all of this," she said.

Lance turned from the grill. "Well, neither of us had eaten, and it doesn't take long to whip something up."

"Oh, yeah, just 'whip up' grilled steak, potatoes, and asparagus," Treva said. "I'd like to see the kind of meals you labor over."

Lance had changed as well before he returned to the hotel to pick her up. In his cargo shorts and Cardinals tee he looked relaxed and in his element.

He set her plate before her. "If it's not done enough, let me know."

He sat next to her at the wrought iron table, took her hand, and bowed his head. "Lord, we thank You for the food we're about to eat, and pray it nourishes. And we thank You for this evening. We pray You accomplish all that You have purposed. In Jesus' name."

"Amen," Treva said.

When she opened her eyes, the sun sat a little lower on the horizon, casting a soft glow on the table. Lance's brother-in-law and his friends were camped out in the lower level of the house, which meant only the two of them were dining together. Her arms shivered a little.

She cut into her steak and took a bite. "Mm, this is perfect. You've got that crisp, caramelized thing going." She smiled at him. "I'm impressed."

He took a bite himself, his eyes smiling back at her.

"By the way, Lance, thank you for spending time with Faith this morning." Treva paused between bites. "You were there for her at a crucial moment."

"I hope it helped," Lance said. "First loves are hard."

"Yeah, and it turned into her first heartbreak two hours later."

"You're kidding," Lance said. "And she's pregnant too. What a nightmare. I'll keep her in my prayers."

"I really appreciate that." Treva took in the surroundings as she ate. "So this is the house? The one you and Kendra lived in?"

Lance nodded. "Believe it or not, her dad gave it to us. He lives in a condo not far from here."

"Oh, wait," Treva said, glancing around again. "Wow, this *is* it." She looked at him. "So, another confession. I googled your wedding."

Lance gave her a look.

"Oh my goodness, it was gorgeous." She spread her hands. "And it was right here, with all this lush landscaping."

"A lot of it was done that very morning," Lance said. "It truly was beautiful."

Treva watched him take it in. "Are you sure you're ready to take this step tonight, Lance? Packing up everything?"

"I'm even more sure after the session today," Lance said, "because of what you said." He set his fork down and focused on her. "I thought about how people love the 'love story' of Lance and Kendra. And when she died, I grieved the fact that that love had come to an end. But this afternoon it hit me. That wasn't the real story."

Treva's brow furrowed a little. "What was the real story?"

"God loving Kendra through me," Lance said. "It was a story of God's love, which can never end. The story didn't stop with Kendra's death."

Treva stared into the distance, meditating on that.

"The crazy thing is that Kendra told me that, moments before she died. She said it was her time to go, but it wasn't mine. And I'll never forget her words: 'Keep letting God use you to love. His well in you is deep.'"

Treva felt slight shivers again. "She said that?"

"It's taken me almost two years, but I get it now. It's time to turn the page. And it starts with this step tonight."

Treva cut into her steak. "I'm sure it'll be interesting for you to discover what the next steps are and then watch them unfold."

"I don't know," Lance said, looking at her. "I can't help but wonder if they're unfolding already."

CHAPTER THIRTY

Faith's insides were a jumble as the elevator descended to the lobby. She'd been in Cyd's suite, having the best time she'd had all weekend, but it all came to a screeching halt when Jesse sent her a text. Stephanie had told her to turn off her phone, but Faith was too curious—would he ignore her altogether or would he reach out? When she got the text asking her to come down, she didn't have strength to resist.

She walked off the elevator, glancing around. Then she saw him, sitting low in a club chair, the bags she'd left at the front desk at his feet.

Faith stopped a few feet away, arms folded. "What did you want, Jesse?"

He touched the chair next to him. "Can you at least sit?" He sounded weary.

"I won't be here long," she said, remaining where she stood. "What is it?"

"I know you won't believe me," Jesse said, "but this is not how I wanted things to go down."

"Of course you didn't," Faith said. "Who wants to get caught in a lie?"

He sighed. "For the record, Brandy and I broke up at the end of last semester, so I wasn't lying. We got back together in April."

"So when you said a friend wanted you to come visit . . ."

"Aaron did want me to visit," Jesse said. "But true, I was mostly thinking about Brandy, because she'd been asking me to go see her in Chicago. She drove down yesterday."

"Meanwhile, you wanted to work on me giving the baby up so you could move on with Brandy, unencumbered."

"It's not that simple," he said. "I kept telling you things were complicated. Yes, I wanted my life 'unencumbered,' as you say, but Brandy's not my sole motivation. I do care about you, Faith."

"You used me." Faith swallowed the emotions trying to surface. "For sex, for a convenient place to stay on campus, for a plane ticket to see Brandy . . ."

"Faith, believe me," Jesse said. "It's not like that. Do you think I'm really that cold?"

"Obviously I don't know you like I thought I did. I saw what I wanted to see . . . I have to go." She turned.

"Faith, wait," Jesse said. "What am I supposed to do tonight?"

She turned back. "Stay with your girlfriend, like you did last night."

Jesse's gaze fell. "She broke up with me."

"Then stay with Aaron."

"Aaron's with his girlfriend, and his phone is turned off." He looked toward the front desk. "They said I can't sleep in the lobby. And you know I don't have money to get a room."

206

"None of this is my problem," she said.

"How would it hurt to let me stay upstairs? I'll sleep in the desk chair."

"How would it hurt?" Faith looked at him. "You don't care the slightest bit that *I'm* hurt, do you?"

Jesse returned her gaze. "I care more than you know."

Faith hated that her heart embraced that. Deep down she wanted to know that there was something there, however small.

"There's something else you should know," Jesse said. "I'm headed for grad school this fall, in Chicago."

"With Brandy." Faith nodded. "So you won't be around for the birth of the baby? Well, what am I saying? You won't be there for the baby at all, will you?"

"I was honest about that, Faith. I'm not ready to be a father."

"It's one thing not to be ready. It's something else entirely to say you won't be a part of your child's life."

Jesse exhaled, staring vaguely at the floor.

"I guess that's it then," Faith said. She turned again to leave.

"So, you're just gonna leave me in the lobby?"

Faith walked away, then turned suddenly and went back. "And one more thing—you didn't have to tell me you loved me. That was just mean."

She left, stifling tears.

"I can't *believe* that boy was whining about needing someplace to stay tonight." Stephanie was sitting on the sofa, polishing her toenails. "He's got more nerve than a little bit." She looked at Faith. "And good for you for not caving."

Faith sat at the table with Cyd, Dana, and Kelli. "I admit I felt a little bad for him, though. I mean, where *is* he gonna stay?"

"You have such a tender heart, Faith," Cyd said. "I hope no matter what happens, you keep that."

Kelli touched Faith's hand. "I know you probably feel totally alone right now . . . I remember that feeling like it was yesterday. I also remember thinking Brian didn't care about any of it, that he was off doing his thing." Her voice was infused with sweetness. "I found out years later that that wasn't the case at all. He was dealing with it at a deep level as well."

"But you and Brian had been best friends," Faith said, "and in a committed relationship. He actually cared about you. That's not the case with Jesse and me. He doesn't really care about me or the baby."

"I guess what I'm saying," Kelli said, "is you can't be one hundred percent sure. Brian and I have heard lots of stories from the guys' point of view. Many of them cared more than they even realized, but they were scared." She got up and opened another bag of chips. "Plus, don't forget, Faith, he's young. He may seem old to you, but he's only twenty-two or so. I'm just saying, we should be praying for Jesse too."

"Well, that's why y'all need to pray for me, too," Stephanie said. "Because that's the last thing that would've come to my mind."

"It hadn't crossed my mind either, to be honest," Faith said. "He's got his future free and clear—he doesn't have to worry about taking care of a baby, he's already got his college degree, he's headed to grad school. If he doesn't get back with Brandy, he'll get someone else. He's got everything."

Stephanie looked up from her toes. "Except a place to stay tonight."

"But Faith, do you think that's really true—that he's got everything?" Dana, Cyd's best friend, spoke up. "It sounds like he may not even have the main thing, a relationship with the Lord."

"I don't know," Faith said. "I thought he did at first, but . . ."

"Okay, fine." Stephanie hopped up, protecting her toes. "I feel kinda bad for what I said, so we hereby interrupt the girls' hangout to pray for Mr. Jesse." She glanced around the room. "Who's gonna lead us?"

CHAPTER THIRTY-ONE

J illian shook her hips to the beat, microphone brush to her mouth, singing out-of-tune four-part harmony with Cyd, Dana, and Stephanie.

"En Vogue better watch out," Kelli said. "You four could go on tour with this."

"Girl, you need to be up here." Cyd laughed, her shoulders feeling the rhythm. "You're the one with the voice."

"Oh, no, this is too entertaining." Kelli had the video going on her phone. "Plus, I can blackmail every one of you later."

"Remember this part?" Jillian said, throwing her head and doing a bouncy turn.

"Right!" Dana mimicked her. "Then they did this little shuffle move."

Dana tried it, and the other three fell in step, cracking up the entire time.

"How do you all remember a video from the early nineties?" Faith was shaking her head at them. "I wasn't even born yet."

"Hey, thanks for that," Stephanie said, pausing from her lip-synch. "I usually feel like the young one around Cyd and Dana."

"Girl, we loved some En Vogue." Cyd was keeping step. "Remember, Dana? That was back when we had tape cassettes."

"Oh, man," Jillian said. "Treva and I used to wait for our favorite songs to come on the radio so we could record them."

"Girl, yes!" Dana said. "Those slow jams especially."

The song faded, Dana clicked Pause on the iPod player, and the four of them collapsed on the sofa.

Kelli laughed. "Really? You all have to work on building stamina."

"That was three songs we did." Dana was winded. "But I'll be ready to go again in a minute. Who should we play next?"

Stephanie looked over at Dana. "Sidebar. You had to be the only white girl on the planet dancing to En Vogue and recording R&B slow jams on the radio. I'm just sayin'."

"If so," Dana said, "then you were the only black girl with no rhythm."

"Ha." Stephanie laughed. "Hey, that might be true, though."

"Nope," Faith said. "I would make it two."

"Okay, fellow partyers," Cyd said, "those with rhythm and those without—it's almost midnight, and somebody's got a closing message to give in the morning. I'd better start winding down."

"Oh, Cyd." Stephanie kicked her feet up. "It's the last session. Live a little. Pull an all-nighter."

Faith was yawning. "I'm tired myself," she said. "I think I'll head to my room. All the day's drama has caught up to me."

"I'll head out with you," Kelli said. "I've got praise and worship in the morning."

"Well, shoot," Stephanie said. "Jillian? Dana? Y'all gonna hang for a little while more?"

Dana kicked up her feet beside Stephanie's. "I took a nap before I got here, so I'm good."

"I'm good too," Jillian said. "I'm trying to stretch out this last night as long as I can before I head home."

The others said good night, and the three who were left replenished their beverages and the bowls of chips and dip before stretching out on the sofa again.

"Jillian, you said you've got four kids?" Dana asked.

Jillian chomped into a Dorito. "Four kids and a straying husband."

Stephanie lifted her head up and looked at her. "*Okay*. Well, let's go there then. Husband talk."

"Sorry," Jillian said. "I shouldn't have said that. I'm over the edge this weekend."

"Girl, I know what it's like to be over the edge where a husband is concerned." Dana pulled her curly dark brown hair into a pony. "If you want to talk, I'm here for you."

Jillian raised her eyebrows. "Well, if you don't mind sharing."

"Oh, the whole church knew," Stephanie said, "so it's cool."

Jillian's eyes widened. "Seriously?"

Dana nodded with a sigh. "My husband and I led the marriage ministry at our church. He was also in the choir, and had an affair with a woman he got to know there."

"Dana caught them in the act," Stephanie said.

"No way," Jillian said, moving to the edge of the sofa. "I can't imagine. Are you still together?"

"We are," Dana said. "And I tell you it was nothing but God . . . because I couldn't stand him afterward." She took a swig of water. "If there's one thing I tell married women all the time, it's that *all things are possible.*"

Jillian stared at the checkered pattern in the sofa for a moment. "My situation hasn't gotten to that point yet, at least if I'm to believe Cecil. But I found out yesterday that he kissed a woman at a conference in March. And they've kept in touch." She sighed. "We've had issues at home. Been married nineteen years and we've grown apart. Little to no intimacy."

"You just found out yesterday?" Dana nodded as if she understood. "So you're angry."

"Good and mad," Jillian said.

"What are you doing with it?" Dana said.

Jillian looked at her. "What do you mean?"

"Well, first I was just *mad*—at my husband, at the woman, at life—and stewing in it. But when I expressed the anger to God, it brought Him into it and made all the difference. Kind of like praying when I didn't feel like praying."

"I sure haven't been praying," Jillian said. "Not since I found out."

"I'm embarrassed to say how long I went without praying," Stephanie said. "Needless to say, I didn't pray about leaving my husband."

Two heads swiveled toward her.

"You left Lindell?" Dana said. "When?"

"When I came to St. Louis a few days ago."

"He's in Haiti, right? Does he know?"

"Nope." Stephanie sighed. "Rather not go into it right now. But I'm claiming abandonment."

"Okay," Dana said, "so Steph *left* home, Jillian doesn't want to *go* home, and what did both of you say you had in common?"

Stephanie dipped a chip. "Girl, it's too late for my brain to be deducing stuff. What?"

Dana pushed her with her foot. "No prayer." She let it sit. "And sisters"—she looked at both, left to right—"how well is anything gonna go without prayer?"

"Can I be real honest?" Jillian stared vaguely as she thought it through. "I think I haven't prayed because I'm not sure I want to do the work to get my marriage to where it needs to be. At this point I don't know if I care that deeply."

Stephanie raised a finger. "Ditto."

"Okay, then." Dana switched her legs to lotus style. "We know where we need to start."

Stephanie gave her a suspicious eye. "We do?"

Dana held out her hands for each to take one. "With prayer."

"See, this was a bait and switch," Stephanie said. "I wanted y'all to stay so we could get fat on junk food and do stupid stuff. It is *so* like God to do this to me."

Jillian took Dana's hand with a big sigh. "The fact that I don't feel like praying tells me I need to. Let's do it."

Stephanie looked at Dana as she took her hand. "Pray I stop turning to alcohol too."

They bowed their heads.

CHAPTER THIRTY-TWO

Treva knew the evening would be emotionally taxing for Lance, but she hadn't realized how greatly it would affect her as well. She found herself in tears at several points, especially as they boxed up memorabilia in the room in which Kendra was raised. Everything had been left intact. Photos of her and her friends. Plaques and awards. Movie stubs and concert tickets. Who would have thought such a vibrant life would end at such a young age?

Lance was determined to finish the bulk of the task tonight, and now they were in the garage sorting trash from recycling, setting aside items to be donated, and taping up boxes.

He glanced at his watch. "It's one in the morning. I apologize. I didn't mean to keep you out this late."

"I actually thought it might take longer," Treva said, labeling a box.

He paused. "So we've got time to talk?"

Treva's insides took a dip. She looked at him. "What do you want to talk about?"

Lance took her through a garage door that opened to the rear of the house. Landscape lighting led the way back to the outdoor patio. They sat again, Lance angling his chair toward her. A few moments of silence passed.

"I'm supposed to be in India right now," he said finally. "We'd been planning for months, then the host ministry encountered a few issues and had to cancel. I was bummed, but it meant I could take part in this conference." He paused. "I thought about that today . . . that if I hadn't been at the conference, I would've never met you."

Treva wasn't sure where he was going, but everything inside of her was on edge.

"Treva, I'm way past needing life to make sense. All I need is to see God, to be moved by God. And being around you, talking to you, praying with you, being vulnerable with you . . . You've turned my world upside down in two days."

Treva dared to meet his gaze straight on. She couldn't remember the last time her heart beat like this.

"Is it just me?" Lance said. "Have you felt it too?"

Treva rubbed the chill bumps on her arms, trying different responses in her head, measured ones. Nothing worked.

"How many confessions are you going to get out of me?" she said finally. "World turned upside down about captures it." She added quickly, "But Lance, it can't go anywhere. Our lives—our worlds—are so different."

His head hung a moment. "I know. You're an attorney, your husband was a college professor, and here I am—"

"I'm not even thinking about that," Treva said. "How old are you? Thirty-eight, thirty-nine?"

"Thirty-eight."

"Do you know I'm forty-five?" Treva said. "At your age, you can marry a young woman and have a huge family. A woman my age would rob you of that. Besides, your life is here in St. Louis, pastoring a church. My life is in Maryland with my girls, and they've got their grandparents near. They love that." She shook her head. "It's too much to get past."

Lance seemed to ponder her words. Then he said, "Can we go back a minute?"

Treva waited.

"You said you felt it too, that your world has been turned upside down. In two days." His brown eyes penetrated hers. "How often does that happen?"

"Probably . . . almost never."

"So we should toss that aside?"

"Tell me how it would work, Lance."

"I don't think we have to know how it would work," he said. "I think we stay in touch and see where it leads. See how the story comes together."

"What about the age factor?"

"I told myself awhile back that I wasn't living in a box anymore," Lance said. "If I wanted the nice box with a wife and five kids, I wouldn't have married Kendra."

"But now you've got another chance, and—"

"So I'm supposed to get inside the box? Why can't I fall in

love with the woman I want to fall in love with?"

His eyes locked with Treva's, and neither of them looked away.

"It would be nice to believe that these two days can be more," Treva said. "That our circumstances could somehow meld together. But reality is too strong. And I'll make one more confession, Lance Alexander. I think I could fall in love with you, easily. But I'm afraid I'd only be setting myself up for more grief." She paused. "This is magical because we're here together. Everything changes when I fly home."

Lance nodded. "Maybe you're right," he said, his voice deflated. "I won't argue. But I might as well give you my first confession. I was already falling for you." He stood and pulled her up by hand. "I'd better get you back."

<hr />

Silence reigned on the ride to the hotel. Lance pulled around the circular drive and put the car in park. With the motor running, he got out and came around to open her door.

"Will you be at the conference tomorrow?" Treva said. "Or, I should say, in a few hours?"

Lance helped her out. "No, our church service starts at eleven."

"Ah, of course. It's Sunday." She could hardly think. His nearness was suddenly overwhelming. "I guess . . . this is it then."

He looked at her. "It was great meeting you, Treva. I mean that sincerely."

The distance in his words . . . She looked into his eyes. If only she weren't leaving tomorrow. If only—

"Mrs. Langston."

Treva turned and saw Jesse move off a bench and come walking toward her.

"Jesse, what are you doing out here?"

"Can you ask Faith to let me in the room? I have nowhere to stay tonight."

"I can't help you, Jesse. I think Faith made the right choice."

Treva glanced at Lance once more then walked into the hotel, wondering if the ladies were still awake in Cyd's suite. When she got to her room she found Jillian fast asleep.

And Treva was glad. Because all she wanted to do was sit alone and cry.

CHAPTER THIRTY-THREE

Sunday, May 22

The vibration of Stephanie's phone woke her from sleep. Groggy, she looked at the clock and groaned—six a.m.? It felt like she'd just gone to bed.

She grabbed at the phone, and it fell off of the nightstand. Picking it up, her heart quickened at the name on the screen—*Lindell*.

"Hello?" she said, realizing it's not how she'd normally answer when her husband called. But he hadn't been calling regularly, and never at six in the morning.

"Steph, we need to talk."

Her insides awakened, wildly, as she wondered if he'd heard that she'd left Hope Springs. Maybe he was *in* Hope Springs, having returned without notice. Was she ready to have this conversation? They hadn't had frank talk about their marriage in a long while. She glanced over at Cyd, who was still asleep, and got out of bed, closing the bedroom door as she moved into the outer area of the suite.

"Okay," she said, sitting at the dining table. "I'm listening."

"I don't know if you've seen it in the news," Lindell said, "but there's a medical crisis down here. Doctors have gone on strike, public hospitals have closed, and the effect on the people in need is devastating."

Stephanie could feel the letdown in her chest. "No, I haven't seen it," she said.

"It's absolutely incredible," Lindell said. "People are having to travel hours with critical conditions, and when they get to a functioning hospital, it's too crowded to admit them. A woman died in my arms yesterday because she'd had a heart attack and the closest hospital had been shut down."

The ambivalence, the guilt, the wondering if she was cold and unfeeling—all of it rose within. The conditions in Haiti truly were unthinkable, and medical help was desperately needed. But what did that mean for her marriage?

"So you need to stay even longer?"

Lindell hesitated. "Three months."

"Can we even afford that?" Stephanie knew they could, since they didn't have a mortgage, their cars were paid for, and with Lindell's reign on the budget, they'd saved a lot. Still, it was worth throwing out there.

"I wish our finances were the main concern." He sighed. "It's hard, because I feel like it's never enough, what I'm able to do down here. I can never see enough patients, can never make the kind of difference that's lasting. But I'm committed to try."

"Are you committed to try to do anything with respect to our marriage?"

"Stephanie, please don't go there." He gave an exasperated sigh. "I go through enough down here without you making me feel like a failure at home."

"I just want to know if you're aware that your wife has been in crisis. Your marriage has been in crisis. Do you ever think about that?"

"What do you want me to do, Steph?" Lindell's voice grew agitated. "Am I supposed to run to your aid whenever you have an emotional breakdown over Sam? I'm dealing with people down here who have life-threatening issues."

Emotion clutched at her voice. "It would've been enough to simply show that you cared." She took a breath. "In my heart and mind, it feels like you've left the marriage, Lindell. So I've left Hope Springs, for good."

Stephanie hung up and buried her head in her hands. She hadn't realized until that call how much she wanted to talk to Lindell, how much she still wanted her marriage . . . how much she'd wanted to believe that she was wrong, that Lindell did care.

And maybe this was all her fault. If she had had the strength to put Sam's tragedy behind her, their marriage would be in a better place. She wouldn't be so needy. If it just hadn't hurt so much . . .

And why wasn't he calling back? She stared down at her phone. She'd just told her husband she'd left, and he didn't even care enough to talk it out.

She got up and went to the kitchenette. In a lower cupboard behind some pots she'd stashed a bottle of white wine she'd bought Friday, before she took Faith to Fitz's. She pulled it out, popped the cork, and poured some into a plastic cup.

She lowered herself to the floor, back against the cabinet, and held it. It seemed official now. The end of Stephanie and Lindell. They were an unlikely pair anyway. She was flighty and temperamental, still figuring out what she wanted to be when she grew up. He was the focused doctor, his mind on things that mattered. Not the coolest guy. Not even her type, since she'd had a thing for pretty boys. Admittedly, it was his doctor status that drew her in the beginning. But somehow they'd come together and grown together, their first year of marriage in particular, focused on growing in the Lord. A few short years later, and she wondered how she'd ever thought it could last.

Stephanie's arms trembled slightly. She brought the cup to her lips, took a sip, and seconds later heard her phone vibrate on the table.

Maybe he cared after all.

She pulled herself up slowly, drink still in her hand, and went to her phone. It was a text from Faith.

Praying & Bible reading first time in a long time . . . thx for being my friend . . . prayed 4 u 2.

Oh, God, what am I doing?

She went to the sink and poured out her cup, then looked long at the bottle. She sighed. *The whole bottle, Lord?*

Holding it over the sink, she let it drain.

CHAPTER THIRTY-FOUR

Treva couldn't wait to get going with the morning session at eight thirty, so they could be one step closer to heading home. A late afternoon flight put them at Baltimore-Washington International Airport at seven p.m. It was time to resume life as usual.

"You're awfully subdued this morning," Jillian said, pulling her shirt over her head. "I thought you'd be on cloud nine."

Treva applied a neutral shade of shadow to her eyes. "Because . . . ?"

"All the time you and Lance spent together last night?" Jillian said. "I mean, I know it was for a somber purpose. But you're clearly smitten with each other, and he's an awesome guy. I'm happy for you."

"Don't be." Treva finished putting on eyeliner, lightly, and picked up the mascara. Then put it down. Might as well look how she felt. *Blah.*

Jillian came closer. "What happened?"

"I don't want to talk about it."

Jillian watched her a moment. "You broke up."

Treva looked at her then cut her eyes back to the mirror. "As if we were together in any way, shape, or form after a whopping *two days*." She flicked light strokes of blush on her cheek. "That's why I hate conferences like this. Nothing but artificial environments that get you amped up, only to crash-land when it's over."

Jillian met her gaze in the mirror. "So you cut it off before that could happen."

Treva walked around her to find her shoes.

"Remember how you did that with Hezekiah?" Jillian followed. "Tried to cut and run when you felt yourself falling for him? If he hadn't been relentless—"

"That was twenty-five years ago, in college." Treva turned. "And you're comparing that to now?"

"You still have a need to be in control. Still afraid of being hurt—"

"I lost my husband, Jillian. The hurt is real. I don't ever want to feel that kind of pain again."

"Meaning what? You'll never love again?"

Treva slipped her feet into wedged sandals. "Not when it doesn't make sense."

"Wow."

Treva shouldered her tote and stood by the door. "Will you hurry up and put on your shoes so we can go? I already called for a late checkout so we can pack when the conference ends."

Her sister didn't move. "I don't know if you and Lance in a relationship would have worked or not. But the last thing I would've said is that it doesn't make sense."

"Think logistics, Jill. Midwest. East Coast." Treva had reminded herself of all the arguments through the night. "And how about, I'm approaching menopause—three kids and a grandkid on the way. Our seasons are on opposite poles."

"How about, spiritually you fit tight as a glove?"

Treva looked away. "You can't know that in two days."

Jillian gave her a look. "Okay." She stepped into her shoes and scooped up her bag as if that was the end of it.

Treva knew better.

Heading for the elevator, she asked, "So what was that yesterday about you losing a friendship?"

"Oh. Tommy." Jillian stared ahead. "I don't feel like talking about it."

"Oh, so it's okay when *you* don't feel like talking about something. When it's me, I get badgered."

"It's for my own sanity," Jillian said. "I get angry when I think about Cecil."

"I thought we were talking about Tommy."

"The two got connected."

They got coffee and made their way to the session. Though it was the final one, conference energy was high still. Treva and Jillian moved to the front row, where they'd grown accustomed to sitting. Stephanie and Faith had beat them there.

"Hey, check us all out," Jillian said.

"I was surprised that both Stephanie and I decided to wear our conference tees," Faith said, "but I'm more surprised to see

Mom in one."

"Me?" Treva said. She gave them each a hug. "Why?"

"Mom," Faith said, "you always *dress*."

"I guess you're right," Treva said, sitting. "I'm not a big T-shirt person."

She'd love to say she'd worn it to get into the spirit. But wearing a tee was more an indication of her mood.

Cyd walked out onto the platform then, and Treva looked up, curious. Typically the praise and worship team kicked off each session.

"I have a quick announcement before we start praise and worship," Cyd said. She waited for some of the chatter to die down. "As you know, the conference ends at ten. Many of you asked about attending church at Living Word, which has a third service at eleven thirty. I'm excited to tell you that the church was able to arrange for a shuttle to take you to the service and back. And the good news is that Pastor Lyles is preaching today."

Shouts and applause went up. So many of the women had done Living Word Bible studies for years and watched Pastor Lyles's teaching on DVD. They all felt they knew him.

"And here's the bonus," Cyd said. "As we've shared, Living Word started a church plant a year ago—Living Hope. There's a second shuttle to take women to that service, which starts at eleven." She paused, giving them an amused look. "A good number of you asked about that one too, so you could hear more from Pastor Lance Alexander."

Louder shouts went up. Treva stared at Cyd's feet.

"We'll have more details at the end of the session," Cyd said, and walked off.

As the praise and worship team came out, Jillian turned toward Treva.

"No," Treva said.

"I didn't say anything yet."

"Just. No."

CHAPTER THIRTY-FIVE

J illian was about to come out of her seat. Seemed everything Cyd had touched on had been crafted just for her. She'd come in with little anticipation, and now was hanging on every word.

"Let me tell you something," Cyd was saying, "don't get discouraged when you leave here and nothing about your situation has changed. The messages you heard this weekend were not geared to change your situation. This isn't magic." Her eyes were steel. "They were geared to change *you*. You need to have a mind set to *run*, no matter the situation. Why do we give circumstances power over us? Why do we let them drive us out of our minds? Ladies, listen." Her voice softened to a whisper. "Stop looking at the circumstances." She lifted a finger to the heavens. "You can't run without your eyes fixed on Jesus!"

"Amen!" rang out as women stood all around the ballroom.

Cyd walked to the edge of the platform. "I'm not making light of your situations. Many of you are going through some serious stuff. Heartbreaking stuff. And yet I say still, without hesitation, why spend your time focused on a mountain you can do nothing about, when you can shift your gaze higher and focus on God who *made* the mountain? On God with all power *over* the mountain!"

Hands waved in the air as women shouted, "Glory!"

"I don't know about you," Cyd said, "but I don't want to live my life acting as if God is not God. I don't want to live like He's not all-powerful, all-wise, in total control, and with full authority over any and everything that comes into my life. That's what we do when we *faint* instead of running our race. We're saying God is not *God*."

She quickened her pace to the other side of the platform. "But when we run *in hot pursuit*, we're saying 'I know my God is who He says He is, and I'm going to trust, I'm going to hope, I'm going to abound and glorify Him *especially* when I'm going through.' Is He God or isn't He?"

Jillian stood, tears streaming, eyes shut. *Lord, forgive me for acting as if You're not God, as if You're not in total control of what's happening with Cecil and me. Help me to run, especially now.*

"Let's be honest, sometimes we stumble. We say the wrong things. Do the wrong things. Think the wrong things. We have a sin nature, and as believers in Jesus we are not immune from falling into temptation and all manner of sin. We will stumble. Amen?"

The women nodded with her.

"That's why I'm so thankful for these verses from Psalm 37," Cyd said. "The psalmist says our steps are established by the Lord, and listen to this." She grabbed her Bible from the podium.

"Verses 24 and 25: 'Though he may stumble, he will not fall, for the Lord upholds him with His hand.'" Cyd looked up, shaking her head in wonder. "Raise your hand if you know about times of stumbling."

Hands shot up quickly.

"Ladies, this is a promise! Say it with me—'Though I may stumble, I will not fall.'" She waited as they repeated it.

"Why?" Cyd said. "Because the Lord, Almighty God, sovereign God, the Alpha and the Omega, our faithful God is upholding *you* by the hand. You're not going anywhere! You *can't*. Not when God's got you like that!"

Jillian fell to her knees, hands uplifted. *Thank You, Lord. Thank You for holding me up when I stumble. Thank You for keeping me in Your grip.* She lost herself in worship, only realizing Cyd had closed when the music started back up.

Jillian stood, wiping her eyes like so many others around her. The message had come at her from so many angles she'd need to listen a few more times to fully process it.

"How did she go from En Vogue at midnight to that?" Stephanie said, pulling out a tissue. "Whew."

Faith looked at Treva. "Mom, we should go to the service," she said. "We've got plenty of time before our flight."

"You mean to Living Word, right?" Treva said. "With Pastor Lyles?"

Stephanie chimed in. "I know this isn't fair to you all, but I grew up with Pastor Lyles. I kind of wanted to check out Lance's church. Not that we need to go to the same place," she added, pouting. "But my time with you all is almost up, and I'm not ready to part."

"That's where I wanted to go anyway," Faith said. "To Pastor Lance's church."

Jillian turned to Treva, who gave her the eye.

Treva hesitated a beat. "I guess that's . . . okay."

Jillian wondered how Treva would handle seeing Lance. Then it occurred to her.

This was Tommy's church too.

CHAPTER THIRTY-SIX

S tephanie was a little surprised by the excitement she felt as she walked into Living Hope Church. Twenty-six women had come from the conference, many still in their tees. Stephanie had assured them that the dress would be casual. From what she'd heard, Lance drew a lot of twentysomethings as well as teens.

"Stephanie!" A greeter came to hug her, a woman she'd grown up with at Living Word. "Girl, I've missed you!"

Stephanie took in a lot of familiar faces milling about as she hugged her friend back. "I've missed you all too."

"Wow, this is nice," Jillian said, glancing around the lobby area. "It took us a few years to move out of the school building we were using when our church was planted."

Stephanie nodded. "It was awesome. This church building was empty, and after hearing Lance's story, the owners gave it to Living Hope."

A bevy of greeters welcomed the women and escorted them into the sanctuary, which had a single aisle up the middle and rows of chairs on either side. Stephanie led the group in then suddenly came to a stop.

"Y'all." She nodded toward a guy seated on the far right. "Is that Jesse?"

The others followed her gaze.

"What is he doing here?" Faith said.

Stephanie cocked her head. "This is stranger than seeing him at Sweetie Pie's with BrandyB."

"Maybe not," Jillian said. She looked at Stephanie. "You're the one who said we should pray for him."

"Shoot, I didn't think anything would happen *that* fast."

"It's still strange, though," Treva said. "Who would have thought?"

They moved up the aisle and into a row of seats to the left.

"Auntie Stephie!"

A little boy came tearing down the aisle toward her. Stephanie held her arms opened wide and scooped up her nephew, big as he was getting, giving him a huge hug. "Chase-man!" She saw Cyd's husband, Cedric, coming toward them and hugged him as well. They all filed into the row together.

"Your wife was on fire this morning," Stephanie said.

Cedric's smile said he was proud of her. "The whole church has been praying for this conference. Both churches. That's awesome to hear." He sat next to Stephanie and bent his head toward hers. "Listen, Cyd told me that you've left Lindell. I'm sorry all of this is happening. I honestly don't know where my brother's head is."

He helped Chase get situated with a book.

"Well," Stephanie said, "you know where it's not."

"I admire his dedication," Cedric said. "I always have. But I had no idea your marriage was suffering like this. I'm praying for him. For both of you."

"He called this morning," Stephanie said.

"Oh, really? So he knows you left?"

"Well, he was calling to say he'd be in Haiti another three months. *Then* I told him I'd left."

"What did he say?"

"I hung up after I said it."

A hand touched her shoulder from behind. "Stephanie Sanders?" The voice added quickly, "I'm sorry, it's London now."

Stephanie turned. "Mrs. Cartwright?" She stood to hug her. "How are you? I didn't know you were at Living Hope now."

"I'm one of the few in the old people crowd," the woman said. "Most all my friends stayed at Living Word, including your parents—oh, how I tried to get them over here."

Cedric looked over his shoulder. "Cyd did too, Mrs. Cartwright. Don't feel bad."

"Well, why did you come?" Stephanie said.

Mrs. Cartwright gave a little shrug, cute in her frosty silver hair. "Roger and I felt like God wanted us to. And I love that the congregation ended up as diverse as Living Word." She leaned in closer, her blue eyes beaming. "But we're making plans to move to Florida. Haven't announced it yet, but we need to set some things in order. That's where you come in."

"Me?" Stephanie said. "How do I figure in?"

Mrs. Cartwright gave her a wink. "After church, let's get a time to meet."

"Okay," Stephanie said. She sat back down, looking at Cedric. "That's odd. Why would Mrs. Cartwright want to meet with me?"

"Whatever it is," Cedric said, "you can be sure it's been prayed over backwards and forwards."

Stephanie nodded. "Ain't that the truth." She looked down the row and saw an empty seat next to Treva. Where had Faith disappeared to? She glanced around the sanctuary then did a double take.

Faith was walking back toward Jesse.

CHAPTER THIRTY-SEVEN

Faith hated that she couldn't ignore Jesse's texts. When he'd asked her to come down to the hotel lobby, she was there. Now he'd asked her to come sit with him, and here she was. She wondered if he asked because he felt alone, then hated that she cared enough to wonder.

Seats were filling, but there was one beside him, and she squeezed in.

"I didn't expect to see you here," Jesse said.

"Likewise." Faith looked at him, in a different pair of jeans and shirt from yesterday. She wondered where he'd changed. "How did you get here?"

"The pastor. Lance."

"What? How?"

"When he dropped your mom off last night, he heard me asking about coming up to your room. He said he knew you and asked if I needed a place to stay." He glanced downward. "He drives a hard bargain, though. Said he'd want me to come to his church this morning."

"Unbelievable."

"What?"

"We prayed for you last night, that you'd have a place to stay," Faith said, "even that you'd go to church. But we weren't thinking here in St. Louis."

"You wouldn't have had to pray for a place to stay," Jesse said, "if you'd just let me come up."

"Jesse, after what happened yesterday, it was crazy that you even asked."

Faith glanced around, thinking how much she'd missed Sunday morning fellowship. There was so much to get back on track. She checked the time. Ten minutes till service started.

"So how'd you like Pastor Lance?" she asked. "Must've been weird, staying with someone you didn't know."

Jesse shrugged. "He was actually pretty dope. I figured he knew about the baby and was ready to give me a sermon. But he made a big breakfast and we debated Cavs versus Warriors."

"Who?"

"Basketball, Faith." Jesse's expression changed.

"What?"

"Just a thought." He glanced at her midsection. "Wondering if it might be a boy."

Faith's heart skipped a beat. She hadn't allowed herself to go there.

"So why'd you text me to come back here?"

Jesse looked away a moment. "My mom called this morning, because Brandy called her, all distraught, and told her what happened yesterday."

"Distraught?" Faith said. "If you two had truly broken up, why would she be surprised that you'd been with someone else? I'm sure she knows how you are."

Jesse stared downward a moment. "Because she's afraid you'll keep the baby . . . like she wanted to."

It took a moment to register. "Brandy was pregnant?"

"Last fall. That's kind of why we broke up, after everything went down."

Faith could only stare at him as emotion surged.

"Anyway, mom was the one who gave me the sermon, and I felt even worse. And I wasn't sure if I'd actually apologized to you . . ." He looked at her, but only briefly. "But I do apologize, Faith."

She stood.

"Where are you going?"

"Back to my seat."

Members of the band started playing, and the praise and worship team took their places.

"Come on, everybody, let's stand and praise the Lord!" one of them said.

"I think Lance is dropping me at the hotel afterward," Jesse said. "Will you be there? And how are you getting to the airport? I'll need a ride."

"You're unbelievable, you know that?" was all she could say as she walked away.

CHAPTER THIRTY-EIGHT

Jillian had ten minutes to get to the shuttle, but she had to talk to Lance first. He'd been surrounded since the end of his message, one person after the next, and she'd decided to hang back and wait. But her time was almost up. She stepped forward and leaned her head in. "Lance, if you have a quick minute?"

Lance nodded and moved toward her as he ended a conversation.

"Hey, Jillian, good to see you," he said, glancing at someone else who'd come near to speak with him.

"I'll make this fast," she said. "First, your message. This wasn't a good weekend for me in terms of my personal life, but between you and Cyd this morning, I feel like I'm charged up and ready to run. Seriously. Thank you."

"I'm sorry it's been a rough weekend." Lance was focused, despite people on his left and right. "But look at God's timing. He wouldn't let the storm hit till you were surrounded by all of this."

Jillian nodded. "I hadn't thought about it like that. Okay, and second . . . I don't know how to say this, but . . ."

There was the other matter of whether she should say it at all, but she'd felt prompted during his message.

Lance walked with her a few feet, away from the others. "What is it?"

"Well. My sister."

Unless Jillian was imagining things, the mention of Treva took him to a different place. "Okay," he said, waiting.

"She's outside, about to hop on the shuttle and head back to the hotel, then to the airport, and I'm so far out of line, and I know she'll kill me—"

"Jillian, what is it?"

"Could you just, talk to her before she leaves?"

Lance seemed taken aback. "You want me to talk to her?"

"See, I kind of know about, you know, the two of you—only a little. But I know Treva—she'd never come in here and wait to talk to you—but I feel like if you'd talk to her once more . . ." She took a breath, looking at him.

"You think so."

"I do. And if I'm wrong, you can kill me too."

He was quiet a moment then gave the slightest of nods. "Okay."

Jillian gave him a quick hug and scurried off, moving through the lobby, which was still somewhat crowded, to catch the shuttle.

"Jilli-Jill."

She stopped, exhaling, but couldn't bring herself to turn around.

Tommy moved in front of her. "You avoided me the entire service."

Jillian glanced up at him, then away. "Isn't that what you wanted?"

"I said it wasn't wise to have a deep friendship with an emotional attachment," Tommy said. "I didn't say we had to be silly about it and avoid each other in the same place."

"I didn't want you to think I came here to see you," Jillian said. "It was a group decision to come to the service."

"Jill, come on. It's cool." Tommy glanced outside, where the shuttle waited at the curb. "So you'll be flying back in a bit."

She nodded, and a few seconds passed. She glanced around the lobby, glad to see two other women from the conference. She wasn't the last one inside.

"This is awkward and so not us, and I hate it," she said. "But Tommy, you were right. Jesus is the one I need to be tight with. It's just . . . too doggone easy with you."

He stifled a smile. "I'm sorry."

She cut her eyes. "I can't stand you."

"Come here, you."

Jillian stuffed emotion as Tommy hugged her.

"Can you at least pray for me," she said, "for when I get home this evening?" Two messages had charged her up today, but she was nervous still about what awaited her.

"Without hesitation," Tommy said. "Always."

Jillian turned and walked out of the church, her heart uttering a prayer.

Jesus, help me to run.

Keep my eyes fixed on You.

CHAPTER THIRTY-NINE

The shuttle pulled away from the curb, transporting the women back to the hotel downtown.

"What just happened?" Treva watched it go, the shuttle rolling down the street and around the corner. She'd been seated when Lance suddenly appeared on the bus, called her off, and told the driver he could leave.

Lance had his car keys in his hand. "I want you to go somewhere with me." He started toward the church parking lot, and Treva moved to catch up.

"How am I getting back to the hotel? I have a flight to catch."

"You'll be fine. I'll get you there."

"I thought you were supposed to be taking Jesse back." Treva paused. "That was really something, by the way, that you'd take him in like that."

"One of the deacons is giving him a ride to the hotel." Lance held the door for her. "And it wasn't a big deal."

He walked to the driver's side as Treva fought to steady herself amidst a conflicted mind and wildly beating heart.

Lance got in and backed the SUV out. "I know you don't have a lot of time," he said. "I just want to go somewhere quiet, to a park not far from here."

"For what?" Treva said.

"So we can talk."

"I thought we said everything there was to say."

He glanced at her. "Did we?"

Treva ignored the reaction she felt within. Staring out of the window, she focused on the houses in the neighborhood, many of them stately. When she'd googled Lance, she'd found an interview where he talked about his ambivalence over living in and planting a church in Clayton, an area far different from where he'd grown up in St. Louis. But this was where he'd been bused to high school for a time, before he was kicked out. And it was where God had opened a door for him to reach students on college campuses minutes away. Ministering here was a form of redemption.

"You're probably hungry," he said. "We can pick up some sandwiches on the way."

On the shuttle she'd told Jillian she was starving. No way could she eat now with her stomach in knots. "I'm fine," she said.

Lance took a somewhat hidden turn and drove through a canopy of majestic oaks that opened to a small park setting. He parked and they got out, walking in silence along a cobblestone path. A waterfall came into view, and they took a bench in front of it. There wasn't another soul around.

Lance looked at her. "I was surprised to see you today."

"Yeah, me too," Treva said. "They announced it this morning, and Faith wanted to come, so . . ."

"What about you?"

She looked at him. "How do you ask questions that seem simple but land where I don't want them to?" She looked away. "I didn't want to . . . want to come."

"Oh, you're a piece of work." Lance shook his head, clearly amused. "Would it kill you to say you wanted to come?"

Treva kicked at a rock beneath her feet. "More like, I was afraid to come."

"Afraid of what?"

She gazed into the rush of the waterfall. "Afraid of cycling back through last night. Afraid of what would happen when I saw you again."

"So what happened?"

Treva let several seconds pass. "Lance, it was never a question whether I was drawn to you. The 'world turned upside down' thing was clearly established. But seeing you today—being with you right now—it's hard."

"Is that *all* it is?" Lance said. "Because being with you is a lot of things, but it's not hard."

"It's hard because this is not real," Treva said. "It's one weekend that's rapidly coming to a close. We'll get back to our separate worlds and I'll have to find a way to stuff all these thoughts."

"Stuff all these thoughts?" Lance quirked a brow. "I thought we'd said all there was to say."

"Okay, correction," Treva said. "I said all I was willing to say."

Lance stared at her.

"What?" she said, refusing to meet his eyes.

"I want to hear what's in that head of yours, without the Treva filter."

Her insides did a double dip.

"As you said, it's all rapidly coming to an end anyway, right?" Lance said. "So let's lay it out there."

She exhaled, glancing at him. "Go ahead, then. You first. But there's no guarantee I'm going after."

"You want what's in my head right now? Without a protective guard?"

She looked at him. As anxious as it made her, she had to admit it. "Yes. I want to know."

Lance blew out a sigh. "Okay. Right now, I'm thinking there's this beautiful woman in my presence that I want to know on every level. I'm thinking how scary it is to risk telling you how I feel, something I almost never do, when you'll probably shoot me down again."

He paused, and every part of Treva stood at attention, wanting to hear more.

"In my head right now," Lance said, "is a picture of us praying together Friday night and again Saturday before the session. And I'm thinking I want us to build on that, for a lifetime. And *then* I'm thinking how crazy that sounds, to be thinking *lifetime* when we've known each other two days . . . But I look at you and I see a strong woman of God, a woman who feels deeply, stubborn yet vulnerable, infuriating yet exhilarating, a woman who has gotten into my head and under my skin and gotten me out of my comfort zone in *two days*. So crazy or not, I can't help but wonder if lifetime is possible."

Treva listened with her eyes closed, feeling every word in the slight tremor down her arms.

"What's in my head right now," he said, "no filter, is that I want to love you." He tucked her hair behind her ear. "I even want to want to love you."

Slow tears coursed Treva's cheeks. "This is what I feared most," she said. "That I wouldn't be able to turn back. That I would have to risk getting hurt because you've taken hold of my heart."

She wiped her tears and took a steadying breath. "I'll go," she said, eyes on the safety zone of the waterfall. "What's in my head is how I was captivated by you at Imo's Pizza. To be honest, my world flipped that first night. Everything . . . your vulnerability, your love for Kendra, the way you listen, anticipate, and ask those way-too-penetrating follow-up questions."

Her heart took over, forging on. "I'm thinking about how I've seen you on the platform at the conference and this morning in the pulpit, and I love that you're the same godly man away from all of that. I love that I'm getting to know aspects of you that most people don't know, and what's in my head is that I want to go deeper." She paused, surprised that she'd admitted that.

Her insides braced for the next one. "With no filter, I'd have to admit that I want to want to love you too." Treva looked at him now. "And I'd have to admit that I'm afraid to pursue any of this. I'm afraid we'll get two months down the road and realize these two days were a mirage."

Lance leaned in and kissed her softly. "I don't think it's a mirage."

Treva stared into his brown eyes, a million butterflies and questions soaring. "So, Lance Alexander, what do we do now?"

CHAPTER FORTY

S tephanie lingered outside the hotel until Lance had put the
last of the luggage into the trunk of his SUV.

"We're all set," he said, closing it.

"I'm keeping this one here," Stephanie said, clutching Faith.

"With the attitude she had on the way out here," Treva said,
"I would've paid you to keep her."

"Faith?" Stephanie put a hand to her chest. "I don't believe
that at all."

Faith wrapped her arms around Stephanie. "Don't forget you
promised to keep in touch."

"You're the one who better not forget," Stephanie said. "I'm
expecting monthly update pics of you and baby."

Jesse glanced back at that as he crouched to get into the rear
seat.

Stephanie continued, "And a biweekly report on what you're
up to." She paused. "I was about to say you might as well jump
on the weekly prayer calls with Jillian, Dana, and me, but that's
grown folks' stuff right there." She gave Jillian the eye.

"Girl, who are you telling?" Jillian said. "I'm so thankful I can
be real with you two."

"What prayer call?" Treva said.

"We talked about it when we got back from Living Hope," Jillian said. "The three of us prayed about marriage stuff the other night and want to keep it up."

Treva nodded. "That's awesome."

"Ladies . . ." Lance said.

"Okay, okay," Stephanie said. "I can't help it that I don't want y'all to go."

She hugged them and watched them pile into the car, and they all waved as the SUV rounded the bend and motored out of sight. Stephanie sighed. With everyone gone, her new life was about to begin. She was no longer here for the conference. She was here. And she needed to figure out what that looked like.

She'd already checked out and loaded her bags into her car, and Cyd was expecting her later at the house. But she had a meeting with Mrs. Cartwright in ten minutes. She'd thought they would pick a date later in the week, but Mrs. Cartwright had zeroed in on today then said they could simply meet where Stephanie was, at the hotel's Starbucks.

Stephanie made her way there now, ordered a chai tea, and picked a spot for two. Minutes later Mrs. Cartwright walked in and gave her a wave before ordering a skinny latte, chatting with the barista as she prepared it. Adding nothing to it, she came to the table with eyes sparkling.

"You have been on my mind, young lady," the older woman said as she sat. "How are you?"

"I'm good, Mrs. Cartwright," Stephanie said. "Intrigued. I'm not sure the two of us have ever met outside of church or a gathering of some sort." She took a sip of tea. "How are you?"

"Good. Busy. Doing too many things at once." Her hands moved frenetically as she said it. "Sold our home a couple of weeks ago, so thank you, Jesus! *But.*" She raised a finger. "Relocating and downsizing have me pulling my hair out." She leaned in. "If you're a hoarder like me, get help now. It's not pretty at seventy-two."

Stephanie chuckled. "My problem is I need to be more sentimental. I throw everything away."

"So. I'll get to it." Mrs. Cartwright tasted her latte first. "We have a second property in the area. Bought it eight years ago and knew it needed a ton of work, but we planned to fix it up and one day move into it to make it a bed-and-breakfast."

"Sounds like a great plan."

"Except we didn't anticipate our daughter and her family moving to Florida," Mrs. Cartwright said. "We visited several times, fell in love with the area and with being near our grandkids. Now we clearly won't be operating a B and B."

"So you're selling that house too?" Did Mrs. Cartwright think she and Lindell might be interested in investment property?

"We debated it. Roger wanted to, but from the beginning I've had this vision of a B and B, yes, but more than that. A special place with the aroma of Jesus." She wrapped her hands around her cup. "I couldn't let that go. After praying, I feel like that's what God still wants for it, even if we can't be the resident care-takers. That's where you come in, and your husband, of course."

"I'm not understanding," Stephanie said.

"Every time I prayed for the Lord to show me whom to ap-proach about moving into the B and B and acting as caretakers, yours was the face I saw."

Stephanie looked at her. "But didn't you know we were in North Carolina?"

Mrs. Cartwright leaned in. "*I know,*" she said, sounding bewil-dered. "That's why it was so strange. I asked your parents if you and Lindell had plans to move back, and they said no. So I tucked it away and kept praying. "Then this morning, there you were at Living Hope. I just had to meet with you."

"The thing is, Mrs. Cartwright, even if we were here, I wouldn't know the first thing about running a B and B. I'm not even the B and B type—being around strangers and what not." Stephanie took a slow sip of her tea. "And I just have to be hon-est. No one has ever said anything about the aroma of Jesus when they're around me."

"Pish-posh," Mrs. Cartwright said, sweeping the air. "I saw that footage of you on CNN, when you spoke at that poor girl's funeral, called those churches to task for being segregated, and led the town in that unity walk. *That* was the aroma of Jesus." Her face was cheery even when she wasn't smiling. "Even the way you befriended the girl—and by the way, *she* was a stranger before you met her—that was the aroma of Jesus. It's in you."

"Okay, well, that aside," Stephanie said, "I might as well be honest with you about something else. This is in confidence."

Mrs. Cartwright folded her hands. "Okay."

"Lindell and I are having marital problems. I'm back here in St. Louis without him." Stephanie told herself to get used to sharing her new arrangement. "So, for many reasons, there's no way I or we could take that on. But I do appreciate your kind words."

Mrs. Cartwright stared at her—though it felt more as if she were staring *through* her, thinking.

"So," she said finally, "when I first started praying about this, you were both on the East Coast. Now one of you is here. And since we know God is able to heal and restore marriages, I'll be praying for you. And believing Lindell will end up here too, moving into the B and B."

"Mrs. Cartwright . . ." Stephanie wanted to make sure she didn't leave any wrong impressions. "Seriously, even if Lindell and I were both here in St. Louis and our marriage was doing amazingly well, a B and B would not be my thing."

"Okay," Mrs. Cartwright said. "I'll be praying for that too, that you catch the vision."

CHAPTER FORTY-ONE

J illian and Cecil were finally alone, and she had no idea what to say.

He had picked up the four of them from the airport and engaged them all about the weekend, his usual friendly self. And after they'd dropped everyone off and gotten home, he'd made a big deal about "Mom being home." Had even encouraged the kids to make a Welcome Home poster board sign, which they held up at the door when she arrived. Lots of talking on top of one another, laughing, tattling, catching up about everything from Sophia's ballet to the latest insect Trevor had caught.

And now, silence.

The kids were scattered to different parts of the house and Cecil was cleaning the kitchen. Jillian wanted to retreat to the bedroom and unpack, but she picked up a dish from the rack instead and started drying.

How long had they been like this? When had their interactions begun to revolve around the kids, solely? She glanced at Cecil, who seemed lost in thought. This was the man who'd swept her off her feet. The man she was sure was an answer to her prayers. They'd been acquainted in college, but it wasn't until a couple of years later that they began seeing one another, both newly walking with the Lord. They'd been through countless seasons together. But this was by far the most challenging yet.

Jillian glanced his way. "So did you get the time you needed, to think and pray?" She placed a dish in the cabinet and reached to dry another.

Cecil looked over at her. "I got some time here and there."

"I figured you got a whole lot more than that, since I haven't talked to you since Friday night." Jillian sighed inwardly at her tone. She'd told herself not to be snarky.

"You could have called too, you know."

"Well, since you didn't want me home, I thought I'd leave the calling to you, whenever you got a moment free from deep meditation."

He rinsed a glass and stacked it. "So you have a problem with the fact that I wanted time to pray?"

Jillian turned to face him. "I have a problem with the fact that you needed to pray because you allowed your heart to stray toward another woman." She kept her voice low. "And now you don't know what to do about the woman you made vows to."

Cecil returned her gaze for only a moment before looking away.

She waited, wanting him to refute her assessment.

"Jillian," he said, staring into the sink, "I was praying long before now. I was praying when it seemed like you had lost all interest in intimacy, in the two of us just being together." He looked at her now. "I was praying when you had time and energy for each of the kids, for the women in your Bible study, and for whatever else you got involved in, but hardly any for me."

Jillian could feel her jaw set. "So I'm to blame, that's what you're saying? Never mind that you never said a word about how you were feeling."

"Really?" Cecil said. "What was I saying when I tried to plan date nights? What was I saying when I wanted you to come to conferences? You weren't *hearing* me."

"You could've made it plain, Cecil." Jillian heard the glass clang as she shelved it. "How was I supposed to know you felt I had no time for you, unless you told me? How was I supposed to know you're ready to give up *on our marriage* and pursue someone else?"

Cecil's expression was even. "I wasn't pursuing anyone."

"Oh, it just happened."

He looked away.

Jillian could feel the erratic pulse of her heart. "So what's going on with you and Regina, Cecil? Is she telling her husband 'I don't know about us' too?"

He looked at her. "How do you know she's married?"

"I just do."

He lapsed into a silence.

Jillian moved closer. "Cecil, I deserve to know. While you're praying about what to do about us, what are you doing about her?"

"I told you before, she's a friend."

"That you kissed."

"At least I was honest."

"So now you want bonus points?" Jillian could hear the bite in her voice. "And anyway, why is she still a 'friend' since you're obviously attracted to her? Why didn't you cut the friendship off?" Her mind went to Tommy. If their friendship had to end, surely this one did.

"We did, for a time."

"What in the world does that mean?"

"We cut off contact, but then . . . it started back up again."

Jillian stared at him. "You're falling for this woman."

Cecil looked down, and Jillian threw her towel on the counter, moved upstairs, and went into the master bathroom, locking the door behind her. Sinking to the floor, she battled the thoughts rising to the surface.

Lord, I want to call Tommy, right now. I want to be able to vent and know that he gets me. I want to hear his no-nonsense advice. And it would be good advice, Lord. Godly advice. How is it fair that I'm cut off from my brother in Christ, but these two get to frolic?

Head buried in her arms, she realized—at least she was venting to God. That's what Tommy had wanted her to do, to run to Him. And if Tommy understood her, Jesus did a thousand times more.

Lord, Cecil is falling for another woman. What am I supposed to do? Show me, please, and then give me grace to do it.

CHAPTER FORTY-TWO

Treva sliced a wicked portion of her mother-in-law's German chocolate cake and drooled as she brought it to the kitchen table.

"And that boy wound up at church after all that?" Darlene had been riveted by the story. "He probably didn't know what hit him, but I'll tell you what it was—*mercy. Only* God. 'Cause if it was up to me, after messing over my granddaughter like that?" She gave them a look. "Somebody would've been throwing a Sweetie Pie's pie at him."

"Oh, Grandma," Faith said, indulging in a piece of cake herself. "You would've been the main one praying for him."

"After I threw the pie."

"As long as you don't throw this cake. It's too good." Treva savored another bite as it went down, knowing she'd be working out extra tomorrow. "I have to admit," she said, "Jesse looked so pitiful today I almost felt sorry for him. And that's saying a lot."

"He's only upset because his girlfriend broke up with him," Faith said, "and it messes up his plans for fall."

"What plans?" Treva said.

"I didn't tell you? He applied to grad school in Chicago to be near Brandy. He got admitted and accepted it before I got pregnant—not that it would've made a difference."

"The good thing," Treva said, "is his mother's here. I know she'll be part of the baby's life regardless of what Jesse does."

Darlene looked at Faith. "I'm just glad you're back. Not back in town, but *back*. I *knew* God would do a work this weekend."

Faith gave her a sheepish look. "I know you were praying."

"Chile, never bombarded heaven more."

"Mom," Faith said, "you haven't shared *your* weekend with Grandma."

Treva's eyes went wide as she wiped chocolate from her lips. She hadn't even had a chance to talk with Faith about it yet.

"You mean besides the testimony and the grief session?" Darlene said. "What happened?"

"Nothing *happened*—"

Faith leaned forward, grinning. "Mom has a boyfriend."

"Oh, good grief," Treva said. "I do not have a *boyfriend*. That is so juvenile. And Faith, why are you even—"

"Wait, whoaaa." Darlene's arms waved the air. "Treva, you met a man this weekend, at a women's conference? And haven't mentioned it yet? What in the world?"

"We met because we were doing the grief session together," Treva said. "He's a pastor, and—"

"Remember, Grandma, the story about the pastor who married the woman with Stage IV breast cancer? And everybody came together to throw them that big wedding. That's the one."

"You are *kidding* me." Darlene looked at Treva, mouth agape.

Treva sat back. "Faith, why don't you go ahead and tell the whole thing. And you watch way too much television."

Darlene resituated herself on the chair, as if that would help her understand better. "So the pastor from the news story did the grief session with you, because, of course, he lost his spouse too. And it developed into something for the two of you . . . in two, three days? Wow."

"Right, that's the thing," Treva said. "We had this indescribable connection, but it was only a weekend. So we're kind of trying to see if, you know"—she shrugged—"anything will come of it." She added, "And I almost refused to try because there are so many hurdles."

"Like what?" Darlene said.

"A major one is he's in the Midwest, and I'm here."

"How is that a hurdle?" Darlene said. "Didn't you live in the Midwest for ten years? It's suddenly a problem now?"

Treva had to pause. She hadn't thought about it that way. "Well, before, I was bent on staying away because I didn't want to be near Mother. Now this is home again. And the girls can see their grandparents whenever they want." She forked up more chocolate goodness. "I *know* you wouldn't want to live hundreds of miles away from your grandbabies."

"Of course I wouldn't *want* to," Darlene said, "but they're getting older themselves and will start venturing here and there. You can't stay here for our sake. You have to live your life."

"It's all way premature anyway," Treva said. "It's far too early to know if this is going somewhere." She looked at Darlene. "But how would you feel, seeing me with someone else?"

"You want to know the God's honest truth?" Darlene said. "If it's someone who loves you like you should be loved, and you love him, it would bless my soul."

"I didn't expect you to say that," Treva said. "Why?"

"Because you have been special to me from the time Hezekiah brought you home. And I've seen you go through so much." Darlene's eyes filled. "I've seen the Lord do wonders in your life, right before my eyes, and He's still doing wonders. God willing, you have lots of living yet to do. And if the Lord brings someone special for you to share it with, all the better."

Treva gave a warm sigh. "And you've been special to me from that very first time I met you." She looked at her daughter. "Faith, I haven't asked how you would feel, seeing me with someone besides your dad."

Faith thought about it. "I think if you asked me in the abstract, it would be hard. But I had seen the story of Pastor Lance, then I heard his message this weekend and he took time to talk to me about it, and *then* I found out the two of you had a thing." She smiled a little at Treva's expression. "At that point, I was like, 'Yeah! I hope Mom doesn't mess this up.'"

"Oh, really? It can't be that *Lance* messes it up?"

"Um, it'd probably be you, Mom."

Treva had to laugh. "That is so wrong."

"Ooh, wait a minute," Darlene said. "I think I heard my phone." She went to her purse and rummaged around.

Treva watched, amused. "Ma, the whole purpose of persuading you to get a smartphone was for you to keep it handy."

"Chile, all those beeps and bleeps work my nerves." Darlene finally pulled it out and put on her reading glasses. "Ha. Russell. He says 'Stop yakking and come home. It's late'."

"Aww, he misses his wife," Treva said. "I can't thank you enough for staying with Hope and Joy this weekend."

Treva had spent time catching up with the younger girls when she first got home, then they'd fallen asleep while watching a movie.

"Oh, we had a good time," Darlene said, gathering her things. "The pleasure was all mine."

Another phone sounded, and Treva and Faith both glanced at theirs.

"It's Lance," Treva said. "I can call him back."

"Go on and answer," Darlene said, waving over her shoulder. "I know my way out."

Treva walked up to her room with the phone, answering before the top stair.

"Hey," she said.

"Hey there."

Two words and her insides flipped.

CHAPTER FORTY-THREE

June

"**S**o what is this, a planned intervention?"

Stephanie had thought she was going to her parents' home for a relaxing Sunday dinner, along with Cyd, Cedric, and little Chase. But an hour into it, the evening was starting to close in on her.

The family sat around the formal dining table in the home in which Cyd and Stephanie had done much of their growing up. Many of Stephanie's favorites adorned the table—barbecued spareribs, macaroni and cheese, collard greens, and candied yams. They'd reminisced and laughed so much that Stephanie had, for a time, been transported beyond her cares. And now the people she was closest to were dumping a fresh new load.

"Of course this isn't an intervention," Claudia said. Her mom sounded convincing. "We're simply concerned. It's been two weeks, and you've essentially done nothing but sit around and watch soap operas."

Stephanie tossed a glance at her sister. "Thank you, Cyd, for filing that report. But to be accurate, I only watch soaps in the afternoon; the rest of the time it's HGTV. And to make it complete, everyone should know I've wasted the same amount of time for the past couple of years, when I wasn't putting in hours at the Hope Springs Diner."

Her dad looked across the table at her. "Steph, our main focus is forward. We want to know how we can help you and Lindell get your lives back on track."

"How did Lindell get into the conversation?"

Her dad gave her a look. "He's your husband. That makes him part of it."

"Not as far as I'm concerned."

Claudia leaned in. "I don't know why you've given up complete hope," she said. "If you want to know the truth, I'm glad you're here in St. Louis. Might as well be while Lindell is in Haiti. But we fully intend to pray for and encourage you in your marriage." Her eyes wore concern. "We're a family of believers, Stephanie. We believe God can heal and restore what's broken."

Stephanie felt the pang of ambivalence. Daily the hurt was compounded, given that Lindell had not contacted her. Yet, on the first weekly call she'd had with Jillian and Dana, they'd prayed specifically for hope.

"So we've got the short term," Bruce said, "which is the period before Lindell returns, and then there's the long term. You need to be thinking and praying proactively about both." He steepled his hands. "I'm with your mom. I'm thrilled you're here. And it makes all the sense in the world for you both to be back, given that there's family on both sides to support you."

Claudia looked at him. "But Lindell works partly in Haiti, partly in North Carolina. He'd need to find a position here again."

"I'm sure Lindell would love to see you two planning out his life," Stephanie said. "And by the way, when I suggested we move back to St. Louis, it got shot down."

"I'm going to see what's out there myself," Cedric said. "I don't typically handle recruitment in the medical field, but I'll talk to a colleague who does."

"Daddy, I want more chicken," Chase said, pointing at the platter.

Cedric checked his plate. "You haven't touched anything else. Let me see you eat some of your greens."

Chase pouted. "I don't *want* greens."

"Okay," Cedric said. "Then I guess you don't want more chicken."

"I'm so confused right now." Stephanie looked around the table, pausing at her nephew, who must've decided he wanted more chicken, given the single leaf of collard greens now on his fork. "Why are you all talking as if these things matter? Lindell is clearly done with the marriage, and he's not interested in coming back to St. Louis."

"Well," Cyd said, looking at her, "you haven't actually heard him say he's done with the marriage. Though, granted, the lack of contact is disappointing, to say the least."

Cedric pushed his plate aside. "I think what we're saying,

Steph—or at least, what I'm saying—is that I'm willing to talk to my brother and strongly suggest he move back, for the sake of his marriage. I plan to strongly suggest some other things as well, but that can remain between him and me. If intervention is needed, it's on *his* part."

"So we're getting somewhere," Bruce said. "Cedric talking to Lindell, seeing what might be available for him here profession-ally—and we should be praying about those things." He looked at Stephanie. "You need a plan as well, beyond a television viewing schedule."

"There's so much you could be doing," Claudia said. "Go out looking for a job, for one."

"But since everyone is praying and believing for my mar-riage," Stephanie said, "we might actually reunite when Lindell returns. And what if we decide to stay in Hope Springs? Wouldn't be fair to commit to working a job, only to have to leave it in three short months, would it?"

"How long did it take you to think up that one?" Cyd asked.

Claudia had a brow raised. "You could always take advan-tage of service opportunities—at Living Word, Living Hope, a plethora of places across the city. They'll take whatever time you can put in."

Stephanie sighed to herself. Were they really going to hound her about how she spent her time? Didn't she get a "currently dealing with trials of life" pass?

But then, she hadn't been able to get Lance's message out of her mind, the one about running to win despite the circumstances. If he could run behind bars, what was her problem?

"Fine, then," Stephanie said. "I have a plan. The one Mrs. Cartwright approached me about."

"The B and B?" Cyd said. "I thought you said you'd never do something like that. And if you can't commit to a job, you certainly can't commit to that."

Stephanie smiled. "I have a plan for that too."

CHAPTER FORTY-FOUR

On crinkly paper in a wafer-thin gown, Faith sat waiting, trembling. "Mom, I'm scared what they'll tell us."

She'd awakened to sheets stained with blood, and the light bleeding had continued throughout the morning. It seemed an eternity to have to wait until one o'clock for an appointment.

Treva stood by the examination table, rubbing her back. "I know, sweetheart. I know. Let's just stay prayerful."

"But I feel bad that I'm having so many different thoughts." Faith fingered the strings on the gown. "If I miscarried, a lot of worries are gone. But if a baby is lifeless inside me, that's heart-breaking."

"What we know for sure is that God is in control, whatever happens. In times like this, it's so abundantly clear."

Faith held her arms, glancing at the door. "What is taking so long?"

The nurse had taken her vitals and asked a ton of questions, but it was the doctor who would tell her what she needed to know. Faith glanced around the room. Little more than a table, chair, a desk, and a few supplies. Yet her life seemed to hang in the balance in this sterile place.

"Mom?"

"Yes, sweetheart."

"I'm really missing Daddy right now."

Treva was silent a moment. "I've been thinking the same thing."

Treva's phone vibrated with a notification. She'd left it on the chair, since they'd been keeping people updated.

"It's Stephanie," she said, looking at it. "She wants to know if we've heard anything. Says she's praying." She looked at Faith. "Did you text Jesse to let him know?"

Faith shook her head. Three weeks since they'd returned from St. Louis, and they hadn't spoken. They weren't seeing each other anymore, or whatever it was they'd been doing. But she'd wondered if he would check in to see how she and the baby were doing.

As if.

"I'll only let him know if I miscarry," she said.

The door opened, and Dr. Warner walked in wearing beige slacks, a summer sweater, and a soft smile. "Two of my favorite patients," she said.

Faith smiled a little. It was her mom who'd been a longtime patient of the doctor's.

"It's good to see you, Dr. Warner," Treva said, moving into the seat. "It's been a rough morning."

"I can imagine." Dr. Warner put a hand to Faith's shoulder. "How are you holding up?"

Faith was suddenly more nervous. "Okay."

The doctor checked her vitals again then brought out a little device. "I want you to lie back," she said. "We're going to see if we can hear a heartbeat."

Faith's own heart rate accelerated. "Really? There would be a heartbeat already?"

"Sure," the doctor said. "You're at ten weeks."

Faith lay back, thoughts rushing. She'd mostly been on auto-pilot thus far during the pregnancy, aware that she needed to eat well and avoid caffeine. But she hadn't embraced the process. She didn't know what should be happening when. Dialing in would only make it more real.

She reached over and grabbed her mother's hand as the doctor guided the device against her belly. Hearing silence, Faith reacted, lifting up a little. "Nothing? The baby's gone?"

The doctor patted her leg and kept listening.

Suddenly they heard it. A soft pulse. Steady. Alive. She looked over at her mom, who had tears welling.

"Praise God," Treva whispered.

Dr. Warner smiled. "Looks like the baby is fine," she said, "and I believe you are too, Faith. Bleeding and spotting happen in pregnancy. We'll run some tests to be sure, but for the rest of the week, at least, I want to put you on bed rest."

Faith nodded, hoping it wouldn't last longer than that. She'd started summer courses to get some of her credits out of the way, since her schooling would be interrupted in a few months.

⁓ ❧ ⁓

Back at home, Faith sat up in her bed, two pillows lodged behind her, her sisters sprawled across the covers. This was their habit, hanging out in Faith's room from the time they were toddlers. Seemed they'd grown by leaps this year alone. At fourteen and twelve, they were maturing before her eyes.

"You haven't said much about what it's like," Joy said, "being pregnant." The middle child, Joy was always sensitive to how others were doing and feeling.

Faith sighed. "I haven't said much of anything to you two about it. I didn't even want you to know at first. I was too ashamed."

"But that's crazy. We're your sisters," Hope said.

"I know," Faith said. "My younger sisters. I was supposed to set the example."

Joy twisted her back, looking up at her. "You are. You're showing us what it's like when you do things you're not proud of, but you keep going. Before, you seemed perfect." She stared back at the ceiling. "This I can follow."

"So what about Joy's question?" Hope said. "What's it like being pregnant?"

"Today was the best day," Faith said. "I heard the baby's heartbeat."

Hope's eyes got big. "What was *that* like?"

"Yeah. What was that like?"

Faith's muscles constricted as she looked toward her bedroom door. "What are you doing here?"

"We keep asking that question," Jesse said. "Your mom told me to go on up. Can I come in?"

Faith nodded, pulling the covers closer. She was sure she looked a mess.

"Joy, Hope, good to see you," Jesse said.

Hope jumped up, smiling. "Good to see you too, Jesse." She'd only met him once, at the Christmas party, which she probably didn't remember. But everyone was a fast friend with Hope.

Joy had heard a little more from Faith about what was happening. She gave him a "Hey" and kept moving.

"Why are you here?" Faith said.

"My mom told me you went to the doctor today because you thought something was wrong with the baby." Jesse stood a few feet from her. "You could've told me."

"The baby's fine."

"But you didn't know that at first."

"And you wouldn't have cared."

Jesse stared at her a moment, then got the chair from her desk, brought it near, and sat down. Seconds passed before he spoke. "I remember the first time I was here, at the Christmas party. We ended up talking for over an hour."

Faith looked at him, wondering what this had to do with anything.

"And I remember thinking how real you were." Jesse focused on her. "And don't take this the wrong way, but it was kind of a corny real . . . You weren't trying to be cute or cool, which threw me because—you're beautiful." He paused, taking her in, before he continued. "But we got into, what was it . . ."

"What didn't we get into?" Faith couldn't help but engage him. "Politics, history, the classics." She paused. "I was surprised you knew so much."

"Ha. The feeling went both ways. And somehow you brought Jesus into it, and I'm thinking I don't know *anyone* like this girl."

Faith frowned a little. She never would've guessed those thoughts had been in his head. But she was reminded of the Jesse she'd been drawn to, the one she could talk to about all sorts of things, before the pregnancy changed the dynamic.

"I knew I wasn't looking to have a relationship with you." Jesse paused, staring off for a moment. "Brandy and I were off and on, plus I was leaving for grad school, though I didn't know where yet." He sighed, looking at her now. "But you kept coming to mind, so I texted you. And we got together, and conversation flowed like before. And I should have stopped it there . . ."

"Why are you telling me all this, Jesse?"

He sighed. "Because you're different, Faith, and it messed me up." He got up, walked toward her shelves. "I could chill with you, be silly if I wanted. I liked getting to know you, with your quirky self." He turned toward her. "I wasn't using you for sex. I could've had sex with a dozen other girls. My problem was, I couldn't stay away from you . . . even though I knew I was all wrong for you."

Faith stared at her peach-colored sheets. She'd been working too hard to pry her heart away from Jesse. Whatever this was that he was sharing, it was meaningless.

"When I heard what happened today, I had to come. If I'm honest, you were on my mind more than the baby. I wanted to see if you were okay, because you wouldn't be . . . you wouldn't be going through all this if it weren't for me." He walked toward her. "Faith, I'm the same selfish guy, I know that. If it were up to me, we'd be making other arrangements for this baby. And I can't make a bunch of promises or long-term commitments."

"I know," Faith said.

"But I can't walk away either." He sat back in the chair. "I know you can't stand the sight of me after all I've done. I get that. But . . . I want to be there for you through this, though I have no idea what that'll look like." He looked into her eyes. "I don't expect you to believe me, and I know it doesn't matter at this point. But you should know—I didn't lie about my feelings for you."

Faith closed her eyes, telling herself to shut out every word. Why was he doing this? Did he enjoy toying with her heart?

"So," Jesse said, "tell me about that heartbeat."

CHAPTER FORTY-FIVE

J illian couldn't believe she was starting to get a little excited. She opened the oven and took out the roasted chicken, smiling at the beautiful golden brown skin, and set the roasting pan on trivets. Scalloped potatoes and green beans were done, as were the sweet potato pie and red velvet cake. She couldn't decide which of Cecil's favorite desserts to make, so she'd done both. The only thing left was to bake Darlene's homemade rolls, the one item she hadn't prepared herself.

She glanced at the clock on the oven. Cecil would be home from work in about forty minutes, and she wanted everything to be perfect for his birthday dinner. It was only God's grace, because left to herself she'd serve him a bowl of cereal. They'd remained distant since she returned a little over three weeks ago, except around the kids. But Jillian had been praying, and as Cecil's birthday weekend loomed, she was moved to make it special. She'd even gotten Treva to keep the kids. She and Cecil had the entire weekend to themselves, and she prayed they could make the most of it.

Jillian walked past the dining table, set with their best china, fresh flowers, and candles. She'd light them when he pulled into the driveway. But right now, her clothing was on her mind. Unlike her sister, casual dress was Jillian's habit, which suited her well since she spent most of her time at home, with younger kids who liked dirt, clay, and paint. Right now she wore yoga pants and a tee, but she wanted to step it up, for the good of her marriage.

She walked into her closet, and her eyes fell on a white shift. She'd bought it while shopping with Treva, who said it looked cute and sexy on her, but she'd never worn it. *Perfect.* She took a quick shower, pampered herself with perfumed body lotion, and slipped into the dress. With minutes remaining, she quickly applied a soft touch of makeup and fluffed her hair with her fingers. She was ready.

She slipped the pan of rolls into the oven, and with it the side dishes to warm. Butterflies stirring, she peered out of the window, glad Cecil had a predictable schedule, which had always worked well with the unpredictable schedules of the kids.

The timer for the rolls went off, and Jillian took everything out. Remembering the cranberry sauce—a favorite of Cecil's year round—she took it out of the refrigerator and dashed it into a serving bowl, careful of her dress.

Minutes later she stood back at the window, watching as cars came and went down their street. When forty-five minutes had passed, she got worried. She picked up her phone and called, but Cecil's went straight to voice mail.

An hour and a half passed, and she called Treva.

"This is so strange," Jillian said. "Where could he be? And

why isn't he answering his phone?"

"Well," Treva said, noise from their kids in the background, "it's his birthday, right? Maybe he decided to hang with friends for a bit after work."

"Maybe," Jillian said. "He does that on occasion, but he always lets me know. I guess this is a sign of how strained things have become, especially that he'd do this on his birthday." She sighed. "I'm so bummed, after all the work I went to."

"The food's not going anywhere," Treva said. "And you've got all weekend to enjoy it."

"True. Okay. I'm glad I called you."

Jillian couldn't bring herself to change out of the dress. She sat by the picture window in the living room, still wanting to catch Cecil when he pulled up. As the summer sun set and shadows filled the room, she retreated to the kitchen, snacking on a veggie tray. By nine o'clock she felt a gnawing in the pit of her stomach.

What if . . . ?

She snatched up her phone and opened her Facebook app. She knew the way: Cecil's profile page, then to Regina's. She didn't have to scroll down. There at the top was the photo and caption: *At the MLK, Jr. monument with the kids.*

Regina was in DC.

Her phone fell from her hand, and her hand went to her mouth as she heaved. She ran to the bathroom and slumped down, head over the toilet, but nothing came out. Just dry, ugly heaves. And tears.

Oh, God . . . He's spending his birthday with her? How could he do this?

She pushed her back against the bathroom wall, sobs pulsing her chest. *Why, God? Why did You move me to go through all this tonight? You knew this would happen . . .*

It all seemed so final. Cecil had made his choice, on his birthday. No more thinking and praying. He knew where he wanted to spend his time, and who with. And he clearly didn't care what Jillian thought about it.

I'm done, Lord. They can have one another. I'm so sick of—
We wrestle not against flesh and blood.

Jillian's head lifted slightly, above her water-stained dress. Treva had reminded her of that in the hotel, that her main struggle wasn't with Cecil or with a failing marriage. It was with the enemy, who wanted Cecil to turn his back on his family . . . and wanted Jillian to give up without a fight.

But now it was the Lord whispering it in her spirit. Telling her to fight. Telling her to *run.*

Jillian's stomach cramped. *How am I supposed to run, Lord? I can't even think straight.*

Lance's words came to mind . . . She'd been crippled, but it was especially now that she needed to run. And not just run, but run to win. And that promise Cyd exhorted them with . . . Jillian forced herself to say it aloud.

"Though I may stumble, I will not fall."

Her voice didn't sound convincing, but the words pulled her to her feet. She moved out of the bathroom, not sure where to go or what to do, knowing there was one thing she needed to believe—

"The Lord upholds me with His hand."

Jillian awakened to steps in the bedroom. She opened her eyes and saw Cecil standing over her.

"Why are you in a dress, asleep on the floor?" he said. "And what's the deal with all the food downstairs? Did you have your Bible study group over?"

Leaving her Bible and journal on the floor beside her, Jillian rose slowly to her feet. "Happy Birthday, Cecil. Dinner was for you." She glanced at the clock and felt a stab of pain. 2:23 a.m. "Where were you?"

"You didn't tell me you were planning something for my birthday."

"I had to tell you, for you to come home? Since when don't you come home?"

"It wasn't planned. A couple of the guys suggested hanging out after work. I didn't expect it to be such a long night."

Jillian could feel her blood ready to boil. "What guys?"

"Jeff and Harold."

She stared at him for long seconds. "I should ask where you

were and what you did so you could keep spinning your little tale. But I know, Cecil. You were with Regina."

"What? What are you talking about?"

Jillian got her phone from the nightstand, went to Regina's Facebook page, and held the picture to his face. "Just a coincidence that she's in town? How long did the two of you plan your special birthday date?"

Cecil sat on the edge of the bed with a heavy sigh. "It wasn't like that, Jillian."

"So you admit it? You were with her?"

Cecil looked aside. "Her kids had some group trip to DC. She and I had dinner in the hotel restaurant and talked in the lobby."

"Till two in the morning." Jillian's arms were shaking. "It's a full-blown affair now. Just say it. You slept with her."

"We didn't sleep together, Jill." Cecil couldn't look at her. "I'm telling the truth about that."

"Oh, because let's make it plain—you tried to lie at first. And you know what? My guess is you're still lying." Jillian paced a little, tears flowing. She turned back to him. "Why did you come home at all? Go back to the hotel. Stay the night with your precious Regina!"

"Jill, I know you're upset, but please . . . the kids."

"The kids aren't here, Cecil." Jillian moved closer. "They're at Treva's. You know why? Because *I* was supposed to celebrate your birthday with you. Your *wife*. It was supposed to be a special weekend for the two of us. But I'm not the one you care about."

"That's not true." Cecil looked up at her. "You have no idea how much I care about you."

"Oh, wow." Jillian laughed, but there was no humor in it. "I mean it, Cecil. You can go back downtown or wherever she's staying. Just get out."

She caught site of her Bible and journal, where she'd written verses to pray over Cecil and her marriage—then headed to the bathroom and slammed the door.

CHAPTER FORTY-SIX

Ith had been more than a month since she'd seen him, but Treva and Lance had talked every day. Always in the evening, after the rest of life had settled, and texting at all times of day besides. But it wasn't too often that they FaceTimed.

Treva smiled as the call came in, wondering what Lance was up to. She clicked on from her kitchen and watched his face appear. "I thought you were at Six Flags today," she said, looking into the phone as she held it aloft.

Lance grinned. "I am! Can't you tell?" He turned the phone's camera and did a panorama of a long line for one of the rides and the youth from his church who mugged the camera, then turned it back on himself. "So we've got a dare happening right now," he said, half shouting above the noise.

"What's the dare?" Treva realized she was half shouting too.

"These young people have dared me to FaceTime while riding this roller coaster." Lance mugged the camera himself. "Like I'm not crazy enough to do it!"

They gathered behind him, shaking their heads. "He's all talk!" one of them said.

Treva laughed. "Don't do it, Lance! You'll drop your phone!"

His grin was contagious. "I *have* to do it. Because they said I wouldn't!" He looked aside, bantering with them for a moment. "So," he said, moving in line, "we're about to get on the ride, and you have to stay on so I can handily win this dare."

"You are *so* gonna drop it," Treva said, "*and* what if you fall out and I have to witness that?"

Lance got a kick out of that. "So I fall to my death. But the problem would be you seeing it." He got into the car, looking at the others with him. "This is gonna be *crazy*."

"*You're* crazy!" Treva said. "I can't believe you're doing this!"

"Mom, why are you shouting?"

Joy and Hope came into the kitchen.

"Oh, she's FaceTiming," Hope said, peering into the phone. "Oh, it's Lance! Hey Lance!"

"Let me see," Joy said, rushing over to wave at the screen. "Wow, are you on a roller coaster?"

"Nice to see you, Joy and Hope! Hey, check this out." Lance turned the camera around, and they watched the car climb a steep track.

"Oh my goodness," Treva said, turning from the view. "I can't with roller coasters."

"This is so crazy cool." Hope had more of her face in the phone than Treva.

"Almost to the top," Lance said. "Then there's a big drop into a loop. Y'all ready?"

"Are *we* ready?" Treva said. "All we have to do is stand here and watch your lunatic self. Lance, hold the phone tight."

"I got it, I got it!"

He turned the camera on himself again, and as the car went over the hill his mouth flew open. All they heard were screams, the car flying down the track, and the roar of the wind.

The three of them stood there in the kitchen, wide-eyed and speechless.

"Whoa!" Lance said, as the car practically jerked into the loop. "I almost lost it!" he said, his voice stuttering as he bounced along at high speed.

Treva shook her head. "He is absolutely nuts."

"Look at his eyes," Joy said. "They look wild!"

When they'd cleared the last hill and slowed down, Lance looked at the others in the car. "Easy money!" he told them.

"We didn't bet any money," one of them yelled back. "That was cool, though, Pastor!"

He did a couple of bows of the head.

"See," he said into the phone, still grinning. "Nothing to worry about!"

Treva smiled back at him. "Except the heart attack you almost gave me."

Lance looked at her. "It was worth it just to see your pretty face." He got out of the car. "I'd better jump off," he said. "Call you later this evening."

"All right, you crazy man."

Treva clicked off, and her girls feigned swooning.

"Oh, stop it," Treva said, chuckling.

"Is this what it was like when you and Dad were dating?" Hope said.

Treva got back to preparing for lunch with her mom. "Hmm, I don't recall anyone FaceTiming from a roller coaster."

"I mean were you happy like this?" Hope said.

The question made Treva pause. "I was happy because I was in love with your dad, but it wasn't a happy time in my life, if that makes sense."

"Because of Grandma Patsy," Joy said.

"You all know the story," Treva said. "There was a heavy cloud over my life for a long time. But I'm thankful she's a different person now."

Treva finished a grilled shrimp Caesar salad and set it on the table as the doorbell rang. The girls had dispersed, but Hope ran down and answered. Her mom entered the kitchen in slacks, a silk shirt, and heels. No one had to wonder where Treva got it from.

"Hey, welcome," Treva said, hugging her. "This was a nice surprise."

She'd called only a couple of hours ago to say she'd be in the area, driving in from Northwest DC. That meant only one thing—she had an appointment at Darlene's hair salon.

"I needed a trim," Patsy said, fingering her hair, "but Darlene cut a little more than I anticipated. What do you think?" She did a full turn.

"I think it's cute," Treva said. "Looks like she layered it a little. Gives you more body."

"You know I try to avoid Saturdays at Darlene's shop." Patsy took a seat at the table. "But I had too much going on during the week." She shook her head. "Just too many folk in there."

"Uh-huh. You mean too many folk outside of your normal circle." She loved that she could be carefree about it now. Her mother's circle of friends had often made Treva feel unwelcome in her own home. "You need to go to the shop more often on Saturdays for your spiritual growth."

Both of them laughed.

"I'm trying to get better," Patsy said. "Thank God He's patient with me."

"Amen to that," Treva said. "I need much of it myself."

"Where is everybody?"

"They should be down shortly." Treva took out bottles of chilled Pellegrino water, her mom's favorite. "Faith was getting dressed last I checked."

"I'm still so heartbroken about that situation," Patsy said. "She had her whole life before her."

"She still does," Treva said.

"But everything will be complicated once she's a single mom. It alters so much."

Treva had had the same thoughts, but it hadn't been helpful to dwell on them. "I'm thinking God will be quite able to help Faith in whatever way she needs. She'll be fine."

"And what about the young man? I understand he's smart, but—oh, goodness, before we get to that . . . Darlene told me you're *dating?*"

Treva would surely take this up with her mother-in-law. "So I'm beauty shop gossip fodder now?"

"No, no, she thought I knew, and I should have. She said he's a pastor in St. Louis?"

Treva nodded. "Yes, he pastors a fairly new church there." She already knew the next question.

"What seminary did he attend?"

Treva had opened the refrigerator to get the salad dressing. Now she wanted to climb inside. "He didn't attend seminary."

"What college then?"

Treva walked over, set the dressing down. Might as well spill it all. "He didn't attend college, Mother. And actually, he dropped out of high school and spent some time in prison."

Patsy looked as if she'd swallowed a frog. "Treva, you can't be serious. How is it fitting for him to pastor a church? And more-over, how can you be dating him?"

Treva sat down. "How is it fitting for him to be a pastor? It's a calling by God. And he's more gifted than many I've heard who are vocationally trained but not Spirit led. He has a heart for people and a bigger heart for God, and He's been discipled and trained by some amazing men of God."

Patsy crossed her legs. "There's no way I could be a member of a church where the pastor dropped out of high school."

Treva's stomach tightened. "Why do you feel the need to even say that, since it's not an option before you?"

"What's before me is my daughter who's dating this man." Patsy looked incredulous. "Treva, Hezekiah had his doctorate in mathematics education—"

"And you had issues with that, because he didn't go to the 'right' schools."

Patsy blinked as if struggling to understand. "I'm simply floored. Darlene said you met during that women's conference, so I assume this is some whirlwind deal that will blow over soon." She shook her head resolutely. "It'll never work, Treva. You're from two separate worlds."

Treva pushed the words away as quickly as they came, words she'd used herself, though for different reasons.

But those words returned throughout the day. By early evening, they were a refrain. That was the forever irony—Treva internalized the very things from Patsy that she sought to reject.

Two separate worlds.

Patsy was right—it had been a whirlwind. Had she gotten too caught up?

CHAPTER FORTY-SEVEN

Stephanie double-checked the address as she pulled in front of the home. Mrs. Cartwright had told her the would-be bed-and-breakfast was located in Lafayette Square, a historic neighborhood in St. Louis. Stephanie thought maybe they'd bought one of the homes off the beaten path. But this . . . She craned her neck around to take it all in. This was one of the Victorian mansions that sat a stone's throw from the immense Lafayette Park.

She parked in front of the house and took the walkway to the entrance. The Cartwrights had been in Florida the past two weeks, and when Stephanie said she'd like to talk again, Mrs. Cartwright suggested they meet as soon as she returned. Stephanie had an idea in mind when she made the call, one she'd admittedly concocted at the family dinner. But now that she was here, she was already concluding it wouldn't work.

The front door swung open, and Mrs. Cartwright smiled broadly as she walked out. "Well, the first thing I'll say before you step inside," she said, "is you're going to have to use your imagination."

"Uh-oh," Stephanie said, stopping short. "That bad?"

"Not *too*"—Mrs. Cartwright grimaced a little—"but, well, you'll see."

"I don't need much imagination for the outdoors, that's for sure." Stephanie turned to view the acres of greenery. "This is gorgeous."

"Isn't it?" The older woman sighed, hands to her hips, staring at the park. "That's what drew us. Well, that and the potential we saw inside. *Plus* restaurants, coffee shops, and such around the corner. I was sad about it at first, once we decided to move, because I could just see this place up and running, people coming and going. But now, with you standing there? There's still hope." She grinned and turned.

"Don't get your hopes up too much, now," Stephanie said, following. She stepped inside, and her gaze went immediately to the grand staircase, then the soaring ceilings, the immense foyer, and the cavernous rooms beyond. "Wow. This is incredible."

Mrs. Cartwright beamed. "I love that that was your first thought, because you might have focused on, well, all of this." She gestured toward wood floors that were scratched and scuffed. Walls covered in flaking paint. Broken banister on the stairway. Every glance cried neglect.

"We've done major repairs here and there over the last few years," she continued, moving into a room with a grime-coated chandelier. "New roof. New plumbing. Upgraded wiring. But as you can see, there's a lot left to do."

"Fireplace in the dining room, huh? Nice." Stephanie checked out the brick, some of it crumbling. "How old is the home?"

"It was built in 1896 by a wealthy financier. But of course, it's passed through many hands. And yes, they loved fireplaces. Three of the bedrooms have them." She kept walking. "And this is one of the sitting rooms, with a rather lovely dilapidated fireplace."

"The character and detailing in these rooms . . ." Stephanie gazed around her, marveling. "Even empty and in disrepair, it feels cozy." She looked at Mrs. Cartwright. "I know that sounded weird."

"Not at all. I feel the same way."

"You said this is *one* of the sitting rooms?"

"There are two here on the first floor and another on the third, in the living quarters up there."

"Hey, why not?" Stephanie said, smiling. "Can't have too many sitting rooms." She paused at the next area. "Look at this kitchen."

Mrs. Cartwright looked side to side, nodding. "This was the next biggie on my list. The cupboards, the counter, the grimy linoleum . . . it's almost depressing."

"Oh, I meant the size," Stephanie said, walking the breadth of it. "I expected a closed-in, boxy space like I've seen in other older homes."

"A renovation was done in the seventies to open it up," Mrs. Cartwright said, "so the space factor is nice. Just needs a facelift."

"What's this in here?" Stephanie stepped into a separate

room off the kitchen that was itself ample.

"Oh, the butler's pantry," Mrs. Cartwright said.

"You're kidding." Stephanie shook her head in wonder. "And if the view from the front wasn't enough, look at this one from the back."

Mrs. Cartwright joined her at the window. "Can't you see weddings in this space back here?"

"Ohh . . . and the wedding design flowing through the lower level. That would be amazing." She sighed. "Mrs. Cartwright, can I tell you why I wanted to meet?"

"I can't wait to hear."

"To be honest," Stephanie said, moving into the kitchen's open space, "my family was hounding me about needing something productive to do. So I thought, even though I can't commit to the B and B thing, maybe I could help oversee the remodeling or something. But I had no idea we were talking *historic mansion*. It's way over my head, even assuming you might've bought into my crazy scheme." She looked at her. "I'm sorry for wasting your time."

"Here's the thing, though," Mrs. Cartwright said. "I've already got a contractor in place, and we've got a plan for tackling repairs like the fireplace, walls, and floors. We even drew up a plan for the kitchen redesign." She held Stephanie's gaze. "I think you could oversee the renovation, no problem. And I think you could do the interior design and have this place jaw-droppingly beautiful. Let me ask you . . ." There was a gleam in her eye. "Do you feel a stirring inside, like this is something that resonates with you? If not, I'll leave it alone."

"I felt a stirring from the time I pulled up in front of the home, but . . . I have to be honest about something else. I'm not the most driven person. I'm in my thirties and still don't know what I want to be when I grow up. So I can be stirred about something one minute, and on to something else the next. I just don't want to disappoint you."

"I hear you," Mrs. Cartwright said. "Tell me about the stirring you feel."

Stephanie took a glance around at her surroundings and sighed. "This place makes me dream. I've always been into style and design, mostly clothes and shoes, mind you, but houses too. So I can't help but picture what these rooms could look like." She gave a mischievous grin. "And to be able to have fun with a design project like this and not be the one paying the bill?"

Mrs. Cartwright smiled. "Not only that, but I'd be paying you to have fun."

"You would pay me?"

"Well, of course. You'd be acting as project manager, interior designer . . . And you'll have a lot of responsibility, because in two weeks we'll be gone."

"Two weeks?" Stephanie felt a rush of excitement and fear rolled together. She took a big breath. "I can't deny I *want* to do this, but I'm overwhelmed just thinking about it—and I've only seen one level."

"If there's one thing I've learned," Mrs. Cartwright said, "it's that when we take on something that's beyond us, God uses it to mold and shape us. I don't know why God put you on my mind. But with all that's going on in your life right now, maybe this old house figures into it somehow, even if you're involved for only a short season. All you can do is take a step at a time."

The words weren't lost on Stephanie. In her mind now, taking one step meant she was moving. In the race. *Running.* And that was far better than the place she'd been.

CHAPTER FORTY-EIGHT

July

Jillian watched as the surgeon and attending nurse wheeled ten-year-old Trevor down a long hallway into emergency surgery.

"Poor little guy," Treva said, standing beside her. "He was trying so hard to be brave."

"As he kept asking, 'Where's Daddy?'" Jillian walked back into the room in which they'd prepped her son for surgery. "I'm so upset with Cecil I can't see straight."

"Jillian, you've got to calm yourself." Their mother had arrived a little while before. "For whatever reason, Cecil hasn't gotten your messages yet. You know he'd be here if he had."

"I don't know any such thing," Jillian said. "I can't predict *what* Cecil might do these days. And if he hasn't gotten messages I've been leaving for the past *five* hours, why not? It's Saturday afternoon. Why don't I have any idea where he is?" She threw her hands up. "He just got up this morning and left."

Patsy frowned. "You can't predict what he might do? What does that mean? What's going on that I don't know about?"

"I don't feel like getting into it." Jillian sat in one of the plastic chairs. She'd had little to say to Cecil in the three weeks since his birthday, but she'd at least thought he cared still about his kids. She popped up again and began to pace. "What if Trevor's appendix had burst? What if his life were hanging by a thread? As it is, he's in the hospital for the very first time, under the knife. And Cecil is off who-knows-where."

"Jillian, for goodness' sake," Patsy said, "stop trotting out the what-ifs and sit down." In a short-sleeved linen dress, she looked regal even in the plastic chair. "Whatever's going on between you and Cecil, you know he loves that boy. He'll be here. Shouldn't you simply be thanking God that they caught this in time?"

"I've thanked Him more times today than I can count," Jillian said, putting Trevor's sneakers, clothes, and the mini iPad he'd used to pass the time into a bag.

"Jillian," Treva said, "I'm sure you haven't eaten. Let's go downstairs and get something. It'll be good for you to take a walk."

"The surgery lasts less than an hour." Jillian tried sitting again. "I'd rather wait here for word as to how it went." She looked at them. "But you two should go."

Patsy opened a magazine. "You know I have no desire to eat cafeteria food."

Jillian's phone vibrated in her hand.

Treva sat forward. "Cecil?"

"Darlene," Jillian said, reading the text. "She's finishing her last client and will be here shortly after." She shook her head. "Darlene the beauty shop owner can get here—on a Saturday— but the boy's own father can't."

"So," Treva said, "I know you're upset. But remember a couple weeks ago you said you were in desperate need of prayer for this very sort of thing—to focus on fighting in prayer and not fighting Cecil?"

Jillian stared ahead.

"I'm just saying, maybe we should pray right now."

"Excuse me," Patsy said, extending her manicured hands between them. "Clearly, I'm the only one who isn't aware of what's been happening here. I know—you two have kept each other's confidences from the time you were young, and my own behavior kept me at a distance. But even if you don't share details, it would be nice to know that *something* is going on, so I can pray too." She added, "I'm sure you've shared it already with Darlene."

"Momma, it's just been a difficult time, and I haven't kept anyone fully updated," Jillian said. "So please don't make this about Darlene."

The door tipped open, and a nurse stuck her head in. "Oh, yes, they're still in here," she said. "Go on in."

The door opened wider, and in walked Cecil, looking harried. "I couldn't find you."

Jillian looked up at him. "For five hours?"

Treva stood. "Mother, let's go to the cafeteria. You can partake of bottled water."

"Where's Trevor?" Cecil said. "Is he already in surgery?"

Jillian realized she hadn't sent that update. But what did it matter, since he hadn't replied to the others. "They took him ten minutes ago."

"I can't believe I missed seeing him." He ran his hands down his face, sighing hard. "What a day."

Jillian chewed her lip. *Help me, Lord. I'm ready to blast him.* "Where've you been, Cecil?"

"On the golf course. I left my phone in the car."

Uh-huh. He hadn't played golf in years.

He took the seat next to her. "So what happened exactly? I got all your messages at once, but I was so thrown I'm sure I didn't catch everything."

"Trevor started complaining about a stomachache day before yesterday," Jillian said, "but this morning he woke up crying because it hurt so badly. Plus he had a fever. So I took him to the pediatric ER."

Cecil's gaze fell. "I wish I had been with him."

"They ended up doing an ultrasound," Jillian said, "and his appendix was swollen and infected. They said it could burst any minute, and they needed to get him to surgery as soon as possible."

"How long is the surgery? Is it invasive?"

"Less than an hour. Thankfully, because it hadn't ruptured, they can do it laparoscopically."

"Was he asking for me?"

"Of course he was asking for you."

Cecil blew out a breath. "I hate that I wasn't there for him."

"Now that's interesting." Jillian stood. "You hate you weren't there for Trevor, but you're not at all bothered about your affair with Regina."

"Jill, how many times do I have to say it?" His eyes pleaded. "I'm not having an affair."

"She's in town again today, isn't she?"

Cecil took her hand and pulled her gently back to the seat next to him, surprising her.

"I wasn't lying, Jill. Harold asked me to go golfing—"

"Right. Harold again."

He held her hand still. "And I went because . . . I needed time to clear my head, to pray—"

"I am so sick of you talking about prayer when it's convenient."

"I promise you, it's not talk." Cecil looked at her. "These last three weeks have been—"

The door opened again and the same nurse stepped in.

"Mr. Mason, you had some questions about post-op activities your son can engage in," she said. "The surgeon's assistant is at the nurses' station, if you want to come talk with her."

Cecil got up, turning to Jillian. "Do you want to come with me?"

She'd already heard the rundown. "No, you go ahead."

Cecil followed the nurse, and Jillian noticed he'd left his

phone in the chair, on the screen that showed her text messages.

She scooped it up and clicked to all of his messages. Not surprisingly, there was a contact right under hers—R.M. She opened, noticing that there weren't many messages. He'd been quick to delete. But there was a thread from yesterday:

Why are you calling our landline?

You wouldn't respond to texts or calls to ur cell.

I told u . . . this can't continue. And what if my wife had been home? She already suspects the worst.

So that's it?

It has to be.

Jillian's heart pounded. She held the phone until Cecil walked back in. "Not having an affair? Then what's the 'this' that can't continue?"

Cecil glanced at his phone in her hand. "The path we were on." He sat down again and stared into her eyes. "I've always loved you, Jillian," he said, his voice soft, "and in nineteen years of marriage, I'd never thought about being with another woman . . . until that night at Regina's hotel."

Her stomach clenched tighter.

"I didn't think I could ever go there . . ."

He trailed off and Jillian waited.

"I knew I was in a vulnerable place. I really was struggling with our lack of intimacy, and when you didn't come with me to the conference, it felt like you didn't care about us." He looked away. "And there was Regina, and she and I were already friendly.

We just started hanging . . . And every little step, I told myself it was nothing. She was married; I was married. It wasn't going anywhere. But I didn't realize the power of temptation."

Jillian listened, her mind calling up Tommy's comment when he cut off their friendship—*I know how sneaky temptation can be.*

"If her kids hadn't been up in her hotel room, we probably would've slept together, and that terrified me," Cecil said. "It was only God's protection."

Jillian shivered slightly. That was something she'd been praying, for Cecil's protection.

"Then I came home and saw what you'd done for my birthday . . ." He looked at her. "I've never felt so bad in my life. I hated that I hurt you like that. I *love* you." He paused. "And yet, I still had these feelings for Regina . . ." Tears filled his eyes. "So yeah, I've been *praying*, Jill. To be free from any thought of her. That's why I told her we had to cut things off. But mostly I'm praying for *us*, that we would enjoy one another again, rekindle not only the passion but the friendship."

Jillian glanced downward. Her prayers had focused on Cecil's behavior and the need for his heart to turn back toward the marriage. Rekindling passion and friendship hadn't exactly made it in.

Cecil took her hand again. "I betrayed your trust and our vows. Jillian, I'm sorry."

Jillian stared at her hand in his, wondering when was the last time they'd done even this. "The Lord's been dealing with me about my part in this, Cecil. I've been defensive about it, but you're right. Intimacy hasn't been a priority." She sighed, looking into his eyes. "I'm sorry for not caring about us in the way I should have."

Cecil stood and brought Jillian to her feet, embracing her. "I want my marriage. I want *us*."

She felt his tears on her neck. "I want us too."

Her own tears fell when she realized how much she meant it.

CHAPTER FORTY-NINE

Faith had told herself not to put any stock into Jesse's words about his feelings for her. Whether real or not, he'd been right—it didn't matter. It'd been a mistake to get involved with him, and she'd be a fool to go there again. Still, she hated that she cared so much about him. She'd wanted him to check on her and the baby, and since that scare at ten weeks, he had. About once a week he texted to ask how they were doing. But that was it, a quick text. No calls. No dropping by. No conversation about anything other than the one he was obliged to have.

Which should have been fine. After all, she'd wanted to get her boundaries back where he was concerned. But it *hurt* that he hadn't told her he was leaving for Chicago.

"When?" Faith asked, in her mom's home office.

"He's driving out tomorrow." Treva sat in her desk chair. "Honey, I'm sorry. His mom mentioned it at Bible study and I assumed you knew. He has to get an apartment and get settled before classes start."

"And get his relationship back on track with Brandy."

"Sweetheart, pull up a chair." Treva's eyes were soft. "Were

306

you hoping still for a future with Jesse?"

Faith got a chair from the office table and brought it near. "Not really." She played with a jagged fingernail. "But I can't stop caring about him."

"I know it's hard," Treva said, "because of what you two shared and the baby you now share. But I'm praying a guy will come into your life who loves God and loves you—fiercely. Someone who protects you and treats you like the beautiful treasure you are."

"But I'll be a single mom," Faith said. "A man like that wouldn't want someone like me."

Treva leaned in. "A young man like that won't be able to resist a young woman like you, because Jesus is strong in you."

Faith pondered that a moment before sharing what else was on her heart. "Mom, I've been thinking about adoption."

"Wow, okay," Treva said. "Tell me what you're thinking."

"I hadn't given it much thought until Jesse brought it up in St. Louis," Faith said, "and then I was upset because it felt like he was trying to distance himself, which he was. But I've been researching adoption sites and praying about it. I don't know . . . One day I want to keep my baby, and the next I know I'm not ready to be a mom. It's hard."

Treva took her hand. "You're fourteen weeks along, so you've got time," she said. "And you've also got a team of praying folk around you. If you don't mind, I'll share this with your Aunt Jillian, your grandparents, even my Bible study group, and we can all be praying with you."

"I'd love that." To her surprise, just hearing her mom's words really did make a difference. Though Jesse was leaving, she didn't have to feel alone on the journey. She got up to head back to her room. "Mom, that prayer you're praying about the kind of guy to come into my life?"

"Yeah?" Treva said.

"I know it's possible, because you've had it happen twice."

CHAPTER FIFTY

Treva sighed, thinking about her daughter's comment. *I know it's possible, because you've had it happen twice.*

She believed that as well, that twice now God had blessed her to have a man in her life who loved Him and desired to live for Him, a man who was everything she could want and more. The problem with both—she was the one who fell short.

Hezekiah had endured it for years, only by the grace of God. He'd put up with Treva's bad attitudes, selfishness, and obsession with her career, to the detriment of her family. Once she'd even told him that she'd take the career over the family, which hurt Hezekiah to his core. It was more than a decade into their marriage before she put any focus on becoming the wife that Hezekiah deserved . . . And that was one of the things that pained her most about losing him. She wished she'd done more with the time they had.

And now there was Lance . . . In her mother's eyes, he wasn't the right man because of his lack of formal education. Treva would've thought the same in years past, but she wasn't that person anymore. Lance had turned her world upside down in two days and had enriched it in the months since. Healing had come as a result of his presence in her life, painfully so at times since with him she faced the hurts and fears head-on. He was often the one who pinpointed them lurking beneath things she did or said. And late into the night, they'd talk it out. And pray. He was more than she could've imagined. *They* were more than she could've imagined, even at a distance.

Still, moments ago, three words came bouncing back: *two separate worlds.*

She turned back to her computer. Before Faith had come in, she'd googled Lance again. It was a small thing that spurred it. At Bible study today his name had come up, and one of the women asked if he was the same Lance who'd spoken at a Bible conference she had attended last year. Curious, Treva did a search to see. But an interview popped up among the finds, one she'd now listened to twice.

Treva's phone rang, her heart reacting immediately. She just knew it was Lance, and looking at the phone confirmed it. For a second she thought of sending the call to voice mail, but there was no point delaying.

"Hey," she said.

Lance paused. "You sound down. Did something happen with Faith?"

"No," Treva said. "Well, it did, but that's not why . . ." She sighed.

"Treva, what's wrong?"

"Um . . ." She melted. His voice. How he knew her. The way

he cared. Her heart was crying already. But she couldn't ignore what she'd heard. "I happened to come across an interview you did."

"Okay . . ."

"The interviewer asked if you ever saw yourself marrying again, and you said it wasn't something you actively thought about, but if and when . . ." The tears were in her chest now, rising, taking her breath. "You always wanted lots of kids, so you hoped God would bless you with someone you could build a family with."

"Treva, that interview was almost two years ago," Lance said, "and I was answering off the cuff."

"You were sharing authentically what was in your heart. And I'm clearly not someone you can build a family with." Treva flicked a tear from her nose. "I'm going on *fifty*, and you're not yet *forty*. What are we doing?"

"Well, for the record, I don't know any thirty-year-olds as fit and fine and—"

"Lance, I'm being serious."

"So am I!" He sighed. "I thought we dealt with this back in St. Louis. Why would I pursue a relationship with you if that were an issue for me? It's not."

"Lance, it's like my mother said, we're caught up in a whirlwind. It's hard to think everything through and see things for what they are. But a relationship with me would mean you'd have *no* kids of your own—and your dream was 'lots.' I couldn't live with myself, taking that from you."

"So with everything you've told me about your mother, including that she thinks we're doomed to failure anyway, you're quoting her on the whirlwind thing?"

"We both said our worlds were turned upside down. That's a whirlwind." Treva grabbed a tissue from the box on her desk. "Lance, this is not a small thing. This is your future. Your dream. I spent too many years thinking only of myself." She took a breath. "You can still have your dream, if I back away."

"We're in my backyard again, with you not listening," Lance said. "Forget the recorded interview. I'm here, live, speaking. Having you in my life is exactly what I want."

Treva stared at the computer screen, wishing she didn't have both Lances in her head. But the Lance who smiled dimples-big when he spoke of his dream scenario if and when he remarried—that was the one front and center in her mind.

"I need you to be absolutely sure," she said, "before we go any further down this road."

"Treva. I *am* absolutely sure."

"We've talked every single day since the conference," Treva said. "I want us to go thirty days with no contact, get the whirlwind out of our system and pray for God's direction." She paused. "And if He's leading us to go our separate ways, we have to be willing to accept that."

Lance sighed. "I'm opposed, but it's looking like I don't get a vote."

"This is important to me, Lance. I need you to step back and be sure."

He was quiet for several seconds. "Thirty days," he said finally. "Can't call to hear your voice first thing in the morning. Won't be able to shoot you a text when you come to mind. No FaceTime so I can see your beautiful smile. And I'm supposed to find something else to do before bed other than spend time on the phone with you."

The nighttime calls. Treva would miss those most. What if this was a big mistake?

Lance exhaled hard. "If this is what you want, Treva."

The phone went dead.

CHAPTER FIFTY-ONE

Stephanie felt as if she were about to take an exam. Mrs. Cartwright had set up a meeting with the general contractor so the three of them could walk through the house and solidify renovation plans prior to the Cartwrights' move to Florida. But she'd also had Stephanie go through again beforehand to note changes she would suggest, which Mrs. Cartwright hadn't. Now, four eyes were on Stephanie to see what she'd come up with.

They were near the dining room, so Stephanie started there. Notebook in hand, she scanned what she'd written and took another look at the room. "Mrs. Cartwright already designated the fireplace repairs and of course the flooring and walls that run throughout." She bit her lip, wondering if what she wrote was too outrageous. Or just dumb.

"This dining area seems to be one of the rooms in least need of renovation, don't you think?" Mrs. Cartwright said, surveying it.

"Well," Stephanie said, "I do have a couple ideas." She walked to the entryway that separated the dining room from the sitting room. "It might be nice to open up this doorway. Create a large cased opening, and make it wider and taller. Guests come down in the morning for breakfast, and it makes for a nice flow between the rooms."

The contractor nodded, stretching out his measuring tape. "That would work well," he said. "The difference would be striking."

"I even thought a glass transom above it might be nice, since they're often seen in older houses," Stephanie continued. "And I would change that window to one that allowed for more natural light." She shrugged. "I have other thoughts, but they're more geared to furniture and accent pieces."

Mrs. Cartwright blank-stared her. "Just a couple thoughts? None of that had occurred to me, and it would enhance the room tremendously." She turned to the contractor. "Let's incorporate those things in the plan. Each one adds to the ambiance we're trying to achieve."

As the contractor busied himself with more precise measurements, Stephanie pulled her aside. "Mrs. Cartwright, are you sure? These really were just thoughts. I don't want you to blow past your budget." She added with a wry smile. "And we haven't gotten to the kitchen and baths yet."

"Believe me, Stephanie, if your suggestions didn't strongly resonate, I wouldn't have incorporated them," Mrs. Cartwright said. "And as for the budget—"

"Oh, I didn't mean for you to get into personal details . . ."

Mrs. Cartwright moved her into the kitchen. "Based on our

conversations and the work we're doing together, I don't mind sharing this with you in confidence. A dear aunt passed a few years ago. Loved the Lord. Never married. No children. More money than any of us realized she had." She was whispering now, her back to the contractor. "Aunt Lucille left it to me with the express direction to use it for the bed-and-breakfast I'd been dreaming about, to remain prayerful, and to glorify God with it. That's why I knew I couldn't let this go."

"Wow . . . I got goose bumps hearing that. This project just went to a whole 'nother level."

"It's quite a task to steward this project responsibly," Mrs. Cartwright said. "I don't want to spend unwisely, and I'll be watching the contractor's expenditures like a hawk. But between you and me, there's no danger of 'blowing past the budget.' I really do want to hear your suggestions."

Stephanie smiled. "I can't wait till we get to the guest bathrooms."

***

Stephanie and Mrs. Cartwright walked the backyard, dreaming up possibilities. They'd spent hours with the contractor, who'd promised to get updated plans to Mrs. Cartwright within the week. Based on the schedule already in place, his crew would get to work in two weeks.

Stephanie sighed in wonder. "I could get a lawn chair and sit back here as-is, enjoying this. It's so peaceful." Her gaze rested on the wooded escape that lay beyond the yard itself.

"But who thought an asphalt walkway was a good idea?" Mrs. Cartwright made a face at it. "Stone would be gorgeous." She looked up. "And I could see a pergola back here."

"Ooh," Stephanie said, nodding. "HGTV had a feature on those recently. That would be nice for weddings." She grinned. "And can't you hear the soothing sounds of a fountain?"

Mrs. Cartwright's eyes widened. "Yes! And I'm thinking for this patio area—oh, you want to get that?"

"It's fine," Stephanie said, ignoring the ringing phone in her pocket, until it rang a second time. She looked at it. "It's Cyd. Should be quick."

She took a step away and put the phone to her ear. "Let me guess. You want me to stop by the grocery store to pick up something for dinner?"

"Steph, you need to get to the hospital. Cedric just called—"

"Oh, no, did something happen to Chase?"

"No," Cyd said. "It's Lindell."

⁂

Stephanie's heart raced on the short drive to Barnes-Jewish Hospital as she tried to make sense of what Cyd had said. Lindell was in St. Louis? In the hospital? Cyd didn't know much herself, so Stephanie would have to wait. But she couldn't think of a scenario that would land him in a St. Louis hospital.

She hadn't heard from Lindell at all in the past two months, which told her he was fine with the split. She knew she must still care, though. Without a second thought, she'd sent up a prayer for him.

Minutes later, she was pulling into the hospital garage and making her way to the fourth-floor waiting area, where Cyd said to meet. When she walked in she saw Cyd and Cedric together.

"Where is he?" Stephanie said.

They both stood.

"The doctor is in with him now," Cedric said.

Stephanie looked from one to the other. "What happened?"

Cedric released a big sigh. "We just got back from Haiti."

"What? You were in Haiti?"

Cedric nodded. "I called Lindell about three weeks ago, and he was stressed, which wasn't surprising, given what he's dealing with down there. Still, something about him didn't sound right to me. I decided to fly down."

Stephanie sat down, overwhelmed. "So what happened?"

"I went from the airport straight to where he was working, at a hospital." Cedric sat as well, along with Cyd. "Except he wasn't working. He was collapsed in a chair suffering from severe chest pains."

Stephanie's hand went to her mouth. "Oh, my Lord . . ."

"And they told me it wasn't the first time," Cedric said. "When it subsided and he seemed to be okay, he got up to go back to work. And I told him we were coming here to have him checked." He shook his head. "It took two days and a nice battle to get him on the plane, but I wouldn't take no for an answer. I've never seen my little brother like that."

"Was it a heart attack?" Stephanie said. "He's not even forty."

"I don't know," Cedric said. "The hospital in Haiti didn't have enough doctors to handle the patients, so Lindell hadn't sought any help. I'm hoping this doctor can give us some answers."

Stephanie could hardly process it. "I can't believe this. What if you hadn't gone down?"

"I shudder to think," Cyd said. "None of us would have guessed—"

"Dr. Malone," Cedric said, standing. "This is Lindell's wife, Stephanie London."

The doctor, a tall, middle-aged gentleman, shook her hand. "Very nice to meet you, Mrs. London," he said. "The good news is that it appears that your husband has not had a heart attack."

Stephanie sighed with relief. "Thank God," she whispered.

"After looking at preliminary testing and talking with him as well as his brother here, I have to tell you I suspect we may be dealing with a form of post-traumatic stress disorder."

"I don't understand," Stephanie said. "Why do you think so?"

"I've seen a fair number of emergency room doctors who suffer from PTSD. They see so much human suffering and tragedy, it can begin to eat away at them like a parasite. And often, they are unable or unwilling to recognize what's happening, because they think they're immune to such things."

"So in Lindell's case," Cedric said, "being in Haiti with human suffering and tragedy to the max . . ."

Dr. Malone nodded. "Yes. It may have taken its toll. It can show up in various ways—dysfunctional and self-destructive behaviors, withdrawal, physical symptoms. With Lindell, he may be dealing with panic attacks, which can involve severe chest pains." He paused. "We'll conduct further tests, but that's my preliminary conclusion."

"Can I see him, Doctor?" Stephanie asked.

"Absolutely," Dr. Malone said. "He's awake."

The doctor left, and the three of them stood for a moment, speechless.

"It's so weird," Stephanie said. "I don't even know what to say to him."

⸙

Stephanie opened the door and walked in slowly, feeling like a stranger. Lindell was staring out of the window, but he turned his head as she approached.

"Steph." His voice sounded scratchy and weak, and he looked as if he'd lost weight.

She took the chair next to him. "How are you feeling?"

Lindell shrugged. "Better for now."

"The doctor told you what he thinks it is?"

Lindell nodded. "He doesn't know for certain, though."

"You're a doctor yourself," Stephanie said. "What do you think?"

He stared outside again. "I thought I was dying the first couple of times it happened. Then I realized it might be panic attacks, because of what I was experiencing in Haiti. But I was so conflicted, because I knew they needed me there." He paused. "I need to say something to you."

Stephanie waited.

"As the doctor explained what might be happening to me," Lindell said, "he said PTSD can arise from a single event or from events over time. I experienced tragedy after tragedy over the past couple of years." He looked at her. "You experienced one, and it was huge given your relationship with Sam."

"What are you saying?"

"I don't know if you were dealing with PTSD," Lindell said, "but whatever it was, it was real. And I didn't take it as seriously as I should have. I wasn't there for you. Steph, I'm sorry."

It took a moment for Stephanie to respond. "It's hard enough processing the fact that you might have PTSD, but to hear that *I* may have suffered some form of that . . ." She looked at him. "But what about when I told you I'd left? You didn't even respond."

"Stephanie, I was stunned. I didn't know what to say or do. Dr. Malone asked if I'd felt detached in any way, and I said it felt like paralysis—emotionally, mentally, even spiritually. I just threw myself into the work, and I see now where that got me." He paused. "Being here now, seeing you . . . Steph, I don't want to lose you."

She stared at him for a few moments. "What does that even mean? What are you willing to change?"

"The doctor said I need a period of rest."

"Then what?"

"Steph, I can't say I'm not going back."

Tears rose to the surface. "Do you not see it? Your actions keep telling me you don't care."

"I do, Steph," Lindell said. "I just need you to understand."

She stared at him, allowing the tears to fall, then turned and left.

CHAPTER FIFTY-TWO

August

Jillian cracked two eggs into the frying pan for Cecil then refreshed her coffee, her mind on the day ahead. Once he left for work, she'd run to the grocery store and the bank. At eleven this morning, their homeschool co-op had a planning meeting for the coming school year—she couldn't believe it was that time already. Sophia had a driving lesson at one o'clock, only her third. She did well as long as Jillian was nowhere near the car to make her nervous. She flipped the eggs. Piano lessons at three. Early evening, a youth soccer meeting—

The doorbell? Nobody dropped by this time of morning.

Jillian slid the eggs onto a plate and turned off the pan. The bell rang again as she walked toward the door. She opened it to see Treva's mother-in-law smiling on the stoop.

"Darlene?"

"Good morning!" Darlene bustled past, bags in hand.

"Did I miss something?"

"You may have," Cecil answered, coming down the steps in athletic shorts. "Morning, Darlene," he said, hugging her.

"Why aren't you dressed for work?" Jillian said. "You're about to be late."

"That thing you missed." Cecil pointed toward the kitchen. "You didn't see the envelope by the coffeepot?"

"No," Jillian said, walking back to it. "How did I miss this?" She lifted a letter-size envelope and looked at Cecil. "What's in it?"

"Chile, open it and see," Darlene said, chuckling.

Jillian tore it open and unfolded the papers inside. Her mouth dropped. "These are boarding passes . . . To Boston? . . . *For this afternoon!*" She turned to Cecil. "Is this real? Are you kidding?"

Cecil smiled. "It's very real."

Jillian looked at Darlene. "You don't know how many times I've said I'd love to visit Boston. The history. The food—oh my gosh, I get to eat for-real New England clam chowder? And it's *summer*. So perfect—but"—she turned to Cecil again—"you could've given me more notice. Do you know how much is on the agenda for today?"

"Piano teacher and driver's ed teacher come to the house—*check*. I talked to the soccer coach and got the parent info he wanted to share—*check*. I saw a homeschool moms' thing on your calendar. You'll have to handle that one."

"That's no problem," Jillian said. "And you're staying here with the kids, Darlene? You are such a blessing. *Oh*, but there's hardly any food."

"I'm headed to the grocery store right now," Cecil said, "while you go pack."

"But Darlene, what about your clients?" Jillian said. "It's Friday, and I know you're busy tomorrow. Are you sure—"

"Girl, if you don't stop worrying about my affairs and get to packing." Darlene turned her in the direction of the stairs. "Everything is covered. Your only job starting now is to *enjoy*."

Jillian could hardly wrap her mind around it. She started toward the stairs then turned back, moving toward Cecil and into his arms. Hugging him, she looked into his eyes. "Thank you."

"Hands down, *the* best so far." Jillian strolled arm-in-arm with Cecil in the heart of downtown Boston on Saturday afternoon. "I didn't even know a Phillis Wheatley exhibit was in the Old South Meeting House. And to see a first edition of her book of poetry on display? From 1773! And a poem I'd never seen—in her actual handwriting! Was that not awesome?" She looked at Cecil, who was smiling at her. "What?"

"I love it when you're like this," Cecil said. "Excited. Chatty. But you do realize you've had a new favorite five times now."

"You know I loved seeing the Lewis and Harriet Hayden House," Jillian said. "The kids and I read about how they helped so many fugitive slaves, as ex-slaves themselves. And let's face it, I could have explored the entire Black Heritage Trail for days." She moved closer to him as someone passed on a bicycle. "But

Phillis? That's my girl. Nothing's topping her." She looked up at him. "I still can't believe you did this."

"I wanted to do something special for you." Cecil slowed their pace a little. "I still can't believe how much I hurt you." He looked at her. "I know this doesn't make up for it. I wish I could do so much more."

Jillian leaned into his arm. "The fact that we've been talking like this is the 'so much more.' Hearing what's on your heart, being able to tell you what's on mine. It's been a long time since we had that."

Cecil walked in silence a few paces. "What you told me last night about Tommy breaking off your friendship," he said, "that was sobering, especially given where I was at the time."

Jillian hesitated to ask. "Have you talked to Regina at all?"

"No," Cecil said. "We haven't been in contact since those messages you saw."

It had been three weeks, and Jillian wanted to believe him, but there was no denying that trust had been eroded.

She watched a trolley roll slowly past, the tour guide announcing to passengers what had occurred more than two hundred years ago on "this very ground." She fingered Cecil's hand. "By the way, last night was amazing. You put some thought into that."

"I know how much you love seafood. And clam chowder." He smiled at her. "It was just a matter of getting some good recommendations."

"But even the coffee and dessert bar afterward were perfect,"

Jillian said. "It had been a long day, but it didn't feel like it. I wanted to linger there with you. It was an answer to prayer."

Cecil looked at her. "What was the prayer?"

Jillian stared vaguely at the family walking in front of them, dad pushing a baby in a stroller, mom telling the toddler son he'd had enough ice cream. Jillian glanced at him, then back to the family. She didn't know how to say it.

"I was praying," she said, "to enjoy you again. To want to be with you, just the two of us." She looked at him. "When we went back to the room, I was a little nervous. We hadn't been together in months, and I didn't know how I would feel or whether I'd be holding onto resentment. But that was an answer to prayer too. It was beautiful."

"All of this is an answer to prayer." Cecil paused, moving them to the side. "Last night was beautiful. This weekend is beautiful." He kissed her. "You're beautiful."

He veered from the sidewalk to a bench among a shady clump of trees. They sat, her hand in his, his eyes on hers. "You were telling me about the conference at dinner last night. And I hadn't asked about it until now because that weekend reminded me of a time I didn't want to think about. I had thoughts of giving up on us, Jill."

"I heard it in your voice," Jillian said, "and it scared me."

Emotion shone in Cecil's eyes. "We hit the roughest road we've ever seen in our marriage. And it was only God who could give you a heart to run while I had lost my mind, nowhere in the race." A single finger wiped a tear from her cheek. "But I've got a new prayer now."

Jillian smiled slightly. "What's that?"

"To up my running game. I'm a phys ed teacher. I'm supposed to know what endurance is about." He kissed her again. "We're in this, babe, running together."

Jillian put her arms around him and held on. "I don't want this weekend to end."

"Well, it ain't over yet," Cecil said.

"What? Why are you smiling like that?"

"You'll see this evening," Cecil said. "There's a reason I chose this particular weekend."

Jillian could hardly stop smiling. Never would she have guessed that Cecil had gotten tickets to see New Edition, in a special hometown concert. The set list was the same, with more interludes with stories of people and places that many in the audience clearly knew. The venue was big but the vibe was personal, the energy electric.

"I'm so glad you got to see this," Jillian said, talking above the song that was ending. "You were always a fan."

"I was in high school when the *Heartbreak* album came out," Cecil said, "and at first I thought, man, all this love talk is a little too mushy for me." He laughed. "But it became a favorite."

Jillian knew what was next and was settling into the groove already. Cecil recognized it seconds later and took her hand, leading her to the aisle. Wrapping his arms around her, they swayed together, and Jillian let herself get lost in his scent, the way his hands felt on her back, the beat of his heart against hers. A crooner by nature, Cecil had a melodic voice. He sang the chorus for her ears only.

Sunny days, everybody loves them.
Tell me, baby, can you stand the rain?
Storms will come, this we know for sure.
Can you stand the rain?

Jillian answered by pressing her lips to his.

CHAPTER FIFTY-THREE

The quarterly girls' night out couldn't have come at a better time for Treva. She and Jillian had taken their girls—all five now that Faith was home—to the movies, and for the past hour there'd been endless chatter at the Cheesecake Factory. Just what she needed. It had been five weeks since she'd talked Lance into a thirty-day break. And every day for the past week she'd awaited his call. Was he counting a month, not days? Was there a misunderstanding—was she supposed to call him? Had he moved on? In the evenings especially, she needed a big healthy dose of distraction.

"No, stand up, so we can see," Courtenay was saying. At seventeen, she was Jillian's oldest.

"I'm not standing up in the middle of the restaurant so you can see a baby bump," Faith said. "I've been with you all evening. You had ample time to look."

"Uh, yeah, but you're wearing that size extra large," Courtenay said, "trying to hide it.

Aunt Treva just said you're showing now. I need you to stand so I can flatten that shirt down and see my little cousin in there."

Joy frowned at her sister. "Are you really trying to hide it?"

Faith sighed. "I was on campus earlier today buying books for the fall. I'm avoiding questions for as long as I can."

"Have you told anyone?" Jillian said.

"Only a couple of close friends."

"People question and judge no matter what you do," Courtenay said. "Didn't you say they were questioning you because you weren't partying like the rest of them?"

Faith nodded.

Courtenay gave her a look. "Now you're worried what these same people might say?"

Treva drained her raspberry lemonade. "I'm glad you're telling her, Courtenay. She needs to move past that."

"So you're a big time junior now." Jillian smiled at Faith. "You ready to start back?"

"I never really stopped," Faith said. "I took twelve credits this summer, since spring semester is up in the air."

"I can't believe how these girls are growing up," Treva said. "Courtenay's a senior this year. Sophia's a sophomore—"

"And I'm now a high schooler, thank you very much." Joy did an upper bow.

"And I'm still the baby," Hope said.

"Baby? You're in seventh grade," Jillian said. "Almost a teenager. That's *crazy.*"

Hope smiled, liking the sound of that.

Faith looked at Courtenay. "So where are you thinking about applying for college?"

As Courtenay rattled off a list of schools, Treva took note of the evening, the blessing it was for the cousins to be able to get together like this. Whatever she and Lance had had, if it had progressed to more they could have ended up moving. This was better, leaving relationships intact. Leaving her life intact. They'd freed themselves from the whirlwind and come to the same conclusion, to go their separate ways.

"Mom must not have heard us," Joy said, snickering.

Treva looked at her. "What?"

"I told Aunt Jillian that Hope and I are homeschooling this year, with Courtenay and Sophia."

"Oh," Treva said, "your Aunt Jillian knew that was nowhere near true."

"Why do you have a problem with it?" Joy said.

"I have absolutely no problem with it, for those who desire to do it. As for me, I happen to have prayed for God to *not* call me to that." Treva chuckled a little. "And why do you bring this up every year?"

"Because I see how Courtenay and Sophia have time to do the stuff they want to do," Joy said. "I would *love* to be able to focus on photography."

Jillian wiggled her eyebrows. "You could even hire Lance as a tutor."

Joy leaned in. "Are you serious? He's a photographer? Why didn't you tell me, Mom?"

Treva gave Jillian the eye.

"Not so much now that he's the senior pastor," Treva said. Or he could be. Who knew what he was doing these days?

Treva jumped a little when her phone rang, and with jittery fingers lifted it from her purse.

She sighed. *1-800* number. Same one that spammed her before, with the automated voice.

She ignored the call and found herself pulling up her photos, scrolling to a selfie she and Lance had taken before they left the park. He'd said he wanted to remember that day. Their decision to see what the future might hold. She stared at the picture, the way he'd leaned in, his cheek touching hers. Those gorgeous eyes. That smile.

Treva dropped the phone back into her purse. If nothing else, her little thirty-day experiment had proven one thing. She'd thought she could never love another man deeply.

She was wrong.

CHAPTER FIFTY-FOUR

Stephanie finished her bowl of cereal, scarfed down a piece of toast, and gulped the last of her orange juice. She rinsed her dishes, put them in the dishwasher, and began filling her thermos with coffee, ready to get going with the day. Lately, she could hardly sleep as her mind filled with the million things that needed to be done to the house. And that was a good thing, since it meant she didn't need to focus on Lindell.

Cyd came into the kitchen in her robe and head scarf, yawning. She stopped, eyeing Stephanie. "I am not used to this. I don't know if I've seen you up this early since you were in grade school."

Stephanie chuckled. "That's probably about right." She grabbed the half-and-half from the refrigerator. "The contractor has a key, but I like to get there early to go over the day's plans. And I need to make final choices on cabinetry, counter tops, and flooring for the kitchen."

"Mrs. Cartwright is giving you that much leeway?"

"I pass everything by her," Stephanie said, "but for some reason, she lets me run with a lot of stuff. Says she loves my design sense." She tossed Cyd a look. "So, ha."

Cyd raised a hand in protest. "I've never said a word about your design sense. I love that you've always been into style, and now you get to use it. I can't wait to see how it all comes together."

"Me either. Seems like it'll take forever." Stephanie added two teaspoons of sugar. "On another note, how long is Lindell going to be here?"

"Steph, we've talked about it." Cyd poured a cup of coffee. "He's as welcome here as you are."

"Hey, as long as he's got his room and I've got mine, we're good."

"Explain this to me," Cyd said. "Aren't you doing a weekly prayer call with Dana and Jillian for the express purpose of praying for your marriage?"

Stephanie sealed the thermos. "Yep."

"But I haven't seen you trying to make any movement toward him."

"I went to his hospital room," Stephanie said. "That was movement. I listened to him tell me he finally had an inkling what I was going through with Sam and hadn't taken it seriously. I was even willing to overlook that he never responded to the tiny fact that his wife had left him—given the state he's apparently been in." She searched her purse for her keys. "*Then* he proceeds to tell me that nothing has changed. It's Haiti or bust once again."

"You forgot the part where he said he didn't want to lose you." Cyd blew steam from her coffee before taking a sip. "Lindell is not himself, Steph. We all see it. Now is when you press in and pray and believe all the more. Whether you realize it or not, as his wife you're in the best position to help him. He needs you."

"He needs to make some changes," Stephanie said, "and he's not willing. He's not even willing to rest for an extended period like the doctor recommended. He's itching to get down to North Carolina and back to work."

"I do wonder when he's planning to leave—"

"Tomorrow," Lindell said, walking into the kitchen in sweat pants and a rumpled shirt. "Three weeks is more than enough extended vacation." He eyed Stephanie's purse on her shoulder as she readied to leave. "I was hoping we could talk this morning. Maybe later today?"

"About?" Stephanie said.

"I'd like you to come with me."

"To Hope Springs? So you can leave me there a couple weeks later? No thanks. And please stop talking like you care. Your actions show something else entirely."

The back door opened, and Cedric came in from walking the dog. "I see the gang's all here."

Cyd looked at him. "Lindell says he's leaving tomorrow, headed to North Carolina."

"When did you decide that?" Cedric unhooked the leash, and Reese padded to her water bowl.

"This morning," Lindell said.

"What about the options we talked about here in St. Louis?"

Cedric asked.

"I don't see why there needs to be a grand shift of my employment and overall life because you all deem it best," Lindell said, opening the fridge.

"How about considering what's best for your wife and your marriage?" Cedric said.

Stephanie waited, wondering what Lindell's response would be.

"You know what," Lindell said, pouring orange juice, "I admit I haven't been the best husband, but you all act as if—" He cried out suddenly, and the jug of juice fell from his hand, splattering the counter, the tile, and the dog. Lindell fell to the floor, clutching his chest, forehead beading with sweat, gasping as if he couldn't breathe.

"Lindell!" Stephanie dropped her purse and thermos on the table and rushed to him.

"Should we call 911?" Cyd said.

Cedric was at his side. "Let's get him to the ER."

From the floor beside Lindell, Stephanie held up a finger to them. "Breathe deeply," she said, lifting Lindell's head. She did it with him. "In . . . out . . ."

Lindell cried out again, writhing in pain. "No, I think this one might really be a heart attack," he said, trying to rise. "I think I do need to get to the ER."

Cedric watched from above. "Steph, we need to—"

"I know it feels like it," Stephanie said, her voice calm. "You'll get through this. Breathe . . . in . . . out. Picture yourself under a clear sky on a sandy beach. Beautiful blue water. Tropical breeze. Not a care in the world."

Lindell grimaced through intermittent groans, sweating profusely.

Stephanie kept talking and rubbing his back as his breathing slowly calmed and the worst of it passed.

"How did you know what to do?" Cyd said.

Stephanie shrugged a little. "Google."

"How are you feeling, Lindell?" Cedric said. "Let's get you to the sofa." He helped his brother to stand.

"Better," Lindell said, moving with Cedric's help.

Stephanie walked slowly beside them. "That was scary, seeing it in real time."

"How did you stay so calm?" Cedric said.

"Something I read said that was key, so . . ."

They got him settled on the sofa, and Cyd brought him some water.

Lindell leaned forward, elbows on thighs, staring downward. "This is out of control," he said. "I never know when it'll hit, and it always seems so real."

"You need to learn ongoing relaxation techniques," Stephanie said. "Everything I read said that's helpful."

Lindell sat back, looking at her. "I appreciate what you did, calming me."

Stephanie nodded. "Well, I need to get to the house."

"You're leaving?" Lindell said. "Right now?"

She looked at him, wanting to walk out the door. Give him a small taste of what she'd felt for so long—that feeling of abandonment. But she couldn't bring herself to do it.

What is this, Lord, a graduation? She lowered herself next to Lindell with a sigh. *One minute I'm getting busted for doing wrong; now You won't even let me do wrong.*

CHAPTER FIFTY-FIVE

Faith pulled into a parking spot in the commuter lot, turned off the engine, and sat. The first day of classes had hit her hard. From the time she awoke this morning, thoughts of her dad had been strong. It had been that way at the start of each year. Her time at the University of Maryland was supposed to be different. Her dad was supposed to be part of it. In high school she'd come visit, bounding up to his office, excited about the day she'd be dropping by as a college student. Well, here she was. And he was gone.

She stared at the students around her who were parking and making their way to class. This was new, this scene. She was used to living in the dorm, walking to class from the other side of campus. But no way would she have stayed in the dorm like this.

She rubbed her stomach through her roomy tee. The baby was twenty weeks, and she was beginning to wonder more and more whether it was a boy or a girl. A pregnancy site said her baby was the size of an artichoke now, and what really got her was that he or she probably had thin eyebrows and hair. Ever since her scare at ten weeks, she'd been praying more for the baby. For excellent health. For God's blessing. To know whether she should be the mom who raised the baby . . . or someone else.

Why was everything so hard and sad and complex?

Lord, one minute I feel strong and ready to run in the midst of all this, and the next I feel alone and overwhelmed. And I'm only halfway through the pregnancy. And if I keep the baby, what then?

She sighed, getting out of the car and bending to lift her backpack from the passenger seat. She threw her keys inside and started walking, and heard her phone. Digging in a front pocket, she pulled it out and stared at it before answering.

"Jesse?" she answered. "Is something wrong?"

"Why do you say that?"

"You never call, so I just figured . . ."

"Last week when I texted, you mentioned being anxious about the start of classes. Thought I'd call to check on you."

"Oh, it's not the kind of anxiousness that would affect the baby," Faith said, walking. "The baby's fine."

"I said I was calling to check on *you.*"

Faith felt a swirl of something and made it go away. "Oh. It's just . . . I'm fine. How's Chicago?"

"Chicago's good. Northwestern's good. I've been trying to learn my way around the city."

"So," Faith said, vacillating about whether to ask, "why didn't you tell me you were leaving? Not that you owed me that."

Jesse was quiet. Then, "My mom sees your mom every week for Bible study, which means she sees you most of the time too . . . which means I get an earful every time she gets back home."

"About what?"

"'Faith is such a sweet girl. You should've never gotten involved with her.'" Jesse's voice took a different tone. "'And don't be sending mixed signals. Stay in your lane and focus on being the father you need to be. Don't mess with her heart.'"

"She said all that?" Faith thought back to when she'd told Stephanie that very thing, that he was sending mixed signals. "Your mom doesn't play."

"I was going to come see you before I left," Jesse said, "but it was purely selfish. I missed you. So I decided to stay in the texting-only lane."

"Except you called just now."

"But this was being self*less*, to see if you were okay. I created an exception."

Faith felt a smile sneaking up. "Hey, did you take Lancelot with you?"

"No way would I leave the knighted beast behind," Jesse said. "I found a pet-friendly complex with a nice park nearby. I'm walking him right now, in fact. He says, 'What up?'"

"Pet him behind the ears for me. He likes that."

"See," Jesse said, "I was about to go there, but I'm staying in my lane." He cleared his throat. "All right, I'm gonna jump off so you can do what you need to do."

Faith slowed to a stop, wanting to linger. Say more. Hear more. "Okay," she said. "And Jesse?"

"Yeah?"

"Thank you."

It took a couple seconds for either of them to hang up.

CHAPTER FIFTY-SIX

September

Dread snaked its way up Jillian's spine. She and Cecil were watching *The Avengers* in the lower level of the house with the kids when the name Dwight Miller popped up on her phone, with a Facebook message that he need-ed to speak with her. She knew who it was—Regina's husband. Jillian eased quietly upstairs to the master bathroom, every awful possibility lodging itself in the pit of her stomach.

What is taking him so long? She'd responded immediately with her number, telling him he could call right away.

This was the last thing Jillian would have expected. She and Cecil's relationship had been steadily improving since Boston. She had dared to hope she'd never hear Regina's name again. Now the woman's husband was about to call?

She paced the bathroom, phone in hand, until finally it vi-brated with an unknown number.

"This is Jillian," she said.

"Jillian, Dwight Miller here," he said. "Thank you for taking my call."

"You said you needed to speak with me?"

"I do," Dwight said, "and forgive me, but this is awkward." He sighed. "Are you at all familiar with my wife, Regina Miller?"

Jillian half rolled her eyes. "Only somewhat."

"Then you must also be somewhat familiar with the situation," he said. "I'll get to the point. She told me today that she's leaving—me, our family—and I won't get into the reasons that pertain to our marriage. But she also says she's in love with another man . . . your husband."

Dwight paused, but Jillian had nothing to say. She stood against the wall, staring at the slightest drip of the faucet.

"Naturally, my desire is to keep my family intact," Dwight said. "I'm reaching out to you to see if you're hearing the same on your end."

"I . . ." Jillian's mouth had gone dry. "I haven't heard that, no. Cecil and I are doing well. I knew of contact between him and Regina, but it's a thing of the past."

"Actually," Dwight said, "I saw where he texted her this week, though she's changed the passcode so I couldn't read it."

"Mom, you're about to miss the good part!" Trevor called from the bedroom.

Jillian muted the phone. "Be right there, Trev!"

"Listen, Dwight," Jillian said, "I'm really sorry about what you're going through, but I can't help you. I really . . . I have to go."

She closed her eyes, her heart and mind a jumble. Regina was leaving her husband? And in love with *her* husband? She could hear her breathing accelerate, along with her heart rate, as she debated what to do. Call Cecil from the movie or wait? Accuse or believe the best? Had she been a fool? She'd had no clue before the women's conference that the two of them had gotten close. If she missed it then, she could have missed it again. Certainly, he'd be slicker about it now.

She moved herself from the wall. On her way to the lower level she spotted Cecil's phone on the kitchen counter. Jillian walked over, eyeing it. She knew the passcode now. He'd given it to her in Boston. Picking it up, she checked for notifications, but the screen was blank. Her thumb input the first letters of his code—

"Mom, it's on pause, we're waiting!"

Jillian pushed the phone back and headed down, returning to her spot next to Cecil on the sofa. He draped his arm around her, and in the darkened room Jillian's eyes fell on her kids—Courtenay, Sophia, David, and Trevor. These evenings were increasingly more rare—all of them interested in watching the same movie— but this is what Jillian cherished. Her family. Together. They'd come so close to a fatal breach. Was the danger present still?

Jillian's arms trembled a little as Dwight's words replayed. Regina had announced her plans today. She and Cecil were back in touch. Was he biding his time, waiting for the right moment to announce his own plans?

"Sweetheart, are you cold?" Cecil said, rubbing her arm.

She shook her head and focused vaguely on the screen, her eyes glazing.

Cecil sat up a little, looking at her. "Jill, what's wrong?" he whispered.

She shook her head again, trying to stifle the emotion.

"Hey, sorry guys," Cecil said. "We need to pause it once more."

"Aw, Dad!" Trevor said.

"I need to talk to your mom."

David looked at them. "Seriously? There's only thirty minutes left. You can't wait?"

"You all go ahead and watch," Cecil said. "We'll catch the end later."

Cecil took Jillian's hand and led her upstairs to their room, closing the door.

"What's going on?" he asked.

Jillian held herself. "I just talked to Dwight Miller."

"What?"

"He contacted me through Facebook and said he needed to talk," Jillian said. "He also said Regina announced today that she's leaving, and that she's in love with you."

Cecil sighed hard. "I can't believe he brought you into this."

"He also said you texted Regina this week. What's going on, Cecil?"

Cecil shook his head. "I don't know. I was shocked. I hadn't heard from her in weeks, and the other day she texted out of the blue. Said she couldn't make it work with her husband." He paused. "She said she wanted to build on what we had. That she realized . . . she had fallen in love with me."

Jillian could hardly stomach hearing him say it. "Why didn't you tell me?"

"Jillian, I had moved on. *We* had moved on. I didn't want to bring her up again, and there was no point. I'm not in love with her." He held her arms. "You're the only one I want."

"Do you know how crazy this is?" Jillian pulled away. "A woman is in love with *my* husband. Because *you* opened the door. You *encouraged* it, with all your calls and texts and *kisses*. Oh, and let's not forget the hotel visit." She looked at him. "Now an entire family is splitting apart."

"I'm not excusing my part in this," Cecil said, "but they were on the verge of splitting long before I came along."

Jillian sighed. "How can we truly move on with her popping up at will? I just want this woman out of our lives."

"One minute," Cecil said, leaving the room.

Jillian stared after him. "Where are you going?"

He was back seconds later with his phone, and held it in front of her.

Jillian saw the texts Regina had sent, that she was leaving, that she loved him. Her eyes moved to Cecil's response.

I'm sorry it's come to this, and I regret my part. But I love my wife. This has to be my last communication.

I really need to talk to you.

There was no text response from Cecil.

Jillian looked at him. "Did you call her?"

"No, I didn't," Cecil said. "And from here out . . ." He went to her contact information and blocked her, then went to Facebook and did the same.

Jillian moved into his arms, sighing into his chest.

Cecil held her. "I'm sorry, babe. You just keep getting hurt."

"I feel bad for that family. It could have easily been us." She thought a moment. "I think we'll pray for them on our prayer call."

Cecil looked at her. "Really?"

"It hadn't occurred to me until just now." Jillian shrugged a little. "Their enemy isn't flesh and blood either."

CHAPTER FIFTY-SEVEN

Treva worked the scrub brush into the stubborn grout stain. Cleaning was her least favorite household chore, but she was tired of seeing the grime in the shower. And she needed something mind-numbing to do on a boring Saturday afternoon. Faith was studying on campus, and Hope and Joy were hanging at Jillian's. Treva would clean every crevice of the house if she had to, which she probably would, to keep her mind off of Lance.

Why is it so hard to clean this stupid thing? Treva sprayed more of what claimed to be a miracle grout stain remover, which, by the looks of it, was doing zilch. She scrubbed more and more then groaned aloud, throwing the brush on the shower seat.

She had a better idea anyway. She brought the vacuum into her bedroom and affixed one of the attachments. She'd tackle the dust and who-knows-what-else under her bed. Then she'd do the hidden spots in the closet, taking out all of her shoes if need be. That would keep her good and busy. She was done wondering what the deal was with Lance anyway. Two weeks past the thirty-day mark and no call? *Fine.* She'd only known him, what, .03% of her life? Easy to erase.

Treva fired up the vacuum and got down on her knees, guiding it under. What did she look like, thinking about some guy like a young schoolgirl. She was a grown woman. With a life. And bills to pay. She flung flip-flops and slippers out. But a little common courtesy would have been nice, letting her know where he stood. *You were right, Treva. It was a whirlwind, and I got my good sense back. Have a nice life.* What did Lance do? Nothing. *Fine.*

Treva pulled out two books and a shirt she'd been looking for. How did that get under there? She coughed from the dust and spider webs, certain she'd feel good by the end of the day. Productive, if nothing else—

Was that her phone?

She flipped off the vacuum and got up, following the sound to the bathroom. She'd left it by the shower door, volume on high, just in case. From where she stood she saw the name, and everything screeched to a halt.

She picked it up, her fingers tingling. "Treva Langston."

"So we're all business now?"

The smile in his voice was infuriating. "It would seem," she said.

"Really? Why is that?"

"Lance, what is this, a game? You acted like you didn't want to do the thirty-day thing, yet when thirty days were up you were nowhere to be found—for two weeks."

"Did you miss me?"

"So *that* was the game? To see how much I'd miss you?"

351

"Actually, no," he said. "I had to take care of some things. It took longer than I expected."

"That's funny," Treva said, "because day to day we're always taking care of lots of things, but somehow we found time to touch base every evening, at least." She paused. "I figured you didn't want to tell me your decision."

"About whether I was sure I wanted you in my life."

Treva's stomach was cramping. "Yes, Lance. That."

"Open your front door."

Treva frowned. "What?"

"Your front door?" Lance said. "Open it."

She threw her phone down and nearly tripped over herself getting down the stairs. And the stupid door knob went wonky at the dumbest times. She turned it left and right until it finally engaged, and pulled it open. And there he was. On her doorstep. With a smile that sent her soaring.

She walked into his arms, and he held her tight.

"I am so mad at you," she said, inhaling his presence. "You could have said *something*. I thought . . . I thought we were through."

"I don't know why you'd think that." Lance took a step back, looking at her. "That was your experiment, not mine. I told you I was sure."

"Still," Treva said, "complete silence, then you just show up?" She eyed his SUV on the front curb. "And what made you drive all the way from St. Louis to Maryland?"

"I wanted to see you."

"That's it?"

"That's not enough?"

His gaze locked with hers, and Treva was sure her heart would explode.

She led him inside, catching a reflection of herself in a picture frame. "Oh, goodness." Her loose bun was frazzled, the cropped sweats and top crumpled. "I look awful."

Lance chuckled, shaking his head. "You couldn't if you tried." He followed her to the kitchen. "This is a beautiful home."

"I can't believe you're here in it."

Treva handed him a cold bottle of water as the doorbell rang. "One sec," she said. "Probably one of Hope's friends looking for her."

She opened the door.

"Heyy," Jillian sang.

Cecil was beside her, and trailing behind were all the kids, save Faith. And Darlene and Russell were walking up the driveway with pans of food.

"Okay, what's going on?" Treva said.

"We can't have Lance coming to town without a welcome meal," Darlene said.

Lance came from the kitchen with a mischievous smile.

"Let me guess," Treva said. "Jillian has been plotting again."

"Nope," her sister said, walking in. "Lance called with plans already made."

"I can't believe you all knew he was coming and nobody told me."

Darlene brushed past her. "It's called a surprise." She leaned toward Lance. "You got her good."

Hope high-fived him, grinning. "She didn't suspect a thing."

Treva narrowed her eyes at the lot of them. "You all have already met Lance?"

"He was at Aunt Jillian's with us," Hope said.

"And at my house before that." Darlene gave a wink. "Where do you think he's staying the night?"

"And he's got his camera." Joy wiggled her shoulders. "Guess who's getting a lesson tomorrow?"

Treva looked past them all to Lance, speechless.

Darlene and crew moved into the kitchen, leaving the two of them in the foyer.

"I don't know what to say," Treva said.

Lance moved closer. "You don't know how many times I wanted to pick up that phone," he said. "But the wait was worth it, to see your face."

She gave him a look. "You could've planned all this for two weeks ago, you know."

"With obligations at church, I couldn't get away for a weekend before now."

Treva looked into his eyes, emotion bubbling to the surface. "I didn't realize how much I . . ."

Her words choked, and Lance brought her near. He spoke

softly into her ear. "That's the longest I'm ever going without hearing your voice."

In casual slacks and a top, Treva watched from the kitchen counter, overcome by the laughter that filled the family room. There was no card game, no board game, nothing on the screen. Just lively fellowship. Stories. Voices interjecting and sharing, even exaggerating, like Darlene's claim that she once had to teach Treva how to boil water. They were probably most taken by Lance's stories of growing up in St. Louis, and the paths he took that led to trouble, driving home for the kids especially the wonders of God's grace.

She set down the dessert plates she'd carried into the kitchen. Darlene never did just enough—she'd made two cakes and a pie along with delicious food they'd be eating for two more days at least. It was a weird dynamic, how she and Russell so easily embraced Lance. But then, their love for Treva was never rooted in the fact that she was Hezekiah's wife. They just *loved*.

"Hey," Lance said, "I wonder if we could all move into the living room. Just a few things I'd like to share, and I thought that space would be nice."

Treva looked over at him, wondering what he was up to now, as everyone got up. They moved through the kitchen, down the hallway, and into the living room with its big picture windows that opened up to the patio outdoors. Lance took Treva by the hand and led her to one of the cushioned chairs, with Faith taking the other. Darlene, Russell, Jillian, and Cecil had the sofa, with the boys plopped down on the floor in front of them. The other girls crammed into the love seat. All of them waited.

Lance sat facing them on the piano bench. He opened his mouth to talk but took a breath instead.

"Okay, I didn't know this would be hard. That snuck up on me." He took another breath. "A question I used to get a lot was how I could marry someone with terminal cancer. What drove me during that time was that I didn't want to live in a box. I didn't want to make a decision just because it 'made sense.' I didn't want to live in fear of what would or wouldn't happen. I wanted to just trust the Lord and *live*, you know?"

Every eye focused on Lance, none more intently than Treva's.

"I wanted to drive out here to Maryland and spend time with all of you," Lance said, "because you're the most important people in Treva's life. I wanted to get to know you a little and hoped you could get to know me. Because otherwise, you'd be saying 'Who is this crazy man proposing to Treva after knowing her for less than four months?'"

Gasps sounded around the room. Treva's hand flew to her mouth.

Lance got up and went to her, kneeling before her chair. "I still have no desire to live my life in a box." He stared into her eyes. "I don't need to wait six months or a year in order for this to make sense. God is *strong* in us, and I have never been more sure of anything in my entire life." He paused, his brown eyes bearing into hers. "Treva, I love you more than you could ever imagine. Will you marry me?"

She nodded through her tears. "Yes."

Lance lifted her to an embrace, and Treva nestled close to him. "I love you more," she said.

Cheers and whistles filled the room as everyone rushed Lance and Treva with hugs.

"Wait a minute, though," Lance said above the noise. His eyes danced. "I do have a ring." He retrieved a velvet box perched near the rear of the piano, took the ring from inside, and placed it on her finger.

Treva gasped, staring at the ring on her hand. Midnight blue sapphire encircled by several diamonds. "Is this . . .? It can't be."

Jillian looked then lifted her hand to examine it closer. "It *has* to be." She looked at Lance. "But how?"

Lance walked to the back patio door and opened it, and Patsy walked in.

"Mother?" Treva's heart rate accelerated. "Have you been out there the whole time?"

"I only got here minutes ago." Patsy winked at Lance. "We timed it well."

Lance smiled. "I still wish you'd been inside with us the entire evening."

"The effect wouldn't have been the same." Patsy hugged

Treva, who had tears streaming down her face.

"I don't understand . . ." Treva said. "What in the world is going on?"

"Lance flew to DC to see me two weeks ago," Patsy said.

Treva felt herself shaking as she looked at them.

"He said he wanted to marry you," Patsy said, "and he hoped to do so with my blessing." She looked at Lance, then back to Treva. "I have many stubborn ways, and I guess God will be dealing with me on those the rest of my life." She sighed. "I was wrong, Treva. I can't begin to tell you all of the things Lance and I discussed. This man ministered to me in a way I've never experienced."

She glanced over at Lance. "He loves you, Treva, and I wanted to give my blessing with more than words." She lifted Treva's hand. "This was your Grandmother Vivian's ring."

"I know." Treva spoke softly, overcome. "I always loved it, but . . ."

"But I said something dreadful to you years ago. I said the ring would go to Jillian because she was my mother's favorite."

Jillian dissolved to tears and moved closer, clutching Treva's hand.

"I still have a lot of learning and growing to do," Patsy said, "but what I can do right now is take another step toward putting that terrible past behind us. I don't say this often, but I know God moved me to do this. This ring is meant for you."

Treva embraced her mother again. "The ring doesn't mean

nearly as much as the words you just spoke. I felt them in my heart. Thank you, Mother. I love you."

"I love you too, Treva," Patsy said. "And I'm so happy for you and Lance."

As everyone mingled, Lance slipped an arm around Treva's waist and walked with her out the front door. The night was turning slightly cool, the sky an inky blue.

"I wanted a few minutes with you to myself," Lance said. "How are you feeling? Are you okay with everything?"

"Am I okay?" Treva looked at him. "Lance, I won't forget this night as long as I live. We're *engaged*. It hasn't sunk in."

He looked at her, their fingers intertwined. "I dare you to call it a mirage."

"No," Treva said, her shoulder brushing his arm. "This is real. The love I feel for you is very real."

Lance paused and brought her close, looking into her eyes before he kissed her. "I love you so much," he whispered.

Treva sighed as they began walking slowly. "I can't believe we only have tomorrow, then we're apart again. That stinks." She looked at him. "How long is this engagement going to be?"

He gave her that smile she loved. "That depends on whether you're willing to think outside the box."

CHAPTER FIFTY-EIGHT

October

Stephanie sat on a scratched and dusty wood floor in the master bedroom on the third floor of the house she was growing to know and love, tuning out the noise of buzz saws and drills below, wrestling with God. Phone in her lap, she had the Bible app opened to Philippians chapter three, to verses Cyd had covered at the conference and which the Lord had reminded her of last night. And all day today.

. . . forgetting what lies behind and reaching forward to what lies ahead, I press on toward the goal for the prize of the upward call of God in Christ Jesus.

Lindell had gone back to Hope Springs three weeks ago, which Stephanie had taken as their final good-bye. Even his sister, Kelli, had tried to talk him into returning to St. Louis, citing the benefits to both him and Stephanie. But Lindell would hear none of it. He was part of a practice in North Carolina. He had obligations, people counting on him. He'd committed to be there when he wasn't in Haiti, and the extended leave had thrown off his schedule with both. Once again he'd asked Stephanie to come with him. Once again she'd refused.

Now God was speaking to her heart, and it was growing heavier by the moment. She couldn't ignore the fact that Lindell was dealing with a medical issue, and had been for who knows how long. She of all people knew what it was like to suffer from seeing a traumatic situation, and he'd seen one after another for years. She'd hated the feeling of Lindell not being there for her when she was in need. Would she, in turn, not be there for him?

But Lord, why am I the one who has to do the right thing? To be understanding and caring. Why can't he be the one for once? I had to suffer through loneliness and sadness for years. Where was he?

Forgetting what lies behind and reaching forward to what lies ahead . . .

Stephanie sighed. God was calling her to take the higher road, to put behind her the hurt her husband had caused, even the heartache of the incident with Sam—and reach forward to what was ahead. *But what is that, Lord? What's ahead? More hurt?*

I press on . . .

Admittedly, she'd done little pressing. She made it on the prayer call each week, but Cyd had been right—she'd made little effort toward Lindell. Once he said he was returning to work, she'd gotten upset and written him off. But where was her faith? Where was the perseverance? The *press?*

Stephanie sighed. *It's not in me to do all that, Lord.*

Christ is in you.

Stephanie sat up straighter. She'd heard Lance mention that verse this past Sunday. She searched her Bible app and found

Colossians 1:27—*Christ in you, the hope of glory.* Well. That was the other thing. It had been hard to keep her eyes fixed on Him.

She stood and glanced around, at the peeling paint on the walls, the dingy bathroom just beyond. If she stayed she'd probably be living here on the third floor, in the owner's quarters. She could easily see how gorgeous the space would be, with three bedrooms, two full baths, plus a living, dining, and kitchen area. It was meant to serve as a retreat away from the guests, and as Mrs. Cartwright had hoped, Stephanie was beginning to see it, to see herself actually running a bed-and-breakfast.

She walked to the window, taking in the view of the Arch. Deep in her heart, she knew. God was telling her to return to Lindell, to reach forward with hope for their marriage. She'd have to leave this project behind. It was good that she'd warned Mrs. Cartwright from the beginning. Now she'd have to find someone else to step in.

She closed her eyes, sighing again.

I can't take a single step without You, Lord. You know that. I can't reach for a single thing unless You help me. And if I'm honest, I'm tired of focusing on the heartache and pain of the past. I'm tired of focusing on myself. Forgive me, Lord. Help me to focus on Jesus, the hope of glory.

Stephanie tucked Chase into bed. She'd read her nephew three storybooks, his way of stalling, but she didn't mind. It had been three days since she'd decided to return to Lindell, and she planned to drive back to Hope Springs this weekend. So she wanted to soak up all the time she could with family. She'd jumped at the chance to babysit while Cyd and Cedric had a date night. She'd miss this little boy.

He rubbed his eyes with two fists. "Good night, Auntie Stephie."

Stephanie kissed his forehead. "Good night, my Chase-man."

Downstairs, she started cleaning the kitchen and heard Reese barking at the front door, her usual greeting the moment Cyd or Cedric's car engine sounded in the driveway.

"Hey, I'm in here," Stephanie called when the door opened and closed.

She waited, hearing nothing, then—

"Hey, Steph."

She turned and stared, her hands in dishwater. "What are you . . . ? How did you get here?"

Lindell walked toward her. "I flew, then took a taxi."

She shut the water off, her heart slipping out of rhythm. "Why?"

"All I can say is God was dealing with me. I kept hearing in my head, 'Love your wife as Christ loved the church,' and 'cherish her.' He came closer. "And as that was happening, I was examining a patient the other day and I was hit with a panic attack."

"What?" Stephanie dried her hands, looking at him. "What happened?"

"Well, the patient was scared out of her mind, thinking I was having a heart attack." He sighed, leaning against the counter. "I couldn't ignore it anymore. I had to make a change." He looked at her. "So I quit. Everything."

Stephanie eyed him. "What does that mean?"

"I'll talk to Cedric about those St. Louis opportunities he's been wanting me to consider." He paused. "And I'm hoping it's not too late for the two of us."

Stephanie was quiet a moment. "God was dealing with me too, so . . . I was coming home."

"I didn't expect to hear that," Lindell said.

"Well. It won't be an easy road."

He nodded vaguely. "I know. I was thinking maybe we need to get help."

Stephanie looked away a moment, thinking how she'd gone that route before, after Sam. Still . . .

"I'm willing to try that," she said.

"I do love you, Stephanie."

She looked at him. "Words are not what I need from you."

He nodded again. "I know."

She turned back to the sink, to washing and rinsing, in awe of God.

CHAPTER FIFTY-NINE

Faith waited anxiously as the technician prepped her for her ultrasound. She was hoping for a clear view, something sure, since everything else about her life had been thrown into upheaval. She'd suspected—hoped even—that her mom and Lance would get engaged, but she hadn't anticipated it happening so quickly. In a blink of an eye, it seemed, the house was on the market and her family was making plans to relocate to St. Louis. Finishing the fall semester at Maryland wouldn't be a problem. But the spring had already been a source of angst, not knowing what she would do about the baby. Now she wasn't even sure where she'd be living.

"We are ready," the technician announced. He smiled at her. "You can make the call now."

Treva stood to get a closer look at the monitor as Faith made the FaceTime call. Jesse's face came into view in seconds.

"It's time?" he said. "I didn't think I'd be this anxious to find out."

"Me either." She held the phone so Jesse could see the monitor.

"Aw, man, is that the baby right there?" he said.

"It sure is," the technician said. "Look, here's a leg." He marked it on the screen.

Faith watched the image swirl on the screen. "Wow, look how the baby is moving."

"Aww, twenty-six weeks," Treva said. "That baby is saying, 'Look at me go.'"

"Here's some hair for you," the technician said, marking that as well.

"This is mind-blowing," Jesse said. "That's our actual baby we're seeing, in real time."

The technician continued to show them the baby from different angles, pronouncing finally, "Looks like you're having a baby girl."

"Oh, wow," Jesse said. "A girl? For real?"

The technician smiled. "For real."

"Look at her," Faith said. "I feel like we're getting a glimpse of God in the midst of creating. She's beautiful."

The technician kept moving around the baby's image, making notations, taking screen shots. When he was done, he told Faith she could get dressed and he left the room. Treva stepped out as well, giving her privacy.

Faith got up from the chair, rubbing her stomach. She looked into the phone. "I'd better go," she said. "I'm glad you got to see."

"I just knew it was a boy," Jesse said. "When he said *girl* I had a moment."

"Why?"

Jesse sighed. "I know it's not logical, but to me, a girl means more responsibility. As in, watching over her like a hawk. Protecting her from . . ." He paused. "Guys like me."

"Not necessarily," Faith said. "You should know I'm seriously considering adoption."

Jesse frowned. "Since when? You haven't mentioned it."

"For a couple months now," Faith said. "I know it's what you wanted, so I guess I didn't feel the need to run it by you."

Jesse looked away for a moment. "I'm really surprised, but . . . okay."

"And what did you mean, more responsibility?" Faith said. "You said you couldn't make any commitments as far as raising the baby."

"I don't know, it just hit me that way when I saw her."

"Well," Faith said, "I have to get dressed."

"Okay."

She put the phone down, her finger ready to end the call. "Faith . . ."

"Yeah?" She looked down at his face on the screen.

"Just noting," Jesse said, "you look cute, with the baby and all."

"Is this self*ish* or self*less*?"

"Oh, no doubt—selfish." Jesse tried not to smile, which made his smile cuter. "I'm way outside my lane, checking you out."

Faith shook her head, hiding her own smile. "Bye, Jesse."

She changed out of the gown, thinking about what she'd seen. A girl. Whether the baby was a girl or boy had no bearing on her ultimate decision. Still, knowing more added to the weight of things.

"Whoa," Faith said softly, feeling a tiny kick. She'd only felt it a couple times before, and each time, it felt like the baby was saying hello. Rubbing her tummy again, she looked down. "Hello there, sweet girl. I'm here. I saw you today." Her own words stirred emotion within. "I love you."

Tears welled suddenly. Probably the hormones. When the baby kicked again, Faith wanted to sit and have a good cry.

CHAPTER SIXTY

November

Jillian had more than fifteen windows open on her laptop, helping Treva search for the perfect, last-minute destination wedding spot. "Does it have to be the first week in December?" She looked across the kitchen, where Treva, Patsy, Darlene, and Faith were busy at work.

"Ideally," Treva said, her head in a bottom kitchen cabinet, sorting things she would give away from things she planned to keep. "We need to be out of the house by the second week. I'd love to be able to move out, head to St. Louis, and leave straightway from there for the wedding." She looked over at her daughter. "If we do it the first week, it works well for Faith."

"Mom, please take me out of the equation," Faith said, cleaning a junk drawer. "You shouldn't be worrying about pregnancy travel restrictions and the timing of final exams. Just plan what's good for you."

Treva set pots and pans from the cabinet onto the counter. "We're not traveling if you can't be there," she said. "We'll find something."

"But Mom, how many islands have you looked at? Every time you get excited about 'the best wedding spot,' you find out it's already booked. You need more options."

"Wait, wait," Jillian said, holding up a finger. "This resort off the coast of Antigua looks amazing. It's secluded, elegant, and you can say your vows on one of three beaches. So there should be at least one spot available, right?" She input the date and groaned. "The resort itself is booked. Let me try this other resort . . ."

"Does it have to be an island?" Patsy had charge of glasses and mugs. "What about a city wedding—London, Paris, Naples?"

"We both really want an island, especially since it's December," Treva said. "Someplace warm and romantic, with endless ocean."

"Flights might be a problem too, you know." Darlene tossed some expired canned goods. "If it's a popular destination, there might not be any seats available. And if there are, they'll be exorbitant."

"I know." Treva sighed. "We knew this was a long shot. We might have to get married at our church here or in St. Louis. The main thing is to be married. Soon. I cannot wait to be with that man."

"Well, now." Patsy looked over, a brow raised. "We do have young ears in the room."

"Really, Grandma?" Faith said.

Jillian chuckled. "To your grandmother, yes, you're still

young."

"I'm glad the house sold so quickly," Darlene said. "You're one step closer to being with the love of your life."

"So," Patsy said, turning toward them, "I'm trying to be as tactful as I can, but I'm not understanding how you can move into the same house—the same bedroom—that Lance shared with his first wife. And didn't she grow up in that house? Why not start fresh?"

"I have to admit, I've wondered about that myself," Darlene said.

"We talked about it," Treva said, pulling out more pans, "and actually, it was Lance who was concerned. But Kendra's father deeded them that house. He even pays the taxes. I couldn't see casting aside a blessing like that. If anything, I was concerned about what *he* would think of my moving in. But he's been so gracious, even welcoming." She looked at them. "Plus, you all do realize I'll be a pastor's wife now. I need to learn fiscal responsibility."

Chortles sounded in the room.

"Uh-huh," Jillian said, "as you plan your destination wedding to some exotic locale. I'll take your clothing budget."

"You wouldn't use it," Treva said.

"I'll buy high-end yoga pants."

"Just so you know," Patsy said, "the wedding will be my gift to you and Lance."

Treva looked at her. "What do you mean?"

"All wedding costs," Patsy said, "including travel and lodging, for guests as well."

"What?" Treva said, with an echo from Jillian and Darlene.

"We didn't bear the cost for your first wedding," Patsy said. "Yet another thing I regret. This is something I want to do."

"Mother," Treva said, "you're taking the reparations thing too far. I'm grown, I've got my own savings—"

"Treva, I'm not taking no for an answer," Patsy said. "In this case I don't mind being stubborn."

"But guests too?" Jillian said. "Do you know how expensive that will be?"

"Treva just told us the guest list, and it's rather small," Patsy said. "Can you let the Lord teach me how to be a blessing?"

Jillian pursed her lips.

"It's incredibly generous, Mother," Treva said. "Thank you."

"I'll say." Darlene tossed a soup can. "I'll have to tell Russell he can go now."

"You two especially," Patsy said. She looked at Darlene. "You took up the slack for me for a lot of years, being a second mom to my daughters, a mom they could look to and learn from and trust. I've been jealous of that at times, even of the relationship you have with our granddaughters. But today, I want to say thank you." Her voice broke a little. "I don't know what's come over me. Treva, this is your fault, with all this marriage and moving and what not."

"That's the truth," Darlene said. "As happy as I am about

it, I'm a little sad we won't have many more times like this in this kitchen." She turned to Patsy. "And Patsy Parker Campbell, I appreciate the kind words, but I see the Lord all over you. I'm reminded of that verse about the Lord restoring the years the locusts have eaten. It's beautiful to behold."

Patsy's eyes widened. "That's what Lance said when we were together. He quoted the very same verse!"

"Look at God," Darlene said. "You cannot tell me God ain't good. *Cannot.*"

"Ooh, this resort in Anguilla is gorgeous," Jillian said, eyeing her screen. "Oh, come on, as soon as I pull up the calendar, peach squares all over the place. Sold out."

"Grandma Patsy," Faith said, "you're doing a lot of looking back and regretting, something I know about too. I've been praying to run my race from where I am today, and I'll start praying the same for you."

Patsy walked over to Faith and hugged her. "You're such an inspiration to me. And I can't tell you how much I love that you'll be staying with me as you finish out the semester."

"I didn't know that," Jillian said, looking up. "Awesome. And then what, Faith? You'll have the baby in St. Louis? What about the doctor you've had here?"

"I love her," Faith said, "but I want Mom with me when I have the baby. And Miss Cyd referred me to her doctor." She paused. "But I don't know what happens after that. It depends on what I decide about the baby."

"Ohh, look," Treva said, phone in hand. "You all have to check this out." She gathered the others around her phone, clicked Play on a video, and Lance and Cedric came on the screen.

"My fiancé told me the women could do a better job of finding the perfect wedding spot." Lance spoke into the camera. "But my man Cedric and I decided to do our own search, and we're thinking you won't be able to beat this one." He smiled. "Sweetheart, get ready. It's beautiful, but if you want to know the truth, I'd marry you *anywhere*, preferably today. I can hardly wait another minute for you to become my wife."

CHAPTER SIXTY-ONE

December

"Oh, Lance, I need a word beyond gorgeous." Treva stepped out of the rental car, doing a full turn as she gawked at the landscape surrounding them. "The photos didn't do it justice. This is *amazingly* stunning."

Lance met her from the driver's side and softly kissed her cheek. "Just like you."

She slipped an arm around his waist, her gaze floating in wonder. "Do you see this?" She'd never been to Oahu, and the northern shore was breathtaking.

"It's crazy," he said, taking it in. "The majestic mountains. The greenery—basically a botanical garden out here. And this is *before* we get to the ocean out back."

"Look at this house, though." Joy had her camera out, taking pictures. "Imagine if we lived here for real."

"Joy, seriously?" Lance said, looking at her. "You're taking pictures of the house when you've got paradise all around? Later today—photography class on capturing and *appreciating* the wonders of creation."

Joy laughed. "Hey, that's cool with me. But have you ever seen a house like this?"

"Never," Lance said with a chuckle. "I'll probably get some pics myself."

"Hope, wake up, we're here." Treva reached into the backseat and gave Hope a shake. "I can't believe she slept through all the scenery from the airport to here."

"Oh, that was amazing," Joy said. She slipped Lance a wry grin. "See. I *was* appreciating."

Treva checked the alarm code as they walked to the front door. The property manager had given detailed instructions, and in short order they were walking inside—and gawking once again.

Treva looked at Lance. "Did I tell you this was a genius idea?"

"You did," he said, "but feel free to share again."

She started moving through the house, not sure where to explore first. When she and Jillian had searched, they'd been thinking resort, with hotel rooms. But Lance's idea was to stay in one house, all of them. With ten bedrooms, six baths, two kitchens, plus living areas, home theater, pickleball and volleyball courts, they would have more than ample space to relax and have fun. The rest of the bunch would arrive tomorrow, including Faith, who was traveling with Patsy and the others from Maryland.

The girls fanned out, claiming they were going to pick out their bedroom.

Treva called after them, "You two get the loft with the twin beds," she said.

"But that faces the front," Joy said. "Not the ocean."

"Hey, look at that," Lance said. "You get to appreciate the mountains."

Treva suddenly knew where she wanted to go first—straight to the back. "Lance, let's go look," she said, extending her hand.

On the lanai, they kicked off their shoes and, since they hadn't yet changed, rolled up their pants a few inches. They walked down a few stairs and along a winding pathway surrounded by more lush gardens, then down to the ocean. They had the beach to themselves.

Treva stared out at the greenish-blue water, relishing the warm breeze on her skin, gripping Lance's hand. "This is overwhelming," she said. "The whole thing. Just standing here with you, knowing you'll be my husband in two days—is *overwhelming*." She looked at him. "How are you feeling? What are you thinking?"

Lance's eyes were on the water. "So many things." He took his time, the sound of sea gulls interrupting the silence. "When I got out of prison and was growing as a Christian, I didn't know if I'd ever get married. I didn't know if a godly woman would want to marry me, given my past." He looked at her. "And I always knew, just being real, that if it hadn't been for Kendra's condition she wouldn't have noticed me, let alone married me. And that was cool. It was all God, the way it happened."

Treva couldn't take her eyes off of him. This was what she

loved about Lance, the way he opened up from the depths of his heart, often when she least expected it.

"Then after Kendra," he said, "I figured the odds of marrying again were slim, for different reasons, and that was okay with me."

"But why would you think that?" Treva asked. "Because I saw for myself—you have a lot of female admirers."

"Admirers?" Lance gave her a look. "I don't know about that, but that kind of stuff doesn't matter to me anyway. I need to connect on a soul level . . . to be able to share from that sacred space and know that I'm receiving that same level of trust and vulnerability." His eyes, always expressive, moved between her and the ocean. "I would hate to feel like I had to hold back what I'm thinking or feeling, hold back how much I'm loving, or hold back on silliness because I'm 'the pastor.' And I hadn't come across anyone I remotely felt I could connect with like that . . . until I met you."

Treva stared into his eyes, her heart swelling.

"I don't have to hold back anything with you," Lance said. "You're way deep down here"—he put her hand to his heart— "and I'm the one who's overwhelmed." He held her hand there. "You want to know what I'm thinking? I'm wondering how God could be so good that He would bless me with a woman who exceeds my wildest dreams."

"But you know how I am, Lance," Treva said. "Stubborn, insecure, irrational at times. I'm so afraid that I'll mess this up.

I'm afraid that I'll—"

He quieted her with a kiss. "Do you love me?"

Treva melted into him. "More than I could ever express."

"Our love is greater than our fears." He kissed her again. "And I don't know if you know, but you're no match for God." The smile appeared. "Even when I can't handle you, He can."

She pushed him a little. "That works both ways, buddy." She wrapped her arms around him again. "And Lance, I've been meaning to tell you . . . Thank you for the way you care for my girls. They love being around you, and it's because you've made them feel special."

"They are special, Treva. I could never take the place of their dad and would never try. He was an incredible man. But I love how Faith, Joy, and Hope are each so unique, and the fact that I get to play a part in their lives is a huge bonus."

"How weird was it, seeing Hope move her things into Kendra's old room?"

"It wasn't weird at all," Lance said. "The night we cleared out that room, I was praying." He paused. "She'll always be in my heart, and I know you get that. But I didn't want there to be a heavy presence that made it hard for me or anybody else to get past."

"It's funny," Treva said. "I was fine until this week. But being there in the guest room a couple nights . . . I suddenly got a little nervous about what it would feel like to move into the bedroom that you and Kendra shared."

"We can sleep in any room in the house," Lance said. "The lower level bedroom works too." He tipped her chin with his finger. "But you need to know that it doesn't matter what room we're in. My one hundred percent focus, mind, body, and soul, will be on you and you alone." He pulled her closer. "Which is actually my problem right now."

They kissed slowly, the waves lapping their ankles, the sun sealing their warmth.

Treva cleared her throat. "We'd better reassess our bedrooms for tonight and tomorrow, make sure they're clear across the house from one another."

"With a moat in between." He kissed her again.

"Okay, really?" a voice said.

"This is so gross," said another.

Treva and Lance turned to see Joy and Hope approaching, arms folded, shaking their heads.

Treva turned back to Lance. "Moat, you say? I think we've got two."

CHAPTER SIXTY-TWO

Stephanie had never felt more alone than here, in what she thought would be paradise. They'd watched the most dazzling sunset she'd ever seen—an orange-bathed sky with brilliant shoots of golden yellow—and now, tiki torches lit, they sat on a gorgeous deck at the foot of the ocean, coupled up. Treva and Lance. Cyd and Cedric. Jillian and Cecil. Each clearly enamored with the other. Snuggling. Stealing kisses. And then there was Stephanie and Lindell.

Their chairs a few inches apart, they might as well have traveled to separate islands. Stephanie had thought this would be the honeymoon she'd never had. And more than that, a chance to turn a corner. It seemed heaven sent, this trip to Hawaii. The entire plane ride she'd felt a growing anticipation. And when they arrived earlier and she saw the house, it was as if she'd been handed a dream. But the day had become nothing short of a letdown.

"I could sit here for hours," Cyd said, "just listening to the waves." She sat against Cedric on one of the love seats. "Everything about this . . . couldn't be more perfect."

"It was eerie to me at first," Jillian said, "being out here by ourselves. We haven't seen a soul on the beach all night. But I think I could get used to this." She leaned into Cecil and kissed him, the two of them in an oversized cushioned chair. "It was so sweet of your mom to fly to DC to take care of the kids so we could come alone."

Stephanie was happy for Jillian and Cecil. She knew how far they'd come, from the women's conference to the times on the weekly prayer calls when Jillian was going out of her mind. Still, it was hard seeing them so freshly head-over-heels while she and Lindell were freshly stuck in the mud.

She stole an irritated glance at her husband who, of all things, was looking up something on his phone. In hindsight, it had been crazy to think this trip could be special. She was the one who'd said they had a long road ahead. They'd had about a month of counseling, which had seen semi-good days and bad days. They were talking more, and staying in the same bedroom. But everything was an effort.

"Hey, Cecil," Lindell said, eyeing his phone, "I knew Cedric was making up the rules as he went. I'm looking at a pickleball site right now."

Stephanie cut her eyes over at him. Nice. *Interrupt everyone else's moment for sports because you can't focus on your own wife.* The guys had been near-obsessed with the game when they discovered it this afternoon.

Cecil sat forward. "Oh, they cheated, huh?"

"Cheated?" Cedric turned to Lance. "Can you believe these

sore losers?"

Lindell looked at his brother. "All those repeat serves you took? Not allowed. And only the team that's serving can win the point. I can keep going." He showed his phone, as if there were a list of infractions. "You do it every time. So competitive you make stuff up."

Cedric looked amused. "First of all, I don't know what site you're on. There's no National Pickleball League, you know. Rules may differ place to place."

"Rematch," Cecil said. "Tomorrow morning."

"Y'all are about to get me in trouble," Lance said, looking at Treva. "It's my wedding day, you know."

"But the wedding is early evening," Cedric said. "Which means he'll play if we can get out there early enough."

Stephanie stood with a sigh as they continued their back-and-forth. She'd have a better time hanging with Faith.

"Gentlemen," Lance said, "you're driving away the women, and after an afternoon of games, this was supposed to be their time. I'm just saying."

Cedric fist-bumped him. "Oh, you'll get big points for that one."

"Steph, don't go yet," Lance said. "I thought it'd be nice to do what we sometimes do in our life groups—affirmations."

Stephanie wasn't sure what he meant. Though she and Lindell had joined Living Hope, they had yet to affiliate with one of those groups.

"I like that," Cedric said. "The men can affirm the wives—and soon-to-be wives—so we can all get points." He put an arm around Cyd.

"How does it work?" Cecil said.

"We just say something that's affirming," Lance said. "Something that'll encourage them."

The idea landed in the pit of Stephanie's stomach.

"I can go first," Cecil said. He waited a few seconds, gathering his thoughts. "I feel like I can say this in front of you all because I know the women are friends. Jillian and I had our roughest year ever, to the point where I wasn't sure we'd make it. And it was because of wrong moves on my part."

Stephanie looked at Jillian, who was focused on her husband.

"And I know there were times Jillian wanted to be through with me," Cecil said, "but I watched her grow more determined. It was almost scary, because she stopped arguing and her tone changed, and I said either she's gone deeper in prayer or she's plotting to kill me."

The group chuckled.

"Jillian's been a strong woman of God for a long time," Cecil said, "and I put that to the test." He turned to her. "I don't deserve you, babe. I thank God for you. If you hadn't been focused on Him, we wouldn't be here together right now." He kissed her.

"So . . . great," Jillian said, wiping an eye, "there are no tissues out here."

"I need some myself," Treva said. "That was beautiful, Cecil."

"I'll go next," Cedric said. "The thing about being married to Cyd is she's always got somebody looking to her, from students on campus to women in ministry. So from the outside, people think Cyd's got everything together, and that's not always the case."

"Uh, bro," Lance said, "this is supposed to be encouraging."

Cedric took Cyd's hand. "What I love about Cyd is, if you truly know her, you know she's not afraid to show you who she is, warts and all. And with me, she's not afraid to talk through, even cry through, her doubts and fears. I love that about my wife." He looked at her. "Sweetheart, you've shown me what it means to be weak, yet strong in the Lord. Thank you for that."

Cyd nestled her head in Cedric's chest as they hugged one another. "I love you, babe," she said.

"Aww, I love that, Cedric," Jillian said. "We should've been recording these."

"Right," Treva said, "and play it back as a reminder when the love isn't flowing quite like tonight." She chuckled a little.

A lull descended, and Stephanie looked at Lance. Surely he wasn't waiting for Lindell.

"Okay, I guess I'm next," Lance said. He turned to Treva, studying her a moment. "I'm trying to think what I can say that I haven't already said." He paused. "I love the way Treva listens. All the months we were apart, talking by phone, she'd remember some small thing I said I was going to do that day, and she'd ask about it. That's why when she tried to act like she wasn't listening—when I told her I was sure about us—I knew she heard me."

"Oh, you think so, huh?" Treva said.

Lance continued. "But more than that, she listens to what's unsaid. She picks up on things that are going on with me, deep down." He kissed her lightly. "Just one of the million things I love about you."

"See, you can't do these kinds of affirmations with engaged folk," Cedric said. "Everything is sweetness and light."

Treva laughed. "Maybe when you're engaged at twenty-two. When you're forty-five, there's a lot of *stuff* mixed in."

"True, true," Cedric said, nodding. "I don't know what I was talking about, since I got married in my forties and I *know* I had some stuff."

Cyd nodded big.

"You didn't have to agree, sweetheart," he said, chuckling.

The rush of the evening waves dominated as they fell into silence. Stephanie wished she had left when she had a mind to. This wasn't Lindell's type of thing to begin with, so there was no way—

"It's no secret that Stephanie and I have had a rough year as well." Lindell looked at no one in particular. "We were separated actually. Not just because Steph left Hope Springs, but because I left her for Haiti, one too many times . . . when she really needed me. It took a medical condition for God to finally get my attention."

Stephanie's gaze drifted toward him.

"One thing I can say about Stephanie is she's passionate," Lindell said. "And I know it's a God-given passion, even though some days she might go off on me." He shrugged as they chuckled lightly then turned to her. "It's that God-given passion that caused you to love Sam so fiercely and grieve her so deeply. It's that passion that moves you to follow Jesus even when your flesh is screaming to go a different way, like when you wanted to walk away from me."

His eyes filled. "I thought you were gone for good, Steph, and I couldn't have blamed you. And I don't know how to get back what we had. I don't feel like myself, but I'm praying to get that back too. I'm just hoping you know how much I love you."

He stood and pulled Stephanie to her feet, embracing her as the months and years rolled into a ball and escaped in one heap of emotion. She heard herself weeping as she held onto him, remembering how it felt to do so, remembering this was the man she still deeply loved.

"Can we pray for Stephanie and Lindell?" Cyd said, walking toward them.

Stephanie felt arms around them on every side. Her head rested on Lindell's shoulder, tears falling as each of them prayed. At the final amen the huddle became a group hug.

Stephanie took a deep breath, wiping her eyes. She caught Treva pulling Lance aside, and a moment later the two of them approached.

"Treva has an idea," Lance said. "We'd like to run it by you two."

CHAPTER SIXTY-THREE

Sand squished through Faith's toes as she walked the beach at sunrise, comfortably warm in maternity shorts and a sleeveless top. She couldn't believe she had this moment to herself. The entire house had been quiet when she'd gotten up and out to capture it. It was so majestic she wanted to freeze it, memorize the colors, the glory, the way God was speaking to her in the midst of it.

She didn't have to worry, about anything—if she could only memorize that in her heart of hearts too. If God could cause the sun to rise each morning, if He could paint it bold colors and make it stunning each time, didn't she think He could care for her and her baby girl?

Is that what You're saying, Lord? Faith meandered closer to the ocean, the water tickling her ankles. *That I shouldn't fear?*

The morning breeze kissed her face as she placed her hands on her stomach. "I love you, sweet girl. Your mommy might be unsure about a lot of things, but I'm sure about that."

"Hey, girlie!" Stephanie called from a few yards back.

Faith turned, smiling. "I'm surprised you're out here so early. Weren't you all up late last night?"

"Till two in the morning." Stephanie shielded her eyes from the sun. "I couldn't sleep, though. Needed to walk and think. And look who I find." She squeezed Faith's shoulders when she caught up to her. "I miss you. I need to be spending all the time with you I can."

"I'll be in St. Louis in a couple weeks," Faith said, "so you won't be rid of me for long. I can't wait to see this house you're excited about."

"I might be a little obsessed," Stephanie said as they started walking. "I've got one of the workers e-mailing pics of the progress while I'm gone. It's come so far from where we started. And now that I know we're staying in St. Louis, I'm over the top with this thing."

Faith looked at her. "So you're actually going to run a bed-and-breakfast? Like, live with strangers, clean up after them . . . ?"

Stephanie laughed. "You're as bad as Cyd. She thinks as soon as somebody rubs me the wrong way, I'll be out of there. Which reminds me . . . I do need to be praying for patience, and a few more things. But things were sealed when Lindell agreed to move in. Kind of a goodwill gesture on his part because he knew I was into it."

"That's a pretty big gesture," Faith said. "He'll be living with strangers too."

Stephanie paused a moment. "Yeah, you're right. I figured we get the benefit of living in a fabulous home for free, but it's still a sacrifice in many respects. I need to show more appreciation for his willingness to do that." She looked over at her. "Enough about me, though. Tell me what's new with you."

Faith stared downward at the footprints she was making in the sand. "Well. I think I just decided to keep the baby."

Stephanie's eyes widened. "Wow, just now?" She hugged her. "That's big. How're you feeling?"

"Scared. I know I'm not in the best position to raise her, and I can't count on Jesse to be there. So it's just me and baby. And God."

"Excuse me?" Stephanie said. "You won't be on an island, sister. Baby Girl's gonna have an Auntie Stephie to spoil her. And I bet I'll have to get in line."

Faith felt tears in her eyes. "It's coming up so soon, and there's so much to think about. This'll mean no school next semester, and who knows when—ooh, she's kicking." Faith took Stephanie's hand and placed it on her stomach.

"Aww, I see you, Baby Girl," Stephanie said, speaking softly, "getting your morning workout on." She looked at Faith. "There's so much grace on you, girl."

"Why do you say that?"

"I don't know *what* I would've done if I'd gotten pregnant at nineteen. But I've seen you grow so much during this pregnancy."

Faith eyed her. "I'm seeing 'so much grace' on you too, and growth in the same amount of time."

"Okay, we're not doing tit-for-tat compliments."

"Seriously," Faith said. "Remember the first day we got together? You were talking about how your life is a mess?"

"Still is."

"Not like it was. Remember that entire bottle of wine? Vomiting in the bathroom stall?"

"Oh, goodness, don't remind me." Stephanie paused. "But wow, I just realized. I haven't had a drink in months."

"See? So much grace." Faith started walking, looking over at her. "I see you, getting your hot pursuit on."

"Haha," Stephanie said, laughing for real. "Girl, I *might* not be bringing up the rear anymore, but you passed me up!"

"Ha." Faith held her tummy. "Walking this slow?"

Stephanie linked arms with her. "Exactly. You and Baby Girl."

CHAPTER SIXTY-FOUR

J illian wrapped the silvery-gray sheer fabric around the chair and tried to make the pretty ruffle in the back. "It's not working," she said, looking over at Stephanie. "This looks nothing like yours."

"Just gather the fabric together like this in the back," Stephanie said, "and ruffle it like this." She undid hers and within seconds had it looking beautiful again.

"Um, basically," Jillian said, "you're going to have to do all the chairs. I'll stick to something I can do, like tossing petals on the ground."

Stephanie chuckled, working the fabric onto another chair. "We're gonna find much more than that for you to do. We're running out of time."

"What was Cyd's last ETA?"

"She said they'd be here in a little over an hour, which was fifteen minutes ago," Stephanie said. "But I need to tell her to find someplace else to stop."

"Where else can they go?" Jillian said. "They did a massage and nails at the spa. Got a last-minute appointment at the hair salon, and went for something to eat."

"I don't care if they go to Pearl Harbor," Stephanie said. "We need another two hours, at least." She picked up her phone and texted.

"Are we forgetting Mom made a big deal of wanting everything simple?" Faith smoothed a silvery cloth across the table.

"Your mom only said that because she knew there wasn't time for any big wedding design scheme." Jillian helped her situate the table covering. "But she didn't know about Stephanie."

"It's still simple," Stephanie said. "Relatively. I'm just glad we found vendors who could help on such short notice. Who knew we could find a place on the island that rented designer table linens and chair covers?"

"And an arch for the ceremony," Jillian said.

"Ohh," Stephanie said. "My mind is going in so many directions, I forgot I still need to decorate the arch. But I'm excited about the idea I have for it."

"Oh, that's striking," Patsy said, coming out to the lanai. "Elegantly done, with just the right amount of ruffle. I've never seen that design on a wedding chair."

Jillian looked at Stephanie. "That's high praise, coming from my mother. She's very, shall we say, particular."

Stephanie looked at Patsy. "I thought it would be a nice touch to dress up the table and chairs, since this is where we'll be eating after the ceremony. But you don't have to do much when you've got this as your canvas." She gestured at the ocean and tropical gardens beyond. "I just hope you all are sure about the color scheme."

"That was Momma's call," Jillian said.

"And it was a tough call, to be sure," Patsy said. "Who knows, really, what wedding colors she might have chosen? But we tend to favor similar things, and this has been my color of late."

Faith frowned. "Gray?"

"Absolutely," Patsy said. "But for the wedding, we also incorporated silver and white elements. And Stephanie, that touch of icy blue with the candles pops."

"When we saw those at the farmers market yesterday, I knew we had to snap them up." Stephanie finished another ruffle, looking at her. "And thank you again for indulging my decorating whims."

"Anybody seen my husband?" Darlene said, joining them. "This house is so big I don't know where to start looking. I need him to run to the grocery store."

"Pickleball court." Faith pointed down and around the bend. "Uncle Cecil said they needed a ref to make sure there was no cheating."

"They've been out there for two hours," Jillian said. "I think they could go another two."

"Then they'll be going without a ref," Darlene said. "I made a list of things I need pronto, and you all have your hands full."

"I can drive Grandma," Joy said, dashing out. "I already know how, and it's less than three miles away."

Darlene barely gave her a glance. "Girl, if you don't sit your fourteen-year-old self down somewhere."

"But I'm almost fifteen," Joy said, "which means soon I'll—" She turned toward the raucous voices floating up toward them.

"Oh, now *we're* the ones who cheated," Lindell was saying. "*With* a ref? You can't handle losing, pure and simple."

"I know for a fact," Cedric said, "that you made those last two serves with your arm above your waist, which means they shouldn't have counted."

Stephanie looked at Jillian. "Sounds like our husbands finally got the best of Cedric and Lance."

The men filed up the stairs leading to the lanai, hot and sweaty.

"That game is addicting," Cedric said, grabbing water from the cooler.

"Where's Russell?" Darlene said, looking.

"He's still down there," Lindell said, "playing with Hope."

Darlene put her hands to her hips. "You've got to be kidding me." She headed down.

Cedric took a swig of water. "We need another rematch."

"No rematches." Lance got a bottle himself. "I'll be on my honeymoon starting tonight. All Treva, all the time."

"Aw, come on, man," Cedric said, "we're here four more days. You can't carve out time for one game?"

"Won't even be here," Lance said.

"What?" several voices chimed at once.

"Where are you two going?" Jillian said.

"We're flying to another island in the morning," Lance said. "I'll let Treva tell you when she finds out. It's my wedding gift to her."

"Hope and I are going too, right?" Joy said. "You can't just leave us."

"It would be unthinkable to leave you . . ." Lance said. "If you weren't surrounded by all these able adults. We'll be back in time to scoop you up for the plane ride back to St. Louis."

Joy shook her head. "That's cold."

Stephanie fanned the air. "Y'all are messing up the wedding vibe we're trying to create here with all that funk. Isn't it time to move to the showers?"

"Almost," Lindell said, before he kissed her.

The men moved into the house, and Jillian looked at Stephanie.

"Affection," Jillian said.

Stephanie's brow rose. "Wow, you're right."

"What?" Faith said.

"On our prayer call last time," Stephanie said, "we prayed specifically for renewed affection in marriages."

"Hmm," Jillian said. "This house is big enough. Maybe the rest of us need to stake out some territory and start honeymooning."

"If you had said that yesterday," Stephanie said, "I would've said there was no way. Now . . . hmm . . ."

Faith piped up. "So much grace."

CHAPTER SIXTY-FIVE

Treva walked a path of rose petals toward an archway draped in sheer white and gray, where the love of her life stood, looking irresistible in white linen. With every step the moment was more breathtaking. The backdrop of an immense ocean. The presence of those she loved most. The gorgeous early evening sky. The lush beauty of the landscape. But mostly—Lance. She couldn't take her eyes off of him. Her heart soared, knowing that in minutes he would be hers and she would be his.

I'm overwhelmed still, Lord. How did this happen? Thank You for surprising me with a love that has left me breathless.

In footless sandals adorned with embroidered crystals, Treva's feet hugged white petals and warm grass as she made her way to Lance. Beside him was Pastor Lyles, making the day extra special. He'd been Lance's pastor and mentor for more than a decade. And he'd been Treva's favorite Bible teacher, his studies changing her from the core. She'd seen him on DVD for years. Now here he was, personally marrying the two of them.

With the intimate number of guests, they simply stood before the archway, on either side of the petaled path. All of it had blown her away—the arch, the flowers, the countless other beautiful touches. Stephanie had outdone herself, and her mother had been spot-on with the colors.

Treva glanced at the photographer and videographer as they scurried to capture her from a different position. They'd come highly recommended by the property manager of the house, and Treva had been glad they were available, though Lance had balked a little about the video guy. His first wedding had been all over the media, with more than a million YouTube views. This ceremony he wanted private. But in Treva's mind there was no way it wouldn't be recorded, for their playback eyes only.

Lance extended his hand, taking hers, pulling her close. His lips grazed her ear. "You've got me going out of my mind up here. You look incredible."

Treva's arms tingled as she held a bouquet of simple white roses. She'd hoped he would like the dress, a sleeveless white silk sheath with a halter neckline and a hemline that hit her at the knee. She smiled, knowing he hadn't yet seen the dip in the back.

"You're not supposed to be talking," she whispered.

"It's my wedding," Lance said. "I can do what I want."

Treva suppressed a chuckle as she faced Pastor Lyles.

The pastor smiled at them, then looked at the guests. "Lance and Treva wanted this to be an informal gathering," he said, "celebrating their union in Christ, yet in a free-flowing way, since we're all family here." The pastor looked at the two of them. "So it's in that spirit that I want to say something to the two of you.

"Lance, you first. You know I couldn't love you more if you were my own son. I conducted your first wedding. I was with you through the love and the sacrifices you made and the loss. I was with you when you wondered if you could love again." He smiled. "And I was wholeheartedly with you when you asked me to pray, because you believed God had given you a love in Treva that was unlike anything you'd ever experienced."

Treva looked at Lance, determined to keep it together.

"Before everyone here, Lance," Pastor Lyles said, "I want to say that this"—he extended his hands—"being here, marrying you two, is an answer to my prayers. Seeing you more joyful than I've ever seen you, and—you were right—experiencing love in a completely different and amazing way. I thank God I can be here to witness it. You've been given a gift. Steward it well."

Lance nodded as his grip tightened on Treva's hand. When he looked at her, his eyes had filled with water.

"And to you, Treva," Pastor Lyles said. "We only met a week ago, but I'd heard so much about you, I felt I already knew you—and I know you felt the same about me." His smile was warm.

"Oh, absolutely," she said softly.

"Treva, from what I know from Lance and from what you shared personally, you've had your share of heartache and loss as well. Yet I see in you such strength in Christ. Such resiliency, I think more than you realize."

Lance rubbed the back of her hand, as if agreeing.

"You two met at the Living Word conference, which I love, by the way." His eyes smiled. "And the theme had to do with running your race to win. Treva, it's so clear to me that you're already running. Now you're becoming one with Lance, and together you will run." He paused. "I want to say to you today—don't stop. You'll leave this pretty scenery, and life will get real. There will be days when Lance disappoints you and marriage gets hard. But remember the God-given strength that's in you, that's in you both. Remember the love that binds you is no ordinary love. It's supernatural. That love is your fuel."

Treva and Lance exchanged a glance, focusing again on Pastor Lyles.

"Remember," he said, "that God gives all things richly to enjoy. I want you to *enjoy* one another. Enjoy the love you've been given in this new season." He smiled at them. "But something tells me that won't be hard."

Lance smiled back at him. "Not at all, sir."

"You think I should get to the vows and make this official?" Pastor Lyles said.

Lance nodded big. "Because I'm about to kiss her, whether it's official or not."

Treva hid her face. "You did not just say that."

"What?" Lance looked at her. "He said *enjoy*."

"Treva Alexander. Treva Alexander . . ." Treva tried the sound of it as she took a late night stroll on the white sands of Ka'anapali Beach with her husband. "I have to get used to that."

"After three days, I'm thinking you should be plenty used to it." Lance hugged her waist. "I'm kidding. I know it's an adjustment." He looked at her. "I imagine there's a lot you have to get used to. You were married to Hezekiah for a long time. Now here's this guy who squeezes his toothpaste differently and sleeps on the wrong side of the bed."

"I was praying about all of that," Treva said. "I didn't want to be comparing you to Hezekiah or comparing any aspect of our relationship to what he and I had." She was silent for a bit, realizing how God had answered those prayers. "What you said about mind, body, and soul . . . That's real for me. I don't know what it is, but I get lost in you."

Lance pulled her to a stop and kissed her, the nighttime roar of the waves engulfing them. It was true. He made every one of her senses come alive.

"I say we stay on Maui, lost in one another." His lips touched hers still. "Let's miss our flight tomorrow."

Treva sighed. "I was trying to forget we had a flight in the morning. The time we've had has been amazing."

They walked, fingers entwined.

"Back to Oahu," Lance said.

"They haven't missed us, that's for sure."

"No kidding. Cedric said the girls and the grandparents took over our pickleball court. Who would have thought! And then you've got all the fellow honeymooners."

"Stephanie and Lindell, especially," Treva said, "I think this week was meant for them as much as us."

"It was awesome being able to pray with them the way we did, and then see them renew their vows." He squeezed her hand. "You were pretty awesome too, by the way. It was your day, but you stepped aside and let them have their moment."

"I thought it was awesome that they wanted to do it," Treva said, "and that Pastor Lyles got to do their vows *again*."

"Yeah, I think 'for better or for worse' had a little more meaning this time around."

Treva looked at him. "I don't even want to think about what our 'for worse' could be."

"We won't think about it," Lance said. He stared into her eyes. "I love what Pastor Lyles said—whatever happens, in Christ we've got what we need to run."

Treva's lips touched his. "Even if we stumble."

"Especially if we stumble." Lance deepened the kiss for a moment then paused. "I'll tell you what, though. I don't know how 'for better' could get any better than this. I love you, Treva Alexander."

She held onto him, everything else fading. "I love being Treva Alexander."

CHAPTER SIXTY-SIX

January

The wind kicked up a little and Faith pulled her coat around her belly, determined to keep walking. With the temperature in the thirties, it wasn't too bad for January anyway. And she wanted to do what she could to speed this delivery along. At thirty-nine weeks, she'd been having contractions for two days. She'd taken two trips to the doctor already, and each time was disappointed to be sent back home. Her contractions needed to be closer apart, the doctor said. Meanwhile, she could be proactive and walk.

She turned down a street she seldom took, eager for detours. She'd grown to know the neighborhood well in the almost month she'd been here. Walking had been beneficial, not only in advancing labor but in keeping her prayerful. The closer she'd gotten to her due date, the more anxious she became. She was about to have a real little person to care for, someone who depended on her. And she didn't even have a job. But somehow when she prayer-walked, she felt a peace. She had to believe God would guide her.

She took the long way back to the house, finally turning down their street. Maybe she'd do the stairs a few times.

She squinted in the fading light of early evening. Whose car was that in their driveway? Moving closer, her heart hammered. Maryland tags. Jesse's car.

The moment she stepped inside she heard his voice—and Lancelot came from the kitchen to greet her.

Faith beamed. "Lancelot, hey boy." She leaned over as best she could to pet him. "It's so good to see you." She looked up as Jesse approached. "What are you doing here?"

"How does the dog get a more cheerful greeting than I do?" Jesse helped her with her coat. "Look at you. Both of you." He hugged her, lingering a moment. "It's been way too long."

They walked to the kitchen, where her mom and Lance were preparing dinner.

Treva looked back at her. "Surprised?" she said.

"You knew he was coming?"

"Only a few hours ago," Treva said.

"You said you were in labor," Jesse said, "and I was texting for updates. Then I said, this is ridiculous. I could just jump in the car and drive down there." He looked at the dog. "But I had to call Lance to make sure it was okay to bring my buddy."

"How could I say no, once you told me his name?" Lance smiled. "It's good to see you again, Jesse."

Jesse looked at Faith. "Can we talk?"

They moved to the living room, Jesse helping her along,

Lancelot at their heels.

"Jesse, I can walk," Faith said. "I've been doing it all this time alone just fine." She paused. "I shouldn't have said it like that. Sorry." She lowered herself to the sofa.

"No, I'm the one who's sorry." Jesse joined her. "I was proud of myself for getting updates every week, *by text*, and here you are, literally carrying all the weight."

"There was nothing else you could've—*ahh*." Faith doubled over as a contraction hit, and began quick breaths in and out.

Jesse jumped up. "What's happening? Is the baby coming?" He moved toward the kitchen. "Mrs. Alexander?"

Treva came in and started rubbing Faith's back. "It's early labor, Jesse. The contractions are irregular, but they've been coming. We're hoping Baby Girl will kick into overdrive soon."

"It might be early labor, but it still *hurts*," Faith said, gripping her mother's hand. "I've never felt pain like this in my *life*."

Jesse stood over them. "What can I do?"

"Here, take my place," Treva said. "Rubbing her back helps."

Jesse sat next to her, leaning toward her stomach. "Little lady, we need you to stop playing around and come on out. I drove all this way to see you." He moved both hands around Faith's back, massaging.

"That feels good." Faith closed her eyes, focusing on breathing as the contraction died down.

"So this is what it's been like?" Jesse shook his head. "It's something, seeing it in person."

"And it only gets worse," Faith said. "So, fun." She glanced down and saw Lancelot at her feet, looking up at her. "You feel my pain, don't you, boy?"

Jesse massaged her back still. "I was just thinking," he said, "how this time last year I was texting you, asking if you wanted to meet for lunch."

"Ugh, don't remind me," Faith said. "If I'd known where I'd be a year later . . ."

He paused, looking at her. "Was it all bad?"

Faith shrugged lightly. "Not much good."

Jesse grew quiet, massaging again.

"So did you and Brandy get back together?" She didn't really want to know the answer, but she'd been curious for months.

"We see each other from time to time," Jesse said, "but nothing like it was." He looked at her. "What about you? Are you seeing anyone?"

Faith cut her eyes over at him. "Right. In my condition."

"Hey, you're still fine."

"Whatever."

Jesse sat forward, looking at her. "What's the update on the adoption process? You haven't said anything lately, but wouldn't you have chosen a family by now? Just wondering who they are, what they're about. And don't I have to sign something?"

Faith hesitated. She hadn't told him yet of her decision to keep the baby, afraid what he would say. "I haven't chosen a family," she said. "There's still time." She swallowed, her mouth suddenly parched. "Can you do me a favor and get me some ice?"

"Absolutely," he said, hopping up.

A moment later, Faith stood. "Ohh! I think my water broke!'

Faith had been in active labor for more than seven hours, and it looked like Baby Girl was finally ready to make an appearance.

"I can see her," the doctor said, standing before her. "We need another good push."

"Almost there," Treva said. "You're doing an awesome job, sweetheart."

Jesse gripped her hand on the other side. "Let's do it. One-two-three-*push!*" He leaned forward with her as she pushed with all her might, groaning loudly. "There you go! I'm so proud of you."

Faith was surprised at what a help Jesse had been, by her side throughout the labor. When he asked if he could be there for the delivery, she had no problem acquiescing.

"Another push," the doctor said. "Gently this time. Here comes her head."

"Oh, wow," Faith said.

"I'm with you," Jesse said. "We're about to see her. One-two-three . . ."

Faith pushed, and through a blur of activity she heard the sound of a newborn's cries. "Is that her?" Tears came to her eyes.

"Is that my baby?"

"Oh, thank you, Jesus," Treva said.

They put the baby in Faith's arms, and she surveyed every inch of her through tears. Every finger. Every toe. Her precious head full of hair. Her little nose.

"Look at her." Jesse stared in wonder. "Look at those eyes."

Treva looked across the bed at him. "They're like yours."

Faith brought the baby close to her chest, heartbeat against heartbeat, cradling her as Jesse leaned in, holding one of her tiny fingers.

"She's got a tight little grip," Jesse said. With his other hand he wiped Faith's tears. "You okay?"

Faith nodded. "I'm just thinking how I said not much good came from us. But this little girl . . ." Faith kissed her forehead. "She's perfect."

***

"I'm surprised you're still here." Faith yawned, looking across her hospital room, where Jesse held the baby in a rocking chair. "How long was I sleep?"

"About two hours," he said. "You needed it. You worked hard to bring her into the world."

"Where is everybody?"

"Your mom and Lance went to grab a bite with Stephanie and Cyd," Jesse said.

Faith half smiled to herself, remembering the first time Stephanie and Jesse had met. They'd gotten to know one another a little today, under different circumstances. She pushed up in the bed to see better. "How is she?"

"She's sleeping." Jesse studied the baby a moment then looked at Faith. "My mom said to tell you she was praying the entire time, getting updates from your mom. I texted her a slew of pics." He frowned at her. "And why are you surprised I'm still here?"

"I don't know," Faith said. "I just figured you'd be needing to get back."

"Not at all." Jesse stared at the baby. "Okay, look, I've been sitting here the entire time you were sleeping, trying to figure out how to say this. I know I'm wrong, maybe I'm tripping because I've been up all night—"

"Jesse, what is it?"

He walked with the baby, to the chair beside Faith's bed. "I think we should keep her."

Faith sat up a little, stunned. "We?" she said. "As in, me? Because I've heard you say a million times you're not ready to—"

"I know what I said." Jesse spoke softly. "Faith, I can't say I'm ready even now. All I can tell you is I'm in love with this little girl. I mean, look at her. She's *part* of me. That blows me away." He paused. "I know I'm not nearby. Everything would fall on you, once again. But I found out how easy it is to jump in my car and drive down here from Chicago. And I need to figure out how to help support her." He looked down at the baby. "I know this is a lot to dump on you. What do you think?"

Faith looked at him. "I um . . . had already decided to keep her. But I thought you'd be upset, so I hadn't said anything yet."

Jesse was quiet, and when he finally looked at her, she was surprised to see tears in his eyes. "That's really sad," he said, "that you thought I'd be upset about keeping this little girl. But I gave you every reason to think that, because of how selfish I've been." He brought the baby closer. "If it were up to me, she wouldn't even be here." He paused, his head buried in his daughter. "I'm sorry, Faith, about so many things."

Faith felt the weight of his emotion. "It's a new year, and you're holding a new life. A new beginning."

Jesse nodded, looking into the baby's eyes. "I feel that already. I don't know what it is with this girl. While you were asleep all I could do while I was holding her was to pray."

CHAPTER SIXTY-SEVEN

May

"Let me refresh that," Stephanie said, lifting the crystal water pitcher.

Lindell rose from the dining room table. "I'll do that, Steph. You've been hosting and moving about all day."

"And beautifully at that," Cyd said. "The day couldn't have been more of a success."

"Here, here!" Mrs. Cartwright lifted her water glass. "To Stephanie, bed-and-breakfast host extraordinaire!"

Glasses were lifted around the table, and cheers of agreement resounded.

Her dad smiled at her. "We couldn't be more proud of you," Bruce said. "All we said was 'Get a job, Steph.' We didn't know God would show you your passion."

"It's superb," her mother said, pinching off a piece of one of the breakfast pastries leftover from the open house. "Every room in this house. I'm so excited for you."

"I had a dream this morning," Stephanie said, "where I woke up for the grand opening and discovered we'd overlooked an entire room that hadn't been redone. My heart was racing."

"A room overlooked?" Mrs. Cartwright said. "You didn't overlook a single detail. Like this beautiful hand-lettered coaster—*He who promised is faithful.*"

"The entire promises theme is captivating," Treva said. "How did you all come up with that?"

"It was Stephanie's idea," Mrs. Cartwright said.

"Well, let's back up," Stephanie said. "It was Mrs. Cartwright's vision from the beginning to have a bed-and-breakfast where people would experience the aroma of Jesus, in the way they were cared for and looked after during their stay." She looked into their faces. "And every bed-and-breakfast promises *something*—a stay like no other, delicious food, restful weekend, superior service. So we started thinking about what we were promising, and it took off from there." She shrugged a little. "We landed on Promises Bed-and-Breakfast."

"You see how many people came out today," Lance said. "The name makes you wonder what it's about."

"Yes!" Mrs. Cartwright said. "I see it as inviting, maybe even mysterious. I've been praying for the Lord to send people who need a special touch of His love and care."

"Oh, I love that," Treva said. "And let's not forget, with the gorgeous way these rooms are decorated? Simply romantic too." She smiled at her husband. "I was ready to book a room for us, babe."

"Hey, they're open tonight, right?" Lance smiled back at her.

"Let's go."

Faith walked in, holding the baby. "Rocked her to sleep after she ate, then she woke back up." She smiled down at her. "She's just too excited about the grand opening."

Stephanie got up, arms extended. "She missed her Aunt Stephie. Come here, pumpkin. I haven't had enough time with you today."

Faith handed her to Stephanie. "Between you and mom, this girl is already super spoiled."

"What? I've done no such thing, have I?" Stephanie said, looking into the baby's eyes.

"I'll admit to spoiling her," Treva said. "And you haven't seen anything yet. Wait till Faith starts school in the fall. Zoe and I will be hanging strong."

"Where will you be attending, Faith?" Mrs. Cartwright asked.

"Wash U," Faith said. "Miss Cyd helped me with the transfer from Maryland."

"Oh, wonderful," Mrs. Cartwright said. "Sounds like you have a great support network here."

Faith nodded. "It's amazing, really."

"I was thinking about setting aside a room for Zoe on the third floor," Stephanie said, rocking her in her arms, "for those times when she wants to do a sleepover. She already told me she's looking forward to that."

"Yeah," Lindell said, "and maybe that'll be next to the room we're setting aside for our own baby."

"What?" Cyd said. "Is this an announcement?"

"Don't get excited," Stephanie said. "At least not yet." She smiled a little. "But we're hoping."

"Especially now that my situation is more stable," Lindell said. "I haven't had a panic attack in months, and I'm loving my new job. I resisted the administrative side of medicine, but it was the right move, at least for now." He looked at Cedric. "You were there for me even when I didn't want you to be. I appreciate that."

"You're my brother," Cedric said. "That's what we do."

The stately chime of the doorbell sounded, startling Stephanie. "Oh, no," she said. "What if it's a guest? We're officially open, but am I really ready? We still have things to put in place, like our registration—"

The chime sounded again.

"Goodness, girl," Cyd said. "It's probably a neighbor wanting to see. I'll get it."

Cyd returned with a young woman clad in denim jeans, a plain navy blue top, and sneakers, her hair tucked under a ball cap.

"She wants to apply for a job," Cyd said.

"Really?" Stephanie transferred Zoe to Faith and ushered the young woman into the kitchen. She extended her hand. "Hi, my name is Stephanie London. I'm the caretaker of Promises Bed-and-Breakfast."

"Cinda," the young woman said, lightly shaking her hand.

"And you're looking for a job here?"

"I heard you just opened, and you probably have all the help you need." Cinda was plain-faced, her eyes weary. "But it's a big house, and if you need help cleaning it . . ."

"Are you with a cleaning service?"

"No," Cinda said. "It's just me."

Stephanie eyed her. She'd never conducted an interview in her life and had no idea what to ask or look for. But the young woman was right—this was a big house and she needed help cleaning it. She and Mrs. Cartwright had just talked today about hiring a service. And this woman shows up?

"Do you have references?" Stephanie asked.

"How would I have references?"

Stephanie gave her a look. "From the owners of the houses you've cleaned."

"Oh," Cinda said. "No. I mainly just cleaned my own house. And the house where I live now. But I clean well. Everybody says so."

Stephanie looked less than convinced. "Everybody."

Cinda shrugged. "I'm just saying."

"Okay, first of all," Stephanie said, "you should've called and made an appointment instead of just showing up. At night. Who does that?" Her eyes swept the young woman from head to toe. "And you show up looking like you don't care one whit about your appearance and acting like you don't care too much whether you get the job. So—"

"No, I do care," Cinda said. "I need this job. Desperately.

That's why I showed up like this." Her face grew animated. "How about this? I'll clean this house for one week. If you like it, you pay me. If you don't, you got a week of the best cleaning job you'll ever see, for free."

"You really want my expectations that high?"

"Yes, ma'am."

Stephanie paused, looking at her. "Deal. But we're not doing the ma'am thing. Just call me Stephanie. We need to talk about all the details, though. Can you be here tomorrow morning at nine?"

"I can be here at eight or eight thirty, if you want," Cinda said.

"Girl, nine is already pushing it for me."

"Yes, ma'am. I mean . . . nine it is." Cinda smiled. "Thank you."

Stephanie walked her to the door, a dozen thoughts in her mind. She'd overseen renovations of the house, worked on making it a bed-and-breakfast, and hosted a grand opening. But this—hiring her first employee—seemed to make it official.

Promises Bed-and-Breakfast was open for business.

CHAPTER SIXTY-EIGHT

"Y ou two should have planned for a longer stay." Treva twisted to see into the backseat. "I can't believe you're leaving tomorrow."

"I know," Jillian said. "But at least we're not leaving till evening. I'm glad we get to be here for baby Zoe's dedication."

"We planned it that way," Treva said, "knowing you were coming for Tommy and Allison's wedding." She covered Lance's hand on the center console. "One of many perks of knowing the pastor."

"I'm glad we came for the wedding," Cecil said. "The ceremony was beautiful, we had a good time, and I got to have a nice convo with Tommy."

"I didn't know that," Jillian said. "What did you say?"

"Basically, I told him I had much respect," Cecil said. "He was a bigger man than I was."

"Tommy's a great brother," Lance said, pulling into the garage. "He's been a blessing to have at Living Hope."

"And crazy as always," Jillian said. "I died when he had the deejay play New Edition and took the mic to sing."

They all laughed as they piled out of the car, Treva leading the way into the entrance off the kitchen. The door opened to the sound of a baby wailing.

"What in the world?" Treva said. "Zoe never cries like that."

Joy was pacing the kitchen with her, a bottle at her lips. "She won't drink it," Joy said, "and I thought Faith would be back by now to nurse her."

"Where is Faith?" Treva said. "I thought Jesse was driving down today for the dedication."

"They went to the movies. And I said I'd babysit." Joy tried the bottle again, and Zoe batted it out of the way, wailing louder.

Treva smiled to herself. Jesse and Faith had been spending more time together, and Treva loved that it was different from before.

"Do you all hear that music?" Lance stood still, trying to listen.

"I don't know how you can hear anything with Zoe crying like that." Treva lifted the baby from Joy's arms, rescuing them both. "Come to Grandma, you little sweetie."

"I hear it," Jillian said. "Coming from the basement."

"Oh," Joy said. "That's Hope. A few of her friends stopped by."

Cecil opened the basement door and the music boomed louder.

"What is Hope thinking?" Treva said, trying the bottle herself to no avail. "Surely the neighbors can hear that. Shoot, maybe that's why Zoe is wailing like this."

"I'll tell them to turn it down," Cecil said, heading downstairs.

Lance smiled at Treva. "Remember when you lamented that you couldn't give me a house full of kids?" Lance spread his arms. "Look at this. I love it."

Treva paced with wailing Zoe, shaking her head. "Only you would love this chaos." She sat with the baby, trying again. "Sweet girl, you can't starve yourself. Come on . . ."

She heard the front door open, and a moment later Faith and Jesse appeared in the kitchen.

"That's not my princess, is it?" Jesse said. "What's going on?"

Joy leaned against the counter. "She wouldn't take the bottle."

Jesse looked at Faith. "I know you're here and can feed her," he said, "but can I try?"

"You have a special thing with her," Faith said. "Let's see what she does."

Jesse took the baby and settled into a chair, cradling her. "Zoe, you're breaking my heart, crying like this." He smiled, his voice soft. "You're my princess, you know that? The most special girl in the world."

Zoe stared into his eyes, her cry moving to a soft whimper. Focusing on Jesse, she started sucking the bottle.

"Zoe's a daddy's girl," Treva said, "just like her mama was."

"The night is still young," Cecil said. "Weren't Lindell and Cedric supposed to be here by now? We have to get that card game going."

"They're on the way," Lance said, checking his phone.

Jillian looked at Treva. "Then we'd better get changed and head over to the B and B for our girls' night. I can't wait to see it."

Treva headed up to the bedroom, Lance alongside, and searched the closet for a change of clothes.

"You know," Lance said, "it was almost exactly a year ago that I met this woman who turned my world upside down in two days."

Treva smiled as she pulled a blouse from a hanger. "Oh, really?"

"She called it a mirage. Said it wasn't real." Lance pulled her from the closet, brought her close, and kissed her. "She said it wouldn't last."

Treva threw the blouse on a chair and wrapped her arms around him. "And what did you say to this deluded woman?"

"I told her it might sound crazy, but I could see myself with her for a lifetime."

"Whoa, an entire lifetime." Treva looked deep into his eyes. "What does that man say today?"

"A lifetime isn't long enough." He kissed her again. "What does the deluded woman say?"

Treva said the words they loved to repeat. "For better or for worse, whether we're running hard or stumbling"—she kissed him—"you're stuck with me, Mr. Alexander."

Reading Group Guide

1. Stephanie experienced profound disappointment after going all-out for Lindell's return, then learning he wouldn't be back any time soon. When Lindell failed to sympathize, Stephanie drowned the hurt in alcohol. In times of great disappointment, do you find yourself stumbling? What does that look like for you? Who or what do you turn to most in disappointment? Do you cling to God?

2. When Faith went to Jesse's home, she'd been somewhat relieved to hear that he was on his way out. When he brought her close and kissed her, she told herself it was as far as she would go, that she couldn't keep to a path that was wrong. Yet, she allowed herself to linger, until temptation had given birth to sin. Have you ever gone into a situation you knew would be tempting? What were you telling yourself? Did you think you would be strong enough to resist? Did you flee?

3. Treva carried the weight of insecurity, which caused her to question whether she could be used by God in certain areas. Have you ever grappled with insecurity? Did you recognize it as a weight in your life, hindering you from running well for Christ? How did you lay aside that

weight and learn to trust God?

4. Jillian knew the truth that her struggle was not against flesh and blood. But when she learned that her husband had befriended another woman and even kissed her, she had no desire to fight by praying for her husband or marriage. Have you had times when you are too upset, angry, or maybe too weary to pray? How do you push past those feelings and pray anyway? Later, Jillian realized that the fact that she didn't want to pray—meant she needed to. Do you ever pray for the desire to pray?

5. In Lance's message at the conference, he testified about a time in his life when he didn't think he could "run to win" because of his circumstances. Have you been there? Have you experienced a season in life where you felt "disabled" because of disappointment, fear, doubt, heartbreak, failure, or a difficult trial? How did you get back in the race? Even now, are you learning to run *despite* your circumstances? Do you believe that God has work for you to do *in the midst of* your circumstances?

6. In the final conference session, Cyd said, "Raise your hand if you know about times of stumbling." Can you identify? Are you aware of times in your life when you've stumbled? Do you stand on the promise from Psalm 32:24 that though you may stumble, you will not fall, be-

cause the Lord upholds you with His hand? Do you have a testimony of how He's done that?

7. Stephanie knew God was telling her to reach forward, to *press*, as Philippians 3:13-14 calls us to do. But she said, "It's not in me to do all that." Do you ever feel that way? Does it seem that you simply don't have the strength or endurance or maybe even the desire to reach forward and *press*? Have you considered that you don't have to do it in your own strength—that the key is "Christ in you, the hope of glory"?

8. Faith told her Grandma Patsy, "you're doing a lot of looking back and regretting, something I know about too. I've been praying to run my race from where I am today . . . ." Do you do a lot of looking back and regretting? Have you asked God to help you run your race from where you are today? Are you looking ahead in faith?

9. What steps are you inspired to take on your own journey, to run "in hot pursuit" for Christ?

ABOUT THE AUTHOR

KIM CASH TATE is the author of several books, including *Cling* (2017) and *Hidden Blessings* (2014). A former practicing attorney, she is also a Bible teacher and homeschooler. She's been married to her husband Bill for more than two decades, and they live in St. Louis with their two young adult children.

Visit Kim's website at kimcashtate.com

Connect with Kim:

Facebook.com/kimcashtate
YouTube.com/kimcashtate
Instagram.com/kimcashtate
Twitter.com/kimcashtate

Made in the USA
Middletown, DE
28 January 2018